Forest of

By

Ralph Whitworth

Copyright © 2018 Ralph Whitworth

ISBN: 978-0-244-41687-4

All rights reserved, including the right to reproduce this book, or portions thereof in any form. No part of this text may be reproduced, transmitted, downloaded, decompiled, reverse engineered, or stored, in any form or introduced into any information storage and retrieval system, in any form or by any means, whether electronic or mechanical without the express written permission of the author.

To my daughters.

Deborah and Lisa,

With Love

Author's Note

Germany invaded Poland in 1939 bringing with it the Nazis.
Their plan was to remove the local population. They treated them as sub-human, going into the villages they killed, tortured and removed them from their farms installing their own Volksdeutsches, (German speaking Poles.) Millions of the population died under their rule.
So the Polish Partisans were born, small groups of like-minded men determined to fight back usually no more than twenty. The war they fought was to the death, no quarter was given on either side.
   This novel is based on a true story of an Englishman fighting behind enemy lines and his involvement with a Polish courier girl.
   A lot has been forgotten and personal details obscured so I have used my imagination taking liberties regarding the fire-fights and the romance.
      The war In Poland left a lot of bad bitter memories amongst those who survived for that reason I have changed all the names of the people, and some of the villages.

CHAPTER 1

JUNE, AUGUST 1942 STALAG 8B

Rance's head pulsated with flashes of pain piercing deep behind his eyes, and rolling on his side he could feel a dull vibration which resounded through him as the floor pitched and jumped, making the pain worse. On opening his eyes he stared at a row of boots four of which were highly polished, while the other two were mud coated and worn. He looked up at McPherson sitting hand-cuffed between two German policemen realizing they were in the back of a lorry and he was on the floor. Daylight streamed through the opening at the back and he could see the tops of the trees flashing by.

'Rance, are you all,'- a heavy fist back-handed McPherson in the mouth and he gurgled lapsing into silence.

He tried to sit up and a German boot pressed him down hard to the floor making him wince at the pain in his ribs and ankles.

For three hours he rode under the boot of the guard until he saw the tops of the barbed wire fence, and knew with a sinking feeling that they were back in Stalag 8B.

They were hurried inside and held up between two guards now facing the Camp Commandant who stared at them in stony silence, while tapping a pencil on the desk in front of him. Rance shuffled his feet in pain.

'Keep still,' the Commandant's voice was harsh quivering with anger. You think being kicked around by the German police is all the punishment you get for escaping from here, well you're mistaken. You two have caused me a lot of trouble now I'm going to cause you a lot of trouble.'

Tossing the pencil back on his desk he stood up. 'Give them a month in solitary confinement only bread and water.'

Turning he stalked out of the room still seething slamming the door behind him.

Rance sat on the hard wooden bunk and surveyed his cell, he'd been in holes like this before and the thought of a month made him want to scream, enough is enough.' What little light there was came in though a small hole cut in the door showing the walls were bare brick with bits of flaking paint.

He grimaced at the small bucket sitting in the corner still full from the last occupant and while peering down at the floor he noticed he had the usual compliment of insects crawling underneath the bed. Lifting his feet he swung himself horizontally onto the bunk gasping when piercing pain stabbed through his chest.

Feeling and prodding he knew he'd got at least two broken ribs, so he took stock of his face gently tracing the swollen cheek bone and split swollen lips.

A month of this! He felt angry and limping across to the door he looked through the hole on to another blank wall. He paced the floor counting four strides by three strides while listening to German voices in the distance and on returning to the door he examined the frame. Made of iron it was tight fitting against the brick-work with the hinges on the outside he knew he could never get out that way.

Sitting back on the bunk he stared at the solid concrete ceiling and started to plan.

First he must recover his strength and wait for the spring, second he and McPherson must save any food they can and get on another working party, thirdly, he tried to stay awake but groaning in pain he turned on his side and drifted off into a restless sleep.

Rance woke to the sound of the door being opened, the cell was in darkness and the blinding beam of a torch shone into his eyes making him blink. He heard metal containers being placed on the floor by the side of the door and then the door slammed with the sound vibrating down the corridor. Feeling his way over to the door he found a full jug of water and a dish with two slices of bread. Carrying them back to the bed he took great gulps of the luke-warm water and bit into the bread before settling back down with the hunger in him easing as the bread started to swell.

His sleep broken he could feel things crawling over him, insects he couldn't see, reaching down he grabbed one and killed it with a savage flick and searched for more as daylight gradually eased its way through the hole in the door bringing relief from the torment. Holding his ribs he slowly climbed to his feet, four paces forward, he turned and counted four back.

One day, became seven days, which became two weeks and so the days slowly passed. The guards came in and without speaking roughly cut his hair bringing instant relief, he knew he had lice and now had lost half of them.

Using a stone he started to draw pictures on the bricks, one picture, for every one stifling, boring, mind destroying day and more than once he sat on the bed rocking backwards and forwards. Once a day the bread and water appeared and he found he could no longer eat the bread so he broke it up into the water and drank it.

He counted his pictures and one month to the day they pulled him blinking into the daylight. Shielding his eyes from the blinding glare he shuffled towards his billet where the guards threw him a clean uniform and left. He gave a lopsided grin to the rest of the silently staring inmates before walking slowly down between the beds of the hut and into the washroom. Pulling off his lice ridden clothes he thankfully sat on the floor in the shower with his back to the wall letting the cold water flow through his hair and over his body.

McPherson came in and sank down beside him Rance stared in disbelief at the once well-built man who was now skinny and gaunt with a face that was no more than a skull, and looking down he realised with a shock that he didn't look any better.

'Jock,' his voice trailed away and he lapsed into silence.

McPherson's eyes seemed twice as large set in his skull like face. He slowly rolled his head on the wall and faced him. 'Whatever you do don't dare ask me to escape tomorrow do you hear me you lice ridden bloody Englishman.'

With that last remark he closed his eyes and let the water run all over him.

He kept his eye on McPherson who he knew was ill and had never really recovered from his stint in solitary confinement. He sat next to him on the bunk where McPherson lay with his eyes shut. He hesitated then put his arm on the Scots shoulder. McPherson opened his eyes. 'Yes, I know what you're going to say and I agree with you. There's no way I can escape in this condition. Out there,'… his voice trailed off, 'Good luck laddie I'm proud to have known you even if you are a bloody Englishman. You do it for my sake as well as your own and when you've gone I'll be with you in my mind. I know you won't let them beat us'.

He wasn't afraid to let McPherson see the tears in his eyes as he nodded. 'Don't worry I'll send you a post-card,' he said quietly.

For weeks he worked the cement barges, and it was now March 1943, He'd sent out word amongst the other prisoners that he was looking for a partner to escape with. He was now fit and had a healthy supply of broken biscuits stored away.

'I hear your looking for a partner,' said the tall man standing over him

Rance, sitting on a bag of cement stared up at the man a few years older than he was perhaps about twenty seven he thought. He was tall over six feet, slim build the eyes staring down at him were blue with a steady serious look.

He climbed to his feet. 'A cement lorry's here let's talk while we load.'

Taking a corner of a cement bag each they grunted their way from the lorry to the barge and then went back for another.

'My names Donald Cross I was a gunner serving with the Royal Artillery. I've never escaped before, but I hear you have several times,' he said taking in Rance's well-built frame, craggy face with brilliant blue eyes, not really tall about five feet ten, but not someone to pick a fight with though.

Rance answered, 'I have also been re-captured several times, and I might add tortured by the Gestapo for my trouble thinking I was a spy.

Cross looked at Rance with a steady eye.

'I would still like a chance,' he said and they threw another bag of cement on to the pile.

Rance noted the man sounded well educated with no discernible accent and liked what he saw. 'I was thinking of going in April that's when the weather is more reliable.'

Donald Cross grinned, 'It sounds more like you're planning a holiday than escaping; he dumped his bag of cement and turned to face him.

'Well, yes or no?

Rance grinned back and shook his hand. 'Start saving your Red Cross biscuits we're off in April'.

They now had enough food hidden away and started to stitch it into their clothes. The weather had improved and seemed calm. 'Don,' Rance paused looking him straight in the eye,

'I think we should be on the next working party that goes outside the wire. If you don't think you're ready, that is if you've changed your mind say so now. I won't think any the less of you.'

Cross flushed with anger. The muscle in his jaw jumped furiously.

'I approached you remember so don't you worry about me,' he said gruffly, 'I know we'll make a great team you and me. Just say when.'

April 1943

Dawn arrived too slowly for Rance who had tossed and turned all night trying to finalize the plan of escape. He lay listening to the snores of the men around him and frowned at the sound of trucks coming through the camp gates.

Soon the guards were entering the huts shouting, 'Aufstehen, du gehst,' nudging the sleeping men awake. Grunting and moaning the men fell in line alongside the trucks. Rance looked along the row estimating there were at least a hundred standing there and was relieved to see Cross further down the line.

He shivered in the early morning air while the German Commandant walked down the ranks of men standing loosely to attention. 'We have a treat for you,' he said stopping in front of Rance looking him up and down with a smirk, before proceeding down the line saying loudly. 'I've decided to let you work in one of our coal mines. You will now be transported to a new camp in Silisia and from there you will serve the Third Reich and believe me you will serve it well.'

Rance edged his way along the line of men until he managed to board the same truck as Cross. When the long convoy moved slowly out through the camp gates his eyes searched the windows of the hospital billet, but of McPherson there was no sign. He turned and stared at the lorry in front with a heavy heart.

It was a tiring journey the truck packed with men standing shoulder to shoulder never stopped until darkness fell and they finally halted. Great arc lights sprang into life and Rance saw the familiar barbed wire. They stiffly disembarked surrounded by guards who split them up into groups of twenty and ushered them into their huts where Rance and Cross slumped onto their bunks.

'What now! this is something we didn't plan for?' exclaimed Cross.

'Rance shrugged, 'Who knows what tomorrow will bring? I don't think anything could surprise me anymore. Let's sleep on it and no doubt we'll find out what happens tomorrow'.

He was up early and saw what looked to be castle walls with one end open but fenced in by barbed wire. Now he could see the outline of the coal-mine and shuddering at the thought of going underground he went from one group of prisoners to the next asking if they knew of any escapes being planned.

He stood and watched as more and more prisoners arrived, and guessed it wouldn't be long before they were all moved down to the mine.

'There's an escape planned for tonight.'

Rance looked at the man who'd spoken. He was tall and thin with a London accent and was standing in the middle of a small group of men.

'There are two of us, and we came in yesterday,' he said, not believing his luck. 'We would like to join you if it's possible; I've been out before so I know what to do. Maybe I can help.'

The tall man hesitated. They'd been around the camps a long time and were fearful of a trick.

One of the men answered for him,

'Why not, the more men that can knock a hole in that wall the better we must get out to-night?'

The tall man shrugged and beckoned with a nod of his head. 'Come with me,' and led the way to an outbuilding against the castle wall where a man was sitting playing a mouth organ while three others were trying to harmonize with loud voices. With a puzzled glance in their direction Rance followed the tall man inside who turned round and grinned.

'They're our lookouts and the noise they're making is to disguise the sound of the hammers. Clouds of dust hung in the air slowly drifting in the semi-darkness of the shed which was empty apart from two shadowy figures crouched against the far wall swinging a hammer each. Rance stooped and examined the hole they'd made in the wall and drew back coughing when the fine dust settled in his lungs.

'How far have you got to go do you know? he asked.

The tall man shrugged. 'These are very old walls we think maybe seven feet. The dust is the main problem each man can only stay ten minutes.' he smiled, 'So the two of you are most welcome.'

Rance returned his smile, 'I'll fetch my partner thanks for letting us join you.' He turned to leave then stopped as an after-thought struck him.

'By the way how many are going.'?

The man's grin widened. 'With you two that makes thirteen. Lucky for some,'

Rance's throat felt dry, they had been working on and off the wall all afternoon and were covered in fine dust. He nudged Cross, 'When we go through the wall stay close to me, we must distance ourselves from the others there are far too many men; it's too dangerous to stay together.'

When the sun finally sank below the horizon the already murky interior of the shed became pitch-black and the men became still and tense each with their own thoughts and fears. Rance and Cross sitting at the rear could just about hear the gentle tapping of the hammers loosening the last of the large stones in the wall to reveal a short open space on the other side beyond which shrubs and trees grew, the sight of which drew a gentle murmur from the men who at last sensed freedom while they crouched waiting for the full security of nightfall.

The tall man looked at his watch timing it until three minutes before the lights illuminated the whole camp. He raised his voice slightly so they could all hear.

'We go out now one at a time, every ten seconds, after that you're on your own good luck to you all. I'll see you back in England.'

Rance and Cross were the last to leave and within seconds were into the cover of the trees. Just ahead of them they could hear the others pushing their way through the undergrowth.

He grabbed Cross by the arm. 'This way,' he said turning right and leading him away from the other men.

They started to run dodging the trees ignoring the branches that snagged their clothes and smacked into their faces before finally coming to a stop at the head of a small valley. With the moon rising Rance could see the outline of the running men on the far side strung out, but still all running the same way.

He came to a decision. 'Don let's keep going to the right, circle the camp and go the other way.'

Twenty minutes later they started to climb a steep hill covered in trees and thick undergrowth while in the distance they heard the heart stopping sound of the camp sirens. Rance paused to listen looking back towards the sound while Cross sank against a tree his breath coming in raw gasps.

'Don,' Rance's voice was full of urgency. 'Listen I think they've let the dogs loose!'

They both stood routed to the spot straining their ears gradually picking up the sound of dogs with the scent of pray in their nostrils.

Not wasting anymore time they started climbing hard, clawing their way up the steep hill while continually having to change direction through the thick undergrowth until they reached the top.

Looking down at the scene below Rance saw the bobbing lights of the guards spreading out across the valley floor, the howling of the dogs increased and the two men on the hillside froze at the sound of men screaming.

Rance held Cross tightly by the arm. 'Let's get the hell out of here when they have a head count they'll be looking for us next.'

All through the night they moved running one hundred yards, and walking one hundred yards several times making a detour when the undergrowth became impenetrable. At last the moon disappeared behind scurrying clouds and Rance could smell rain. He stopped and looked back listening intently, but all he could hear was the wind gathering strength whistling though the treetops.

Dawn came slowly with it a light drizzle which pleased Rance, it would hide their scent from the dogs when they came. They sat letting it cool their aching muscles before reluctantly clambering back on their feet and moving on.

Finding the going easier in the daylight they started to run again, and every stream they came to they waded up or down just to be sure their tracks would be impossible to follow. Two hours later Rance pulled himself up a steep bank and lay gasping for breath while waiting for Cross to join him. The clouds were breaking up and the sky was turning blue he guessed it would be hot later. Cross rolled over the top and lay with his face pressed into the soft wet grass his face hot and flushed with exhaustion.

Rance shielding his eyes from the glare of the rising sun sat up.

'I can hear a train,' he said in astonishment. 'We must be right next to a railway line.'

The noise grew to a steady roar, the rails hidden by a slight incline started to hum. Now they saw it, travelling fast it appeared from around a bend in a cloud of steam pulling coaches packed with German troops. Swaying from side to side it hurtled down towards the two men sitting transfixed by the track.

The driver spotting them, sent a greeting whistle echoing through the surrounding hills and the vibration from the train shook the earth while the air exploded in their ears with clouds of steam and smoke billowed high above their heads.

Waving hard they stepped back with the coaches flashing by. German troops stared out of every window.

'Look they're waving back,' shouted Cross giving them the victory sign until it thundered into the distance leaving them staring after it.

'What we need now is a slow goods train that will take us miles away from here,' said Rance glancing back down the track. 'We don't stand a chance getting on one here; it's too flat the trains go to fast. Let's find an incline so the next train has to slow down.'

'Where do you think this track leads to?' Cross asked.

Rance shrugged, 'I don't even know what country we're in never mind where it goes to. All I know is it will get us away from that camp and the dogs'.

Cross strode off down the track, 'let's get out of here,' he said over his shoulder.

Six hours later he and Cross sat on the track with the blazing orb of the sun high overhead sucking greedily at the moisture in their hot aching bodies.

Cross groaned, 'If we don't get a train soon I'm not going to have the strength to climb aboard.'

Rance licked at his dried parched lips. 'You're right we must rest.' Finding a patch of trees near the line he slumped in the cooling shade and promptly fell asleep.

Through a fog of tiredness Rance stirred uneasily his brain trying to register the sounds around him. Startled! his eyes opened wide, the light was beginning to fade and the sun was well below the horizon. He looked across at Cross who was sitting with his head on one side listening intently.

'There's another train coming,' he exclaimed and it's a lot slower than the other one.'

They moved to the edge and looked along the track.

'Here it comes and it's going the same way,' Cross said excitedly. So they stepped back into the shadow of the trees and waited while it rumbled towards them at half the speed of the troop train.

'It's a goods train but is it going slow enough?' Cross was unsure.

'But we may not get another chance,' he said watching as the engine laboured struggling with its weight of heavily loaded wagons.

Waiting impatiently until half the wagons had passed they ran alongside grabbing at the rungs. Rance's fingers grasped and held a rung feeling the fierce wrench which pulled him off his feet and almost under the wheels forcing him to let go.

The train started to gather speed. Rance tried again and was flung away where he rolled at the side of the passing wagons. Desperately he regained his feet and ran alongside the last three. He wanted to look for Cross but needed all his concentration for getting on board. He jumped high for another rung and his legs swung inwards towards the wheels and he cursed lifting his knees to his chest he clambered onto a narrow ledge. He looked for Cross but failed see him.

CHAPTER 2

Piotrekow central Poland

No Izabel you can't go it's too dangerous the Germans are everywhere.' Anya's eyes were fierce and staring, frightened for the safety of her nineteen year old daughter.
'I could go with grandfather they wouldn't bother with an old man and a young girl,' answered Izabel defiantly, 'Anyway we need the food, our cousin with her farm said she would help us, it's only a few kilometres away.'
Her grandfather Edward was nodding in agreement, 'She's right, we've nothing to eat. Jarek your son is only twenty; the Germans will surely take him for the labour camps if he leaves the apartment now. Anya moved over to the kitchen table pulled out a wooden chair and slumped down holding her head in her hands.
'I'm frightened since your father died I keep thinking you or Jarek will be next,' she whispered looking up at her daughter through tear stained eyes realizing that the awkwardness of a young girl had gone and in its place a beautiful young woman was emerging. Tall and slim with breasts already full and firm. Her long black hair tumbled down to her shoulders, framing the high cheek bones and large brown eyes with lips that were full and perfectly formed over brilliant white teeth. Her mother already knew that when she entered a room every man's head turned to gaze in admiration.
I will go to the priest tomorrow and pray for you and your grandfather.'
Izabel and her grandfather left the apartment the next morning and turning a corner they were confronted by a row of burnt out houses. Nobody had attempted to put out the fires which must have raged all night. The grandfather griped Izabel's arm tightly, 'Jews lived there I can smell death we must move away quickly.'

It was only then did she realise what the sickly smell was. 'I feel I'm living in a nightmare.' she shuddered.

Edward's grip tightened, 'Nothing can bring them back. One day we'll drive these Nazi monsters back into the slime from where they came.'

Twenty minutes later they reached the outskirts of the town and were met by her grandfather's friend. 'I've borrowed a small Panje cart for you; I know it's not very large and the horse is old but the horse has a strong heart and will get you there and back,'

. Twenty minutes later they approached a German road block Edward glanced anxiously at Izabel relieved to see that she showed no sign of nervousness.

A young soldier caught the reins holding out his hand. He was curt and to the point speaking German, 'Lass mich deine papiere sehan,'

Edward handed the papers over while Izabel sat quietly looking at the floor of the cart. Two other soldiers wondered over and stared at the young girl. 'Gdze idziesz tak wczesnie rano?' asked the young soldier speaking in Polish.

The grandfather was startled! He'd never heard a German soldier speak Polish before obviously a Volksdeutche a German speaking Pole his lip curled in contempt.

'My friend lives on a farm near Golesze and is very ill so we're going to visit her,' he answered not taking his eyes off the two soldiers who were moving to the girl's side of the cart.

Grinning broadly one of them reached down and lifting the blanket looked underneath Izabel stiffened and pulled it back sharply causing the soldiers to burst out laughing before slapping the horse's rump and jeering it on its way.

'I don't think I'll ever get used to those pigs,' she said her voice shaking in suppressed anger.

Within half an hour they turned off the main road on to a sandy track and entered a pine forest. Another hour they left the gloom of the forest and moved into open fields. The dark clouds had cleared leaving it breathtakingly beautiful with the azure coloured sky enhancing the multi-hued greens of the trees spreading out before them. A river sparkled and danced adding movement and life as they lumbered up an incline in the track and stopped to let the horse rest.

'That's the village of Kalnik just below us.' The grandfather's voice suddenly rose in alarm watching German troops moving between the houses.

The sound of gunfire and screaming drifted up to them while they sat transfixed on the cart watching men being thrown into the backs of trucks. A Gestapo officer sat in the back of an open topped staff car and Izabel could hear him shouting orders while pointing at two elderly people clutching each other at the side of the road.

A soldier walked forward and swung his rifle butt into the old man's face sending him unconscious into the dirt while the old woman screamed in anguish and threw herself over him trying to lift his blooded head. The Gestapo officer climbed out of the car and walked casually towards the couple drawing his pistol making the old lady flinch back in terror when bending down he shot them both in the head before walking back down the road without a another glance.

'Quickly we must get to our cousin and warn her before they move on,' Izabel wept urging her grandfather to move faster while they skirted the village and made for the farm.

Sweeping into the farmyard Izabel jumped off the momentum throwing her headlong to the ground, but the farm was deserted.

Edward shouted a warning, Daj spokoj, quickly get back on the Germans are here.'

The horse and cart bolted back out of the the gate only to find it blocked by a German troop carrier. The soldiers leapt down and raced for the cart causing the horse to swerve violently to the right tipping Edward and Izabel into the mud. Izabel reached for her grandfather but was too late a German boot swung into her kneecap, while rough hands grabbed her throwing her backwards where she lay in the mud kicking out at them in desperation when they bent down towards her squirming body.

'Nein, dort,' shouted one pointing towards the house. Realizing what they intended to do, she started to struggle screaming for her grandfather. Laughing two more soldiers grabbed her feet and ran towards the house.

Izabel never heard the gunfire until two of the soldiers staggered sideways before pitching forward on to their faces. In confusion the remaining two fumbled for their rifles while the sound of a dozen more shots filled the air sending them sprawling backwards into the mud.

She lay paralyzed with fear as more shooting followed and the remaining troops fell into the farmyard dirt.

Izabel ran to her grandfather and held him as he tried to speak the words drying in his mouth when they looked up at the group of men approaching. She stared at them with fearful eyes.

'Oh, God, what now?' she whispered to herself as they approached.

Filthy clothes, unshaven faces, hair long and uncombed. She shuddered and pulled her grandfather closer as they bent down towards her.

'Welcome to the Polish Home Army,' one of them said smiling, 'we must get away from here it's not safe,' he continued.

'My cousin lives here but I don't know where she is,' said Izabel recovering her composure.

'I'm afraid I have some bad news,' said the man, 'The Gestapo got here yesterday we were too late to save them.'

Izabel felt sick. 'Not the children as well?' she shivered.

The man couldn't look at her, 'We had to bury them in the woods.

I think these,' he nodded at the soldiers, 'had come to finish what they'd started yesterday.'

Suddenly they were in a hurry. For three hours they travelled, no one spoke. Overcome with grief Izabel sat stiffly upright. There were no tears just the start of a burning anger and hatred for the soldiers that had overrun her country.

Studying the men around her she noticed that their ages ranged from early twenties to late forties. Their leader was young perhaps twenty five she couldn't be sure. He was tall with broad shoulders and a face that was rather handsome.

Stopping the horse he came back to her. 'Where do you live?' he asked.

'Piotrkow,' she replied blushing thinking he'd noticed her staring.

'Just ahead is the main Piotrkow road this is as far as we can take you,' he said apologetically.

At that moment she knew she had to do something. 'I want to join you, what can I do to help?' the determination strong in her voice.

He stared at her, hesitating for a second before making up his mind.

'Give me your address we may be able give you something to do.'

Writing down the address she held it out and he lent forward to take it. On impulse she reached up and lightly kissed his cheek. 'Thank you for saving our lives,' she whispered. What's your name?'

'My code name is Marek,' he answered in a strained voice.

Seeing them safely on their way he beckoned to his men and they turned disappearing back into the forest. He touched his cheek smiling to himself; all he could see in front of him was the face of a most beautiful girl.

Coming to the edge of Piotrkow Izabel breathed a sigh of relief seeing an empty road. On reaching the stable she jumped down.

'You get home girl,' said the friend. 'I'll keep your grandfather here with me

Bursting through the main door of her apartment block she made her lungs ache racing up the three flights of stairs before stopping outside the door to compose herself. Slowly she opened the door and walked in.

'Izabel thank God you're here,' Anya ran towards her from the bedroom stopping suddenly seeing the state her daughter was in.

'What's happened? Where's your grandfather?' Izabel didn't answer straight away she stared hard at her mother's face and could tell she'd been crying. 'Something happened here to-day mother, what is it?' she asked in alarm.

'Your brother went out for some fresh air. The Gestapo took him.

Izabel pushed through the crowds thronging the main square looking at each of the thirty hanging men gagging in horror at the bulging eyes and bloated faces. When the ordeal was over she weakly walked away relieved that her brother wasn't amongst them.

A loud speaker blasted out over the square warning the local population about helping the 'Bandits' that roamed the area and that for every German killed thirty civilians would hang.

Silently she walked down the main street towards her home passing the German police HQ situated in the town hall. She glanced at the armed sentries and open doorway hesitating before acting on impulse she turned and entered the dark hallway.

With heart racing and trembling limbs she approached a police sergeant sitting at a desk in the entrance.

'Dobrze, czego chcesz?' he glared at the young girl standing in front of him.

She swallowed hard. 'My brother is missing can you tell me if he has been taken for any work in the area?' Avoiding his gaze she stared at the floor.

'Nobody is ever taken for work', he sneered 'They all volunteer to serve the Third Reich.' He picked up a pen and rifled around for a form in his desk.

'What's his name?'

She now wished she hadn't come in. The hallway had suddenly become stiflingly hot and she was starting to perspire. Slowly she stammered his name, 'Jarek Markowitz, he's twenty.'

'Jego adres?' he snapped impatiently shuffling his papers.

She knew by his attitude that it had been a mistake and wished she hadn't been so impulsive. He stood up and came around the desk towards her. 'Now if you were to be friendly towards me I could make enquiries with the Gestapo upstairs.'

'Sergeant what's going on here who is this girl?'

The sharp tone brought the sergeant smartly to attention. Izabel turned round to see three Gestapo officers walk through the entrance and with a sudden feeling of revulsion and fear she recognised the one in front as the officer who had been in the village of Kalnik.

'It's only a stupid Polish girl looking for her brother she seems to think we've taken him away,' the sergeant stammered.

'Get rid of her,' the officer snapped and went to walk passed then suddenly stopped and studied the girl standing submissively in front of him.

He'd had beautiful women from all over Europe but this one struck him as one of the best he'd seen, and young, he stared at her figure so fresh and firm.

A feeling moved inside him a feeling he hadn't felt for a long time. A new game was about to start and he relished the thought particularly the end result when she would come to him without force. He almost licked his lips it was the game that counted when he had someone they loved as hostage and would do anything to get them back.

She lifted her head and stared into the coldest and cruellest eyes she'd ever seen they reminded her of a dead fish and it took all her self-control to stop from shuddering.

'Get her name and address,' he said curtly to the sergeant, 'I'll look into it.' then he was gone moving up the stairs two at a time.

The sergeant glared at her, 'Aren't you the lucky one. That was Major Schneller a powerful man. Get on the wrong side of him, well,'…

Izabel didn't wait to hear anymore she turned and ran.

Upstairs Major Schneller turned to a large map of Piotrkow and the surrounding district.

'I want you to remember what the chief of the Reich Central Security Office Reinhard Heydrich said. That the ultimate aim of our plan is to be kept secret. All the Jews are to be rounded up and disposed of by the end of the year and the Polish villagers and farmers will be removed one way or another to be replaced by our own Volksdeutsche.

He turned his attention to Franz Lohr his Lieutenant in command of the special motorised Einsatzkommando units. Well over six feet tall with broad shoulders and thick neck he was a bull of a man with a nose that at some time in the past had been broken more than once. His lips were fat and turned down at the corners and his eyes were hard and ice blue.

'We're not getting on removing the Jews fast enough there are far too many left. Also our collaborators inform me of increased bandit activity here he drew large circles on the map. I have requested more Einsatzkommando units to be brought in and any bandits caught must be interrogated more carefully and kept alive longer so as to get as much information as possible.' Lieutenant Lohr kept his eyes firmly fixed on the map in front of him thus avoiding the staring dead eyes, and his face was inscrutable when he turned away scribbling in a small note book.

Schneller looked at the other Lieutenant disliking him intensely. Schmidt he couldn't be bothered to find out his first name. He'd put him in charge of the local forced labour camps, but was now having second thoughts on the matter. 'I want you to find out if we have that young girl's brother in one of our camps. Get her name and address from the sergeant downstairs and find out all you can about her.'

Schmidt nodded and hurriedly left the room with relief he was afraid of the Major. He'd seen it all before with other women and began to pity the young girl even if she was a Pole.

Izabel sat facing the two men at the kitchen table in her apartment.

'Marek has sent us to see you,' said one of the men by way of an introduction. She stared at the two men shocked at the mention of his name. 'I thought he'd forgotten me it's been such a long time,' she answered eyes wide with surprise.

The man smiled, 'He hasn't done that I can assure you,' he observed dryly. 'Do you still want to help?' he asked at length.

'Yes what do you want me to do?' As soon as she said it she felt frightened but she also had a sense of exhilaration.

The two men sat back in their chairs nodding approvingly. 'Curan, that's the code name for our commander here in Piotrkow wants you to act as our courier carrying messages to the partisans living in the forest. He also understands that you have been studying English that could be useful in the future.' said the man.

'Curan will obtain all the necessary papers saying you work on a farm near Blezun. Its on the road to Sulejow as you know. 'We,' he nodded at his silent companion fight with Marek. My code name is Krolik and this is Pies.

A week later she received her papers all seemingly genuine as far as she could tell. Three days after that she had her first assignment.

It was with a feeling of fear and excitement that morning when she took the road to Sulejow she found riding a bicycle hot and tiring work and the perspiration ran down her neck and into the valley of her breasts making the thin dress she was wearing cling to the contours of her body. Occasionally a truck would pass carrying young Polish men to work in the labour camps making her think of her brother wondering if he was amongst them.

She approached the first road block with mixed feelings hoping Curan had got the papers right. The very thought of being tortured frightened her how would she stand up to it she couldn't possibly know. The partisans had guns; they could shoot themselves if they were caught, but a courier that was a different matter.

'Dokumenty tozsamosci', the young soldier eyed the young girl standing perspiring in front of him with something akin to awe he didn't even bother to read them. He'd never seen such a girl with her figure hugging dress showing every line and contour of a perfect body.

She smiled at him and he was flustered, handing back her papers he let her proceed.

Once through the road block Izabel drop her pretence at a smile she was through and that was enough.

Halfway to Blezun she found the turning she been instructed to take and entered a narrow forest track feeling it refreshingly cool in the shade of the giant pine trees. The track became narrower and the trees grew closer together blocking out the light.

She was becoming frightened not sure how far she was supposed to go. She dismounted and rested, leaning her bicycle against a tree her fear replaced by an excitement at the thought of seeing the young partisan leader again. She ran a comb through her hair.

'Leave it you look nice as you are,' a voice whispered in her ear making her jump she whirled round to see Marek standing there.

'I'm sorry I didn't mean to frighten you', he said.

She snapped, 'Don't ever creep up on me like that again,' but seeing the look on his face instantly regretted her outburst and tried to make amends.

'It's me that should be sorry this is my first time and I'm very nervous,'

His sudden smile made her relax although she noticed it never really touched his eyes. 'Come, meet the others.' he said.

A short walk brought them into a clearing with a foresters hut in the middle. A small group of men stood up to welcome her amongst them she recognised Krolic and Pies. Marek introduced her to the others all using code names. They were dressed in an odd mixture of clothes some of them from the old Polish army and some obviously taken from the Germans. There were various assortments of weapons, ranging from old hunting shotguns and rifles to German Schmeisser machine-guns and bandoliers full of cartridges were slung casually over their shoulders, they nearly all sported German calf length boots.

'Will I be meeting the rest of your men Marek?' she inquired; looking round.

'Marek laughed, 'This is it my army, it's too dangerous to have more, twenty is about right, but we keep losing men and have to replace them when we can. We're hunted by the Gestapo, police, and Waffen SS troops so we can never stay in one place long, hence the need for couriers like you.'

Izabel was shocked she didn't realise until now how much the odds were stacked against them. After the introductions were over she gave him the messages and they walked alone in the forest.

He turned to her with an explanation, 'The reason why I finally decided to fight was because my family had been forcibly removed from our farm to make way for the Volksdeutches. They came one morning with German troops and I hid in the wood-shed watching ashamed as they took my family. I believe them to be in a German labour camp somewhere in Germany or dead.'

Izabel could hear the bitterness in his voice and touched his arm in sympathy. Marek although solemn and serious most of the time had a boyishness about him that she found attractive. He was handsome also there was an aura of danger about him which she found strangely exciting.

Walking by his side she was keenly aware of his arm brushing against hers. Somehow it seemed an intimate gesture and she chastised herself for being too imaginative. But it wasn't imagination when she caught him looking at her out of the corner of his eye. Sometimes he would be lost for words when facing her almost shy. It annoyed her that was the reaction she had on most men blaming her looks.

Marek was tongue tied angry with himself he seemed to be acting like an oaf in front of her. God, but she was beautiful he felt miserable that he couldn't be natural and at ease in her presence. She must think of him as a savage he thought, fingering his week's growth of beard and glancing down at his dirty clothes. When she touched his arm he felt as if he were on fire and had an impulse to take her in his arms, but fought off the desire she would be shocked and horrified he was sure.

The next time when they met he would smarten himself up and look the part of a leader then perhaps he would have the nerve. Have the nerve him a leader of men not afraid to fight, but goes to pieces in front of a woman.

She finally left with Marek walking her back to where she'd left the bicycle when he suddenly held her and bending his head kissed her full on the lips. Startled! She started to struggle then suddenly with her legs feeling like water she answered to her feelings, clinging to him her body pressing warmly against his chest she returned his kiss with passion. His grip tightened and he started breathing heavily. Gently she pushed him away.

'Steady my fighting friend I have to go now,' she whispered breathlessly. Still blushing she rode away calling over her shoulder

'Be careful until we meet again'.

He stood watching her until she was out of sight, a half smile on his lips. Now did she mean, ' Careful until we meet again, or not so careful when we do meet.' The thought sent a surge of adrenaline through his body that made him want to run after her instead he walked back to his men and noticing their amused expressions, brought him back to reality.

'What are you all grinning at, haven't you seen a woman before?' he said gruffly.

'Yes we have, but we don't think you have,' Krolik retorted and the men burst out laughing.

'Don't be stupid, I was just being kind to the young girl that's all.' stammered Marek and again enraged when they laughed. He stormed into the hut slamming the door behind him.

Izabel felt uneasy. The curfew began at five o'clock and there was still a long way to go which made her curse herself for being such a fool staying so late on her first assignment.

There were new soldiers manning the road block with no sign of the young soldier she'd met going out. In his place was a surly older man who was taking his time. Izabel moved slowly up the queue until she stood in front of him and handed over her papers. He took them without a glance in her direction. 'These papers are recent, why do you travel so far for work?'

With a start she realised he was now staring at her suspiciously. She tried smiling but that didn't work on him. He appeared more suspicious than ever.

'Sir, I have tried everywhere in Piotrkow to find work which I am suitable for but there is nothing at all. My father and brother are both away working for the Third Reich, but that leaves me to feed my mother and grandfather,' she answered.

The man stared hard at her perspiring red face then shrugged, reluctantly handing back her papers.

It was on a hill that she lost control with her front wheel bouncing into a hole. She stared in dismay at the ruined wheel and looked at her watch half an hour to curfew.

Throwing the bicycle into a ditch she started to run aware of blood running down her leg and into her shoe. A German troop carrier passed horn blaring and the soldiers sitting in the back realized why she was running and pretended to shoot her.

'Run Pole run, only half an hour to go,' they whistled and shouted until they were out of sight.

'Oh for a gun, I would fight you, I would fight you,' she cried bitterly glancing at her watch again.

Fifteen minutes to go although she was now on the outskirts she was at least twenty minutes from home. Finding a low wall she sat with her head between her legs gasping for breath. Ten minutes to go she felt a deep dread knowing the Germans showed no mercy, would tolerate no excuses for breaking the curfew she would be shot. She started to panic and in desperation started knocking on the nearest doors to no avail. Turning a corner into the next street she stopped in shock. It was five o'clock and deserted she had run out of time. At the far end of the street stood a German patrol. Desperately she tried to return to the corner,

The corner Izabel was running for seemed but a distant dream when gunfire echoed through the deserted streets like a sharp clap of thunder bringing her screaming to a crouch on the pavement in sheer terror.
In utter bewilderment she found herself untouched while staring down the street watching the Germans running for cover. The firing continued from an upstairs window of a building opposite while a slightly built man appeared next to the corner beckoning furiously with one hand and grasping a pistol in the other. Scrambling to her feet she sob with relief on recognising Krolik whose face was totally devoid of any emotion, until she looked into his eyes and saw the raw hatred while watching the running Germans.
He pushed her roughly away from the line of fire and holding her tightly by the arm ran to the next block before turning into a small courtyard and up a flight of stairs. Once there they crossed a balcony and entered a small room containing two old chairs, a wardrobe, and a single bed. On the opposite side was a cooker that had seen better days, and a kitchen sideboard with a couple of pots and pans hanging above.
He spoke without any sign of emotion. 'This is my home such as it is, you'll be safe here, but you must wait until the curfew finishes in the morning.
'Out there in the gunfire you had so much hatred in your eyes?' said Izabel softly. It was more a question than a statement.
Krolik gave her a fixed unblinking stare.
'They killed my son.' he answered woodenly.

'I'm sorry,' she stammered.
'So will they be'.
'How did you know where to find me?' she asked quickly changing the subject..
'Marek realised after you'd gone that you wouldn't reach safety before the curfew so he sent us after you. It would seem we only just got here in time. That was Pies in the building opposite.'
'I hope he gets away safely,' concern showing in her voice.
'Don't worry about Pies he can look after himself, he'll be long gone by now'. He walked to the door turning to face her with the door half open.
'Don't worry, you'll do fine, it's a good lesson you've learnt today.'
With that last remark he fully opened the door and disappeared into the night.
She spent a disturbed night before breathing a sigh of relief when the sun rose and the curfew was lifted for another day. Leaving the room she made her way through the now crowded streets back to her own apartment.
'Where have you been? I've not slept all night worrying about you. Your grandfather has been out of his mind.' cried Anya tearfully from across the kitchen table.
'I'm sorry mother, I had to stay with friends because I missed the curfew, I couldn't get word to you,' she lied.

They both jumped at the loud knock on the door. Anya opened it and stared at the German officer standing there with a sergeant behind him.
Brushing passed Anya they strode into the room. Izabel stood up and faced them her face pale and drawn conscious of the officer's penetrating gaze as his eyes roved over her face and then slowly down her body before returning to her face.
Inwardly she squirmed with embarrassment and her face started to flush with anger. She glanced across at her mother who stood with her hand to her mouth, her eyes wide with concern. Izabel struggled to regain her composure staring back at the officer with cold defiant eyes.

'Izabel Markowitz, I am Lieutenant Schmidt, I have been ordered by my superior Major Schneller to trace your brother who volunteered to work for the Third Reich,' he said using his sergeant interpreter

Izabel felt uncomfortable she wanted to spit into his smirking face,

'We're worried about him we haven't seen or heard from him since he disappeared,' she replied stiffly.

'I want a full description of him including his age and the date he was supposed to have disappeared?' he smirked at that. Also the district he was in that day?'

Izabel retorted 'The police took him from outside this apartment.'

With the sergeant taking notes he asked her where she worked and about her immediate family, and had she got any boyfriends?

Finally the lieutenant turned to go. At the door he stopped, 'You're lucky Herr Schneller has taken an interest in you. When we find your brother I'm sure you'll be suitably grateful for his safe return.'

Izabel listened to his mocking laughter when he left the door open and sauntered down the stairs. Feeling sick and close to tears she sank back on a kitchen chair. Now she understood the purpose of his visit.

Gestapo HQ. Piotrkow Central Poland.

Major Schneller finished reading the report placing it carefully on his desk in front of him, his lips parting in what Schmidt took to be a smile,

'You've done well Schmidt now all you have to do is find the girl's brother. I'm sure you'll be successful in doing that won't you?' he said softly.

Schmidt didn't miss the threat in Schneller's voice. He swallowed.

'Yes sir, I'll get on it right away.'

Schneller stood up, 'No you won't we have a meeting to attend. Come with me,' he strode out of the room with Schmidt almost running to catch up.

Major Schneller entered the operations room with a flustered Schmidt trailing behind. Claus Ritschel head of the Gestapo for that area and Schneller's immediate boss was already waiting impatiently.

A thin dour man going bald and whose hat always seemed to be too big for him, like Schneller he had lost his sense of humour years ago.

Sitting near him was the director of SS Outposts Captain Herman Braun and his second lieutenant Adam Grieb both always immaculate and efficient. Lieutenant Franz Lohr, who was in command of the special motorised detachment sat opposite. Schneller strode into their midst and studied the map in front of them.

Claus Ritschel spoke softly but there was no mistaking the authority in his voice.

'You're to be congratulated on the work done in the village of Kalnik, but you did lose some men near there why was that Major Schneller?'

'The men got careless they learned a hard lesson which the rest of the detachment won't repeat.' he paused. Claus Ritschel interrupted. 'What did you do about it you know it's not good for moral?'

Schneller retorted, 'We took thirty hostages off the streets of Piotrkow and the surrounding villages and hung them in the main square with a warning to the rest of the population of the consequences of harming any German soldiers, besides which-'.

'That hasn't stopped the partisans from attacking my outposts,' interrupted Captain Herman Braun loudly. 'All it seems to do is make it worse and so it goes on.'

Inflamed with rage Schneller rounded on him,

'You wait and see it hasn't even started yet. These stupid Poles don't know what's going to hit them. We'll grind them into the mud, they're not human so we'll not treat them as such.

Impatiently Claus Ritschel waved him into silence. 'So now what's your next step?' he asked frowning.

'I propose to move on the farms south of Piotrkow clear them out and install our own farmers there.' Schneller paused staring at Herman Braun 'It's your job as Director of SS outposts to see that our new farmers are protected from these bandits, who aren't partisans I might add.'

Infuriated at the jibe Braun's face went red with anger, 'It wasn't me that lost eight men Schneller.' he retorted icily.

Claus Ritschel moved angrily between them.

'Stop it, try and act like German officers will you,' he snapped, 'Save the fighting for the Poles, we have a job to do and I'm here to make sure you do it.'

In the silence that followed he turned to Schneller.

'Now tell me what are you proposing?'

Schneller pointed with his baton. 'I aim to set a trap for the so called bandits roaming the forests east of the River Luciaza. The village of Lutowo is close to that river on the north bank. I'll cause so much trouble there that the bandits in the vicinity will hear the noise. They can't help but respond and will be drawn across the river

He threw his batten down glancing at Herman Braun, 'And with your troops lying in wait we'll have them,' he said gloatingly.

Braun sniffed, 'What if they don't respond?'

'We will still have a cleaned out village,' retorted Schneller sardonically, refusing to be drawn into another fight.

Izabel woke to a gentle tapping on her bedroom door,

'There's a man to see you,' her mother whispered.

She hurriedly dressed and entering the kitchen found Krolik sitting at the table wreathed in smiles.

'I have a new bicycle for you,' he said by way of a greeting. 'Come and look.' She stared in dismay at the rusty looking bicycle leaning against the wall of the courtyard. Krolik seeing the look on her face, joked. 'It's not what it seems it's almost new and very sturdy.'

He pointed to the frame, 'In there is a secret hiding space, in it is orders for Marek.'

Tomorrow you go to Blezun then take the road to the east alongside the River.' He grinned again, 'This time watch out for the curfew.'

'You won't be there,' she said it as a statement.

'Perhaps,' he answered.

She was worried there seemed an unusually high number of Germans on the road that morning. Another convoy of troop carriers led by an open topped car came up behind her so she pulled onto the grass verge to get out of the way, stiffening in shock when she recognised Schneller and the officer who was at her apartment. The sergeant interpreter was driving, she didn't know the other lieutenant sitting in the front seat next to him as they swept passed without a second glance.

She watched them turn off towards the villages of Witow and Lutowo and a feeling of alarm came over her, there was nothing but villages and farms down there. She remembered Kalnik and her face went white.

It was over an hour before she arrived in Blezun before turning right on the east side of the river. A figure stepped out in front of the bicycle and she almost lost her balance regognizing Pies. Gasping for breath she related what she'd seen and what she suspected.

Pies nodded, 'We heard firing from across the river, Marek has taken the men to investigate. He asked me to look after you until he returns.'

Taking her arm he said, 'Come we must get away from here, don't worry about Marek he'll be fine.'

The heavy drone of many trucks filled the air as a German convoy led by a staff car entered Lutowo. German troops quickly spread out through the village and three men who were working on a barn were forcibly joined by forty other villagers, a mixture of men women and children. Major Schneller stood by the unfinished barn shouting over the sound of the screaming women and children his face was a mask of madness.

'Now burn them do you hear me, burn them,' he shrieked.

Black smoke billowed and twisted though the village as the barn caught alight bringing with it the stinking smell of burning flesh.

Spurred on by the gunfire and screaming that rose in an ever increasing noise Marek and the fifteen men with him ran as they'd never run before wading the shallow river their lungs gasping, searching for precious air. Reaching the far bank Marek signalled them to spread out as dense smoke drifted down through the trees and a fresh wave of gunfire and screaming made them cast caution to the wind and run faster.

The smoke lingered, thickening in the still morning air Second Lieutenant Adam Grieb waiting with his troops for the partisans to arrive rubbed his smarting eyes. He was dubious that they would even come it was a gamble that he hoped wouldn't come off so he wouldn't have to fight.
A machine-gun opened up on his left with a short sharp distinctive clatter he could now see shadowy figures running towards their positions sending him into a blind panic.
'Fire, fire now, but who was the fucking fool who opened fire before my command,' he screamed.

When the first machine-gun opened up and the man next to Marek fell, he dropped and rolled desperately trying to escape the bullets that whistled through the air all round him.
He cursed himself furiously for a fool, falling into such a trap while around him he could see his men dying.
They'd lost the element of surprise and were paying for it with their lives, already those that were left had turned in retreat.
Taking advantage of the thick smoke cover which drifted between him and the machine gun he turned and ran half blinded by blood from a scalp wound.
He emerged into fresh clean air and saw his men ahead of him nearing the river. He counted eight and his mind cried in despair and remorse, seven men he had led to their deaths while behind him he heard the Germans calling to each other in the acrid smoke.

Izabel pulled herself free from Pies grasp.
'Take me to the river there must be something I can do to help,' she said.
Pies looked at her in alarm his face showing apprehension. 'No, Marek will kill me if I put you in any danger.'
Her eyes flashed with anger and her face became white and taut.

'Remember this I volunteered to join the Polish Home Army not to hide behind a tree at the first sound of a gun.' she stuttered.

'If you won't come with me then I'll go on my own.'

Pies stared in astonishment watching her run for the river. Then groaning in exasperation he slipped his German machine-pistol off his shoulder and hurried to catch up. The firing stopped as they approached the river bank and thin wisps of stinking smoke drifted through the trees.

Izabel caught her breath at the sight of Marek and some of his men wading waist deep back towards her.

She looked beyond them to see the Germans emerging from the thick smoke screen on the opposite bank and fire at the men in the water

Izabel cried out in anguish watching Marek sink out of sight while Pies threw himself to the ground and opened fire sending two of the German soldiers spinning backwards forcing the rest to scatter.

Changing direction she ran downstream keeping the trees between her and the Germans, staring into the brown swirling water.

Sobbing with relief she saw Marek surface holding onto a wounded man. Without thinking she slid into the water beside him. Marek's face was covered in blood his eyes opened wide in disbelief. 'Czym jestes,'--

Izabel didn't reply struggling to help hold the wounded man.

She heard the anger in Marek's voice when he shouted at her to let go. Glancing down she realised the man was dead.

Marek held her roughly by the arm and ran up the bank and into the trees where she glanced back to see Pies following.

Marek never faltered gripping her hard when she stumbled and nearly fell. It was another ten minutes before he called a halt. Izabel sank to the ground and rolled on her back fighting to get air into her tortured lungs. Marek sitting with his back to a tree felt his anger at her slowly diminish. He couldn't help but stare at the beautiful young woman gasping for air at his feet.

Marek turned his head away his anger returning this time at himself. He'd led his men to their deaths how could he have been such a fool. His feelings suddenly gave way to remorse he stared unseeing at the ground.

Isabel went over and sat beside him gently laying a hand on his arm. 'Please don't blame yourself. This is war you were desperate to help those poor villagers. You weren't to know it was a trap, the other villagers still need you,' she faltered. 'I need you.' She blushed, it was something she hadn't bargained on saying. It just came out.

Marek straightened and turned towards her she could sense his strength and resolve returning. 'Yes your right its war and things like this do happen,' he said it bitterly, 'but I'll make them pay for this day there'll be no mercy for any of them.' he retorted harshly.

He held her close and looked into her eyes, the anger and bitterness disappearing to be replaced by something else. A feeling that made both their pulses quicken.

'Marek we must move on we need to get to the forester's hut before it gets dark the rest of the men have scattered,' interrupted Pies coming up silently behind them.

'Where are we going?' she asked almost having to run to keep up with his long strides. Looking down at her hot flushed face he again felt the groin twisting agony of desire and quickly turned away lest she see it in his eyes.

'I'm taking you to a forester's house, the family help us and sometimes we rest there. They have a daughter about your age so you'll be safe for the night. It isn't possible for you to return to the road it will be alive with German troops'.

'You're not staying?' Izabel tried to keep the disappointment out of her voice.

Marek's laugh was hollow and void of any humour.

'After this next assignment, I have been ordered to travel to the Lodz area to help train new recruits. Me, the man who lost most of his men in one action,' his voice scarcely above a whisper sounded hard and bitter. Izabel felt his pain .

'We're here,' said Marek his voice almost back to normal.

They had emerged into a large clearing in the forest. Growing in the centre was the largest oak tree Izabel had ever seen and standing in its shadow were three small wooden houses which were grey and weather beaten. To one side there were vegetable gardens being tended by a man and a girl. 'Marek, doze ice widia,' cried the man, sticking his spade deep into the earth and striding across to greet them while rubbing his sweat stained hands on his trousers. Marek introduced Izabel to Jozef, his wife Julia, and their daughter Marian. telling them what had happened.

'Will this killing never end,' muttered Jozef grim-faced and sombre. 'Of course you must stay with us tonight and rest.

'No, only Izabel must stay I have to go.'

Izabel walked with Marek as far as the giant oak tree fighting to hold back the tears.

'You will come back won't you.' her voice trembled.

Stealing himself to remain calm he took her in his arms and looked into her beautiful sad eyes that glistened with tears. Her warm body pressing against his trembled with emotion when he kissed her full on the lips, her head spun and she started to wilt. She felt his strong tender mouth moving over hers slowly at first then with fire and passion that sent her senses reeling. Suddenly he was gone she stood alone the tears at last falling slowly down her cheeks.

CHAPTER 3

Buffeted by the wind Rance hauled himself up the rungs and sat on the top, there was still no sign of Cross. If he wasn't on the train it would mean Rance having to jump off, he ran across the top towards the front end and looked down between the wagons and with a feeling of relief he found Cross sitting on a small platform bracing him-self against the lurching of the train.

Cross stared up at him grinning, 'I didn't think you were going to make it, I almost jumped back off when I saw you in trouble.'

'I'm glad you didn't,' said Rance dryly.

With the fading light giving way to darkness the temperature began to drop and Rance shivered bringing his knees up close to his chest trying to sleep, only to jerk wide awake when he nearly fell between the wheels.

Dawn broke slowly leaving a night which Rance thought would never end. Bleary eyed he stared out at pine forests that ran for miles in all directions broken occasionally with wide mud coloured rivers which tumbled and twisted between the trees, carving out islands and deep swollen pools. Open fields appeared each with its own small wooden house and barn.

Dirt roads crossed the rail track along which people drove small four wheeled carts or sat on bicycles watching the wagons rolling passed. It was mid-day before they came to the first big town the fields were now giving way to houses and factories which made him uneasy when the train finally started to slow down. He peered round the edge of the wagon and stared at a station platform they were approaching in a cloud of steam.

'Don, there are German troops standing on the platform ahead,' he whispered. His first thought was to jump off on the far side but discounted the idea as being too close to the station.

Not knowing what else to do both removed their uniform tops and covered their faces in grease. The train had slowed to a crawl and now they could hear German voices as they lay on the narrow ledge pretending to work on the linkages between the two wagons.

The noise from the troops grew louder jostling and joking with each other only feet from where they were crouching. The brakes squealed and the train started to judder to a halt.

They were going to be caught Rance saw the dread on Cross's face. He touched his arm and moved to climb underneath aware of the stares from the troops lining the platform. The train jumped forward with a sudden hiss of steam and the wheels spun on the track. Startled! he swung himself back on board as it gathered speed and moved out of the station.

'I don't believe we got away with that,' Cross choked.

The train emerge from the sprawl of the town into more open fields with forests and rivers much the same as before. Rance felt the pain of hunger clutching at his stomach and the craving for a drink was now becoming an obsession with him more than the hunger. It was two hours before the train slowed down again this time the incline was steep and the train almost ground to a halt.

In the distant fields they could see people working so they waited until it rounded a bend then jumped listening to the sound of the departing train. Cross stared round at the rolling countryside. 'I wish to God I knew where we were.'

'Or even which country we're in,' replied Rance. 'Come on let's get moving.'

They approached the men working in the field with caution hands kept well away from their bodies in a surrender motion. The men stopped what they were doing and watched them approach in silence.

'We are English soldiers, English do you understand, we need your help, we are English?' said Rance .

A heated argument started between the men. Rance couldn't understand a word they were saying. One of the men stepped forward his head on one side studying them closely.

'German?' his voice crackled, choking out the question.

Rance shook his head violently, 'No, no, English, English, at the same time showing him his uniform jacket.

There was another discussion, the man smiled and held out his hand. Rance grasped the hand in relief and the rest of the men gathered round talking loudly full of smiles fingering their uniforms.

'I hope they don't think we've come to liberate them,' cracked Cross, laughing.

The man gestured for them to follow him and strode off across the fields. For over an hour they walked with the man talking most of the way. Rance could only smile weakly and shake his head not understanding a word. On entering a wood the man became silent and walked quickly down a narrow path He raised his voice, shouting loudly sending the birds scattering from the branches above them. He stopped to listen and was answered by another shout in the distance. The man turned smiled at them and hurried on.

Six bearded and heavily armed men stood facing them in a clearing behind them were pitched two tents. Their guide spoke rapidly gesturing towards Rance and Cross. A tall man obviously their leader looked at them with hard weary eyes.

'Welcome our camp you rest with us,' he said in broken English. 'But you no stay we Jew, everybody enemy is better we show other partisans, they help, OK.'.

Rance thanked him, 'One thing I would like to know,' he asked, 'Which country are we in?'

The man looked surprised at such a question, 'Why Poland of course.'

Now shown to one of the tents they slept.

The screams in his dream were true and vivid, he was back in Boulogne 1940 sliding down the roof of a house with Anna his girlfriend sitting on the top held tightly by a German soldier, she was crying and screaming, he too screamed when he went over the edge and felt himself grabbed by the shoulder.

He woke with a start perspiration drenching his body to find the tall Jew shaking him. Bleary eyed he staggered to his feet waking Cross. The Jew handed them some old clothes that were well worn and dirty,

'Put on we burn uniforms you no trace, you get caught now with these old clothes,' he said, drawing a finger across his throat to emphasise the point, 'They shoot you a spy that the risk you take. There small railway station not far here we arranged the railway guard you travel in back he hide you. Not be afraid he good man.'

'Train go Czestochowa, from there we not know, but he will know, OK,'

They shook hands and followed the tall Jew for three miles to the small halt and waited for the train. Rance and Cross spent the twelve hours it took to reach Czestochwa dozing having given up trying to speak to the guard who understood no English and sat whittling a piece of wood. It was dark and raining when they arrived and upon leaving the railway yard they entered a maze of streets before being ushered into a small house. The guard shook their hands grinned and promptly disappeared into the rain swept night.

Their host was a portly built man with a sallow skin and slightly stooped. Rance thought he looked ill and probably was. He couldn't speak any English either and waving them to a seat he disappeared, leaving them wondering what was going to happen next.

Dawn broke with the sun shining weakly through the scurrying clouds the portly man reappeared with a cart pulled by two horses that looked as if they'd seen better days and another man who sat smiling on the seat beside him.

Using sign language the two Poles made them lie in the back covering them with dirty sacking. Rance fought the urge to vomit as it stank of pig manure and rotten cabbage and feeling Cross moving uneasily by his side he resisted the urge to jump out. The rattling wheels on the cobbled stones gave way to a swishing sound as they moved on to a dirt track while he lay listening to the sounds of other carts passing going the other way.

The sun had started to set and at last they were allowed to sit up and survey their surroundings. It appeared they were entering the courtyard of a large house. Rance stared up at the building in wonder. Not a house. A chateau. It towered above them in the fading light its dozens of windows glinting in the dying sun's rays with turrets that pointed sharp fingers of light grey stone towards the darkening sky.

The driver jumped down from the cart in front of two giant double doors and rang the bell. A butler appeared and after a short discussion he went away and reappeared with a tall distinguished looking man. Another discussion followed ending with the tall man beckoning Rance and Cross to join him. Rance looking at the tall distinguished man noted that he wore expensive tailor made clothes, and his silvery grey hair was carefully groomed and neat. He spoke in English without a trace of an accent.

'Welcome to my home but first things first. A bath some clean clothes then food.' He lifted his arm and motioned to the servants.

'They'll show you to your rooms we dine at eight afterwards we'll talk.'

He turned and left the great hall.

Rance followed the servants looking round in awe. Beautiful antique furniture stood against the walls. Large mirrors in golden ornate frames reflected the lights from two chandeliers hanging elegantly from the high moulded ceilings where hundreds of crystals threw back a dazzling display of colourful rainbows and two staircases curved gracefully down to meet the highly polished floor.

He stood in his richly furnished bedroom not believing the luxury while a servant proceeded to run his bath in an adjoining room. Rance caught sight of himself in a full length mirror it was like looking at a stranger. A thin brown skull stared back with eyes that had a grim hardness about them, eyes that were normally brilliant blue but now seemed to be slate grey.

Sliding out of the filthy clothes he examined the sores and insect bites on his thin and emancipated body with disgust. When he stepped into the hot steaming bath the servant gingerly picked up his clothes between thumb and forefinger and carried them from the room. The hot soapy water flowed over his aching body soothing him making him feel drowsy.

He started to doze relaxing in the luxury of his first bath in-- he tried to remember how long, but failed. So much had happened since his escape the first time in 1940. A vision of Anna, her mother and the Le Becs in Boulogne crowded in on his thoughts. The memory of her screaming his name when the Gestapo dragged her away the blood running down his badly cut arm, which made him suddenly sit up and rub fiercely at his body and the jagged scar with the soap, blinking back the mist in his eyes.

His mind drifted into the death cells of the Belgium prison where he was kept and tortured both mentally and physically before the Gestapo pretended to shoot him.

The servant returned with new clean clothes breaking his mood. He shaved away the stubble on his face and looked at the new man emerging. Satisfied with his appearance he carefully dressed and joined Cross in the dining room with their host.

'Gentlemen, this is my wife, I apologise for not giving our names but it is safer this way.' said the distinguished man who was now dressed in a black dinner jacket and bow tie. His wife was also tall and elegant her long black dress almost touching the floor complete with a single strand of pearls around her neck and her hair although starting to turn grey was beautifully styled shoulder length. In these surroundings Rance thought she should have been wearing a crown, he almost bowed.

Seated at a long table covered with a brilliant white table cloth he stared at the silver knives, forks, and spoons that seemed to stretch for miles on either side. Two servants, not the ones that had shown them to their rooms scurried round serving the several courses. Rance carefully noted which piece of cutlery was being used and followed suite. He could see Cross was completely relaxed and at ease with it all.

They discussed the war their host asked them if they had any recent news. They shook their heads telling of their escape and journey which took up the rest of the conversation until their meal ended and their host's wife excused herself and left the table. The grey haired man leaned back in his chair and lit a cigarette before turning and dismissing the servants. He stared hard and long at his guests before speaking.

'The German's grip on my country is becoming tighter every day. They have left me alone because of who I am which doesn't concern you my identity you are best not knowing. Needless to say it is only a matter of time before they turn their attention to me.'

Pausing to draw on his cigarette he continued, 'It will not be safe for you to stay here so I will put you in touch with the Polish Home Army or the AK as we call them. They are partisans split into small groups living rough in the forests. Their aim is to disrupt the German lines of communication in any way they can. Also they try to protect the farmers and villagers from the Einsatzgruppen, Nazi mobile killer squads. All psychopaths under the command of psychopath officers.'

His voice became hard and bitter, The Gestapo and German police along with their troops are committing mass murder amongst our villages and farmers. They destroy whole communities and install their own people. That is why we must fight back or very soon there won't be anybody left.'

His voice was trailing into silence and he stood up throwing the remains of his cigarette into the fire place. 'I must tell you that I can't see any chance of you getting back to England. Not that I can foresee the future but things are getting worse, I fear for us all. 'He poured them a brandy and sat down again.

'The day after tomorrow you will be taken to meet some of the partisans, there you will be given a choice, either hide until the war finishes one way or the other or you can fight with us against our common enemy. He paused again and sipped at his drink..

'If you decide to fight you must know there is no quarter given on either side. In other words there are no prisoners taken. The golden rule to remember is never be taken alive. If you are you'll be tortured for information then shot. His face broke into a grim smile. 'The choice is yours.'

Rance felt his stomach churning, he stared at Cross who was sitting opposite. He already knew the answer and could see it in his friend's eyes. Their host glanced at his watch, 'It's getting late, I have a lot to do tomorrow and you must get some rest. I bid you good night.'

He found it hard to sleep despite feeling exhausted. He was about to re-join the war this time hundreds of miles behind enemy lines. Was he really in central Poland? Would he ever see England again? He finally drifted off into a restless nightmare of being chased by a pack of howling dogs and screaming men. The Gestapo were at him again thinking he was a spy forcibly pouring warm urine down his throat at the same time slashing at him across the head with their pistols.

Waking with a start he found himself covered in sweat with most of the blankets on the floor then he relaxed realising that dawn had broken and the sun was shining brightly through the window.

The two of them spent the morning walking round the well-tended gardens with lawns that had never seen a weed. The grey haired man joined them for lunch.

'I'm sorry but you'll have to move to-night. I've made the arrangements and one of my best men will accompany you. Once again you'll travel by cart,' he smiled, 'but this time you'll be covered in clean sacks. I'll say goodbye now because I have to entertain the local German Commander to-night. 'Good luck and may God go with you both.'

It was still daylight when they left the chateau, their cart was the same one they arrived in, but as promised the sacks were clean. The sun finally sank behind the trees and darkness closed round them like a protecting blanket making it impossible to see the track ahead, but the horses never missed a step, weaving ever deeper into the forest.

An hour later they entered a clearing with the faint outline of a small building in the centre. The cart halted and a man stepped out of the darkness behind them. There was a whispered discussion between him and the driver before Rance and Cross followed the guide into the building. The room was lit by one small oil lamp that cast jumping shadows round a room containing another three men. Thick cigarette smoke hung like smog above their heads mixing with the smell of stale sweat which pervaded the air. A man in the centre of the room spoke quickly, the driver answered, speaking slowly and quietly while Rance studied the men. All were heavily armed with German machine pistols and wearing German made boots. It didn't take much brain power to guess how they acquired them. Their clothes were sweat stained and well worn. A heated discussion broke out with the men looking grimly at the two Englishmen.

'I think our future is being discussed,' Rance whispered to Cross.

The talking stopped and the man who had spoken first beckoned them to come forward where they were met with a huge grin and a fierce slap on the back.

Bottles of homemade Vodka appeared and Rance found himself with his head back gulping down the fiery liquid as if it was his last night on earth. It hit the back of his throat and roared down to his stomach like a time bomb which exploded and sent the whole lot back, he choked, gagged, and was promptly sick joining Cross against the hut wall. The room vibrated with the whooping laughter of the men. Rance walked slowly back into the centre of the room and gingerly took another swallow this time it stayed down, leaving him with a warm glow and a flushed face.

The men crowded round each one slapping his back and offering a toast. Cross joined in and the two of them offered toast for toast with the liquid quickly working on their empty stomachs. Rance tried to focus his eyes on their leader sitting next to him on the edge of the table. The room moved up down and round. He attempted to stand and promptly rolled off on to the dirt floor. Lying there he couldn't stop laughing he didn't understand what they were saying and laughing about, but it sounded funny to him.

He woke up to a pain that throbbed and poked into every corner of his brain. Groaning he staggered outside breathing in the clean morning air. Cross was sitting on a bench looking a picture of misery. A man with a week's growth of stubble on his chin thrust a steaming hot mug of an evil tasting drink into his hand. He sipped at it cautiously unsure about the smell.

'It's supposed to be soup at least, that's what I think it is.' said Cross. 'There are bits of cabbage and Swede floating about and maybe crushed acorns or nuts, I'm not sure which. Anyway I can't touch the stuff.'

Rance forced himself to drink half before throwing the rest away.

Their horse and cart was wheeled into the clearing and they were made to sit in the back. Two armed horsemen rode behind and they wheeled out of the clearing to the shouts and cheers of the men left behind.

For two days they kept moving north through almost flat countryside interspersed with small farms and villages, It was mid-afternoon on the third day with the weather blowing a full gale before they finally arrived at a dilapidated barn. The men swung open the large double doors and the horse and cart was wheeled inside. Rance clambered down soaked and half frozen sniffing at the smell of cow dung and fresh hay. Part of the roof leaked but most of the barn was dry. He helped the men close the heavy barn doors leaving them in semi-darkness. They sat shivering on a bed of hay, unable to converse with their guides.

'I could do with a mug of that soup now,' mumbled Cross. 'I wonder how long we'll be here they seem to be waiting for someone.'

Two hours later they were alerted by a long low whistle from outside. One of the guides opened a small door at the back of the barn and two men entered. The first was slightly built with sharp features, wearing a flat hat that dripped rain onto an already soaked dirty raincoat that was once white but now had deteriated into a muddy stained brown. Over his left shoulder was slung a German sub machine gun and his pockets bulged with what Rance could only assume was spare ammunition. The other was younger, about twenty five with broad shoulders, wearing similar clothes but without a hat.

His rain soaked hair was plastered with water droplets running down his tough and mean looking face.

A long conversation ensued with frequent glances in their direction. The talking ended, and the slightly built man walked over and pointed to himself. 'Krolik,' turning, he pointed to his partner, ' Pies,' he said, starting to speak rapidly in Polish.

Rance, shrugging, held his arms open to show he didn't understand.

The man called Krolik grinned, and shook their hands while Pies stood back eyeing them suspiciously.

Krolik turned up his collar and walked to the door, beckoning them to follow. Most of the day they walked along narrow farm tracks and it was late afternoon when they entered the suburbs of a small town. He noticed Krolik nervously looking at his watch while they walked through the narrow streets. German troops were everywhere, Rance was reminded of the time in 1940 when he was brought into Boulogne in a similar fashion. It started to rain heavily again when they entered a courtyard surrounded by a three story block of apartments, each with its own small balcony.

The courtyard was deserted, the bad weather keeping everyone inside. Entering through a narrow doorway with peeling paintwork and a broken hinge they climbed the three flights of stairs to the top. Krolik tapped lightly on a door facing the stairs. An old man let them in, who despite his age held himself upright and was dressed in clean well pressed clothes. Krolik spoke to the two women standing near a well-scrubbed kitchen table.

The older woman had a kindly but worn looking face showing worry and suffering, there was sadness to her eyes while nervously fiddling with her apron. Rance's attention became riveted on the young woman at her side, marvelling at her beauty.

He used all his will power to avoid staring down the length of her perfectly formed body, instead he looked into her large deep fathomless brown eyes and was lost. Her hair, just washed and groomed shone with a black lustre framing a pale oval face with high cheek bones. He reluctantly pulled his gaze away from the girl and addressed the older woman.

'Me Rance, him Donald, we no Polish, we English.' He stopped and waited for a reaction.

"That's all right, I speak a little English,' said the young woman quietly.

Rance swung round to face her, gaping in astonishment.

Her eyes were studying him with a calm dispassionate look.

He fidgeted, conscious of his dirty unshaven appearance.

'This is our home, what we have is also yours,' she said at last smiling, showing perfectly formed white teeth. 'We have been asked by our commander to give you shelter.

Rance shook her hand feeling it cool and firm and becoming tongue tied he felt like an idiot with nothing to say.

Speaking to Cross she said, 'Unfortunately we can't keep the two of you here,' she motioned to Krolik. 'This man will take you to another place where you will be safe. After a while you will be together again but first we will teach you a little Polish, because without that knowledge you stand no chance.'

Rance shook Cross's hand gripping it hard.

'Until we meet again my friend, by the way you'd better get used to that soup,' he said trying to joke.

Cross grinned, 'I wonder if I'll have as much luck as you. Don't make a pig of yourself.' he responded.

Rance thumped him playfully when Cross accompanied Krolik and Pies out through the door.

'My mother says you must be hungry, she will make you something to eat. Please sit at the table,' the young woman said sitting opposite him.

Much to his relief the meal was a hot thick stew with a little bread although he didn't think there was much meat in it, but the vegetables were fresh. Rance tried to eat slowly aware of those beautiful big brown eyes watching him, but his stomach unaccustomed to the rich food made him choke.

'My name is Izabel this is my mother Anya and my grandfather Edward. When was the last time you had any food ?' she asked.

'I'm afraid I can't remember' he said trying to think, 'but this is lovely tell your mother she's a good cook, and please will you tell her how grateful I am for your hospitality.

She leaned forward with her arms resting on the table top.

'What did your friend mean when he said, 'Don't make a pig of yourself?' I'm unfamiliar with that expression.'

Rance coughed to hide his embarrassment and avoided her inquisitive eyes by staring down at his empty plate.

'He was meaning not to eat too much I think,' he replied gruffly.

A sudden realisation dawned on him, he stood up his face white.

'Why didn't you eat with me, is it because you have no food and that I have eaten the last? he asked dismayed at the thought.

He stared at them his face a miserable picture of remorse. Izabel came round the table and made him sit down.

'Please don't be sorry we wanted to. It was our way of saying welcome,' she said softly then quickly changed the subject.

'Excuse me for staring, but although I speak a little English I have never met an Englishman before, I would-'

Rance interrupted , 'And the first one you do meet, eats you out of house and home.'

'That's another expression I've never heard of,' she retorted.

Rance gave up, he didn't want to fall out with this beautiful woman sitting opposite him. 'I'm sorry if I've upset you I feel terrible knowing I'd eaten the last of your food. Please forgive me.' he said apologetically.

Izabel was furious with herself for being so unthinking and letting him know. Her mother had always criticised her impulsive behaviour. She'd felt sorry for him standing there so thin with his face showing suffering far beyond the ravages of the weather. She smiled at him trying to put him at ease.

'I'm not upset, come I will show you to your room.'

She opened a door to reveal a small room containing two beds a wardrobe, bedside cabinet and one chair. 'You will be sharing with my grandfather the other bed was my brother's.'

'Where is your brother now,?' he asked .

She turned her face from him and didn't answer.

'Tomorrow we start your first lesson in Polish, we do not have very long because it's too dangerous here for you and us. When you have learnt enough to get by I will take you to your friend. She stopped and stared up into his face 'It must be hard for you not knowing the language and so far from your home. To want to fight with us against the Germans in such circumstances makes you a very brave man.'

She turned and left him, softly closing the door behind her.

CHAPTER 4

Izabel enjoyed teaching the Englishman basic Polish, he learned quickly the words and short sentences becoming quite proficient in the few weeks he'd been staying with them.

Some days she would keep up the pretence of going to work on the farm at Blezun where she became friends with the farmer and his family, enabling her to bring back small bundles of food for them all.

Rance received his false papers on the fourth week and puzzled over the name Volksdeutche stamped inside.

Izabel explained it was the German way of identifying all Poles of German origin, and that it made it easier at road blocks and even getting more food. She warned him that ordinary Poles hated them and to be careful. When he was ready to join the partisans he would be issued with an ordinary Polish ID and to use the two when circumstances warranted it.

He became bored trying to study by himself when Izabel was away, even practising on Anya and Edward didn't help matters so he would pace the floor waiting for Izabel to return.

He still felt a prisoner shut in the apartment and there were times when she wouldn't return for two days and he worried for her safety guessing she was on a mission. Despite his attempt to be dispassionate and impassive towards her he couldn't help his feelings towards her grow.

Bending over the Polish books together he was conscious of the sweet clean smell of her hair when it gently brushed against his cheek, and sitting opposite he would become lost in the beautiful large brown eyes that swung from a mischievous twinkle into something more, a sensual passion which Rance sensed was just beneath the surface, unsettling him bringing back emotions which he thought he'd left in France.

Deliberately he kept his distance trying hard not to show his new feelings towards her, and he knew now he must move away, that he couldn't risk her life if he was caught in her apartment. There was no way he would want her to be dragged away, to die under torture like he was sure Anna had back in Boulogne.

He had to leave, it was time to fight.

Izabel had worked hard that day stacking the hay on the farm near Blezun. She was tired but her mind was focused on the lone Englishman back in her apartment.

At first he seemed cold and remote as she'd imagined all Englishmen to be. When as time progressed she got to know him better, she realised that something had happened in his recent past that he didn't want to talk about she knew from what little things he'd said that he'd suffered at the hands of the Gestapo and could sense the tension in him. Even so he had a good sense of humour and they would laugh together whenever he got his Polish words wrong. Sometimes she would catch him staring at her with something more than friendship in his eyes and it excited her which made her angry with herself. There had been no word from Marek since he'd kissed her goodbye all those weeks ago, she'd had news that he'd been back in the area, so why hadn't he contacted her? Now he'd gone again and she was left to wonder.

Izabel returned to Piotrkow. Tonight she would try and get him to talk about his past perhaps that would help him. She turned into her street and found it strangely deserted and her heart beat faster with trepidation at the sight of a German staff car parked outside her apartment.

She dismounted and with trembling limbs walked towards the entrance, faltering at the sight of the German lieutenant and his Sergeant interpreter standing at the bottom of the stairs. Hiding her feelings she tried to walk past but felt herself gripped forcibly by the arm and taken swiftly towards the car. 'It's not everybody gets to ride in a staff car,' the lieutenant smirked in her ear. 'Major Schneller wants to see you regarding a personal matter and we wouldn't want to keep him waiting would we?'

Had they found the Englishman? Was her mother and grandfather safe? Fearfully she entered the Gestapo HQ and followed the fat lieutenant into a large office. The Major sat behind his polished desk where she stood silently facing him, hating the figure who was busily writing a letter, totally ignoring her.

Putting down the pen his eyes slowly moved up and fixed on her face, once again the dead fish like eyes sent shivers of revulsion through her body.

He leaned back in his chair, 'Well, fetch the lady a chair then,' he ordered the lieutenant who hastily placed a seat behind her. She was surprised at how good his Polish was and wondered if he was a Volksdeutche. She sat down.

'You wish to speak to me sir?' she asked her voice hardly above a whisper.

He didn't answer, instead he snapped his fingers at the lieutenant, 'I'll call you when I need you, Schmidt,' he said dismissively.

Schneller walked around the desk and sat on the corner swinging his highly polished boot.

Izabel stared at the floor not daring to look at him afraid she would show the loathing in her eyes. He didn't speak and the seconds ticked by making her feel sick the tension growing. Finally he rose to his feet and walking behind her put a cold clammy hand on her shoulder, she froze in terror.

'I have some good news for you, I've found your brother,' he hissed in her ear. 'He's in a camp in Germany, so I've requested he be sent back to work here. At the moment he's quite well.'

Izabel understood the hidden threat in Schneller's voice.

'I promise that you'll be able to see him when he returns.' he said silkily, his fingers moving from her shoulder to the nape of her neck. Catching hold of her hair he steadily pulled her head backwards so she was forced to stare up into his face. White spittle gathered at the corners of his mouth and when he spoke it fell on her forehead. 'I know you will be suitably grateful'

'You're hurting me sir,' she whispered her voice surprisingly level and calm, no sign of the hatred and anger that now consumed her.

Surprised at her remark, Schneller let go of her hair and returned to his desk picking up his pen, 'Schmidt will take you home, I'm sure you'll dwell on what I've just said,' he remarked coldly.

Izabel sat in the back seat on the way home keeping well away from the fat lieutenant conscious of his leering stare.

'Herr Schneller likes his women to come to him gratefully even if they are blackmailed into it,' the Lieutenant sneered and laughing at his own joke placed a hand on her knee.

'It's a game he plays with women you see.' His hand moved further up her leg and leaning forward he smirked into her face,

'Don't you worry, I'll look after you,' he crowed.

Izabel sat further back in her seat away from his stinking breath and clawing hands. Her eyes were flashing in anger and disgust.

'I'm sure Herr Schneller would be interested in what you have just said,' she snapped and thought he would explode. First he went white then dark red in anger, now she realised she'd made a very bad enemy. Oh why was she so impulsive! it was with relief she saw they'd stopped outside her apartment block. Schmidt flung open the car door.

'Geh raus du schampe, get out you Polish bitch,' he shouted, pushing her out onto the pavement, then thumping on the side of the car with his fist he shouted at the driver to move.

Still shaking she stood on the pavement watching the car drive away with Schmidt sitting in the back mouthing obscenities. Running up the stairs slamming the door behind her, she calmly told Rance and her mother almost all of what had happened. They listened in silence. Rance stiffened. 'Are you sure you're all right, they haven't hurt you.'?

She shook her head, 'They were just trying to frighten me.'

Rance remained unconvinced, 'I must leave here and join Don, the risk is too great for you and your family, I know enough of the language to get by.'

Izabel reluctantly agreed, 'I will have to clear it with Commander Curen, that's his code name, they all have code names,' she informed him.

'You'll be safer in the forest, here in Piotrkow there are too many spies and informers. I'll take you to Don.'

She put a hand over his mouth when he started to protest that it would be too dangerous for her.

'Don is with a girl friend of mine in a village called Blezun about fifteen kilometres from here, I would like to visit her anyway it's near the farm where I work so it's much safer for me than you think,' she said convincingly.

Two days later with a new set of travel papers and a newly acquired bicycle for Rance they set off early in the morning and queued at the first road block. As his turn for inspection approached his hands became moist and his breathing quickened. Izabel went through and rode off without giving any sign that they were together. His turn came, it was an anti-climax. The German soldier glanced quickly at his papers and waved him though.

Peddling at a leisurely pace in the fresh clean air breathed new life into him. Confined to the small apartment for weeks had nearly driven him mad. He felt the hot sun on his back and the wind in his face while watching enthralled by Izabel's lithe youthful figure riding along ahead of him. A passion stirred again in him, easing away the pain of France, bringing him new hope and a new lease on life.

They entered the village of Blezun just before mid-day where the road was joined by a narrow gauge railway line and a clear wide river that ran alongside them both. Near the far end of the village Izabel opened a gate and they walked into a farmyard. The house was single story and built of wood that was grey and weather beaten. At the far end of the dried mud-coated yard stood a dilapidated barn with large double doors and a small window near the roof top. There were no sign of any animals and everything looked overgrown and neglected.

'Marie, Marie, masz towareytwo,' shouted Izabel, excitedly.

A tall slender woman came to the door drying her hands and with cries of delight they hugged each other. Cross appeared from behind her and joined in the welcome.

'Rance, you young dog, you've put on weight and had a haircut. Mind you, you're still as ugly as ever but it's still good to see you,' he laughed, shaking Rance's hand and they sparred with each other, grinning like Cheshire cats.

'He's not ugly,' Izabel said impulsively, 'I think he's very handsome.'

Cross looked knowingly at her, 'Oh you think so do you?' he said with a sly smile.

Izabel blushed and became flustered. 'Well, I mean,'-

Rance saved her, 'Take no notice of him he's always pulling someone's leg.'

'He's not going to pull one of my legs,' gasped Izabel, horrified at the thought. The two girls looked on in astonishment when the men collapsed with laughter.

The afternoon was spent with the four of them swimming and playing together in the river. For the two men it was like a dream and that they would soon wake up in a prison cell again, or worse. To Rance the war seemed a thing of the past, a bad memory something to thrust into ones subconscious and forget. He didn't want this day to end and when he and Izabel swam together their bodies occasionally touched, Rance felt his whole body become charged with fire.

It was the middle of the afternoon when Cross pulled Rance to one side, 'Let's take a walk,' he said quietly, and the two of them wondered off down the river bank.

'I'm glad we're together again Rance, but I feel we won't be here much longer,' said Cross solemnly. 'Marie tells me things are getting even worse with the Germans and a new partisan group is being formed and we're going to be part of it.'

He paused, looking sheepishly at Rance. 'Marie and me have become very close these last few weeks,' he paused again, turning to face his friend.

'Well the truth is we are more than friends, and there is only one bedroom,' he was becoming embarrassed pulling at the branch of a tree.

Rance burst out laughing pushing his friend so hard that he nearly fell in the river, 'Is that all, I thought you were going to tell me something terrible had happened,' he exclaimed before pointing an accusing finger in Cross's face.

'You were the one that told me not to make a pig of myself.'

Cross's look of embarrassment turned into a grin. 'I don't know how far your relationship has got, but at this moment in time Marie is asking Izabel if she wants to stay over for a couple of days,' he murmured sagely.

Now it was Rance who looked sheepish. 'We didn't get that far, I didn't want to abuse the family's hospitality by making an advance that she might not like.'

Cross stared at his friend in amazement.

It was Rance who now fiddled with the tree branch; he looked a picture of misery. 'The truth of the matter Don is that back in Boulogne just after the start of the war, when I escaped the first time. I became very fond of a French girl who sheltered me from the Germans. We were together nearly a year.'

He faltered, regaining the memories, a bitter note crept into his voice. 'One day we were betrayed and I managed to escape, but the Gestapo arrested her and her mother. They killed her mother under torture that I know for sure, and Anna, that's the girl's name just disappeared. The French people who befriended me afterwards said the same fate happened to her. Rance stopped to regain his composure. 'I don't want that to happen to Izabel.'

Cross felt saddened for his friend. 'I'm sorry Rance, I didn't know. War causes some terrible things to happen. I know it's easy for me to say.' But for you,' --- he lapsed into silence.

On returning to the girls Marie said, smiling at him, 'Rance, I've asked Izabel to stay for a few days. It's so nice and peaceful here.'

'I'm sure Don has told you that he and I are together so if you don't mind, I've made you two lovely comfortable beds in the hayloft at the top of the yard.

Rance walked over to Izabel, 'I think that's a wonderful idea, what do you think?' he said disarmingly.

'Yes, I think it's a lovely idea,' she answered lightly trying to keep her voice steady.

What was left of the afternoon Rance and Izabel spent walking alone in the forest, careful to keep away from the main road. Excitedly she pointed out the different kinds of birds nesting high in the branches. Deer and even wild boar crossed their path while they stood in silence with shafts of sunlight finding their way to the forest floor.

Rance listening to the many birds singing their hearts out as if they were in tune with him, combined with the gentle breeze rustling the branches felt at peace with himself.

He became conscious of her hand in his and all the pain in his mind slowly ebbed away. Looking down into that beautiful upturned face and large brown eyes made his head swim, he gentle put his arms around her waist pulling her close. Her eyes became half closed when he bent forward and kissed her full moist lips that were suddenly full of hidden passionate promise, he could feel her shaking when the contours of their bodies merged together.

Gently she pulled away her face flushed and radiant.

'Come on I'll race you to the river bank,' she laughed her eyes sparkling, and together they ran like children.

She was like a deer bounding through the trees he found it impossible to catch her.

Izabel was in love she knew it, it overwhelmed her right through to her very soul. She'd fought against it. Marek had been gone long ago. What she thought of as love she now realised was just the romantic dreams of a young girl who had been rescued by him.

This was different. Her whole body was alive and tingling the war, just a bad dream. The war,-

She stopped in mid-flight gasping for air, her face now chalk white, she turned to face Rance, who startled by the sudden change, came to a halt in front of her. 'What is it, what's the matter?' he asked his face full of concern. She came to him he could feel her shaking. She started to cry.

Her body shook, the tears rolled down her cheeks.

'Rance, I don't want you to die please don't fight. They said that if you wanted to you could stay in hiding.' She clung to him, her tears soaking his shirt.

Rance gently stroked her long black hair, his heart going out to her.

'I can't do that it isn't the way. I wouldn't be able to live with myself if I did. Until the Germans are defeated we can only live for today.'

She started crying again her heart pounding. She knew deep inside that he would have to fight, that he wanted to fight, and that nothing would stop him. They only had a few days and he would be gone, as Marek had gone. This war had altered all her thoughts and dreams.

'Let's go back to the house, they'll be getting worried,' she whispered.

In the evening after dinner, the two men and Marie sat sipping her home made beer, which Rance found to be particularly strong, while Izabel declined, saying she found it too much for her stomach, They laughed and joked, nobody wanted to be serious that night. Eventually Rance stood up,

'I'm going to get some fresh air before I go to bed.' He looked at Izabel, 'Would you like to come for a walk'

Neither wanted to go for a walk, instead they went hand in hand towards the barn where Marie had left a small lantern burning just inside the door. They climbed a ladder and found a little room had been prepared with two beds made of straw covered with a blanket. The window overlooked the yard and down towards the river. The moon had risen and its silvery rays made the water sparkle and dance, it seemed just for them. Arm in arm with heads touching they marvelled at the scene before them.

Slowly they turned to face each other with Izabel's beauty enhanced by the flickering oil lamp, her eyes seemed luminous when they caught and reflected the rich glow.

'Rance,' her voice was barely above a whisper, 'We both know that we can't go any further with this at the moment. For me because I'm not ready, and I don't know how I'll feel afterwards. And for you there is something that happened in France that you need to come to terms with first.

He felt crushed but he knew deep down that what she said was true. They were trapped in circumstances beyond their control.

Gentle he touched her face staring down into the deep luminous eyes. 'You're right it's something that we'll work out. Fate will take its course.

CHAPTER 5

With the weather hot and humid, the four spent most days playing and swimming together. Gradually the bitterness of the past eased for Rance who was happy with the laughter and joy of living. Sometimes the urge to be alone made him and Izabel break away from the other two strolling arm in arm through the forest, lost in each other's dreams, talking about everything and nothing, just happy to be together and alone.

Although always mindful of the German patrols they stayed away from the road and made sure they were back in the house before dusk. The days flew by too fast for Rance who was now fit and strong. Looking in a mirror he noted with satisfaction that he was almost back to his usual self, with an even healthier suntan as a bonus.

On the fifteenth day he walked in to Maria's house and found Izabel standing with her back to him staring out of the kitchen window. He admired the shape of her slender figure, until he saw her shoulders shaking and realised she was crying. Silently he walked up behind her and grasped her tightly round the waist. 'What's the matter, why the tears, aren't you happy?' he whispered.

'I've never been so happy,' Izabel sobbed, 'but today I have to take you and Don into the forest to meet the partisans. A new group is being formed and you're to be part of that group.'

Rance's heart missed a beat feeling the sudden surge of adrenaline. At last after all the months even years in prison and on the run with all the degradation that went with it, a chance to fight back.

Izabel choked, turning round she gripped him tightly.

'These two weeks have been the happiest days of my life, which I'll always remember,' she said weakly though her tears. But now you must go.'

It was mid-day before Rance, Izabel, and Donald Cross set off on bicycles. Rance noticed the sky had turned leaden, storm clouds reared like giant mountains on the horizon, he could smell rain in the air which had become still and oppressive. He'd never been superstitious but he hoped it wasn't an omen. The road they were on followed the banks of the river for three miles then turned sharply away.

It was there they left the road, turning on to a track which twisted between the huge pine trees of a forest. He felt the mosquitoes start to bite and gave up trying to fight them. The tops of the trees started to sway bending in a stiff breeze that heralded the coming of rain.

The huge drops hurtled down like missiles thrown by the Gods angered by the intrusion of humans in their domain, exploding in fury on the dry parched earth. Within seconds the three were soaked and their track turned into great puddles with mud coloured water. Rance didn't mind the rain for it got rid of the oppressive stifling heat and kept the mosquitoes at bay.

An hour later, thoroughly soaked Izabel led them into a large clearing with three small wooden houses, and standing in the centre was a giant oak tree its branches towering over them. Beyond the houses Rance could see rows of vegetables. A figure emerged from behind one of the houses and beckoned them to approach.

Rance recognised the man he'd met before as Krolik and tried out the polish he'd been taught, offering greetings. He received a fast response in return, none of which he understood, he shrugged in embarrassment.

Izabel chided Krolik, telling him to speak more slowly.

Krolik, thinking it funny, burst out laughing and slapped Rance on the back making him wince. 'Now you Pole, yes, welcome to Kalow,' he chortled.

They all laughed and followed Krolik into the middle house.

'Meet our new recruits,' he shouted loudly over the noise of talking men. They fell silent. The light was dim, and the room full of cigarette smoke which mingled with the smell of cooking from a small stove at the far end of the room. The men were sat or lounging against the walls on all sides. Sitting at a table was a teenage girl and an older woman that Rance assumed to be her mother. A tall well-built young man older than Rance stepped forward holding out his hand.

'Welcome to the Polish Home Army, my name is Marek,' he said.

Rance heard Izabel's sharp intake of breath and looked at her with a puzzled expression, she was staring transfixed at the young man.

'You!' she blurted, 'I thought you'd gone forever.'

Marek put his arm round her smiling. 'I've been a long way from here, there was no way of contacting you,' he said by way of explanation bending his head to kiss her.

Alarmed at this sudden turn of events Rance stepped between them.

'Izabel, what's this all about, how well do you know this man?' he asked angrily.

Izabel flushed, 'This is not the time to discuss it,' she stammered, trying to remain calm.

'What have you to do with my girlfriend?' snapped Marek, rounding on Rance.

'You're girlfriend, you've got it wrong! Why don't you ask her?' countered Rance, his eyes turning grey and cold.

Marek moved closer, his own eyes starting to burn with anger.

The room became deathly quiet, the startled men watched expectantly, sensing a fight. Izabel went to move between the two men as Marek struck.

Rance saw it coming but didn't move fast enough and Marek's fist exploded on the side of his head sending him reeling backwards against the table. Dimly he heard the teenage girl screaming and the older lady shouting. 'Not in my home,' before he was manhandled outside by some of the men and thrown off the porch..

Marek ran down the steps with fists swinging, forcing Rance to duck clear and bring his own fist up in a vicious upper cut which caught Marek full on the side of the jaw. He grunted in pain and fell backwards in the mud. Rance moving swiftly after him, only to be caught in the groin when Marek kicked upwards.

'Stop them, stop them, they're killing each other,' screamed Izabel wildly jumping in between the fighting men. It brought another round of cheering encouragement from the watching partisans who had started to take bets on the outcome.

'I'll give odds that the girl will win,' one shouted, and the other men collapsed in fits of laughter.

'You idiots, save your fighting for the Germans,' she sobbed frantically swinging her small fists at them both.

'You bloody stupid Pole,' Rance snarled at Marek in English, under a barrage of blows.

'What did he say?' cried Marek still enraged, falling back as Rance retaliated.

'He said you're a bloody stupid Pole,' Izabel screamed back, adding, 'Which you are.'

That reply bought whoops of laughter from the surrounding crowd while Rance and Marek looked around in astonishment at the men, who still laughing moved between them holding them apart. Izabel glowered at them both.

'I think we should talk,' she exclaimed sharply. 'You first,' nodding at Rance and walked into the forest, while he simmered walking angrily after her.

She told him in no uncertain terms what she thought of his behaviour, before explaining that she now had no interest in Marek. Satisfied by this he walked back to the others who by now had gone inside. He nodded to Marek. 'You next.' Marek glowered and went to her.

Rance stared round self-consciously at the men who couldn't hide their amusement, prodding each other and grinning.

Cross sat against the wall and Rance joined him. 'At least they have a sense of humour, I thought they were going to shoot us' said Cross out the corner of his mouth trying hard not to smile,' but Rance had spotted it.

'Don't you start, 'I'm not having a good day,' he growled rubbing his head.

Cross burst out laughing, Rance climbed to his feet and stalked off outside where he waited still simmering with anger for Izabel and Marek to return.

Izabel was first, she brushed passed him without a word and went inside. He stiffened at Marek's approach waiting with clenched fists. They stood warily eyeing each other, Marek's face showing a red mark where Rance fist had landed.

'Izabel has told me how she feels about you Englishman,' Marek said speaking slowly so Rance could understand,

'But I am also in love with her,' he stopped, searching for the right words.

'It's because for that reason I will not fight with you, but I must warn you, I'll try to get her back and one day I will. In the meantime no more will be said. Our fight is with the Germans and that's what we must do.' He stopped, staring at him sullenly.

Rance didn't understand all that was said but he got the general idea. They turned and walked back inside to join the grinning men, neither attempting to shake hands.

Izabel disappeared with the other women, no doubt to gossip about him and Marek thought Rance despondently, and picking a space on the floor tried to sleep.

The next morning Izabel had gone, having left a message with the young girl Marian. He opened it and read that she couldn't stand saying goodbye. That she would see him soon she hoped and to be careful. She pleaded with him not to judge Marek too harshly because he too had suffered in this war.

Rance carefully folded the letter and put it away before meeting Cross and the partisans round the kitchen table.

When he faced Marek there was no sign of any animosity in the man, just a cold politeness. The rest of the men stood round grinning expectantly looking from one to the other. Marek ignored them, carefully placing two German machine guns on the table and two bags holding spare ammunition. He looked at Rance. 'Have you ever used one of these?'

Rance picked one up shaking his head while he ran his fingers along the barrel and onto the butt which gave him a sense of excitement, an elation that he hadn't felt for a long time, a chance to fight back.

Running his hand down the butt he felt for the trigger.

'Be careful, it's loaded,' warned Marek, taking it off him.

'This is the standard weapon used by the SS, this particular one is an old blow back model, it's different from some of the others because its cocking handle is at the rear of the action. Its rotated and pulled back like so.'

His hands were quick and sure as he demonstrated.

'The advantage is that unlike the others you can't get your fingers caught. There is a second trigger behind the first, the first trigger is for semi-automatic fire, when you pull it further it engages the second trigger for fully automatic.' He laid the gun back on the table.

'When you use this weapon never fire at the head, keep it low, stomach and chest wounds are what we're after. This is how you load.'

The instruction went on all day with rifles, pistols and hand grenades. It soon became obvious to Rance that most of the others, apart from Krolik and Pies were also new men and very nervous.

He knew they would have to be led and sensed that Marek was the man to do it. He wondered what Marek had in store for him, could he be trusted? He counted fifteen in the group besides himself and Cross. At least three were over forty years old, two under twenty with the rest in between. Marek stripped down a German rifle cleaned it and put it back together again before handing it over to Rance.

'Show me what you can do,' he said with a thin smile on his lips.

Rance had never forgotten the old Sergeant's teachings over their three years together, the hours spent blindfolded, sitting cross legged on the floor with his own rifle, stripping and feeling the parts, cleaning, and putting them back together, telling him, 'One day you may have to do this in the dark and it could save your life.'

He also taught him how to fire falling, rolling and firing again, sitting, crawling, and lying on his back still firing. The knowledge which he retained he would now put to use. Running his fingers over the rifle he noticed it was slightly different from the English models but not much. Lifting his eyes, he kept them firmly fixed on Marek's face. Slowly at first, then with speed the rifle came apart, his fingers never fumbled he cleaned and replaced the gleaming parts in one swift and continuous movement still with his eyes fixed on Marek, who slowly lost his smile.

Rance finished with a flourish, spinning the rifle, presenting it butt first.

Marek ignored the offering, turning to the other men.

'There is one golden rule which we all must obey,' he said, holding up a bullet for all to see.

'If you're trapped and you know there's no escape, you must use the last bullet on yourself. To be captured alive means you'll face torture to find out what you know and when you've told them, as inevitable you will, only then will they shoot you, or hang you. Just remember that in this war there are no prisoners kept alive,'

He looked round at the silent men as if expecting a question, when none came he continued, 'I know most of you are new to this and have much to learn, so take your orders from me, Krolik or Pies.'

He paused, looking at Rance. 'It seems the Englishman can teach you something too, so when we rest, ask him.'

He turned and walked to the door followed by Pies and Krolik,

'Now gather your things we move out in an hour.'

With his bundle containing food, spare ammunition and his rifle slung over his shoulder Rance walked over to the young girl Marian who stood with a small group of people under the giant oak.

He nodded and Marian shyly introduced them all.

'This is my father Jozef,' Rance found his hand grasped in a tight firm grip by the large man in front of him, the man carried no excess fat on his lean but strong looking body and his eyes twinkled with humour. Rance instantly liked him.

'Welcome to my home Englishman,' he boomed, from now on you will always be a friend and I thank you for coming to fight with us, even if you did start fighting with our leader first,' and they all roared with laughter.

Hurriedly she turned to the next man,

'This is our neighbour, Radice, and these are his two sons.'

Rance shook hands with the tall thin man who was still grinning.

'Take no notice of us, we have a strange sense of humour here, it's probably due to the war. We blame everything on the war. I don't know what we'll do when it finishes. Anyway it was good entertainment last night,' he said, nudging Jozef. Marian gave him a disapproving look which he totally ignored.

'You all live here in the forest?' Rance asked hurriedly, changing the subject.

'Yes, nodded Radice, we worked to keep the forest in order, it was paid for by the government and these are our homes. Now since the Germans came we give our time to the partisans.'

The last man stepped forward, Marian introduced him as Skubisz, a quiet man of medium build who shook hands without smiling but his grip was firm, he nodded a greeting.

Rance joined the group as they moved out into the forest with Marek in the lead a hundred yards ahead and Krolik bringing up the rear. Two hours later Pies changed places with Marek, and Rance found himself walking by Marek's side. The two of them were silent for several awkward minutes before Marek spoke. 'You can handle a gun Englishman, but can you fight, can you kill?'

'Yes I can fight I had the best teacher, an old Sergeant, he'd been through many battles in his lifetime some behind enemy lines. Unfortunately he was too old for this one. He died in my arms on the battle fields of France. As to the other question, yes I can kill, I'm a regular in the army and that's my training whether I want to is another matter but I will play my part have no fear of that.'

Marek walked in silence for a while pondering on Rance's answer before coming to a decision.

'I want you to help me teach these men. Teach them what you know, how to fight and survive, they already know how to die. They are only farmers and workers against well trained and well supplied troops. We have already lost many men.'

Rance realised Marek had swallowed his pride in asking for his help for the sake of his men, his estimate of the man grew.

'How much time do I have?' he asked quietly.

Marek shrugged, 'We have no time, the time is now but you and Cross won't always be with me. You will move between us and another group whose commander is a great man, far more experienced than me. His code name is Viktor all his men respect him for his courage and cunning against the enemy. You will meet him soon.'

For two days they headed northwest skirting the town of Tomaszw where they kept to the forest during daylight hours, only coming into the open at night to scavenge for food amongst the German run farms in that area. Once they stole a pig which they cut up sharing it amongst themselves, roasting the pieces over open fires, which were only lit at night for fear the Germans would see the smoke.

When they stopped to rest the men gathered round Rance and Cross trying to learn the rudimentary rules of warfare. While they learned quickly Rance knew they had run out of time some of it would help but many would have to learn the hard way, while others wouldn't live long enough.

Passing over a railway line they came by a large area of swamp land before joining another line that ran west. There Marek called a halt and briefed them by drawing a map in the sandy soil.

'Not far from here is a railway junction where two lines meet. We have orders to join forces with men from the Konski region to sabotage those lines as a troop train passes through. At this junction there is a German outpost which we have been detailed to take first.

'If we do that the Germans will take hostages from the surrounding farms and hang them,' interrupted one of the older men.

'If they do all well and good,' said Krolik reassuringly, 'for they are all Volkdeutches, who have taken over the farms in the area. The original farmers are either dead or in a forced labour camp.'

Rance glanced at his watch, four thirty am and with the sun still below the horizon dawn was like a grey stillness, silent except for the chorus of birds each marking its own territory. Laying in the tall grass soaked by the early morning dew he could just about see the German bunker and surrounding barbed wire, beyond which ran the faint outline of the railway tracks. To the right of the bunker sat a squat observation tower built of logs.

He turned his attention back to the bunker to see another soldier patrolling inside the wire. Slowly he wriggled forword mindful of the waving grass above his head and aware of Cross on his right hand side. He didn't know where the others were. He stopped when the grass gave way to barren sandy soil which he guessed had been cleared by the Germans all the way to the bunker which lay two hundred yards in front of him.

Sliding his rifle forward he rested it on his left arm after adjusting the sights and centred it on the sentry in the observation tower, waiting for Marek's signal.

When it came he gently squeezed the trigger. The sharp retort of the rifle sent the birds wheeling crying high into the air and the sentry tumbled out of sight. Before the echo of the shot had died away he was up and running with Marek, Cross, and the other men spread out in a line, firing as they ran.

Gunfire resounded all around him as the hapless soldier by the fence at first startled managed to get off two shots before he was catapulted backwards by a fusillade of bullets.

The German troops caught in their beds tumbled bleary eyed out of the bunker, the first were met by a withering blast of machine pistols, leaving the rest to retreat back inside. He reached the wire and throwing himself on his back pushed it up with his rifle before slipping underneath and twisting back onto his stomach. On his left he saw one of Marek's men attempting to climb the wire, only to be caught by a machine gun firing rapidly from a slit in the bunker throwing him backwards and leaving him screaming, hanging upside down.

The machine gun traversed the open space cutting into the Partisans, sending them diving for cover and throwing up clods of earth into his face. Coming to his feet he ran crab like towards the bunker out of the line of fire and bending down he inched to the slit where the machine gun fired continuously raking the ground in front.

Rance looked for Cross and saw him crouched by the bunker door, while over on his right he heard the sounds of a fierce fire fight. Pulling the pin from a hand-grenade he reached up and tossed it through the slit and listened to the screams of the troops inside fighting each other to escape.

Those that made the door were met by Cross's machine pistol bullets which smashed into the luckless men jammed in the doorway. Within seconds the bunker erupted and Rance threw in a second one for good measure, sending debris out through the slits. The fierce fighting on the other side of the bunker ceased as he ran towards the corner with Cross following close behind.

A fire was burning in another smaller bunker and through the smoke he saw Marek triumphantly emerging. 'We've done it,' he shouted, unable to keep the exultation out of his voice.

Rance was impressed, such had been the element of surprise that the whole action had taken but minutes and the outpost was theirs.

'I can still hear shooting,?' said Rance, a question in his voice.

'That's Krolik and Pies with the German wounded,' Marek answered stiffly.

'What about our men? I saw at least one of them die.' queried Rance.

'Any dead we will bury in the forest, any wounded that are fit enough to move we take with us, if not,-'- he turned away, the sentence unfinished, but Rance knew and felt a chill run down his spine. That last unfinished sentence and the shooting of the German wounded brought home to him the appalling savagery of this war that he and Cross were now in. There was no such thing as the Geneva Convention here. You could run, fight, or die. No other choice.

Cross returned from a head count, his face grim. 'We suffered two wounded, one looks in a bad way, but the worst is we lost the two youngest men neither of them yet eighteen,' he said quietly.

Rance felt saddened what a waste of young life, forgetting he was only twenty two years old himself. He seemed to have been living forever.

From the opposite side of the track he could see movement as the Konski partisans moved down to mine the railway line at the junction and feeder lines branching off.

Marek ordered their departure from the captured outpost. Heavily laden down with the wounded and as much spare ammunition and guns as they could carry they started back. An hour later they stopped turning at the sound of two explosions and watching as a tall column of black smoke rose over the tree tops.

'The troop train has arrived,' Krolik said while the others stared, grim-faced.

'Come we must hurry,' Marek said abruptly 'they'll be hunting us, I'm afraid this action isn't over yet.' He sent Pies back as rear guard and Krolik ahead as a scout, then for two hours they maintained a punishing pace taking it in turns to carry the wounded.

Marek at last called a halt and gratefully they rested until Pies returned in a hurry with the news that a German patrol was fast approaching from the direction of the train.

'How much time have we got?' Marek snapped.

Pies paused, fighting for breath, 'Not long, only a few minutes.'

'How many in the patrol?

'I'm not sure, perhaps more than twenty, I don't know.'

Marek wasted no time, 'Take four men and the wounded and go after Krolik. 'Tell him to keep going back the way we came and we'll try to catch up later.'

He turned to Rance and Cross. 'You'll come with me, we must fight and run, delay them and lead them in a different direction.'

He looked at their rifles. 'Forget those, use the sub machine guns and make sure you have plenty of spare ammunition.'

They followed Marek while he hunted for the best killing ground. A spot where the trees had thinned out and only saplings grew. They spread out on the other side of the partly cleared ground hiding in the denser part of the forest and waited.

Rance lay amongst the roots of a giant pine tree straining his ears and eyes for any sound or movement from the German patrol. Shafts of sunlight lit the forest floor highlighting the thousands of flying insects and butterflies that swooped and dived in endless formations. The only other sounds were of the birds that flitted high in the branches above him.

The air was still and calm the leaves of the trees dappled in shafts of light, sporting untold shades of green which turned into camouflaged forms, darting between the trees. But still only fleeting shadows, they gradually turned into running men that emerged from the denser forest opposite as they ran amongst the saplings. Rance tensed at their approach spread out in a line to the right and left of him.

His gut twisted, his throat felt dry, they were Waffen SS, the most hated and feared of all German troops in the area. He waited. At one hundred yards he took aim, at seventy five yards he started to slowly squeeze the trigger. At fifty yards he couldn't miss and the fear disappeared when he pulled the trigger, right through the single shots to fully automatic.

The shattering roar almost drowned the screams of men all but cut in half by the deadly fire at such close quarters. The beautiful tranquil scene set by nature was now transformed into a bloody hell as men rolled and died in agony on the forest floor.

Jumping a fallen tree it disintegrated behind him as the heavy calibre bullets from a machine gun chased his fleeing figure, the trees closed in offering their protection and the firing died away leaving just the sound of the crying wounded.

He looked for Marek and Cross and much to his relief saw them running together on his left hand side. It was twenty minutes before they stopped unable to run anymore. It was a further two minutes before Marek could speak. 'They'll be more careful now and will proceed with caution, afraid of another ambush, but they'll still come. It took them three hours to skirt the swamp and cross the main railway line that ran though the town of Tomaszow and a further half an hour to catch up with Pies and the wounded who were resting in a barn.

'Where's Krolik?' Marek asked Pies.

Pies shrugged, not even asking how they fared. To him the very fact that they were there was enough.

'He's gone ahead to a village he knows someone there who'll give help to the wounded and hide them.'

Gunfire echoed through the forest coming from Krolik's direction, they all became nervous and alert. Marek climbed to his feet lifting his gun, 'Someone's coming and in a hurry,' he whispered tersely.

Krolik stumbled through the undergrowth wheezing for air before collapsing at their feet. 'There's an Einsatzgruppen squad in the village ahead,' he gasped, fighting for breath, 'I think they're Ukraine with a German officer in charge.' He stared hard at Marek. 'They're killing the villagers' he stated grimly.

CHAPTER 6

Piotrekow July 1943

It was stifling hot in the operations room despite all the windows and doors being propped open. Claus Ritschel fanning himself with a sheaf of papers beamed at Major Schneller.

'All of us here must congratulate you on the success of your plan Herr Schneller,' he said, looking across at Captain Braun and his second Lieutenant who reluctantly acknowledged with a curt nod.

'We've had no more trouble west of the River Luciaza area since,' continued Claus Ritschel smugly. 'So I'm speeding up our schedule.

You'll have three more squads at your disposal; they will consist of the usual Ukrainian troops, each with a German officer of the SS.

He turned his attention to Captain Herman Braun.

'As each village is emptied and our own people installed, you will build outposts, not that you'll really need them but as a precautionary measure only, to give our farmers peace of mind.

'You'll take any advice about the areas in question from Major Schneller, is that understood?.

Braun nodded sullenly keeping his eyes fixed on Claus Ritschel, so avoiding Schneller's sardonic gaze.

'Now to a different subject Herr Schneller, I've had a request from Berlin for more young people to work in the factories, so I want you to double your efforts in that respect. Whilst we're on that subject Herr Schneller, I've been informed that you've had a young man Jarek Markowitz brought back from Germany and put in one of our local labour camps. What would be the purpose of that exercise may I ask?'

Schneller glared icily at Herman Braun before looking Claus Ritschel straight in the eye. 'I have information from one of my collaborators that this young man can lead us to other bandits that maybe left in the area and I can assure you I'll be most vigorous in pursuing this information,' he said firmly.

Herman Braun stared at him in astonishment while Claus Ritschel looked suitably impressed and changed the subject again.

'I read from your last report that you've already got some Ukrainian troops working in the area South of Tomaszow. What is the situation there now?'.

'It's my intention to eventually clear all the Poles in the villages from the boundary marked by the Sulejow to Radom road, and from where the railway line crosses that road up to Tomaszow Mas', Schneller explained.

'That means it will be easier for him,' nodding disdainfully at Herman Braun, 'to build his outposts around the outside of the whole area and not in every village like he does now.'

'An excellent idea Schneller,' Claus Ritschel rubbed his hands together in delight. 'I will report your idea to Berlin perhaps we can use it in other areas.'

Schneller walked back to his office in a good mood everything was going well he thought. He gave Lieutenant Schmidt a grimace of welcome which totally unnerved the man. He called for a cup of coffee, but didn't offer Schmidt one.

'Well, what have you to report about the girl?' he asked, slumping in his chair behind the highly polished desk staring at Schmidt who was looking nervous and wouldn't stand still.

Schneller sensed he wasn't going to like what he was about to hear. 'Speak up man, what's the matter with you?' he snapped, with sudden impatience.

'She's gone from her apartment,' Schmidt blurted, 'Nobody has seen her for two weeks. Her mother and grandfather have both been questioned and they only say she has gone to stay with a friend for a rest.'

Schmidt watched the change in Schneller's face with alarm. He wanted to turn and get out of that office as fast as possible while he stuttered the rest of his report. 'They said she was going to let them know where she was going, but as yet she hasn't.'

Schneller, beside himself with fury brought his batten down with such force on to the desk top that it broke in half and sent the coffee flying over Schmidt. The cold eyes seemed to burn into Schmidt's brain making him shudder but he was too frightened to move.

'Now you listen to me you have two days to find her and I don't want any excuses. I don't care how you do it but get results. Standing up he sent his chair crashing back against the wall and coming round the desk he pushed his face close to Schmidt's.

'Get moving you fat pig or I'll have you shovelling shit for the rest of this war,' he snarled.

Schmidt's nerve broke he turned and ran from the room wiping Schneller's spittle from his face.

Schneller sat back heavily in his chair struggling for air thinking he was going to have a heart attack. It was five minutes before he settled down to do some paper work. His orderly timidly knocked on the door.

'Come in, don't just stand there, what is it?' he grunted sourly.

The orderly placed a report on the desk and hurriedly departed. Schneller had to read it twice.

It was for Herman Braun with instructions for it to be passed to him.

Quote, 'Bandits attacked an outpost west of Tomaszow, destroying it and killing all twenty men there. Stop. They then proceeded to sabotage a troop train. Stop. On being pursued they killed and wounded a further seven German troops. Stop. The bandits are currently being hunted south of Tomaszow. Stop. End of report.

Schneller's rage returned and a black cloud engulfed his mind, he again sent his chair crashing backwards while screaming orders to get a company of his troops together. Within twenty minutes they were rolling out of Piotrkow on the Radom road with Schneller in his staff car, leading eight Troop carriers each carrying ten soldiers.

Krolik gripped Marek's arm, asking him again, 'Marek, they're killing the villagers, what are we going to do?'

Marek's slight hesitation disappeared bending over one of the wounded he thrust a pistol into his hand.

'We have no choice but to leave you here, we have to help the villagers and get help for you, so keep alert we'll be back soon,'

The two men nodded their eyes showing no emotion, knowing that if Marek failed they would be left to die.

Marek picked up his machine pistol,' Let's go,' he said tersely.

They approached the village with care spreading out fifty yards apart and Rance saw the wooden houses between the trees with one on fire. Two personnel carriers sat in the centre of the village and on one side of the road stood a group of women and children. Against the side of a house were a pile of bodies and in the back of one troop carrier under guard were a group of young men.

An officer strode before them shouting orders to his troops who were now pushing the women and children into the sights of a machine gun. Rance could hear them crying and the men in the back of the truck urging them to run. One man unable to control himself any longer jumped down and ran towards the soldier manning the machine gun. The officer walked behind him grinning and fired one shot to the head, the man staggered tried to keep running before collapsing. The officer stepped contemptuously over the still twitching body and shouted an order to the machine gunner.

Rance heard the screams of the women and children before he broke from the cover of the trees and ran out into the open between the houses.

The officer didn't see Rance, but the machine gunner did and his eyes opened wide with shock as he desperately tried to swivel the gun.

Rance, unaware that he was now screaming himself kept running towards him his machine pistol held waist high with the trigger on fully automatic. The bullets smashed into the man and gun, churning up the earth behind him.

The nerve jumping grip of the dead soldier forced the barrel into the air as it continued to pump bullets aimlessly into the sky. The officer at first paralyzed with shock acted quickly turning around, his eyes widened with fear as he lifted his pistol in panic.

Cross running alongside Rance shot the man in the chest, the force of the bullet throwing him onto his back next to the dead villager where he lay whimpering, his arms stretched out in terrified surrender. Marek ran past them with the other partisans who were spreading out through the village. Marek fired at two soldiers crouched by the corner of the house killing one, while Rance fired at the other and missed, so he turned his attention to the trucks where the villagers had overpowered their guards and were running across the road looking for their families.

Dimly he heard Marek screaming at them to get out of the way, before he came under fire from the soldier he'd missed earlier. He fired back at the soldier cursing when he missed again unable to get a clear shot. Two partisans died in a cross fire and Rance turned round desperately looking for the source and saw three German troopers at the far end of the village disappearing behind the houses with Marek and Cross running after them.

Rance shouted for one of the partisans to follow running at an angle between the houses trying to cut them off.

There were four of them wide eyed and panting scattering towards the forest, fear lending wings to their feet. Cross and Marek close behind shouted and opened fire, bringing two down before the remaining two reached the forest disappearing between the trees. Cross started to run after them but Marek shouting for him to return.

Leave them there isn't time for a man hunt. We have to get the surviving villagers out of here the Germans will want revenge for this day.'

Cross looked at Rance nonplussed. 'I wish to hell I could understand more of the language, did he say we're moving, or the villagers or what?'

'More like all of us, the Germans will be swarming over this place and God help anybody they catch here.' answered Rance looking around at the dead and dying Germans.

They hurried back to the village centre where the German officer lay. Rance looked down and turned his head away, someone had cut his throat. Marek was shouting at the remaining villagers urging them to leave, already some were moving out carrying what meagre possessions they could.

'Where will they go Marek?' Rance asked, staring around at the people.

Marek spread his hands despairingly, 'Anywhere away from here maybe relatives in another area if they're lucky.'

73

Krolik reported to Marek his face bleak. 'We've lost two more men.'

Marek suddenly looked old, he turned and walked away. Krolik walked after him, 'Marek, four of the men from the village want to join us.'

Marek didn't look round. 'Tell them to pick up as many weapons and ammunition as they can carry, for now we must bury our dead.'

The graves were shallow with no markers just two pieces of wood in the form of a cross nailed to the nearest tree.

The sun had set below the horizon, it was getting dark and Marek was in a hurry to return to the two wounded men they'd left behind earlier. They halted tense and uneasy at the sound of two pistol shots vibrating through the forest gloom coming from the direction of the barn.

Marek crossed himself. 'The German patrol has found them. Now we have no wounded,' he said with a voice that had become devoid of any emotion. 'We must leave before that patrol catches us too.' He looked at the darkening sky. 'They won't find us in the dark or even dare to follow us too closely so if we walk all night we should be clear by the morning.' He turned leading them South towards the Radom road.

It was almost dark by the time Major Schneller and his troops came across the deserted village strewn with their dead comrades. In an ever increasing rage he watched while his men carried out the dead laying them in a neat row at his feet. He counted eight, and one officer who'd had his throat cut. There was a commotion at the far end of the village one of his lieutenants came forward, bringing two frightened and exhausted soldiers with him.

'Sir, we found these two hiding in the forest, they're all that's left of the squad.'

Schneller eyed them with distaste he didn't like Ukrainians, but they were necessary for the new plan he just wished he could have pure Germans for this work.

He walked around them not bothering to keep the contempt he felt out of his voice. 'Well you miserable pair what have you to say for yourselves?' he said pointing his pistol and they shrank back in terror. 'You deserted didn't you, you fucking pieces of pig-shit?' he ranted.

'No sir, no,' the one nearest to him quavered 'we were overwhelmed, caught by surprise, there were at least fifty of them.' he said, close to tears.

'We couldn't believe it, some were English,' stuttered the other one.

Schneller froze with shock. 'Say that again!' he shouted.

'We heard some of them speaking in English and thought there'd been an invasion sir.'

'Now I know your lying,' snapped Schneller, "There isn't an English soldier within hundreds of kilometres of here.'

He turned to his Lieutenant who had been listening with amusement.

'Take these deserters away and hold them for a court martial. I will hear no more of it.'

Schneller felt uneasy they didn't sound as if they making it up. Had a fifth column been parachuted in. Perhaps even now they were organising real resistance. No, he again shook his head in disbelief at the thought.

He called his Lieutenant and together they studied his map. Schneller pointed to the spot where the train had been derailed.

'This is the first contact,' he said tracing their route with his finger.

'They ambushed a patrol there now we have this one. They came West, now they've turned South towards the Radom road.'

'Sir, there's a patrol coming in,' a sergeant reported.

They came out of the forest looking tired and dirty, a bedraggled sergeant saluted.

'Where is your commanding officer?' Schneller fumed his mood getting uglier.

'Dead sir,' answered the sergeant still standing stiffly to attention.

'We were ambushed in the forest sir.'

'Yes I know all about that,' said Schneller impatiently,

'How many bandits were there?'

'We only saw three sir.'

'What!' Schneller shrieked, 'three men,' he shook his head again in disbelief. 'Waste no time sergeant, keep going South though the forest towards the Radom road all night if you have to-' he folded the map.

'I'll take the Troop carriers and see if we can cut them off.'

He returned the sergeants salute and walked back towards his staff car.

The sergeant looked grey, only a fool would venture into the forest at night looking for desperate and heavily armed men.

'Yes sir,' he whispered to himself knowing Schneller of old who didn't give a damn for any of them.

He went to return to his exhausted men, but Schneller called him back to the car.

'Just one more thing sergeant, have you heard of any Englishmen in the area?'

The sergeant looked bewildered by the question, 'Why no sir.'

Schneller waved him away and led the Troop carriers back towards the Radom road. It was now dark and they were forced to drive on headlights which failed to pierce behind the first rows of densely packed trees giving the area a dark and forbidding feeling.

The bandits were in there somewhere, even now they might be preparing an ambush. The thought made Schneller squirm in his seat for he was an open target for them sitting in the back. A cold feeling overcame him, he sank further down in his seat. 'Faster driver,' he snapped suddenly having an overwhelming urge to get out of that forest of fear.

The sergeant sat with his back to a tree and watched Schneller disappear down the dirt track with a feeling of disquiet. There was no way he was going to lead his already exhausted men into that forest at night unless it was at a very slow pace and with scouts out.

The bandits knew every inch of it and he didn't, besides which, they had nothing to lose and he had.

'To hell with you Schneller,' he thought spitting after the departing personnel carriers before settling down for a rest.

They were pushed for three hours before deciding it was safe enough to rest. Posting guards, they lit a small fire and cooked their strips of dried pork, it tasted rancid to Rance and smelt off but starvation made him force it down. He grimaced, listening to Cross vomiting it back up.

Marek came over and told them it was time to move, not always understanding what was said, they took their cue from the man next to them.

Cross groaned rubbing at his stiff muscles. 'Rance, just think we could be lying in a nice soft prisoner of war camp now,' he said looking around at the men gathering their weapons.

'And not only that,' he grumbled, 'With people we can have a decent conversation with, someone we can understand. Most of their words I can't even pronounce.'

Rance prodded him in the ribs, 'Come on, you know you'd only be bored stuck in a camp that's why you volunteered to go walking in Poland.' .

Cross grunted, not impressed. .

There was no moon that night, Rance found it difficult to see the man in front but knew they were on a narrow track that weaved its way southwards while his stumbling feet made no sound on the thick carpet of pine leaves scattered over the uneven ground. Occasionally he heard the sound of animals in the undergrowth and guessed it was either deer or wild boar.

Dawn broke and Krolik came back with a warning they were approaching the Radom road.

They lay at the edge of the forest for two hours watching the German patrols on the road ahead. The sun had risen burning off the early morning dew and the mist patches that swirled round in the near still air.

Marek ordered Pies back to scout their rear, convinced there would be a German patrol still following their trail. He felt uneasy they were in a precarious position, unable to cross the road ahead and somewhere behind, an untold number of the patrol they had fought earlier.

If they headed west there was the garrison town of Sulejow and to the east there was a large area of open farmland. He really had no choice they would have to retrace their steps and risk another fight with that patrol, but this time they could be the ones caught in a trap.

He felt himself being nudged in the ribs by the grinning Englishman Rance, who pointed at the road. The Germans were pulling out. A staff car with a Major sitting in the back was leading a convoy of eight Troop carriers which were stopping and picking up the patrols before moving on in the direction of Piotrkow.

With relief he watched them disappear into the morning mist. Sending one of the men to fetch Pies they crossed the now empty road and entered the security of the forest on the other side.

Half an hour later the German Sergeant led his men out of the forest behind Marek, where he stood, unsure of which way to go. The mist had cleared and the road was deserted as far as he could tell. He shrugged and led his men in the direction of Sulejow.

CHAPTER 7

Izabel returned home to face a distraught mother and grandfather, listening in growing alarm at the news she was wanted by the Gestapo. Pacing the floor she was worried, horrified at the thought of being taken for questioning.
    She grew tired and went to bed but found she was unable to sleep. Restlessly she kept turning over biting her lips until the tears came.
    'Rance,' she whispered, 'where are you? I need you now,'
    The next morning Izabel sat at the kitchen table red eyed but listening with mounting joy to the news from a messenger that her brother had been brought back from Germany and was now in a labour camp west of Piotrkow near a town called Belchatow.
    He was well, but kept away from the other prisoners, for what purpose the messenger didn't know, but she knew, now she realised why she was wanted by the Gestapo. It was Schneller behind all this and she shuddered at the thought of his hands on her. She thanked the messenger and showed him to the door. Her mother and grandfather were out so she scribbled a quick message, saying that she had gone to stay with friends and would be back shortly.
    Taking her bicycle she turned onto the Sulejow Radom road determined to go back to where she had last seen Rance and Marek.
    Once there she hoped to get a message to them. If anybody could help, they could.
    She was half way to the turn off at Przglow when she was forced off the road by a convoy of German Personnel Carriers led by a German staff car. She froze at the sight of Schneller fast asleep in the back and wondered where he'd been so early in the morning he was obviously heading back to Piotrkow.
    It was mid-morning before she reached Kalow. Jozef, his wife and daughter welcomed her warmly.
    'Is there any news of Marek and the others?' she asked hesitantly, Jozef grinned. 'You mean the Englishman don't you?' he said teasingly.
    Izabel felt herself flush, Jozef was kicked in the shin by his wife.

'You take no notice of him,' interrupted his wife, he's just a savage peasant at heart.'

Jozef became serious, 'A courier came this morning, saying there'd been heavy fighting near Tomaszow. Whether it's Marek or not I couldn't say, but they were in that area. We can only wait and see. Anyway its better if you stay the night with us, it will be safer.

She woke having spent a disturbed night, imagining all sorts of things happening to the men fighting in the forest. A messenger had arrived with a sealed letter from Curen, addressed to Marek which Jozef carefully hid away while his wife cooked them all breakfast.

Three hours later Izabel's heart missed a beat when she saw Rance and the others walk wearily into the clearing. Marek walked past her pretending not to notice her interest in the Englishman, but he was glowing with anger. He snatched the letter off Jozef and went into the house, slamming the door behind him.

Rance slept like a dead man for the next six hours, then after eating he and Izabel walked into the forest, to a small glade with a river running through it. It was now past mid-day and the sun was hot overhead, he stripped off his clothes and washed, standing naked up to his waist in the cold slow running water. Izabel lay on the bank watching him through half closed eyes. Although he was thin and undernourished his body looked strong and his muscles were firm. She saw the terrible scar on his forearm and wondered why he would never speak of it.

Grinning, he walked out the of river and stood over her dripping wet, making her squeal, 'Oh you, now I'm all wet.' she laughed.

While walking hand in hand back to join the others she told him about her brother Jarek and the Gestapo chief Schneller.

Rance fumed in anger, his normally brilliantly blue eyes were now an icy grey.

For a second, Izabel was frightened by the passion of hate she had aroused, wishing she hadn't said anything.

'I'll get your brother out, with or without Marek's help. Just don't go home until I can get him free. Then I will deal with Herr Schneller,' he said.

Izabel became more frightened at his words.

Marek met them at the oak tree, he was icily polite his face giving no hint of his thoughts. 'Rance, we have a small job to do in the village of Przglow.' he said glancing casually at Izabel. 'It's the village where you all stayed I believe,' he said curtly.

She flushed, and looked away not answering.

He continued, 'There's a new family just arrived there. Our intelligence suggests that they maybe Volksdeutsche, it's our job to go and warn them of the consequences if they were to be in league with the Gestapo.'

Rance opened his mouth to speak but Marek waved him into silence. 'I know what you're going to say, and the answer is no, we won't hurt them. If we did, the Gestapo would destroy Przglow.' He paused choosing his words carefully. 'All we'll do is frighten them a little.'

Izabel now told Marek about her brother and Schneller and for the first time he showed emotion. Ignoring Rance he held her hand.

'I promise we'll get him out, and we'll protect you and your family. Don't worry, you'll be safe. I'll gather information on where he's being kept and make plans.'

He squeezed her hand tightly, his eyes pleading, 'Trust me,' he whispered.

Overcome, she reached up and kissed him gently on the cheek.

'I do Marek,' she whispered huskily.

Eight o'clock the next evening, Rance and Pies walked silently down the rear of the houses in Przglow treading carefully ever mindful not to disturb the dogs that most people kept. Marek and some of his men were positioned at either end of the dirt track standing watch for any passing German patrol. The house they wanted was near the end of the row with a light from an oil lamp shining through a crack in a broken shutter, illuminating the rutted yard and old dilapidated barn. Cautiously, they walked round to the front of the house and knocked on the door.

The talking within stopped, 'Who's that, what do you want?' a voice shouted gruffly.

Pies didn't bother to reply, instead he lifted his foot and sent the door flying open to rebound against the wall with a crash, quickly stepping inside he was followed by Rance.

The Volksdeutsche was just picking up a hunting rifle, but at the sight of the two heavily armed men he immediately dropped it, throwing his hands in the air. 'Don't shoot, don't shoot, I have my wife and family here,' he shouted, his face ashen.

Rance looked across at his frightened wife and children, and feeling sorry for them lowered his rifle.

Pies snarled, 'We have a warning for you,' picking up the table with their half-eaten meal he threw it across the room and lifting his rifle he drew back the bolt.

Alarmed by this, Rance stepped between them.

'I won't be a party to shooting women and children,' he said, forgetting speaking in English.

Pies didn't understand and looked puzzled, shrugging his shoulders.

They both stiffened at the nerve shattering sound of gunfire echoing through the village. Pies blew out the light and crept to the front door peering outside. He quickly drew back. 'German SS and Police coming this way,' he whispered.

They moved to the rear of the house, kicking open one of the shutters as the Volksdeutsche ran out the front door crying for help.

Pies, cursing loudly jumped out of the window followed by Rance, who promptly lost him in the darkness. He heard the Germans coming in through the front door so he ran. He wanted to go left the way they'd come but he could see the lights of the troops searching the houses so he turned right.

Running over the back gardens of the houses he jumped over a small wooden fence and fell into a deep ditch.

A thin trickle of water covered the bottom and slipping in the mud he followed it, finding it led away from the buildings towards the River Luciaza.

He recognised the station masters house looming out of the darkness and hammered on the door, but received no answer.

Behind him, he could hear German voices, then the howling of dogs, while all around gunfire and screaming rent the air. Realizing it was impossible for him to return to the partisans he ran back to the ditch and down to the river.

Running along the bank he came to a small foot-bridge which he ignored choosing to wade across underneath gasping as the cold water came up to his armpits. He paused in the centre sinking below the surface when the bridge above filled with Germans shining their torches over the dark water.

Unable to hold out any longer he emerged choking only to see the Germans heading back to the village.

Climbing the river bank he ran into the forest and followed a narrow track. Twenty minutes later he stopped to listen for sounds of pursuit, but only silence surrounded him in the pitch-blackness. He shivered and walked on away from the village. An hour later he was totally lost with the forest seeming to close in all around him. Despite the walk he still shivered in his wet clothes and knew he had to keep moving.

It was nearly two hours later before the track emerged onto a dirt road. Looking both ways he could see nothing in the blackness but the never ending forest, now hearing rustling in the undergrowth he brought his rifle up to his chest gripping it tightly. It came from behind him. He spun round with a shout making the wild deer he had disturbed run down the track in fright.

He decided to go right and realising he couldn't walk about with his rifle and grenades, walked a short distance into the woods and hid them amongst a tree root, marking the spot with crossed twigs then went back and marked the dirt road so he could find them later. For another hour he walked until dawn broke before sitting down to rest.

Overcome with fatigue he dozed and finally slept. He awoke to find himself looking down the barrel of a shotgun. Two men stood over him, he tried to stand but one of them pushed him back with a prod from his gun.

Both men were young about his age well built and by the state of their clothes, which were rough and worn, they obviously worked on the land. One had shaved that morning but the other sported at least three days growth and needed a wash.

'Who are you, and what are you doing? You must be a stranger, because we know everybody around here,' snapped the clean shaven one, eyeing him with suspicion

Rance nodded, trying to smile. 'I was visiting friends in the village of Przglow and in the dark I got lost and didn't-.

'You're not a Pole, I can tell, you can hardly speak the language,' interrupted the unshaven one, his eyes widening in shock. The two men took a step backwards. 'You're a stinking German spy,' he snarled, swiftly lifting his gun he began to squeeze the trigger.

Rance sat bolt upright. 'No wait, listen to me first, then you can decide to shoot me if you wish.' He was trying to appear calm but he could feel the sweat on his brow. 'He lifted his arms, 'Look I'm unarmed you've nothing to lose.'

The man slowly lowered his shotgun, Rance gave a sigh of relief.

'Firstly I am English.'

The two Poles looked at each other in stunned disbelief. 'You're a liar, everybody knows there are no Englishmen within hundreds of kilometres of here,' the unshaven one shouted belligerently again lifting his shotgun.

'No wait, I can prove it,' said Rance, in desperation. 'I'm a partisan, we were on a mission and I got lost. I've hidden my rifle and grenades because I didn't want the Germans to find them on me.' He looked at both of them in turn.

'I can take you to the guns.'

They hesitated at first, finally agreeing. So Rance set off back the way he'd come, closely followed by his captors.

He searched for an hour but was unable to locate his marks on the track.

Losing patience, the clean shaven one angrily thrust his shotgun into Rance's back. 'You're playing for time, we'll go back to my village, there, we'll get the truth out of you.'

Rance sat with his back against the wall of an old wooden house. Standing in a semi-circle in front of him were six men, three holding hunting rifles. They were arguing amongst themselves, speaking so fast that he couldn't follow what was being said. Guessing some of them wanted to shoot him there and then he interrupted, speaking slowly so there would be no misunderstanding. They stopped arguing and turned to listen.

'There's a house in Przglow where I have a friend, her name is Marie she will vouch for me and if you want to go to meet any of my group she will take you.'

A heated discussion followed while he sat watching trying to weigh up his chances of survival. An older man turned to face him and the others fell silent.

'We want to believe you, but it's difficult with some of these younger hot heads, but for now we will give you the benefit of the doubt.'

His face darkened. 'If we find you have lied to us believe me I will be the one to shoot you.'

He turned and left shouting back over his shoulder

'You'd better pray that we find your friend at home and that she hasn't gone away.'

Rance found himself locked in a shed, there were no windows and only one door and the men had posted a guard. He examined his prison. It had at some time in the past been used to keep chickens. There were none there now he guessed the villagers had them well hidden away from the Germans. Darkness came he was given a mug of water but no food. Lying on the hard earth floor he tried to rest but felt insects running over him then the scratching of a rat. It made him sit upright thrashing his legs about to scare it away.

The night was a torment bringing back memories of the German cells. Claustrophobia was overwhelming making him shut his eyes while beads of sweat gathered on his brow, he tried to imagine he was back in England walking in the green fields and on the beaches of Cornwall. Then the rat came back and he kicked out as it ran across his legs, bringing him back to reality.

Daylight came through a crack in the door with agonising slowness, and the heat built up with the sun rising higher in the cloudless sky.

His fame seemed to be spreading, people from the village began to gather in small groups at the chicken shed. Rumours were spreading like wildfire. Most were convinced he was a German agent and even knew Hitler.

Somebody said he was maybe an Englishman dropped by the RAF to prepare for a larger force that would be coming later.

He was starting to lose patience he had only been given water and was starving. He kicked at the door demanding to be let out. His guards kicked back shouting at him to keep quiet. When that happened the villagers cheered and little boys ran up kicking the shed as well.

There was a commotion outside and Rance dived to look through the crack in the door. The older man had returned bringing Pies back with him. He breathed a sigh of relief another reprieve how many lives had he left he wondered?

The door flew open and he was dragged out. Startled! he started to struggle thinking they were still going to shoot him, then stopped when the villagers surged forward shaking his hand and slapping his back. Everybody was grinning and laughing thrusting pieces of pork and bottles of the usual homemade Vodka into his hand. Wisely he declined the drink catching sight of Pies who stood at the back of the crowd nodding a greeting with a slight smile on his face. Rance couldn't believe it, Pies smiling at him, he was honoured.

The old man stepped forward holding out his hand, 'We're sorry we did this to you, but the Germans make us suspicious of every stranger. We know now that you've come a long dangerous way to help us.'

He put his arm round Rance's shoulder and walked with him towards the grinning Pies. 'From now on you are our brother and will always be welcome here. Remember this well, if you're ever in trouble, send for us and we'll be there to help you. Now go in peace my friend we will pray to God for you and good luck.'

He felt drained and at the same time relieved that he had lived to see another day.

He returned to a tumultuous reception from his group, even Marek shook his hand and Cross couldn't stop laughing with relief at his safe return. 'Rance, don't do that to me again you bugger, who will I have to talk to if you get killed,' he joked punching him hard on the shoulder.

Izabel met him at the edge of the clearing, 'I thought you were dead, we all did. I've been out of my mind with worry,' she was sobbing with relief.

Arm in arm they walked back into the clearing and stood beneath the giant oak where Jozef met them.

'I'm sorry, I know you've only just returned, but we've received information that Schneller is going to have Izabel's brother moved into Piotrkow where it will be much harder to free him. I've been in touch with Curen and he thinks it would be a good idea. to turn it into a major raid to free all the prisoners held in that camp.

'From the information we have things are looking bad there many die. He thinks many of the prisoners will want to join us if we can free them. We'll be joining forces with a much larger group than ours from the Konskie region. The same ones that blew up the troop train. That will make us at least fifty strong.'

He nodded at Izabel. 'You'd better say goodbye again, we leave in one hour, it's a three day walk to our meeting with the Konskie group.

Staying close to the edge of the forest, Rance noted they moved south before crossing the River Luciaza and turning northwest towards Belchatow. Four new recruits had joined them and Rance was given the task of teaching them to fight.

'We're not going to have enough time to train them for the finer points of killing and survival, are we Rance?' observed Cross watching the recruits fumbling clumsily with the unfamiliar weapons.

Rance took the rifle off one when he almost shot himself.

'We have to try we're all they've got. They'll learn a little and have to trust to luck, like everyone else,' he muttered.

Their group of ten were joined by Jozef and his neighbours Radice and his two sons, Edmond the youngest who was only sixteen, and his brother Jan eighteen. The other neighbour Skubisz travelled alone, after the usual greetings and exchanges of Vodka they crossed the main Czestochowa road and railway line before meeting the Konskie group in a small clearing near the village of Borowa.

Rance counted forty-five including themselves. Like his group their ages ranged from teenage up to their forties all were dirty unshaven and obviously undernourished and he could tell by the way they continually scratched at themselves that they too were infested with lice.

The meeting was a grand affair with much back slapping and shaking of hands. The Konskie leader was a short stocky built man, going by the code name of Losos. A captain's hat of the old Polish army was perched jauntily on the back of his head while a jacket too large for him also bore the rank of captain. Round his waist keeping up a pair of riding breeches was a wide leather belt supporting a giant machete strapped to his side.

Brandishing a large bottle of home-made Vodka he insisted they all drank to toast each other's health. His men gathered round sharing their bottles and discussing the latest news.

'And which village are you from?' asked one offering his bottle to Cross.

Cross and Rance looked with resignation at each other, and each took a swig of the fiery brew.

'We're English,' said Cross grinning at the man's astounded expression.

'Losos, Loso,' the man shouted.

Rance and Cross stepped back in alarm and the rest turned and stared.

Loso bounded up to them, 'What's the matter with you, you look as if you've seen a ghost.'

'Te dwie sa po Angielsku,' shouted the man dancing round thrusting the bottle back at Cross and the whole camp roared its delight.

Loso grabbed them both in a giant bear hug laughing, 'Witajcir powikani, Anglicy co za mile widziany widok jaki jestescie oboje, miecej wodki,' he cried, 'we must celebrate with our two new friends.'

He pushed two more bottles into their hands and tilted his back letting it run like a torrent down his throat.

He slapped their backs. 'Now you my friends, drink,' he ordered.

Cross slowly upended his bottle and Rance followed his example, managing to spill most of it but still felt the fire in his belly when the liquid hit and rebounded up to his brain.

Sitting with his back to a tree Rance found it an awesome sight watching these men dancing round the fire with bandoleers full of ammunition across their chests a rifle in one hand and a bottle of Vodka in the other.

As the fire grew brighter and the sparks flew it enhanced the feeling of unreality as the fiery liquid took effect. The flickering flames made the men's twisting leaping shadows even more menacing as they cavorted round the fire. He was thankful that he was on their side for these Poles were enough to frighten the bravest of men. The fires glow combined with the dancing figures of the wild drunken men brought home to his blurred brain once again, the utter savagery of this war he was in.

Shaking his head he staggered thankfully away cutting branches from a tree to form his bed. In a haze he watched Cross weaving towards him and picking up an axe swung it at a tree missed and fell flat on his face. Cursing he tried again this time losing the head off the axe.

He laughed watching as Cross sat down heavily before rolling on his back giggling loudly slurring his words,

'Wash sher smatter with sho? sho lice ridden-,'

Rance woke the next morning to the sound of men getting ready to move. He felt like hell thinking for a moment he was already there, when he looked across at Cross's deathly white face and red swollen eyes.

Groaning he looked away swearing never again to touch another drop of their Vodka. He squinted at the men moving about none of them seemed to be suffering like he and Cross were.

Marek and Losos were studying a plan of the labour camp, so he and Cross walked over to look although neither could understand what was being said because the two leaders were talking to fast, although Rance did notice that the camp was out in the open with no cover.

. The prisoners were in a separate compound to the guards joined by a wired walk-way between them. Around both compounds were the usual barbed wire fence which enclosed the two. Four watch towers gave the guards a clear view of the area.

Marek looked up slowly explaining their plan.

First they would attack at night knocking out the four watch towers. The Konskie group led by Losos would try and keep the main reserve guards from reaching the prisoner compound by cutting off the wire walk-way. Marek's group would break through the circling fence and deal with the guards already there, freeing the prisoners from the huts of which there were six.

Rance and Cross nodded their understanding while Marek studied them with a hard look in his eye.

'One more thing any prisoner who is ill or isn't capable of moving fast we leave. If either of you are injured or wounded and can't be helped, you must not be caught alive. If you are not capable of shooting yourself then your friend must do it for you. Believe me when I say he will be doing you a favour.'

'What about Izabel's brother do we know which hut he's in?' queried Rance.

Marek shook his head. 'That we don't know all we know is that he was still in the camp four days ago.

When darkness came they silently came out from their forest refuge splitting into two groups then into groups of four. The lights around the wire came on glowing dimly at first but getting brighter as they approached.

The one searchlight the camp possessed forced them to the ground its beam swinging backwards and forwards erratically across the open space.

Rance grew impatient as the time passed but he knew they dare not get any nearer with the searchlight on.

Suddenly the camp was plunged into darkness when Loso's men cut the power. Rance was running for the nearest tower listening to German voices shouting to each other asking about the problem.

Crouching beneath the tower he cut the wire fence before he was joined by Cross who quickly climbed up the ladder towards the platform. Radice and his youngest son came through the hole and

Rance motioned to the sixteen year old to stay and guard their escape route. Cross reached the underside of the platform as gunfire erupted from the main compound and a siren started to wail directly above him.

A star flare burst high above them and a German stood transfixed with shock before screaming a warning to the watchtower. Radice shot him, aiming low to make sure of a hit. Panicking, the guards in the tower opened the trap door in the platform to fire at the men underneath.

Cross sitting within a metre couldn't miss empting the magazine of his machine pistol up through the hole the sheer volume of bullets sent both guards over the safety rail to crash at Rance feet who was cutting through the second fence.

He pushed the last strands aside and was in. The night was lit with a series of fire flashes gunfire rolled like claps of thunder all around him. Cross firing from the platform with the dead guard's heavy machine gun adding to the noise.

Rance shouted up to him to stay on the platform to cover their retreat as he and Radice ran to the first hut and blew off the lock, shouting at the startled inmates to get out.

Now running to the second hut he could hear the cheering when the first hut emptied. He shot off the lock on the second hut nearly being crushed in the rush when the prisoners joined the others. The hole at the fence became a bottle neck as too many men tried to get out at once.

A German machine-gunner caught them in his sights and opened fire at the struggling mass, men screamed and died while the wounded sank beneath the crush of the panic stricken survivors. Making for the third hut he came face to face with Krolik who signalled they had freed the others.

He moved amongst the escaping men shouting for Izabel's brother while men shook their heads still running, almost knocking him over. One prisoner stopped and pointed. 'There's a man kept in a small hut inside the main compound, I've seen him sometimes when they let him out for exercise. I've heard his name was Jarek Markowitz.'

Rance grabbed the man's arm. 'Which hut, show me?' he demanded but the man pulled himself free and disappeared.

Rance ran after Krolik, 'Where's Marek? they've got Izabel's brother in the main compound.'

Krolik shook his head. 'There's no hope of getting to him there,' he answered.

Rance snapped back, 'Of course there's hope. Find Marek. We're inside the camp so we can go through the wire passage that joins the two together.'

He turned and ran not waiting for an answer as the firing on all sides intensified. Another star shell turned the compounds into daylight and ahead he could see the other opened gate, the entrance filled with dead troops killed by Losos and his men when the guards tried to reach the prisoners compound.

The gate swung open while a gigantic explosion sent shock waves through the air almost blowing him off his feet a giant fireball lit up the night sky sending dancing shadows along the side of a hut wall. He entered the hut and stared around at the empty room before running for the next hut which was slightly hidden by other buildings out of the main line of fire. It was secured by a large padlock which he blew apart with two quick shots.

'Rance, Rance,' a voice shouted he whirled round his gun raised, only to lower it when he saw Marek, Krolik and Pies coming up behind him.

Without answering he rolled through the door, his gun ready to fire at a shadowy figure standing against the far wall.

'Jarek Markowitz,' Rance shouted swiftly aiming at the silent figure moving to his left and then running towards him.

CHAPTER 8

The flames from the burning labour camp rose higher into the night sky its flickering light illuminating the figure coming towards him.
He started to sweat maybe it wasn't Izabel's brother.
'It's all right Jarek we're friends of your sister,' he shouted before diving to one side.
Marek entered the hut shouting hoarsely. The dark figure changed direction. 'Thank God you're Polish, I thought he was a German,' Jarek cried with relief.
Rance let the air out of his lungs. How close he had come to killing the boy, his hand shook.
Running from the hut they made their way back to the wire passage. With the flames slowly dying came the smoke, drifting thickly on the night air stinging their eyes making it difficult to see.
Rance counted it a blessing for without it they would now be dead. The partisans raced for the cover of the huts making their way back to the hole in the fence where Radice and his sixteen year old son were anxiously waiting. Rance shouted to Cross and was answered by the heavy machine gun in the tower above his head its clattering roar drowning out any other noise. Cross traversed the machine gun slowly across the camp tearing into buildings window and doorways, hunting out and finding any German foolish enough to expose himself. Then finally satisfied with his work he swung down to join Rance, slapping him on the back.
'What kept you?' he said his eyes wide his body still filled with adrenalin.
Rance's reply was drowned in more gunfire and they ran for the sanctuary of the forest. Two partisans fell on Rance's left he stopped but a look was enough to see one was beyond help while the other writhed helplessly on the ground his legs and back shattered. He bent over him but the man immediately thrust a pistol into his own mouth and pulled the trigger.

Rance reeled back in shock covered in the man's blood and choking back vomit he ran for cover and entered the clearing, finding chaos with dozens of bewildered men wondering aimlessly about.

Rance looked for Marek and found him with Pies and Krolik who were trying to get some sort of discipline into the escaped prisoners some of whom were wounded: four unable to move.

'Where's Losos, he should be here by now?' said Rance.

Marek looked around with a harassed expression, 'How the hell should I know, I've got enough problems getting these men into smaller groups,'

Losos raced through the trees waving the machete over his head his eyes gleaming with blood lust closely followed by his men. They still looked an awesome sight punching the air with their guns shouting in triumph eyes staring with the lust to kill.

Watching, he couldn't help but feel the excitement the adrenaline coursing through his body he had to physically shake himself realising he was becoming swept away with the same emotion.

Gradually a sort of order prevailed they split the escaped prisoners into five groups each with a small party of partisans to cover their retreat.

Now with the glow from the burning camp on the horizon they started the perilous return journey knowing they would now be hunted ruthlessly receiving no mercy if they were caught.

Gestapo HQ Piotrekow

The Nazis were always particular with their records.

Major Schneller listened intently to Lieutenant Lohr's report on the collection and execution of villagers in retaliation for the recent deaths of the German soldiers south of Tomszow. It mattered little to him that they were all from a different district they were Poles and expendable.

'Eight babies up to two years old, twenty three children up to twelve years old, thirty teenagers up to seventeen years, fifty-five women from eighteen to seventy-five years, eighty-seven men up to eighty-seven years. The total in number, two hundred and three executed by firing squad.'

Lohr's flat emotionless voice lapsed into silence.

Schneller idly picked at his nail, annoyed that it had broken.

'What about hostages, don't tell me you didn't take any?' he said, still aggrieved at the sharp piece of nail.

'My men did get carried away in that village I'm afraid but we did manage to keep fourteen,' answered Lohr with a slight smile.

'We did teach them a lesson they won't forget.'

Lieutenant Schmidt, standing in the background listened with contempt although he didn't care about the Poles he knew from other sources that acts of that sort only made things worse.

He stiffened to attention when Schneller turned to face him.

'Send a message to Captain Herman Cathman requesting he set up his outposts in the last area we spoke of,' Schneller ordered.

Schmidt nodded and began to scribble furiously anxious to appear busy. Schneller brought his attention back to Lieutenant Lohr.

'Before you go about your business in that area, there is one little job you can do for me,' he said, pointing at his map.

'There's a farm near Przglow that I want destroyed and everyone found in it with the exception of any young women who you will bring in for questioning. Do you understand?'

Schmidt noted that Lieutenant Lohr didn't even blink at the order, he shuddered at the coldness of the man when he answered. 'Yes sir, I understand, what do you want me to do with the bodies?'

Schneller shrugged. 'I don't really care hang them from the nearest tree it will be a warning to others.'

Lieutenant Lohr saluted and left the room with Schmidt turning to follow.

'Just a moment Schmidt, I want a word with you,' said Schneller sharply.

Schmidt blinked hard before turning and walking back into the room.

'What have you done about the girl?' asked Schneller.

Schmidt felt smug and at ease with himself. At last he felt he might have done something right.

'I've had the girl's grandfather arrested and brought here. He's been in the cells all day and I'll keep him awake all night. Tomorrow, I'll start to question him about the girl, I'm sure he knows where she is.' He stopped and looked with satisfaction at his superior before continuing, 'I've sent out an order requesting that her brother be brought to Piotrkow as soon as possible.' He smirked. 'Double pressure so to speak.'

Schneller closed his eyes. Why did he have to put up with the fat smirking idiot he thought before changing to a more important matter. 'I want you to find out from our spies in the districts if they have heard of any rumours or stories of any Englishmen in the area.'

He saw the look on Schmidt's face, 'I know it sounds far-fetched, but you never know in war what the enemy might do. Just get them to report back to me.'

The old man was tired and also puzzled why the Gestapo had kept him awake all night, trying to think if he'd done anything wrong in their eyes. The bare bulb over his head blurred his vision of the fat Lieutenant standing in front of him it hadn't helped when they'd taken his glasses away. The officer dropped his cigarette on the floor making no attempt to put it out and spoke in German which was translated by an SS Sergeant.

'Your name is Edmund Michnik and you have a granddaughter whose name is Izabel Markowitz, is that correct?'

The old man didn't answer dropping his gaze to the floor.

Lieutenant Schmidt leaned forward and grasped the old man's face digging his nails deep into the man's cheeks forcing his head up.

'Look at me when I'm talking to you, you stupid Pole,' he snarled, between clenched teeth.

Edmund Michnik's eyes watered, mumbling 'Yes', between Schmidt's dirty cigarette stained fingers.

'Where is she you fucking old bastard?'' Schmidt shouted.

'She's gone to see a friend she didn't say where,' whispered Edward numbly.

The back of Schmidt's hand smashed across Edmund's face jolting back his head drawing blood from his crushed lips.

'When will she be back?' Schmidt scowled clenching his fist.

'She didn't say'.

The savagery of the attack nearly sent Edmund toppling backwards out of the chair. The room spun as he desperately tried to regain his senses almost sick with the pain. He knew he was too old and weak to resist but he still had his pride he would never tell them anything. In a daze he felt somebody lift his hand on to the table top and screamed as the Lieutenant slowly broke his fingers one by one using the butt of his pistol. Pain roared through his brain lancing like red hot irons up his arm.

'Where is she?' the voice seemed a long way off with the pain deadened all other sound.

'I don't know,' he tried to sound defiant but it came out only as a whisper. Sweat covered his brow running down into his eyes blinding him.

He felt his other hand being lifted and was powerless to resist someone was screaming in the distance, 'Where is she?.

Pain sent his mind spinning into darkness and he felt at peace.

A pin point of light appeared and widening he found himself in a sunlit field. It must have been springtime because wild flowers carpeted the ground their colours shimmering into the distance amongst the gentle waving grasses. Ahead of him a little girl of about five years old danced amongst the blooms crying out in wonder at natures display.

Holding out his arms he called to her, 'Izabel let's dance together,' and he smiled when she turned and ran towards him.

Darkness blurred the vision and he found himself falling into a pit of blackness he struggled for a second to get out before finally giving up.

Schmidt shouted, violently shaking the old mans crumpled body staring in shocked disbelief, realizing the man had died. The face was composed now free from the pain and torment and a slight smile seemed to linger round the old man's swollen lips.

'Don't you die on me you old bastard!' cried Schmidt beside himself with anger. He looked at the Sergeant in frustration,

'The old devil must have had a weak heart,' he muttered.

The Sergeant stared straight ahead with an impassive expression.

'Yes sir, I think your right,' he answered coldly.

Schmidt felt panic setting in when he thought of what Schneller would do or say when he found out. If he found out.

'Sergeant, get a doctor in and make sure that he's certified as having a heart attack and that's all do you understand me?'

The Sergeant's voice was non-committal, 'Yes sir I understand you.' Then he said guardedly. 'What about the body sir?'

Schmidt hesitated, 'Take it to the cemetery and bury it, after that I want you to forget about today Sergeant. We wouldn't want you to get into trouble now would we?' he said a menacing tone reflecting in his voice.

The Sergeant kept the loathing out of his eyes while he stared at the fat Lieutenant, 'Yes sir, I think I understand what you mean sir,' was his wooden reply.

It was four hours before Schmidt could pluck up enough courage to report to Schneller's office where he stood uneasily to attention.

'Well,' Schneller snapped he was in a bad mood and could hardly bare to look at the man.

Schmidt swallowed with difficulty feeling his throat dry. 'As yet there is nothing to report about the old man we're letting him sweat so to speak,' he swallowed again under the gaze of those fish eyes.

Schneller was puzzled. Why was Schmidt so nervous and why wouldn't the fat idiot stand still. He shrugged there was more important things to think about.

'Schmidt, I've been ordered to go back to Berlin I don't know how long I'll be there but you will be under the command of Captain Cathman until I return. I don't have to remind you of where your loyalties lie so just remember. I'll be back.'

Schmidt heard the hidden threat in Schneller's voice but ignored it, not believing his luck.

Forcing himself to appear calm and detached he nodded coolly,

'I'll have the utmost discretion about your affairs sir and I'll have everything in order for when you return ,'

Schneller waved his baton impatiently, 'In the meantime let the old man go and leave the girl's brother where he is for the moment. Last and not least, leave the girl alone. I'll deal with her when I return'.

Schmidt drove Schneller to the train that afternoon carefully placing his bags on the rack above his head in the private compartment.

'Have a good journey sir,' said Schmidt unable to keep the smile off his face. Schneller eyed him suspiciously and refrained from answering.

Schmidt slammed the carriage door shut saluting as the train pulled slowly away from the platform.

Kalow

After Izabel said her goodbye to Rance watching him depart with the others to free her brother and the prisoners at Bechatow she knew she couldn't just sit and wait for their return so she decide to visit her friend Marie in Blezun where she spent two enjoyable hours recalling their time with the Englishmen.

Finally looking at her watch she rode out to the farm near the village where Jan Milosz and his wife met her by the gate. Straight away she could tell something was wrong by the expression on their faces. A feeling of dread overcame her and a cold shiver ran down her spine. 'What is it, what's the matter? she whispered.

Jan Milosz spoke gently putting his arm round her shoulder. 'I've received some bad news from Curen. The Gestapo have taken your grandfather away. He was last seen in their Headquarters but has since disappeared nobody knows where.'

The shock news brought a deep sob from Izabel and the tears welled up into her eyes. Jan and his wife helped her into the house where their two young children sat watching wide eyed at the kitchen table their half-eaten meal lying forgotten. Jan's wife tried to comfort her. 'It may not be anything important after all what could he know that would interest them he's too old to be an active threat. They must have made a mistake.'

Izabel lifted her tear stained face looking a picture of misery. 'This has nothing to do with the war. It's one maniac Gestapo officer and for some perverted reason he wants me,' she sobbed.

'First he uses my brother and now my grandfather. Oh God I know it's him. It's some terrible game he's playing.'

'Daddy, there are some soldiers outside and they're hitting one of our workmen.' The little boys voice stunned them into silence, Jan ran to the window pushing his son down. He turned away his face ashen.

'Get the children away and into the woods. It's a German patrol and they've just killed one of my men.'

He climbed on a chair and reaching up into the rafters took down an old hunting rifle.

'Go with my wife and the children it's your only chance,' he whispered frantically to Izabel his eyes full of fear.

She shook her head her defiantly her face white and drawn.

'No, it's your duty to look after your wife and family you go I'll delay them.'

He shook his head desperately trying to think full of indecision.

'Go damn you look after your family,' Izabel screamed at him.

Jan stared look at her before running after his wife and children. Defiantly she stood in the centre of the room and waited, jumping in fright when the door was kicked open and a German infantryman of the Waffen SS cautiously entered covering her with his rifle. A hard faced Lieutenant followed making her cringe when she stared into his cold grey eyes.

'Bist du allein?' she shrugged, 'I don't speak German,' she answered.

'Answer him', snapped the infantryman in Polish, 'He asked you if you were alone?

Before she could answer, gunfire and screams echoed from the rear of the house. The Lieutenant spoke again before running out of the back door.

The infantryman smirked at her. 'The lieutenant said, 'Never mind, we've found them'.

Izabel screamed and ignoring the soldier ran in the direction of the woods where the German's had gathered in a circle around the bodies of Jan, his wife and the two children.

Izabel screamed again and fought the infantryman who had caught up with her. He cried out in agony as her nails raked his face. Throwing her to the ground he drew his knife and his face twisting in anger he pulled back her head, exposing her throat to the blade.

Izabel looked up and seeing death closed her eyes but then was conscious of him falling. She opened her eyes with the Lieutenant standing over them both his face contorted with rage shouting at the stunned soldier.

'What the fuck do you think you're doing? Your orders were not to kill the woman. I'll have you court-marshalled for this how dare you disobey an order,' Lohr spluttered his eyes bulging in rage.

The infantryman tried to stutter an excuse but the Lieutenant cut him short. 'Put the girl in the back of the car with me, then hang those things to the nearest tree,' he snapped nodding at the bodies.

Izabel was oblivious to anything on the journey back to Piotrkow, her mind in a complete state of shock with the picture of Jan and his family lying in front of her she couldn't control her shivering body.

She stole a glance at the silent Lieutenant completely ignoring her his gaze fixed on the road ahead. Arriving at the Gestapo HQ Lieutenant Lohr gripped her tightly by the arm and marched her in front of the duty Sergeant at the front desk.

He spoke rapidly to the man before going without a backward glance leaving her looking at the amused face of the Sergeant sitting behind his desk, remembering him as the one she'd met there previously.

His grin was lopsided and malicious as he leaned back in his chair.

'Well, well my beauty what have you been up to then?' he said picking up his pen and laughing. 'Seen your brother yet?.

The laughter dried in his throat as she stared back silently with eyes full of contempt, he put pen to paper. 'Name? he snapped.

Her eyes focused on the wall behind him as she droned out her name and address. He stopped writing and glared at her angrily.

'Well you are a sullen little thing aren't you? You must have done something really bad to have been brought in by Lieutenant Lohr, mind you you we're lucky he brought you in at all,' he sneered. 'No doubt we'll find out in due course,' he said calling a guard. 'Show Miss Sullen to her room,' he quipped.

'I'll deal with this Sergeant,' said a voice behind her.

She turned; coming face to face with Lieutenant Schmidt, her face became white with fury.

'What have you done with my grandfather where is he?' she hissed.

'Shut up you stupid bitch how dare you speak to me like that,' he shouted back.

The desk Sergeant stared at them both in astonishment before hurriedly bending his head to his paperwork. Schmidt motioned to the bewildered guard, 'Bring her to my office.'

He sat down behind Schneller's desk his fat face ugly in simmering anger. 'You stinking bitch you have caused me a lot of trouble do you know that?' He said, working himself into a rage.

Izabel faced him all fear gone almost beside herself in her own anger. 'Where is he where is my grandfather?' she screamed at him.

Schmidt jumped out of his chair unable to contain himself any longer.

'I'll cut that pretty face to shreds and take pleasure doing it then we'll see how much Schneller wants you,' he shouted harshly coming round the desk and pushing her back into the chair.

He grabbed her right breast squeezing so hard she gasped in pain. His now red and bloated face was an inch away from hers, and smelling his stale sweat and stinking breath she turned her head away in disgust.

'I'm going to do what Schneller should have done a long time ago instead of playing stupid games,' he grunted.

She couldn't understand what he was saying but she guessed what his intentions were.

She struggled to get up but he pushed her back down and grabbing her legs pulled her towards him opening them at the same time. As her white thighs became exposed he grunted with lust.

She screamed and lashed out with her fist catching him on the cheek bone. Brutally he smacked her in the face then tore at her dress exposing her breasts just as the door to the office flew open and in strode Lieutenant Lohr.

'Schmidt, what the fuck are you doing,' Didn't you hear the alarm, there's a full scale attack on the labour camp at Belchatow?' he shouted eyeing him in disgust.

Schmidt jumped away from the girl as if she was red hot.

'That's not possible our intelligence informs us that there is no bandit group strong enough for such an attack,' he stuttered trying to compose himself.

Lohr stared at him with contempt completely ignoring Izabel who was trying to pull her dress together.

'You fat fool they were wrong. You're in charge of that camp and you've just lost over one hundred prisoners,' said Lohr stiffly.

Schmidt's face slowly lost all colour. He shouted for the guard,

'Lock her up until I return.'

Lohr intervened waving a piece of paper under Schmidt's nose.

'Read that it's a direct order from Major Schneller that if we find this woman we're to let her go unarmed. I've just discovered her name from the desk Sergeant downstairs and what do I find?' you up here almost wetting yourself over her.'

'That's nonsense I was just interrogating her,' said Schmidt, flustered trying to make excuses. He straightened his tie. 'Get this bitch out of here, let her go I've had enough,' Turning to follow Lohr He stopped staring at Izabel,

'You'll not be forgotten,' he whispered with venom his eye full of hate.

She shivered at his words her legs felt weak and her body trembled.

Schmidt sat sullenly in the staff car next to Lieutenant Lohr, he leaned forward and muttered impatiently to the driver,

'Just how long will it take to reach Belchatow?'

'Under one hour sir,' the driver replied his voice low and respectful.

'Can't you go any faster?' Schmidt moaned.

'It's the troop carriers in front and behind sir we're limited to their speed.'

Schmidt sat back and bit his finger nails nervously. He hated Poland, he hated the army, he hated Schneller and that bitch he was on heat for. Why Schneller just didn't take her was beyond his comprehension.

Now he'd lost the grandfather and was about to lose the brother.

He broke into a sweat at the thought of what would happen when Schneller returned. Perhaps he would never come back perhaps he would be bombed by the RAF while in Berlin. Even that thought couldn't cheer him up. No, his best way out would be to arrange a transfer before that.

He noticed the red glow in the sky from the burning labour camp ten minutes before they arrived there and his fear deepened when he stepped out of the staff car in dismay. Everywhere he looked there were dead, dying, and wounded troops, half the camp had been destroyed. He ran to the hut that had contained the girl's brother arriving there panting and out of breath, only to find it empty. He stormed back to the staff car and smashed his fist hard on the bonnet in frustration. Lieutenant Lohr moved amongst his men splitting them into groups of fifty and sending them out into the forest in pursuit of the escaping prisoners and partisans. He totally ignored Schmidt.

CHAPTER 9

Belchatow

With one last look at the burning camp Rance moved away with Cross to join Marek who together with Izabel's brother and twenty of the prisoners started the return journey back towards Kalow leaving the rest to split into smaller groups.

Gradually the noise from the camp died away as they moved deeper into the forest where the light from the moon never penetrated and the silence was only broken by the laborious breathing of the men. They followed a narrow track which twisted and turned amongst the pines and whose roots grew in confusion, writhing out of the earth to trip the unwary. Occasionally they left the old track to cut deeper into the forest before emerging onto a new one. Rance now had the greatest respect for Marek's knowledge of the forest and his instinct on direction. Two hours later sudden gunfire and screaming on their right brought them to a watchful halt. Marek looked tense.

'How far away do you think?' Rance asked.

'Quarter of a kilometre no more than that,' Marek answered, staring uneasily into the surrounding darkness. 'The Germans must have got more reinforcements out we must move on quickly.'

He walked down the line checking the men and finding two who were weak and unsteady on their feet made sure the others took it in turns to help them. He sent two men back to cover their rear and two ahead to act as scouts.

The night seemed endless then gradually the bright yellow orb of the sun came up slowly from the horizon its warming rays piercing the forest gloom with shafts of light burning off the early morning mist which swirled through the trees like ghostly figures in torment. Rance felt exhaustion gripping him when they crossed the main Czetochowa road and railway line. Here the tension increased when they lost the protection of the forest and were forced into the open. They halted warily at the sound of more firing this time from their left but much further away.

Some of the ex-prisoners were now beginning to falter so Marek called a halt in one of the groups of trees. The scouts came in reporting movements of German troops ahead and to their right so Marek decide to wait for nightfall before continuing.

While the men sank gratefully onto the dew soaked earth and slept Rance and Cross were given first sentry duty. They lay together at the edge of the woods looking over open grass meadows to a small lake that shimmered in the rising heat haze. Rance felt the hot sun's rays on his back when the sun climbed higher in the dazzling blue sky bringing out the flying insects which danced and fed hungrily on his body.

Scratching and raking his chest he looked in disgust at the sight of lice running through his clothing and began to hunt them down killing them one by one between his fingernails. He watched as German troops fanned out moving from left to right of their position.

Cross put down the binoculars. 'They're moving north and away from us which is good news but it means we'll have to go further west before we can turn towards Piotrkow,' he whispered slapping at an insect that was trying to devour his cheek, 'Damn these bugs,' he growled rolling over on his back and staring thoughtfully into the shimmering blue sky. 'I wish we were swimming in that river with the two girls,' he said longingly before rolling back over and looking at Rance. 'Better still I wish we were in England with the two girls,' He paused his eyes serious. 'I had another thought that we might not live to see that day Rance,'

Rance opened his mouth to speak but Cross continued. 'Promise me one thing will you? Don't let the buggers take me alive I've heard what they do to their prisoners before they kill them and I don't want any of that'.

Rance nodded his face sober in thought knowing what he'd heard from the other partisans that their chances of living one year were less than even, two years never.

He tried to remember some of the things he did in England and of Anna in France but his mind kept closing down as if to protect him from that bitter memory. It made him think only of the present and of the dangers they faced.

It had been dark for over an hour before they set off still travelling west. Rance quenched his raving thirst in the first stream he came to the cold water filled his empty stomach quelling the hunger pains that tormented him.

A commotion further down the line of men made him hurry back to find the two weakened men lying on the ground unable to go any further. Marek decided to leave them at the nearest farmhouse but the frightened farmer refused, then on seeing their condition finally agreed to keep them hidden for two days when Marek promised to send help.

They left the farm and Rance walked with Izabel's brother Jarek.

'You have the same colour hair and eyes as your sister,' said Rance, unsure of what to say as an opening to a conversation.

Jarek looked at him in surprise. 'You speak Polish and how do you know my sister?' he asked in astonishment.

Rance coughed to hide his embarrassment. 'Err well, she taught me to speak a little Polish before I could join the Partisans. I stayed with your family for a few weeks, in your room as a matter of fact.'

Jarek turned and stared at Rance with thoughtful eyes.

'And how well did you get on with my sister?' he asked.

'Err very well as it happens, your sister is a lovely woman,' stuttered Rance, feeling himself getting hot and bothered under the gaze of the boys amused eyes.

'Oh how time flies before I was taken prisoner she seemed to me to be just a young girl. Now you say she's a woman,' exclaimed Jarek now grinning broadly.

Rance felt himself reddening. 'Well if you must know your sister and me have become quite fond of each other.'

Jarek's grin widened and he held out his hand. 'Welcome to the family you do realise that my sister can be quite strong willed for a young girl, err I mean a woman that is,' he said trying to keep a straight face.

Rance hurriedly excused himself and moved back to the front of the line.

There was no moon that night so they were able to make better progress by skirting the woods and staying out in the open fields. Three hours later when the dawn showed its first glimmer on the horizon they were again forced to hide and wait for nightfall spending the time sleeping. Now once more they marched at night finally heading north until they walked into the clearing at Kalow in the early hours of the morning.

Seven hours later Rance woke and looked at his watch, ten-thirty. Stiffly he rose and after a wash wondered round the clearing finding Jozef chopping wood. Rance said he thought Izabel would have been there to meet them.

Jozef stuck his axe in a log and wiped his brow. 'There's always work to do in the forest,' he moaned holding his back, 'I think I'm getting too old for this you know. Perhaps when the war is over I'll move to Piotrkow.' He put his arm round Rance shoulder, 'Come my friend let's go get breakfast, Marek is already at my house eating me out of all my food so why shouldn't you have some.'

They entered the house sitting down opposite Marek.

'Rance thought Izabel might be here,' said Jozef grinning mischievously at Marek.

Marek grunted sourly. 'I've already sent a message about the release of her brother and I apologise for her not being here,' he said, the sarcasm heavy in his voice.

Rance kept his temper in check while Jozef sat back grinning watching the two of them. Marek ignored Rance, who sat uncomfortably drinking from a hot mug that Jozef's wife put before him. She shook her head at her husband, eyes flashing angrily warning him not to interfere.

'I've decided to move all our men further into the forest because now there are thirty-five of us it's too dangerous to remain here with all the German patrols about in the area. We'll make camp two kilometres away and operate from there,' said Marek climbing to his feet ignoring Rance.

'I'll send you food and messages through my daughter Marian,' answered Jozef now serious. 'Curen will be pleased with what we've accomplished I think.'

Marek walked outside calling back over his shoulder. 'So he should be,' and slammed the door making Rance wince staring after him.

'He's mad at you isn't he?' chuckled Jozef enjoying the sport then jumped as his wife banged a saucepan down hard on the table.

'That's enough Jozef, I know you and the other men think it's a big joke but you can go too far sometimes,' she snapped.

'Don't pay any attention to them they're just ignorant,' she said to Rance in sympathy,

'Marek will come round wait and see his stupid manly pride has been hurt that's all.' She glared at Jozef who instantly wiped the grin off his face and stared back owlishly before standing up and quickly walking to the door.

'I must finish chopping the wood,' he spluttered trying not to laugh.

Rance hurriedly excused himself and went in search of Cross.

Marek moved them all away from the comfort of Kalow and set up camp in the forest only cooking at night so the smoke wouldn't attract attention. He now settled down to await new orders from Curen who knew they needed more weapons for their new recruits. While they waited Rance and Cross started to teach the new men how to use the different weapons they had, spending time patiently with each one. Rance noted they were all young specially taken by the Germans for that reason so they could work them hard. All were under thirty some obviously farm workers, but most were from the local towns and villages and all were adamant they wanted to fight. Marek split the group into three, giving Pies and Krolik twelve men each and their own territory north and south of his position.

A savage game of hit and run developed between the partisans and the German patrols hunting them. Usually the German patrols were comprised of twenty to twenty-five men of the Waffen SS, each heavily armed battle harden troops who had seen fighting all over Europe.

For weeks Rance and Cross marched with either Viktor's group or Marek's moving only at night, attacking and sabotaging the enemy at dawn, then disappearing back into the forest to hide ready to move out again at dusk. Sleeping rough on the ground they were at the mercy of the weather and when hungry raided the farms of the Volksdeutche.

The Polish farmers and villagers helped with feeding with what little they had, warning them of any immediate danger often paying with their lives. The fighting was hard and bitter with neither side taking any prisoners except when the Germans wanted information.

Marek's group often down to six or seven men would be replenished by more recruits running from the Gestapo killer squads who were also looking for men to work as slave labour in their factories back in Germany.

Rance and Cross trained them, never making friends finding it too painful when they died. It was still hot in September when Rance stood guard watching his group wash the dirt and lice out of their clothes in a stream that had almost dried up in the hot humid weather. He noted that they were all thin as rakes their bones protruding in ugly lines through their toughened flesh. Feeling the sharp bite of an insect on the back of his neck he ignored it. Things like that didn't bother him anymore he was part of the forest, his home.

It seemed to Rance that he'd always lived there for he knew the sounds the forest made in daylight and the totally different sounds at night. He could sense danger a kilometre away, idly he watched Cross sitting in the river laughing with one of the young partisans, what was his name? he was new. Rance gave up thinking about it, there had been so many. Cross was like a brother to him now they fought well together each one looking out for the other.

He froze the sound of the forest had changed he gave a long low whistle and the men scattered. Crouching by the river bank he watched one of their scouts come into view. The man had been running hard and was near to collapse when Marek caught him by the arm.

'What's the matter man that's happened?' he said looking in the direction the man had come from.

The man fought for breath taking great gasps of air into his tortured lungs. 'There's an Einsatzgruppen patrol in the village of Sadinki, about three Kilometres from here and I could hear gunfire and screaming so I came for you.'

Marek turned to his men but no order was necessary for they were already reaching for their guns.

Running silently through the trees Rance automatically checked his machine pistol then the pistol at his waist. He looked for the others but only saw them as fleeting shadows in the sun dappled half-light of the forest. An hour later they cautiously approached the village spreading out moving slowly into the centre. It was unnaturally quiet. Rance felt his stomach muscles tightened and he felt the sick feeling in his gut. The village was small the houses with an assortment of outbuildings and barns seemingly scattered about at random with a dirt track running through the centre. He glanced inside two of the nearest houses and found them empty their doors swinging ajar. Bullet holes penetrated the walls and ceilings and the broken oil lamps slowly dripped fuel onto the stone floors. Walking through the second house and out though the back door into the yard he was followed by one of the younger men.

His stomach lurched a shiver ran down his spine at the sight of a heaped mound of bodies almost filling the yard which were already becoming bloated in the heat.

A dense swarm of flies rose in a sickening buzzing cloud from the gaping and blackened wounds of the dead villagers. He leaned against the wall of the house bile rising in his throat his eyes blurred as he fought to clear his senses. The young man following behind was immediately sick crying unashamedly into his hands.

The pile of death moved Rance swiftly bent forward pulling away two of the bodies to reveal a small boy about five years old who had been shot in the throat. Gently lifting him he carried the boy into the house and cleared a space on the floor with his feet before laying him down.

'I need water,' he snapped at the young partisan who pulled himself together and fetched a bowl full. With care Rance tried to wash the boy's wound. The five year old opened his eyes and screamed in terror, the wound opened pumping blood over Rance's hand while he desperately fought to stem the flow but the screaming died to a gurgle and the life slowly ebbed from the young body. He gentle closed the boy's eyes and walked outside blinded by tears. Sitting down on the ground he cried out in anger and despair.

'I was sure I could have saved him but I was wrong to move him. It's my fault,' he whispered, Cross sat down beside him and laid a hand on his shoulder. 'It's not your fault Rance blame the Nazis that came to torture and kill, not you', he said his grip tightening with his fingers digging into Rance shoulder. 'It's up to us Rance to stop this bloody slaughter, you, me and the partisans.'

Rance climbed to his feet all emotion drained from his face his eye were ice grey cold and hard. 'Where's Marek?' he said quietly his lips were thin and tight with a small nerve jumping in the side of his jaw.

Marek, when he found him looked white and drawn old before his time.

'There are another forty two bodies over there,' he choked nodding behind him. 'There were a few survivors hiding in the forest, we found one and he told me the Germans were looking for us. He overheard them say something about the village of Wielbark then they moved off in that direction following the road.'

Marek wiped the sweat off his brow using the back of his hand.

'They only left about half an hour ago if we hurry we can cut them off by using the forest tracks.

'They ran like men possessed of madness in ice cold anger. The narrow track that led through the dense undergrowth was rough and uneven and the low overhanging branches whiplashing their faces they totally ignored.

An hour later Marek called a halt when the trees thinned and the road appeared in front of them. Marek sucked air into his torture lungs.

'Spread out and make sure you don't get caught in any crossfire,' he said addressing his latest recruits, 'In other words don't position yourselves opposite one of your own men.'

Rance picked himself a giant pine tree and sat down leaning against the cool rough bark. He looked across at Cross ten feet away, and even from that distance he could see the nerve jumping in his cheek, Cross stared back with eyes that were as cold and hard as his own.

The German patrol was a long time coming and after an hour he closed his eyes thinking of Izabel. He was bitterly disappointed not seeing her after her brother was freed also he worried for her safety, she risked her life nearly every day delivering messages and in his mind's eye he looked down at her breath-taking beautiful face into the dark brown sparkling eyes that would turn and show sensual smouldering passion when aroused. He could taste her soft lips-.

The rifle shot jarred him back to reality. Flattening himself close to the ground he heard Marek cursing one of the new men for firing to soon. Looking down the road he could see the German patrol scattering for cover and was angry for not keeping a watch himself.

Clutching his gun he ran for the thicker cover of the forest undergrowth somewhere behind him a heavy calibre machine gun opened up its clatter loud and harsh amongst the tree, with bullets chewing up everything in sight he dived into the thick undergrowth while they thrashed at the branches above his head like a giant reaper.

Rance crawled deeper into the forest before getting to his feet and working his way around behind the machine gunner finally crawling to within fifty feet of his position. With care he checked his machine pistol was fully loaded before rising to a kneeling position. All the fear and tension drained away to be replaced by a cold feeling of revenge.

His hands holding the weapon were steady, he lined up the sights on the man behind the machine gun and gently squeezed the trigger bringing it back to fully automatic sending a stream of bullets into the man who jerked like a puppet and rolled over his loader companion who in turn screamed and in panic tried to hide behind the still twitching body. Rance showing no trace of emotion continued firing and the bullets smashed through the first body and reached the crying man underneath who twisted and jumped before falling back limply.

The remainder of the German patrol stopped their advance looking back in confusion at the now still machine gun. Suddenly it started firing again this time killing two of their own, forcing them to go to ground before it jammed and Rance had to abandon it. The gap between the two sides narrowed to less than fifty feet amongst the trees. It was now a deadly game of hide and kill, while he, together with the other partisans ruthlessly hunted them down.

The Nazi officer in charge desperately tried to keep his men together while they slowly retreated but their nerve broke and they ran in all directions.

For Rance, the next two hours were a nightmare of killing as the partisans took their revenge. The remaining troops ran until exhausted and fell as Marek's men closed in making no sound no cheers of victory just a deadly intent, and so the killing went on and the bullets flew until finally came the silence. Where no birds sang and where no man spoke.

Rance sat with his back to a tree, his mind numb, he felt no joy in revenge just a cold purpose, a job to do. 'No more would they kill another child,' were his thoughts. He watched Marek and the others as they moved amongst the fallen troops and he joined them, removing their guns and all the spare ammunition they could carry. He watched in silence as Marek walked round checking each body to make sure they were dead before they were dragged out into the open and laid out in the shape of a swastika. Rance counted twenty five. He felt empty inside and walked away.

'This bloody war will it ever end?' he whispered to Cross feeling sick at heart and counting their own loses. Five, including the one Cross had been sharing a joke with in the river such a short time ago. There were also four wounded including one seriously.

After burying their dead and heavily laden down with spare arms, ammunition and supporting their wounded they slowly made their way back to Kalow.

'At last we may have a chance of seeing the girls soon,' said Cross unable to keep the excitement out of his voice.

Rance felt elated, it must mean that Izabel may be there to meet them. He looked with dismay at Cross's gaunt unshaven face and dirty lice ridden clothes. 'It must be a reflection of me,' he thought, hoping that he would have time to clean up before she saw him.

Marek stopped in the village of Pniewo and dropped off the wounded promising to send back a doctor. He avoided the village of Dabrowa preferring the deep cover of the forest and they sweated in the close energy sapping heat of the late afternoon.

It was dark by the time they entered the clearing at Kalow, gratefully answering Jozef's guarded challenge having left the captured guns and ammunition hidden at the edge of the forest. To celebrate their return Jozef and his neighbours shared what food they had and opened several bottles of his home made Vodka. Rance tried to look grateful when one was thrust into his hand. He looked across at Cross's stricken face and burst out laughing before taking a huge swallow from the bottle then waited for the explosion in his belly. When it came, it hit with the force of a hand-grenade making him blink rapidly forcing the tears from his eyes.

Cross stared at him in astonishment, 'I thought you were never going to touch the stuff again, what changed your mind?' he said bemused.

Rance grinned. 'Tomorrow we'll see our girlfriends, so it's time for a celebration.'

With the Vodka quickly taking effect on their empty stomachs, Rance and Cross started to sing in English giving their own version of 'Hang out the washing on the Siegfried line.' Their Polish hosts couldn't understand a word but they clapped and danced anyway.

Chapter 10

It was the pounding in Rance's head that woke him, bleary eyed he forced one eye open swearing once more not to touch the evil brew again, he squinted at Cross sitting on his bed of tree branches.

Cross this time was quite the opposite feeling none the worse with not even a twinge of remorse he took great delight in teasing him.

'I don't understand a man that can't take his drink it shows a poor upbringing,' he laughed watching Rance stagger down to the river and plunge his head in the fast flowing cold water. Rance brought his head back out gasping for air and sat forlornly on the bank it was two hours before he could face anything to eat.

There was no word from Izabel so Marek decided to move back into the forest for safety. Rance became more nervous and apprehensive. It was four days since their return and still no sign of her.

He approached Marek and asked him if there was anything he could do. Marek shook his head angrily telling him not to be so impatient and wait. Disgruntled by Marek's attitude who he was sure took great delight in watching him suffer Rance took to walking in the woods only to be involved in another row with Marek over the fact that he should stay in the camp.

'I don't know why you and him don't have a bloody good fight and get it over with,' Cross said despairingly, 'The pair of you are upsetting the whole camp.'

Rance grunted moodily and went for another walk.

Another two days passed before a man brought news and asked to speak to Marek. They spoke so quickly he gave up trying to understand what was being said and stood impatiently to one side staring at them both in frustration. Watching Marek's face change, he realised the man was bringing bad news.

'What's happened, where's Izabel, why isn't she here?' he asked apprehensively.

Marek stepped back with a look of annoyance on his face. 'The Gestapo have arrested Izabel's grandfather, he's disappeared. She loved the old man and has become overwhelmed with worry. It's also very bad for the people in Piotrkow there's no food and she's become very ill with something and can't move from her bed. She also has a temperature and there is no medicine.'

Marek stopped and looked at Rance to see if he understood, he nodded, Marek continued, 'The town is alive with new German troops and more are arriving every day. Curan has information that they are doubling their patrols. They seem to think there are British troops fighting with the partisans here'. Marek smiled grimly, 'At least while they look for us they might leave the villagers alone.'

Rance didn't hear the last remark his mind was in turmoil he had to go to her she needed him. 'I have to go to her,' he said determinedly.

'No,' Marek snapped, his eyes full of anger. 'It's out of the question.' He nodded at the courier, 'You heard what he said. The place is crawling with German troops.' His voice grew firmer when the expression on Rance's face became more stubborn. 'You're a foreigner and your Polish is lousy, you would endanger us all if you were caught.'

Rance went white and he felt his anger boil over. 'You would call me a traitor, you idiot of a Pole, there's no way I would tell those bloody Nazis anything,' he shouted in disgust.

'You're not going and that's final,' snarled Marek, his face now red with rage. Rance prodded him hard in the chest with one finger. 'I'm going, so don't even try to stop me.'

Marek, his expression now one of total fury lashed out with his fist. Rance saw it coming trying to move his head but was only partially successful. It felt like a sledgehammer when it connected with the side of his face sending him flying backwards onto the hard sandy soil.

He rolled aware of Marek's incoming boot and came up on his knees grabbing at Marek's leg catching it on the swing. Marek slipped and fell dragging Rance down on top of him while bringing his knee up viciously searching for Rance's groin who blocked it with his leg punching Marek hard in the face making him grunt.

Cross and the others came running up in alarm only to stop and gather round to cheer the fighters on. Dimly Rance heard the shouting and Cross's voice yelling encouragement as they stood toe to toe slugging it out. He saw Marek's bloody nose and split lips and then a fist exploded between his eyes almost fetching him to his knees. Grimly he hung on jabbing Marek in the throat with the side of his hand, Marek gagged and staggered back fighting for air. Now Rance felt himself being dragged away by the crowd of men who were laughing holding the two of them apart.

'What's the matter with you two? As if I didn't know,' Cross groaned despairingly.

To everyone's surprise Rance suddenly relaxed and faced Marek.

'OK, so I don't go now,' he shrugged, 'We'll discuss it tomorrow'.

Marek dabbed his bloodied lips with a dirty cloth eyeing him suspiciously.

'It will be no again tomorrow,' he said curtly.

Rance didn't reply and walked away with Cross glancing sideways at him

'It's not like you to give up that easily Rance?' he said more of a question than a statement.

Rance's face broke into a twisted smile. 'Who said anything about giving up, I'll leave first thing in the morning after I borrow a bicycle from Jozef.' Seeing the look of concern on Cross's face he held him by the arm.

'Don't worry my friend I have Volkdeutche identity papers, and can speak German better than I can speak Polish,' he said reassuringly.

'Why didn't you tell Marek you could speak German?' Cross queried with a note of exasperation in his voice.

Rance grew angry again. 'The man is jealous he wouldn't listen to reason, that's why.'

'Rance, I think this time you're wrong'. Cross looked towards where Marek was talking to Marian.

'I think he's genuinely concerned for your safety after all its one hell of a risk you're going to take.' Cross waved his hand to stop Rance from speaking.

'I'll give you two days my friend and if you're not back by then I'll come looking for you'.

Rance rose at the first glimmer of dawn shivering in the coldness of the early morning air. It was deathly quiet as he gathered together the bundle of food for Izabel and her Mother and with a last cautious look round at the sleeping men he stealthily worked his way around the guards before finding the path leading to Kalow.

Relieved he'd left the camp behind undetected he lengthened his stride. The sharp click of a pistol being cocked stopped him dead in his tracks and Marek stepped from behind a tree grasping a Walther P38 pistol which was pointed unwaveringly at Rance chest, his face was an inscrutably mask as he stood there in silence.

'The only way to stop me is to use that thing,' said Rance trying to stay calm but his gut twisted he could feel the tension.

Marek didn't blink, 'Don't think I won't, you disobeyed a direct order. What you're doing is putting all of us at risk,' he stated with a voice that was full of menace.

Rance spoke slowly trying to find the words with his limited Polish.

'I've calculated the risk and understand what you're saying but I should have told you before, I speak German. I learnt when I was a prisoner of war in Paris and Brussels. With my Volkdeutche papers, I'll pass as one of their farmers so the risk is limited.'

The seconds ticked slowly by with Marek pondering on his words.

Rance moved uneasily from one foot to the other calculating his chances of reaching Marek by surprise.

Marek lowered his pistol, Rance suddenly breathed freely, realising how close he'd come to death.

'I'll let you go for one reason only that's because I love her too, but you must promise me, swear on her life that if you're caught you must immediately use this on yourself,'

Marek reversed the pistol and presented it to Rance butt first. 'I've have said it before no one can withstand the torture of the Gestapo, in the end you would beg them to let you speak.'

Rance took the pistol and pushed it into the waist band at the back of his trousers so it would be concealed by his coat. Marek nodded towards Kalow. 'You'd better get moving you've a long way to go,' he said flatly.

They stared at each other unsure what to say next. Rance half lifted his hand thought better of it and turned away without a backward glance.

Marek stood and watched him walk out of sight wishing he was the one going. Instead he moodily returned to his men.

Rance picked up a bicycle and more food from Jozef before setting off on the track leading to Blezun. The sun climbed higher bringing with it the bird's dawn chorus and for the tenth time he felt for his papers making sure he still had them.

It was ten thirty before he reached the road in Blezun. He resisted the temptation to stop at Maria's house to reassure her that Cross was well, becoming uneasy at the sight of the man they had threatened sitting in the front of his house. Keeping his head turned the other way he cycled slowly past conscious of the man's careful scrutiny. The man looked long and hard at the scruffy farm labourer cycling past his front door there was something familiar about him, what was it, he knew him but from where? His wife called. He shook his head and went back inside his house.

The road was busy with German convoys coming and going to Piotrkow but as yet there were few civilians going his way, he could now feel the familiar tightening of his stomach muscles. The first sign of fear making the palms of his hands damp and clammy holding the handle bars.

The feeling he had that everyone knew who he was persisted, he felt highly vulnerable which made him more conscious of the pistol digging into his flesh. He arched his back to relieve the discomfort.

If anybody had said to him before he left England that he would now be riding a bicycle amongst thousands of German troops in central Poland he would have called them mad.

His pulse rate increased approaching the first road block situated at the top of a small hill. Dismounting half way up he walked the rest of the way pushing his bicycle with the bundle of food tied on the back. It was hot now but he still kept his coat on for fear they would see the pistol.

Coming up to the barrier he could feel his heart pounding and the adrenaline surging urging him to run. His face flushed with the mounting tension when he counted five soldiers manning the barrier.

They were all young, four armed with Mauser Kar 98K standard rifles and one with a Schmeisser sub machine gun. Two were checking papers while the other three stood watching, cradling their guns across their chests making Rance wonder how many he could take before turning the pistol on himself.

He avoided their stare concentrating on the guards checking the papers. When his turn came they looked at him with contempt. 'Papiere',

Rance fumbled in his pocket mumbling in German an abject apology for being so slow.

'Oh, ein weiterer Volksdeutche Hans,' the trooper said to his companion. 'Why are you German Poles so unkempt and dirty haven't you heard of soap and water?' he snapped flicking at Rance coat, 'Whats the matter with you, aren't you hot in that?'

Rance stiffened as the trooper prodded him in the chest with his finger.

'You have German blood in you, why don't you have some self-respect for yourself?' said the soldier starting to enjoy himself at Rance's expense.

He pulled at the bundle tied on the back of the bicycle, 'What's this you've got in here, more rags I suppose?'

Rance put a whine in his voice. 'Please sir, it's all the food I have', fixing the trooper with a pleading stare, 'I'll willingly share it if you leave me a little.'

The young soldier's face broke into a smirk fingering the dried meat.

'Do you honestly think that I could eat this rubbish,' he said glowering at the thought, he stepped back in disgust.

'Get going I have better things to do than talk to you all day,' he sneered.

Rance nodded lowering his eyes. 'Yes sir, thank you sir,' he muttered showing due respect. He pushed the grubby papers back into his pocket and careful not to hurry pushed the bicycle between the troopers before mounting and free-wheeling downhill feeling the breeze cooling his flushed face, resisting the urge to glance behind him. Although he was sure he'd already been forgotten.

It was mid-day before he reached the outskirts of the town, and closer to the centre German troops and civilians started to crowd in on him so he stepped into the road noticing the only cars being driven were by German soldiers. The tension in him increased at the sight of police patrols on every corner periodically stopping and searching people at random. He tried to remember where Izabel's street was knowing it was almost opposite a cemetery, but as yet he hadn't seen one.

There was a commotion behind him and turning round he saw someone being detained by the police before being bundled into a car and driven away. No one stopped they just hurried on with their heads down. Rance did the same.

He was stopped twice in twenty minutes by the police but allowed to proceed. It didn't get any easier, his nerves were screaming with tension.

It had become hot and humid the air hanging lifeless in the narrow street making the perspiration run down his back and around the butt of the pistol, which rubbed ceaselessly on his spine. Looking up at the sky he saw storm clouds gathering sometimes blotting out the sun.

He couldn't find the street and was now lost he would have to ask someone. Who? he chose an old man.

'Excuse me, where can I find Sieokawicza Street?'

'Co'? shouted the old man lifting his hand to his ear.

Rance wished the road would open and swallow him.

'Co powiedziales?' bawled the man his voice loud and shaking,

Rance winced when passers-by turned and stared.

He hurriedly waved his arms. 'Niewazne, ze to nie znaczenia,' he said and went to walk away.

The old man caught him in a claw like grip, 'Co powiedziales?' Rance shook him off and hurriedly turning round found two German policemen blocking his path.

'Warum die eile?' said one stepping closer. Rance's stomach turned upside down his pulse rate went up through the roof.

'I'm sorry sir but I've lost my way,' he whispered shuffling sideways putting his bicycle between them and him.

'Lass mich sehen, dass du papiere bist,' snapped the larger of the two men, he was a sergeant with broad shoulders and a bent nose that had obviously been broken more than once. Rance didn't fancy his chances taking him on so he meekly handed them over. The sergeant studied them at length fixing him with a penetrating stare.

'Now why would you be lost in such a small town as this?' he asked, suspiciously.

Rance became aware of his companion walking behind him. Feeling a sharp prod in the back just above the hidden pistol took all his self-control to appear calm; shuffling sideways away from the prodding finger he weighed up his chances of reaching the gun before they could hold him.

'Where do you want to get to?' asked the man with the prodding finger.

He was young and arrogant, obviously wanting to impress his sergeant.

Rance ignored him and spoke to the sergeant,

'I'm looking for the cemetery, my mother is buried there'.

The Sergeant scratched his broken nose. 'Why haven't you been before this, weren't you at her funeral when she was buried?' he queried belligerently.

'Sir, I had the honour of working for the Fatherland in Germany, so I couldn't get to the funeral.'

'Well, why aren't you still in Germany now?' interrupted the young one still standing behind him.

"My family have always been farmers so when the Fatherland asked for volunteers for this area they chose to come. I was given permission to join them later. Unfortunately I was too late to see my mother,'

The Sergeant wasn't impressed and turning his attention to the bundle tied on the back of the bicycle he pulled it open revealing the food.

'What's all this food, I don't think your mother will be that hungry, do you?' he guffawed winking at his companion and they both laughed loudly at his joke.

'It's all I have I heard there wasn't any food in Piotrkow,' stuttered Rance hanging his head.

The Sergeant's face became ugly. 'You know it's an offence punishable by death to have black market goods about your person, indeed it's an offence to store food,' he snapped.

'I wasn't going to sell any of it,' Rance was beginning to sweat he could feel his palms becoming moist.

He watched in dismay when the Sergeant took half and dropping it on the floor ground it into the pavement with his boot.

'The cemetery is down there on the right,' the Sergeant said, pointing. The food on the pavement we have confiscated. We wouldn't want you to get into trouble now would we?' still laughing they walked away leaving Rance with his depleted bundle.

His relief at being free overcame his anger at losing half the food, he hurried to the cemetery where he walked up and down pretending to search for the grave until he was sure the police wouldn't return.

He found Sieokawicza Street ten minutes later and climbed the stairs to Izabel's apartment.

Satisfied there were no strangers about he knocked in trepidation, not knowing what to expect.

'Kto to jest?' a frightened voice answered.

'Jego Rance,' he whispered.

The sound of a bolt being drawn back echoed in the empty hallway, the door opened two inches to reveal Anya's frightened face peering out at him. Quickly she opened the door wide and pulled him inside her face white and drawn with fear.

'What are you doing here?' she whispered her voice shaking and uneven.

Rance didn't answer walking past he entered Izabel's bedroom to find the curtains drawn and the room in semi-darkness. She seemed asleep her breathing shallow and laboured with her body bathed in perspiration, he sat on the edge of the bed gently wiping her forehead.

She opened her eyes gasping with shock at seeing him sitting there.

'Rance,' she whispered tears coming to her eyes while she tried to sit up.

Gently he restrained her. 'Don't worry I'm here now everything will be all right,' he said softly.

'You shouldn't be here its too dangerous,' she gasped laying her head back on the pillow closing her eyes.

'I'm sorry, but the whole German army couldn't keep me away,' he murmured kissing her burning forehead. Quietly he left the room and joined Anya in the kitchen where she sat at the table biting her lip.

'What does the doctor say?' he asked.

'She has a virus, there is a lot of illness about but he has no drugs or medicine to treat her. He gave me a note for the German chemist.'

Anya started to cry. 'I went to see him but he just laughed, saying he didn't treat Poles.'

Rance looked at his watch. 'It is three thirty now an hour and a half before curfew. Where's the note and tell me how to find this chemist?'

Anya looked at him in shock, horror showing on her face.

'You haven't a chance of seeing him and even if you did he would have you arrested immediately,' she cried.

'Anya, give me the note and address of the chemist,' he asked again. Hurriedly she scribbled the address on the back of the note and handed it to him with shaking hands.

'Oh please be careful or you're a dead man,' she cried her eyes filling with tears. He looked at the address she'd written. It was in the main square, she gave him directions.

'How long to walk there?'

'About ten minutes but that would mean going past the Gestapo HQ, it would be better if you detoured through the back streets which would be fifteen minutes.

He chose the back streets careful not to show any haste thinking fifteen minutes there, fifteen minutes back. He glanced at his watch, twenty five to four. That gave him fifty five minutes to deal with the chemist. Plenty of time.

He noticed he was on a busy road not what he would call a back street. Had he taken a wrong turning, no he couldn't have there were no other turnings. He cursed his limited Polish he must have misunderstood Anya. Walking on with an uneasy feeling he ignored the first and second right turns as instructed. At the third corner he hesitated made up his mind and turned right. Now he was in a back street. His heart pounded when German troops in twos and threes sauntered passed. He stood on the corner of the next junction and looked left it must be that way he thought staring at his watch trying to keep down the panic. Five to four. The palms of his hands felt damp and his heart rate increased. A few spots of rain fell, he'd forgotten the storm that had been brewing all afternoon. Glancing at the sky he noticed the sun had disappeared and giant black clouds were building menacingly on the skyline as if to warn him of things to come.

Chapter 11

He cursed his luck bad weather was the worst thing that could happen, it would drive people indoors leaving just him and the German patrols out on the streets. He frowned at the thought and as if to taunt him a low growl of thunder rumbled menacingly in the distance. He walked left conscious of people already hurrying for shelter and entered the almost deserted town square walking slowly round the edge looking for the chemist.

Finally the rain came great spots fell exploding on the cobbles quickly soaking up the dust making rivers of mud. A group of soldiers on the opposite side of the square hurriedly reached for their capes running for shelter.

He almost missed the chemist with its small unimposing shop front. Trying the door he found it locked and while peering through the grime covered window that had begun to streak with rain water he saw a middle aged woman dressed in a white coat busily writing at a desk. Impatiently he hammered on the glass, she glanced at the window her face showing extreme annoyance.

Frantically he waved the note at her but she shook her head vigorously waving him away, mouthing that they were closed. Rance continued to hammer until angrily she rose and walked through a door into another room situated at the rear of the shop.

Annoyed at her reaction he stepped back and looked along the shop fronts seeing an arched gateway between the buildings. On entering he discovered it led to a courtyard behind the shops, countingthe doors he came to the rear of the chemist.

The rain was now falling heavily the overflowing drains causing huge pools in the courtyard; he studied the surrounding buildings all of which seemed deserted the windows staring back at him with sightless eyes.

Taking out his pistol he reversed it knocking with authority on the back door of the shop before standing to one side so whoever opened it would have to let it swing wide to see him.

'Who is it, don't you know we're closed?' rasped a man's voice, annoyed and angry.

Rance grasped the pistol butt tightly. 'Police, we have an emergency open up damn you,' he growled.

The man behind the door hesitated. Rance hammered on the door again. 'Hurry up, we have a wounded soldier here,' he shouted impatiently.

The man slid back the bolts cautiously peering out into the rain soaked air

A dark figure loomed in the doorway catching him by the throat stifling his scream. With bulging eyes he felt himself being thrust backwards until an inner door jamb brought him to a violent stop, he groaned in pain unable to shout staring in terror at the pistol pointing between his eyes.

The middle aged lady came into the hallway Rance turned the pistol pointing it at her, silencing the cry she was about to make, instead her hand flew to her throat and her eyes rolled.

Rance thought she was going to faint.

'Move back into the other room,' he whispered.

She backed away he followed still clutching the terrified chemist by the throat who was short, balding, with a very thin neck and he was also choking to death, going purple in the face.

Rance relaxed his grip to look at his watch. Twenty passed four, he mentally fought down the signs of panic. Pointing the gun between the chemist's eyes he passed the note to the woman.

'Give me the medicine and drugs written down there or I'll kill you both,'

She stared with dread at the savage looking man standing before her, rain water was running off his long hair and down his unshaven face, the cold hard eyes seemed to burn into her very soul.

She started to whimper the chemist stopped choking.

Rance savagely thrust them together.

'I haven't got time to play games move damn you.'

They scurried to the drugs cabinet their fingers shaking making up the prescription while pills rolled over the floor. He opened the door at the front of the shop staring out at the deserted rain lashed square.

The trembling chemist handed him a small bottle of pills and a large bottle containing a dark liquid.

'Take one tablet four times a day and a tablespoon of the liquid every four hours,' he mumbled eyes wide with fear wondering what was to become of him. Rance glanced round the room stuffing the medicine into his coat pocket. 'Where does that lead to,' he asked nodding at another door.

'It's the cellar,' murmured the chemist apprehensively.

Rance levelled his pistol cocking it. 'Open it and get inside,' he snapped.

The chemist started to cry 'Bitte tote uns nicht,' he blubbered while a wet patch appeared at the front of his trousers slowly widening down his leg. Rance looked at him in disgust and pushed them both down the cellar steps into a small dark store room without any windows.

Using old wiring that lay in a heap on the floor he tied them tightly together face to face.

'If you get out of here before dawn I'll return one day and kill you both,' he threatened.

The petrified chemist shook his head violently from side to side to reassure his tormentor that was the last thing on his mind. With one last look around Rance quietly slipped out of the back door and entered the empty square. Bracing himself against the cold wet wind he turned into a side street only to find it blocked by a police patrol coming the other way.

Forced to detour he found himself on the main street with the Gestapo HQ in the town hall ahead of him. He turned to walk away and was again forced to go forward by the same patrol coming up behind him. Quickening his step trying to keep ahead of them brought him ever nearer the main entrance and the sentries standing by the large wrought iron gates.

Glancing at his watch his nerves went haywire and the tension in him grew. Ten minutes to five curfew time.

There were two civilians in front of him, they too were in a hurry. The sentries stepped forward raising their arms bringing them and Rance to a halt. His nerves were now screaming and the adrenaline surged, he turned placing his back to the railings feeling behind him for the pistol which he moved to his side pocket.

A German staff car drew to a halt at the curb and the sentries saluted a high ranking Gestapo officer who swept passed without a second glance. Rance glanced quickly behind him towards the police patrol recognising the large sergeant and his companion whom he'd met earlier. He turned his attention back to the sentries who were now examining the two civilian's papers and waited his turn conscious of the two policemen now standing behind him.

'Well, well, if it isn't our little grave friend,' the sergeant laughed at his own joke. The sentries waved the civilians on and turned their attention to Rance who calculated he'd only a split second to reach his gun and use it on himself. He stepped backwards and pressed against the fence.

One of the sentries held out his hand. 'Papieres'.

Rance started to reach for the pistol.

'Oh don't worry about him, we've seen them already,' said the sergeant in a loud brash voice.

The two sentries hesitated and shrugged before returning to the HQ entrance.

'Eaten all your food?' the sergeant's companion inquired with a snigger.

'Yes sir I was hungry,' answered Rance.

'You're lying, we know what you've done with it, don't we?' said the sergeant turning knowingly to the younger man who looked at his watch. 'Five to five, let's keep him here until five passed then shoot him for breaking the curfew,' he quipped, they both laughed at the joke.

Rance put on an expression of horror. 'Please sir I've only to go to my friend's house round the corner, two minutes sir.'

The sergeant grinned, he was enjoying himself.

'I'll tell you what we'll do,' he winked at his companion, 'We'll give you a minutes start then come looking for you.'

Rance didn't wait to hear any more.

'Thank you sir,' he shouted over his shoulder and ran down the road.

'Hey wait!' shouted the startled sergeant before the two of them burst out laughing, and entered the Gestapo HQ.

Anya welcomed him at the door. Quietly he entered Izabel's bedroom, although she seemed to be asleep he gently lifted her head and administered the medicine. Barely conscious she whispered his name before sinking back on the pillow.

He sat by her bedside all night stroking her hair and bathing her flushed face with cold water refusing Anya's offer to take over. Every four hours he gave her more medicine and the pills until gradually her fever started to subside, by mid-day she had settled into a normal sleep. He slept in a chair next to the bed and woke with a nagging pain in his neck. Blinking his bleary eyes he stretched rolling his head from side to side realising he'd slept awkwardly in the small chair. He looked at his watch, three o'clock in the afternoon.

'Rance,' Izabel was wide awake her large dark eyes were misty and showed alarm, her face pale and drawn.

He got up and sat on the edge of the bed.

'Thank God your fever has gone,' he said bending down kissing her forehead which was cool without a trace of the fever that had tormented her body.

'You shouldn't have come', her tone was angry.

He looked startled. 'You needed me nobody could have kept me away,' he whispered.

'I wasn't thinking about anybody what about the Gestapo?' she countered, 'They're everywhere.'

'I couldn't stop myself your life is my life. As far as I was concerned there was no other way,' said Rance, unrepentant.

'You fool you endanger us all. Me, my mother,' Izabel was close to tears.

Rance didn't know what to say. 'I thought that,'--

She wouldn't let him continue. 'Rance please for all our sakes, please get back into the forest,' she started to cry.

Totally confused Rance walked out of the room and sent in her mother while he sat in the kitchen upset at the turn of events unsure what to do next.

Anya came back and kissed him on the cheek. 'Thank you for saving my daughter's life, I will be forever in your debt.'

'She's angry that I came,' he said getting up and pacing the floor restlessly. 'Do you think I did the wrong thing?'

She nodded, 'Yes I do there are a lot of people's lives at stake including your own.' She paused looking at him with a curious expression on her face.

'It would have been a dangerous thing for a local man to do what you did to-day, but you an Englishman in central Poland in 1943,'-- she shook her head in wonder. 'You're a very brave man Rance God bless you for it but you were wrong, now you must leave.' She hugged him, 'God go with you I shall pray to the saints that they watch over you.'

She returned to her daughter who was lying on her stomach sobbing.

'Oh mother what have I done sending him away like that, what a fool he was risking his life in such a dangerous way,' she cried her tears soaking the pillow.

Anya stroked her daughter's hair. 'Hush girl the man is in love with you, he did save your life,' she whispered.

Izabel sobbed even louder. 'Oh I wish I hadn't said anything but I was worried out of my mind for his safety'.

Anya bit her lip, 'I know you love him too,' she said with tears in her eyes.

'Yes I do I would die for him, but I don't want him to die for me,' Izabel said in anguish grasping her mother tightly. 'Oh please God let him get back to the forest safely'.

Chastened, depressed, and in a dangerous mood, Rance walked away from the apartment looking at his watch. Three thirty, he would make the forest but not Kalow. He could smell rain again in the air and hoped it would hold off already the rivers would be in full flood from the rains yesterday. The streets were full of German troops standing talking in groups, or sitting in cafes idly watching the passers-by.

The hidden pistol against his back gave him little comfort knowing that if he pulled it, it would be to shoot.

A large crowd had gathered outside a shop with someone shouting that there might be bread. Rance pushing his bicycle walked to the other side of the road as tempers flared and scuffles broke out with people fighting for a place, police moved in swinging their battens. Men shouted and women and children cried as more fighting broke out spilling into the road.

He felt the stinging blow from a batten across his back making him stagger then he was running with the rest. Turning into a side street he left the chaos behind and keeping well away from the main road he made his way to the outskirts where he debated whether to abandon the bicycle and strike out across country or stay with the road. In the end he decided it was too close to the town, he would be too conspicuous out on his own so he stayed with the road and at four thirty he cleared the last of the road blocks without further trouble.

A little later he looked at his watch again, four fifty, curfew time.

Hiding the bicycle he struck off into the forest keeping the road in view on his left. Occasionally he stood watching German patrols pass relying on the shadows cast by the trees to conceal his presence. The first drops of rain fell slanting through the trees while he looked at the heavily laden sky turning the evening light into a murky gloom. Now the remaining light faded turning his forest sanctuary into a black hole of misery.

He skirted the village of Przglow, twice losing his way in the rain soaked blackness before almost falling in the River Luciaza. Slowly he waded into the fast flowing water struggling to keep his balance when the current threatened to sweep him away. Now exhausted he climbed the river bank on the opposite side and after the oppressive heat of the day he felt frozen, shivering in the rain-drenched blackness of the forest. He was tired, so it was with relief he found the track leading to Kalow, an hour later he was hammering on Jozef's door.

Gratefully he sipped a scalding hot drink made by Marian, and was joined later by their neighbours Radice and his two sons who listened in stony silence when Rance told them of the build-up of troops in the area and the food shortages in Piotrkow. Jozef informed him that another courier had arrived from Curen bringing orders for another assignment for Marek, and that he should return first thing in the morning.

He returned to the camp to be met by Cross who grasped his hand in delight, smacking him on the back with gusto. 'If you hadn't returned to-day I swear the whole camp would have come with me,' he said laughing with relief.

Rance told them the news. Marek listened in silence until he'd finished. 'It's good for all our sakes that you have returned safely. It's also possible that we might find your ability to pass as a Volksdeutche very useful in the future,' he said thoughtfully.

Rance wasn't sure he liked the sound of that last remark.

The next few weeks were a nightmare with the deadly game of ambush continuing while new German patrols appeared almost every day.

Marek avoided speaking, content to sit on his own. They lost more men and had to periodically return to Kalow for new recruits and pick up orders for their next assignment.

Rance was overjoyed to hear that Izabel was now back as a courier and had been asking about him. He left a message telling her how glad he was about her recovery and hoped to see her soon.

He noticed the weather gradually changing becoming more wet and windy with the leaves starting to fall in profusion.

At first the autumn colours were dazzling in their diversity with the greens turning to gold, orange, and yellows but now the trees looked drab in their winter bareness. Early morning frosts were now commonplace and Rance sported an old overcoat given to him by a farmer. It was worn out and smelt of horse and mouse droppings, but it was warm. Cross had fared somewhat better, an ex-German greatcoat given to him by Marek that once was grey and full of bullet holes. It had been dyed a muddy brown and stitched up, making it look quite respectable.

Cross paraded up and down in front of Rance.

'Don't you wish you had influence in this army like me?' he chortled, 'Instead of being put at the back all the time.'

Rance grunted disdainfully. 'Marek is a petty idiot, he might be a good leader, but as a human being he's a cretin'.

'You like him then,' laughed Cross.

CHAPTER 12

'Where are we going Marek?' Rance asked.

It was dusk they'd been heading south for the past hour without being informed on what was happening which was unusual.

Marek looked at him and was about to make a sharp retort then thought better of it.

'We've been ordered to attack a machine tool factory near the town of Radomsko,' he answered shortly.

'How far is that?' queried Rance choosing to ignore Marek's curt reply.

Marek shrugged, 'The way we travel, two days'.

Rance counted the men, 'There are only ten of us will that be enough?'

'We're joining up with Krolik and Pies, for this one. As you know they have their own men.

We'll meet in the village of Niwy, there will be over thirty of us,' he looked at Rance with distaste. 'Anything else you want to know?.

Rance stared at him in anger, 'It's nice to know what we might be dying for that's all,' he said, turning his back on Marek and walking away.

Two of the more experienced partisans, Golab and Moskit were acting as scouts while Rance and Cross brought up the rear. They walked slowly all night skirting the many small villages with only the occasional dog barking to mark their passage.

Dawn came and with it a heavy flurry of snow. Rance glanced apprehensively at the dark and brooding overcast sky, the clouds racing each other all seemingly anxious to rid themselves of their heavy burden.

Cross read his thoughts, 'I don't think we're going to like this assignment, do you?' he said soulfully.

Rance shook his head. 'Let's hope it will slow the Germans as it will slow us,' he retorted.

Cross looked sour faced, 'We'll leave a trail in the snow, it will be as good as saying, 'Here we are, come and get us.'

An hour later Krolik and Pies welcomed them with the usual bottle of Vodka. Krolik grinned shaking Rance and Cross's hand with gusto.

'Welcome Englishmen how do you like our Polish winter eh?' he roared.

'It's something I could do without,' Rance answered.

Pies, heavily wrapped against the cold was his usual unsmiling self giving a brief nod before stepping back in silence, offering no greeting. Krolik slapped Marek on the back motioning towards his men.

'We have seventeen men between us, we lost a few in the last two weeks and haven't had any replacements yet,' he said.

Marek nodded. 'That makes twenty seven in all, that should be enough. We'll stay here until dusk then follow the railway line down to Radomsko and aim to arrive there at dawn.'

Rance was pleased to see Jarek, Izabel's brother, who welcomed him with a huge grin and a vigorous handshake.

'I'm pleased to see you're still around, I heard what you did for my sister. It seems my family owes you a lot and I thank you for it. My sister is very lucky to have found a man like you', he said with sincerity.

'Try telling that to Marek,' chuckled Cross making Izabel's brother smile, for it was common knowledge about the fight.

Rance pulled a face and quickly changed the subject.

'You're looking well, how is Krolik treating you,' he asked.

'He knows the forest almost as well as Marek and he's a good leader, his men have confidence in him and so do I,' Jarek answered.

'Krolik keeps you well supplied with weapons,' said Cross nodding at the heavily armed men.

'Well, we had a bit of luck there,' said Jarek. 'Four days ago we attacked a German outpost that was poorly guarded and found a surprisingly large amount that had been stored, for what purpose we don't know.'

'What's in the sacks strapped on the backs of those two?' Rance asked curiously as two men walked passed. 'That's something else we found there. Explosives, more than we could carry which was a pity we had to leave so much. Krolik thinks we can use it at the factory.'

'Have you seen your sister and mother at all?' he said.

'No I haven't, but I've heard that she's active again. Jarek looked wistful, 'but it would be nice to see them again.'

Yes, thought Rance it certainly would but would she want to see him again?' he felt despondent thinking about it.

Rance and Cross cut branches to form a bed then cut more to cover themselves. As Rance pulled his knees up to his chest in an attempt to keep warm the last thing he heard was Cross cursing, 'Bloody Polish weather.'

He woke feeling a heavy weight pressing down and opening his eyes he thought it was still dark. He could smell the freshly cut pine with the branches lying on his face. Pushing them away he found himself covered in six inches of snow.

Someone had lit a fire so he threw his make shift bed on to it and warmed himself when the flames leapt towards the snow filled sky.

The temperature continued to drop and the shivering men pushed sticks through their pieces of dried pork thrusting them into the glowing embers. Rance could feel his stomach rumbling with hunger while he chewed at the half cooked, half charcoaled meat.

The men sat cross legged around the fire and the now familiar Vodka bottle was offered which Rance and Cross politely declined.

Marek stood facing them his peaked cap pulled low over his eyes and his scarf tied tightly round his neck to keep out the swirling snow.

'From now on we walk in line one behind the other and only step in the footprints of the man in front that way the Germans won't know how many we are. If it snows much more then we will take turns to break a path through it. He paused rubbing at his unshaven chin.

'I remind you again about being caught you must save a bullet for yourself, his voice thickened, growing harder. 'Don't hesitate, don't stop to think, do it quickly before they can get to you that way your death will be painless. He stopped and looked around at their strained white faces, no one spoke as the snow swirled across the fire. Rance felt the queasy feeling of dread at the blunt words, once again bringing home the utter savagery of the war he and Cross were in. Shaking his head he brought his attention back to Marek.

'This factory is important to the Germans it makes machine tools for their weapons and repairs them when they go wrong we have been given the job of destroying it. He picked up his machine pistol and bag of spare ammunition. 'Let's go,' he said quietly.

They headed west keeping to the forest where the snow wasn't deep and made good progress. On reaching the railway line they skirted the small station and clambered onto the track.

The moon stayed hidden behind the heavy snow filled clouds while occasional flurries blew off the nearby trees coating them in a fine white film which blended them into formless rambling shapes.

The snow was deeper now on the railway line with the frost making the top layer hard and brittle. He found it difficult to walk stumbling over the hidden sleepers. No one spoke all he could hear was the laboured breathing of the man in front and Cross behind. Three times they had to detour around a station building which sometimes was no more than a shed, but all were guarded. Marek called a halt resting for twenty minutes, wearily sinking onto the snow covered track.

Rance adjusted his boots thankful that the Germans made them strong and almost water tight. Rubbing his hand over the stubble on his chin he was surprised to find it coated in icicles from the moisture of his breath. He wondered if he would get frostbite but decided he had more important things to worry about as they resumed their journey.

Dawn was still an hour away when Marek called another halt.

Leaving the track they lit a small fire and ate what was left of the pork. Rance took the first bite and yet again it tasted rancid so he charcoaled it almost to a cinder before forcing it down with a swig of Vodka struggling not to fetch it back.

Marek drew a map of the factory, at the same time outlining what each man had to do. The plan was to place an explosive charge in the ammunition store to the rear of the factory as a diversion before attacking the main buildings.

'Who wants the job,' Marek asked looking round.

'I'll do it,' answered Pies his voice hard as if to stifle any objections.

'You know it will be the most heavily guarded,' said Marek.

'I know that's why I'll take three men with me,' he countered and to Rance's surprise he actually smiled. 'We'll be in and out before they know it'.

'The bugger's actually enjoying this,' whispered Cross. 'I always knew he was mental. Come to think of it so are we. We could be sitting in some nice prisoner of war camp right now.'

'Or we could be stuck down some bloody German coal mine,' joked Rance trying to keep his voice light but already he could feel the first twinge in his stomach and his palms becoming moist. It never got any easier this waiting just before a fight but he knew that once it started he would become calm and the fear would subside, but not go away. Death could be just around the corner, waiting.

Dawn was just a faint glimmer in the sky and the snow was beginning to fall steadily. Pies and his men had been gone an hour when Rance stood rocking on Moskit's shoulders enabling him to look over the wall.

The factory building itself was a long one storey construction that had seen better days with partly boarded windows and a wide yard leading from the wall to a large pair of double doors almost opposite him.

In the yard were scattered parts of old rusting machinery and lengths of steel, a start had been made to repair one wall of the building and scaffolding was placed against it with piles of red bricks ready for use.

In the growing daylight he could make out the silhouette of a guard tower at the far end of the wall on his left, while on his right were the main gates to the factory guarded by two machine gun posts surrounded by sandbags.

Rance reported to Marek who immediately despatched two men with explosives to deal with the tower the rest he took with him for a frontal diversionary attack on the main gate, leaving Rance and Cross with six men two of whom carried the main explosives.

The falling snow was now turning into a blizzard making it hard for the guards to see. Rance blessed their luck while crouching against the outer wall waiting for Pies to blow the ammunition store. Restlessly he checked his machine pistol for the fourth time, the tension building and with the minutes seeming to tick by so slowly he started to sweat.

The store blew up! He reached the top of the wall and lay on the top. It was impossible to see what was going on in the yard by the main gate with the blizzard conditions sweeping around him but he could hear firing on his right then another explosion from the direction of the tower.

He dropped to the yard below and caught the sacks of explosive charges that were thrown down to him. Now joined by the others he ran in the direction of the double doors. Somewhere near a siren started its warning wail, which quickly rose to an ear shattering scream dying to a whisper when it reached its highest point and dropping to a murmur before starting all over again. The blizzard swirled in as Cross and Rance fired blindly across the yard before turning their guns on the lock to blow it apart. Abruptly the siren fell silent and Rance was dimly aware of the sound of a fierce fire fight by the main gate and for a fleeting second he wondered how Marek and the rest were doing before he entered the building.

Rows of machines and tools glistened coldly in the gloom with machine-guns and rifles partly dismantled lying scattered on benches around the edge. Over on the far side he could see parts of field-guns and their carriages. There were no guards in the building and he stood watching as the charges were laid down the length of the machines and against the pillars holding up the roof.

A door behind the field-guns opened and German troops moved scattering amongst the machines. The partisan with the explosives lit the main fuse and ran towards Rance when a German bullet caught the man in the back catapulting him forward onto his face. Reaching for the partisan Rance grabbed him by the leg trying to drag him out of the line of fire while watching Cross make it to the outside door before turning to give him covering fire.

The partisan screamed for Rance to leave him, his blood pumping from the wound leaving an ever widening pool on the oil stained floor.

Rance shook his head still firing at the advancing troops and watched in horror as the partisan pulled out his pistol and with eyes closed pushed the barrel into his mouth and pulled the trigger.

letting the body go he threw himself at the outside door feeling the bullets pull and tug at his clothing. A blast of hot air hit him in the back throwing him forward onto his face, in a daze he was aware of Cross pulling him to his feet and together they ran with the building behind them blowing up, the fuses having run their length. Now slowly at first then in one continuous roar it sent shards of glass and splinters of jagged wood into the troops caught inside.

Rance crouching low trying to avoid the lumps of masonry and slates flying like missiles all around him anxiously looked for Cross and saw him as a dim figure running through the snow on his right.

The fire-fight near the gate had spread into the yard with men flitting like shadows through the blinding snow storm. The shape of a man loomed in front of him and he swung his gun almost shooting Marek, who mouthed something he couldn't hear, still deaf from the explosion.

Frantically Marek signalled a retreat pointing in the direction of the main gate. Rance nodded that he understood and together with Cross ran past the dead sentries lying across the sandbagged entrance and out into the open.

With the blizzard continuing the visibility was down to less than seventy five yards. Rance clawed his way up the embankment and found Pies the only survivor from the explosive store raid.

Marek, Cross, and Izabel's brother Jarek appeared and together they crouched on the top of the bank firing back at the shadowy figures fading in and out of the snow storm. More partisans reach the top while some caught on the bank screamed and slid down leaving a trail of blood, turning the bank into a slide of death.

The survivors retreated along the track until finally Marek gave orders to abandon it for the safety of the forest.

Rance found the going easier under the trees where the snow lay thinner on the ground and as the forest closed in around them the firing became sporadic, finally dying out altogether. Looking back at their trail in the snow he frowned thinking it wouldn't be long before the Germans regrouped and with reinforcements would follow their tracks.

Marek ordered four men to act as rear guards and did a head count. Sixteen and that included four wounded. Rance shook his head they had lost eleven men and it wasn't over yet. He looked at the snow filtering slowly through the trees and wondered if it would cover their tracks in time? The answer came with a sudden burst of firing from the rear guards, so struggling with the wounded they moved on.

He was joined by Cross and Jarek who were silent as they stumbled and slipped amongst the snow laden trees. Pies just ahead of them faltered holding his stomach his face white and drawn. Marek called a halt at a wide but shallow river which had icicles hanging from the frozen banks his was face taunt with indecision.

He hesitated, before making up his mind. 'I don't think we have any choice we must use the river to hide our tracks,' he said reluctantly.

'Rance took a deep breath and slid down the bank into the freezing water and although he was expecting it the shock made him gasp in pain when it came over the tops of his boots instantly freezing his feet and legs.

 The going was treacherous with the ice covered boulders and the loose stones underfoot, Rance slipped falling to his knees, again feeling the shock of the icy water round his lower body.

 The two men in front half carried half dragged one of the wounded before they too finally fell dropping him in the river where he lay partly submerged, his screams sounding like a wounded animal and the water running red with his blood.

The column of men halted while he was pulled up the bank and they attended to his wound. The trees that had protected them had thinned and the blizzard swirled in a white blinding fury making it almost impossible to see more than a few feet. Marek decided to use it to their advantage and left the river hoping it would now hide their tracks.

Rance stared back down the river. 'Where are the Germans? I would have thought they'd have caught us up by now,' he said to Krolik.

'They'll come, but slowly they don't give up that easily. They're experienced soldiers and fear an ambush,' answered Krolik. 'Half of them will have gone upstream to look for our tracks so they'll be more cautious not having so many men.'

'Marek', one of the men called, 'it's Moskit, he's dead'.

They gathered round and Rance stared down at the man they'd dropped in the river. His clothes were stiff, solid with ice and frozen blood covered his neck and chest. He realised the man had bled internally and the fall had brought the blood up through his mouth.

Pies crumpled falling to his knees clutching at his stomach before rolling over on his back. Marek knelt beside him and gently moved away his fingers undoing the man's coat and trousers to expose his belly. A bullet had sliced it open as if it were a knife allowing the intestines to squeeze out like a giant snake. Some of the men gagged and turned away.

Rance forced himself down on his knees and held Pies while Marek washed the wound in Vodka and tried to push the intestines back in.

Pies rolled his eyes and arched his back in agony his screams echoing through the frozen forest before he relapsed into unconsciousness.

Marek climbed to his feet and retched, his face a white mask as he gave orders for Moskit's body to be hidden and four men to carry Pies.

Rance marvelled at Pies courage in getting this far but couldn't understand how he did it. Slowly the men moved into the forest while he stayed back with the rear guard listening and watching for any pursuit, but all he heard was the sound of the river.

He hurried to catch up with the main party and noticed that their tracks were already disappearing under the falling snow. Would it be enough before the Germans came, he wasn't so sure?

Keeping to the forest they skirted any open spaces with care as the snow was already over eighteen inches deep and drifting higher in places. An hour later they entered a village and Marek hammered on the door of a small wooden house.

The frightened face of an old woman peered round the open door and nervously let them in. Rance looked round the almost barren room that contained a table two chairs and a single bed that was pushed against the far wall. After the cold outside the room was almost unbearably hot, heated by a stove burning bright on the opposite wall while on the right was a door leading to what looked like a small kitchen.

Marek had the men place Pies on the bed and spoke to the old woman.

'You must look after our friend who's badly wounded. We'll go for a doctor and return as soon as possible but in the meantime you must do your best is that understood?'.

The old woman looked at the wound and stared at Marek with knowing eyes. 'You won't be back you know it and I know it. This man is dying,' she stated.

Rance looked at Pies realizing with shock that he was conscious and listening to them his face ashen with pain.

Marek gave him a pistol which he held loosely by his side his breathing sharp and fast like a wounded animal. Then he took the old woman to one side.

'We're not doctors, we can't be certain he's dying so we must try and get help for him. If the Germans come which is no means certain then you must immediately leave our friend to deal with it himself and go to a neighbour. You know nothing it's not your house. Do you understand?.

The old woman nodded with relief.

Rance, the last to leave stood in the doorway and looked back.

The man's eyes hard and expressionless as ever didn't blink.

'Goodbye Englishman I hope one day you'll return to England and find peace,' his voice strained with pain. He groaned and sweat ran down the side of his face. 'I think I'll find peace quicker than you.'

'Goodbye Pies,' murmured Rance gruffly quietly closing the door behind him.

'Can we get a doctor to him, is it possible? He asked but knowing in his own mind that it was already too late.

Marek's face showed the strain of the last few hours.

'We can try but with this weather and the Germans so close behind,'-- his voice trailed into silence.

144

Rance looked at his watch. Three o'clock in the afternoon and it hadn't stopped snowing. Already it was getting dark and the heavily laden clouds still raced each other overhead. Feeling the temperature start to plummet he shivered, it was going to be a long cold night. His mind felt numb with fatigue his body cried out for rest and sleep but still Marek pushed them on through the unrelenting freezing snow.

Darkness came suddenly or so it seemed to his tortured mind and aching limbs. Marek led them into a dense part of the forest where the branches of the huge trees bent almost to the ground with the weight of the snow.

'It's dark enough now to stop and rest. Light a fire he ordered his exhausted men. 'We'll need its heat before this night is out'.

They stumbled like zombies cutting wood for the fire and branches for a bed. Marek gave the first sentry duty to Rance and Cross.

'He never gives up on you does he?' grumbled Cross morosely. 'Sometimes Rance its moments like this that I wish I wasn't your friend.'

Together they crouched as close to the fire as they could without burning. Cross tried blinking the tiredness from his eyes which were red and sore. 'God, this is one hell of a war were fighting Rance,' he said throwing more wood on the fire which spat sparks at the night sky. 'I despair that we'll never see the end of it but if we do I want both of us to have a bloody good holiday together along with the girls. We'll drink real English beer in a real English pub'.

They lapsed into silence each with their own thoughts back in England a million miles away.

The old woman wiped the sweat from Pies feverish brow. It was almost four hours since the partisans had left and she looked at his wound again shuddering at the sight. He was going into a coma with the blood congealing over an hour ago. She stiffened in alarm at the sound of voices and went outside staring towards the far end of the village. It was dark and difficult to see but there was no mistaking the German troops searching her neighbour's houses. Turning she ran inside and slamming the door stood with her back to it her face showing sheer terror. Startled she realised the man was wide awake and staring at her with cold fathomless eyes.

'Zostaw mnie', his voice was cold and lifeless, 'go to your neighbour. Tell the Germans when they come that the people who lived here ran away you don't know why.'

The old lady started to cry. 'What about you! What will you do'? she sobbed, almost losing control.

'Idz do diabla, zanim beddzie za pozno,' he snarled.

With a choking cry she pulled a shawl over her head and fled in panic from the house.

Pies lay breathing heavily his whole body seemed on fire with waves of pain rolling over him. He listened to the sounds of breaking furniture and the screams of the occupants as the Germans ransacked the house next door. Slowly he struggled to lift the pistol across his chest pointing it at his head. His bowels sent shafts of screaming pain into his very soul and he bit deep into his lower lip to stifle the cry that stuck in his parched throat.

His fingers tightened on the trigger slowly forcing it back. He could now hear them outside on the porch a window smashed letting in a blast of cold air. The trigger went right back resounding with a deadening click. His hand shook, he let go the weapon which had jammed.

When the door finally burst open he reached down to his belly and tore at the wound, screaming in pure mortal agony when it burst, sending blood and guts onto the bed and floor.

The first soldier into the room turned and vomited over his companions at the sickening sight. A German officer strode in, looking in disgust at the dead partisan lying on the bed. He shook his head in wonder.

'How the hell could he do that?' he said speaking to his Sergeant.

It's a pity we couldn't have taken him alive, he could have told us so much.'

He looked round the room and shrugged in resignation.

CHAPTER 13

Gestapo HQ Piotrekow

Lieutenant Schmidt read the two signals which had landed on his desk with some consternation.
The first from Radomsko. Telling of an attack by bandits on a factory and asking for reinforcements as the group responsible was believed to be heading north towards Piotrkow.
It was the other one that made him nervous. The one from Berlin.
{Arriving 10 December on the afternoon train from Warsaw.} STOP.
{Have a car ready to meet me.} STOP.
{I want a full report ready and waiting for that evening.} STOP.
{Major Schneller.} STOP.
He bit his finger nail and read it for the second time.
'So you're coming back are you, you bastard.' he whispered.
The sergeant sitting opposite him looked up with a startled expression.
Schmidt sighed despondently and reaching for the telephone spoke to Lieutenant Lohr and Captain Braun informing them of the situation.
Having got the reinforcements under way he turned his attention to writing a long and detailed report which included a short private one on a separate piece of paper about the girl.
He hadn't much to say about her because he'd kept well away. He was now worried about what Franz Lohr would say to Schneller regarding the episode in his office. He threw down his pen in anger.
'I suppose I'd better check if the bitch is still there,' he said to himself, reaching for his hat and coat.
'Get me a car, we're going for a ride,' he snapped at the sergeant.

Anya was worried about her daughter. Ever since she'd sent Rance away her daughter had become withdrawn and despite her recovery was still pale and listless. Anya knew she bitterly regretted that day tearfully confiding she was frightened she'd lost him. There had been no real news for weeks even from Jarek, although Curen had sent word assuring her that he was well.

At first they didn't hear the gentle tapping on their apartment door until it got progressively louder, annoyed, Izabel walked across the kitchen room and opened it. Her eyes opened wide with shock when Lieutenant Schmidt strode purposely into the room closely followed by the Sergeant interpreter carrying a large box.

'My dear girl it's been such a long time since our unfortunate misunderstanding,' he said apologetically.

His attempt at a smile was a disaster. Izabel looked with distaste at the curling upper lip which parted from the lower one revealing his dirty discoloured teeth.

'What do you want?' she exclaimed angrily her eyes flashing and her cheeks going red.

Anya looked on in amazement at the change in her daughter.

This was the real Izabel returned from a shadow to someone full of spirit and life and although Anya was overjoyed at the transformation she was now afraid that her head-strong daughter would go too far.

She stepped between them.

'What is it you want of us sir?' she asked politely ignoring Izabel's grunt of disgust at calling him sir.

Sighing with relief at avoiding a confrontation Schmidt turned to the mother.

'Madam, these are hard times and I have been an admirer of your daughter for some time. I promised my superior that I would help you both so I have filled this box with good food and drink for your enjoyment.'

'You don't have to worry about making it last there's plenty more where that came from,' he said silkily and snapping his fingers he motioning for the sergeant to place the box on the kitchen table.

'I trust you and your daughter are well. Please don't hesitate to call me if you need anything more'.

Anya looked anxiously at her daughter who was standing speechless beside herself with fury.

An embarrassing silence followed.

'I, err, I don't know when my superior will be returning but I'm sure he'll wish to see you both,' he said nodding.

'Let's go,' he snapped and walked stiffly from the room without a backward glance.

Waiting for the door to shut behind him Izabel walked to the table and looked inside the box at the fresh fruit, eggs, chocolate, meat, a whole chicken, ham, even a bottle of wine.

Lieutenant Schmidt stepped into the street pulling on his costly handmade leather gloves. He felt pleased being now able to report to Schneller that he'd helped her with food and generally looked after her while he'd been away.

'Oh Lieutenant Schmidt,' the voice came from above and he looked up smirking with satisfaction just in time to see his box of food come hurtling down. Shouting in alarm he jumped sideways as the box shattered at his feet. 'You forgot your box,' shouted Izabel, from the third floor.

'You bitch, you fucking bitch,' Schmidt screamed beside himself with sudden rage shaking his fist. He stuttered and spat his face red and bloated.

'You wait you, you,' he hunted for words. 'I'll come back you bitch, you-.' He jumped in the car.

'Move, damn you move,' he hissed at the sergeant through gritted teeth.

The sergeant looked though the rear view mirror at the fury on the Lieutenant's face while he wiped the wine off his trousers and boots.

 Serves you right you fat pig, he thought to himself and started to whistle silently. It had turned out to be a good day after all.

Anya looked on in horror when Izabel opened the window and threw out the box of food. 'Izabel, what have you done? he'll come back and have us arrested,' she cried.

Izabel walked away from the window her face still showing signs of anger. 'Mother get packed, his visit means Schneller is returning and I don't want to be here when he does,' she exclaimed storming into her bedroom shouting over her shoulder. 'We'll go to my friend Maria in Blezun for a while. Curen will help us to get papers for the trip I'm sure.'

Izabel waited impatiently but it was the next day before their new papers arrived with a message from Curen that the road to Blezun was blocked by snowdrifts and the German army had forbidden anyone to use it. He suggested they use Krolik's home because it would be some time before he returned.

Hurriedly they gathered together a few clothes and mementoes which Anya resolutely refused to leave behind and stood in the doorway casting tear filled eyes around what once had been a happy place, but now was just an empty shell, a thing of the past. Gently they closed the door and carrying their bundles walked the few streets to Krolik's flat.

Izabel remembered climbing the stairway recalling the day she was nearly shot and entering Krolik's room she looked round in dismay.

It had obviously been empty for months and had a closed musty smell about it. It was also freezing. Anya gingerly sat on the edge of the bed wringing her hands. Izabel putting on a brave face came and sat beside her.

'It's going to be all right mother, you'll see,' she whispered reassuringly.

Anya fought back the tears while Izabel got up and searched the room, coming up with a small heater.

Shaking it she guessed it to be half full of paraffin. With care it would last at least two days. As the warmth invaded the room Anya regained her composure and helped hang the bedding in front of the heater to air.

Izabel tried to light the stove in the kitchen pulling a face when it didn't work. They sat back on the edge of the bed and shared their bit of bread and cheese that Izabel had bought with the last of her money. Paying ten times its real worth

Anya stared at it wistfully. 'We should have kept the box.'

Izabel reacted with a fury that left her mother speechless and in tears.

'No no! No way. I couldn't have taken anything from that horrible German pig,' she said storming round the room like a woman possessed. 'Mother, I think he's the one that took grandfather, her face was a picture of misery. 'Him and that evil man Schneller are responsible for the deaths of hundreds if not thousands of innocent men women and children.' She shook with anger and her voice grew louder.

'Even now they might be killing Rance, Marek, my brother and your son. Oh God mother, how could you think of taking anything from them?'.

Anya's head was lowered. When she looked up Izabel saw her face pale and drawn, her eyes stricken in shame. She melted at the sight all the anger evaporated. 'I'm sorry mother, I didn't mean to shout, but there is nothing on this earth that could have made me touch his gift,'

Anya nodded silently, 'I know my love I don't know what made me say it.'

Izabel sat holding her mother's arm biting her lower lip. She felt helpless unsure what to do next. Her thoughts went to Rance, out there somewhere in the bleak snow covered forest fighting not just for himself but for all of them. A guilty feeling overcame her, remembering how she'd sent him away.

Piotrekow railway station

It had started to snow again. Lieutenant Schmidt's feet were freezing standing on the platform waiting for Schneller's train.

'Come on where are you?' he whispered cursing the train for being an hour late and for the tenth time he walked the full length of the platform. He gave gave a sigh of relief hearing the sound of an engine in the distance.

Grinding to a halt it spewed out smoke and steam over his already grubby uniform, doors opened disgorging civilians and German troops alike. Schneller came towards him with his familiar stilted walk.

Schmidt saluted trying to smile a welcome.

Schneller ignored the salute staring slowly up and down the fat Lieutenant's slovenly figure a look of disdain on his face.

'Bring my luggage,' he snapped pointing with an ivory handle cane. 'It's in the guards van at the back.'

'Yes sir,' Schmidt turned to his sergeant. 'Get two men and bring it to the car,' before running after Schneller who was already half way down the platform.

They sat in silence on the way back to the Gestapo HQ. Schmidt glanced sideways at the grim faced man sitting next to him and felt an uncontrollable twitch start in his left eye.

Schneller sat back in his seat staring at Schmidt with his dead fish eyes who now wished he was on the Russian front.

Schneller was silent until he reached his office and by that time Schmidt was a nervous wreck.

'Reports have reached me in Berlin that you've been a lazy man Schmidt'

Schmidt squirmed in his chair. 'I've done my best sir,' he stuttered 'I thought things had gone quite well.'

Schneller smashed his cane down hard on the highly polished desk top. His voice came in a deadly whisper to Schmidt's ears.

'Oh no you haven't.'

Schmidt winced sinking further into his chair.

'I've been sent back to speed things up and I'm not a happy man Schmidt.' Schneller's face became ugly with anger.

'I was hoping to spend Christmas in Berlin this year. Now because of your incompetence, I'm back here in this God forsaken hole'. 'I want a meeting tomorrow with Franz Lohr, Herman Braun, and you at nine o'clock sharp. He stood up to leave.

'I also want a full report from you on all matters regarding this office including anything I left with you. Do you understand me?'.

Schmidt nodded afraid to speak. His mouth felt dry he tried to swallow and failed. Finally he managed to stutter. 'I've sent Lohr and Captain Braun on a mission.'

Schneller's eyes bulged, he screamed at the cowering Lieutenant,

'I said nine o'clock sharp I don't care where they are get them back!' he stormed out slamming the door with such force that he made the desk sergeant jump.

Weakly Schmidt spoke down the telephone. 'Get a message to Lohr and Captain Braun. They're to report back here nine o'clock sharp in the morning. I don't care how they do it but they'd better be here. Tell them Schnellers back'.

He replaced the telephone on its cradle and leaning back in the chair nervously bit the remains of his finger nails.

Dawn came slowly revealing to Rance's blurred vision the still heavily laden clouds which were again gathering on the horizon. The fire had been put out but his boots and socks were already dry and back on his feet, he marvelled that he hadn't got frost bite. Now looking across at Jarek, he thought about Izabel. The boy tried to smile but failed, Rance felt sympathy it must be hard for the young lad. He sipped cautiously at the hot black liquid a partisan had pushed into his hand. His eyes searched for Cross whom he saw staring into the dead ashes of the fire.

'You all right Don?' Rance asked.

His voice made Cross start and he looked up at Rance with red eyes and a white face. 'I'm bloody freezing Rance. I can't remember ever being as cold as this. It's only the beginning of winter and someone said it can go to below minus twenty, I never did like the cold.'

Before Rance could form a reply Marek gave orders to move out.

An hour later they found themselves lying in the snow at the edge of the forest staring at the village of Wilkoszewice, beyond that lay open countryside broken by an occasional group of trees and farmhouses. Rance lowered the field glasses and passed them to Cross who stared at the village centre. He stroked the thick stubble on his chin. 'That's a troop train your looking at.'

Cross stared hard at the main railway line running through the centre of the village and Rance heard his sharp intake of breath watching the German troops disembarking with dogs and their handlers.

Supporting the wounded they moved away with Rance and Cross acting as rear guard and the forest closed round them silent and comforting. They back-tracked and moved west while Rance glanced back at their foot prints.

'Pray for snow Don to cover our tracks or we're dead men.'

His voice was low but carried in the still morning air earning him a rebuke from Marek.

Two hours later Marek called a halt. One of the wounded had become delirious and started to cry. 'Gag him,' Marek hissed.

'The man's dying,' someone muttered.

'Gag him,' Marek snapped and moved on through the trees with the others trailing behind. Rance looked at the gagged man who now stared sightless at the snow filled sky.

Another fell to his knees before pitching face down into the drifting snow his blood turning it pink.

Marek called another halt and his voice cracked with the strain.

'We can't take them much further without rest and medical help.

His men looked at him in silence all reluctant to give advice. He was the leader the decision was his.

One of the scouts came back reporting open pasture land ahead. Marek cursed under his breath. 'How far is it to the next forest'?

The man shrugged. 'One kilometre perhaps'.

Marek stared at his men with bloodshot eyes the strain clearly visible.

'As I see it we have no choice but to go on. We'll cross the open space and some of us will lay an ambush on the other side. The Germans will have to come across if they want us and some of them will die. In any case they will be delayed and it will give us more time to find a hiding place for the wounded. Any questions?'

No one spoke the decision was made.

Rance's heart was pounding while his nerves screamed danger when they left the protection of the trees and moved out into the open carefully treading in each other's footprints.

The snow was nearly eighteen inches deep in places hiding the uneven ground, a man stumbled bringing a cry of pain from one of the wounded. Rance glanced up at the clouds racing overhead and as the wind increased, he prayed for it to snow.

They reached the other side and Marek detailed Krolik and six others including Rance and Cross to stay behind while he and the rest went on with the wounded.

Krolik spread them out over a hundred metre section of forest and they settled down to wait. Rance stared back along the line of footprints to the other side and wondered if the Germans would risk following or detour the spot. A few snowflakes drifted down, he looked to windward and saw giant black clouds towering in layers on the skyline rolling and twisting towards him. A shout from the other side of the open space brought his attention back to the forest. Grey uniformed shapes fanned out from the snow laden trees. Dogs barked in their excitement held tight on long leather leashes as they ran confident and alert.

Rance lay down his rifle in favour of the machine-pistol. He studied the strength of the wind and waited, calmly lining the sights against a running figure. They were close Rance could clearly see their faces.

He gently squeezed the trigger to automatic shot and felt the rebound. The man in his sights threw up his arms and fell over backwards. Gunfire roared across the open space as the partisans turned the pasture land into a blood bath and the German line faltered before falling back in headlong retreat.

The unmistakable sound of a machine-gun opening up on the other side made him crawl backwards looking for better cover as the heavy calibre bullets demolished everything in their path.

He stared across the open space they were coming again. Once more he took careful aim and waited. The next man in his sights rolled in agony clutching his shattered knee.

Krolik pointed at more troops crossing further away from their line of fire and motioned for them to move out. He bent double and ran relieved to see Cross ahead of him. Looking behind he saw Krolik and one other. There was no one else. Another three gone. Rance ran faster.

The sound of firing lessened when they retreated following Marek's trail. It had started to snow heavily the wind whistled and wailed its way through the tree tops sending the snow twisting and swirling around them. Rance gritted his teeth bending his head into the storm driven wind. Within fifteen minutes the snow quickly drifted and they were down to a slow walk. Rance felt the biting cold strike though his overcoat while he tried to keep moving.

Marek's trail disappeared so Krolik decide to turned north and for the rest of the day they stumbled frozen and exhausted into the teeth of the blizzard.

CHAPTER 14

Piotrkow

Izabel entered Krolik's flat closing the door quietly so as not to wake her mother asleep on the bed. Dropping her empty basket on the floor she sank gratefully on to a chair feeling tired and exhausted. She slipped off her shoes gently massaging her aching feet. There was no food to be had anywhere in Piotrkow and holding her stomach the hunger pains stirred, she was sure her stomach was shrinking. Her mother moved uneasily muttering at some dream or nightmare. She worried about her mother it was only four thirty yet she'd slept nearly all day. Gently she shook her awake and Anya sat up with a startled cry.

'Hush mother it's only me,' she whispered quietly.

'I had a dreadful dream about you being taken by the Gestapo and having your fingers cut off. It was horrible,' her mother sobbed.

Izabel kissed her. 'Don't worry so much it won't happen,' she reassured her.

'Mother I have to go away for two days, I have to visit Marie to make arrangements for us to move there and I've been told that the road to Blezun is now open.'

She hated lying to her mother avoiding her anguished eyes. For her own sake she couldn't tell her she'd received orders from Curen that she was to proceed to Kalow with a message, Informing Marek of an arms convoy bound for the garrison in Radom. He'd also warned her of the danger involved as the weather was so unpredictable and not to take any chances.

Anya clutched her daughter's arm making her wince at the hard grip.

'The weather might change; you know what it's like here'.

Izabel kissed her wet cheek. 'Hush now mother I'll be all right, I'm going to borrow the horse and Panje from grandfather's friend.

Mentioning her grandfather made Anya cry even more and Izabel bit her bottom lip to stop herself from crying too. She forced herself to smile although her eyes shone with tears.

Anya still clung hard to her daughter fighting back the flow of tears.

'Please be careful there is only you and your brother left now,' she exclaimed.

The next morning having left her mother in a deep sleep Izabel made her way to the outskirts of town picked up the horse and Panje and wheeled it out onto the main road where the wheels crunched in the packed down frozen snow. The road was open for single line traffic with passing places every few metres, gangs of men of all ages from the labour camps sweated over their shovels to keep it clear under the watchful eyes of the German guards, their breath turning to ice crystals in the early morning air.

The guards manning the check point at the edge of town took little notice of the heavily wrapped figure sitting on the cart, giving her papers a fleeting glance before waving her on stamping their feet to keep warm.

Izabel looked apprehensively at the overcast sky. 'Please don't let it snow,' she whispered to herself.

Her progress was slow, having to continually pull in to allow others to pass coming the other way. The old horse laboured up a slight incline its sweat steaming, forming ice crystals on its shaggy main.

Izabel looked in wonder at the beautiful scenery unfolding before her eyes. The great open spaces carpeted in brilliant white, broken by forests which stretched in every direction with the branches of the trees heavily weighted down with their burden of sparkling frozen snow. The river running alongside the road was festooned with giant icicles which hung over the banks and boulders shining with a thousand lights, she gave a sigh and turned her attention back to the task ahead.

It was an hour before she reached the first of the woodland and the weak sunlight she had enjoyed disappeared behind the trees. She shivered at the sudden drop in temperature and pulling the blanket closer around her gently urged the horse to move a little faster.

The conditions on the road slowed her progress so it was two o'clock before she reached Blezun. On entering the village she became uneasy at the sight of a German patrol lingering near the station master's house. On the opposite side of the road she was aware of a man standing in the doorway of his house. Her pulse quickened suspecting him to be the informer. Aware of their stares she urged the horse forward round the bend in the road, breathing a sigh of relief when they disappeared from view. It had been her intention to stay with Maria but now that was out of the question. They may come to find out who she was.

Passing Maria's house she came to the turning towards Kalow. Hesitating she stopped the horse. The road was down to two narrow cart tracks and looking at the sky she noticed the black overcast skyline. Biting her lower lip her mind raced trying to make a decision. She climbed down and walked around the horse and Panje checking the harness and casting her eyes once more at the sky. It was no more than eight Kilometres to Kalow but the last two would be virgin snow, perhaps not too deep because of the thickness of the forest. She looked back at the deserted road. No, it was impossible to go back it would arouse too much suspicion. Climbing back on to the rough seat she prodded the tired horse on.

Gestapo HQ Piotrekow

Nine o'clock in the morning, the operations room was full. If Schneller noticed the tension pervading the atmosphere he gave no sign, he nodded to Claus Ritschel who curtly nodded back.

Claus Ritschel disliked Schneller intensely, but the man had connections in Berlin so it was prudent to feign friendship. Captain Braun sat next to Adam Grieb and they both stared sullenly at the map behind him. Only Lohr managed a weak smile. Schmidt sat at the back of the room holding a note pad in his sweating palm.

'With your permission sir,' Schneller addressed Claus Ritschel. 'Berlin has sent me back here earlier than planned'. His eyes stopped moving fixing on Schmidt who stired uneasily in his seat.

'The reports reaching Berlin are of increased bandit activity in this area and beyond, for example the raid on our factory in

Radomsko to name but one.' He paused to give his next statement more effect. 'The reports go on to say there are English troops operating with these bandits as yet we don't know how many.'

A startled murmur swept the room and Schneller held up his hand for silence. 'It's important that we find these men. We need to know their strength and what their intentions are. So we have two tasks. The first is to destroy these bandits which goes without saying. The second is to catch and interrogate the Englishmen.'

He pointed to the map with his baton. 'My information points to the villages in this area that help the bandits most', his baton traced an area south east of the River Pilica.

'We are going to show these peasants that it doesn't pay to help them,' again the white spittle appeared at the corners of his mouth. 'Winter is here so we take away all the food we can find. We take hostages from one village to another and show them that we mean business. We will make them tell us what we want to know.'

Captain Braun interrupted his voice petulant. 'We almost had the bandits that attacked Radomsko until you pulled us away for this meeting.'

Angrily Schneller rounded on him. 'That isn't what I heard. You led your men into a trap. You were lucky you left when you did'.

Herman Braun jumped to his feet his face grey with fury.

'I will not stand for remarks like that.'

'Sit down and shut up.' Claus Ritschel said quietly.

Herman Braun promptly sat down looking around at Lieutenant Lohr for support, but Lohr's eyes were fixed on the map deliberately refusing to make eye contact.

Braun looked back at Major Schneller with malice, but Schneller continued as if nothing had happened. Pointing his baton at Lieutenant Lohr he said,

'I'm putting you in charge of this operation although I will come along occasionally to monitor your progress. Make no mistake I want your best effort on this.'

He turned his attention to Captain Braun and Second lieutenant Grieb. 'After every village he has been to you will set up a police post and monitor every person that comes and goes.'

Now addressing the whole room he turned back to the map and drew a large circle round the area in question. His voice became vicious and demanding.

'I want at least five squads to join together to show strength to these peasants. Above all I want them frightened so much that they will betray their own mothers.'

'Lieutenant Lohr finished scribbling in his note book and put it away.

'When do we start this exercise?' he asked 'and have I got full authority on this one?'

The room was silent they all knew what he had in mind.

Schneller's answer was short and sharp. 'You have it and you start tomorrow.,

The road to Kalow

It had been snowing for an hour and the light was fading. The cart sat in the middle of the road with one of its wheels broken at the hub.

Izabel gave up trying a repair kicking it in frustration.

Gently whispering to the old horse she freed it from the harness pulling it clear of the shafts. The icy wind whipped amongst the tall pines driving the snow into a frenzy causing the heavily weighted branches to shed their load, quickly filling in the two tracks which had made the going easier.

Slowly, talking quietly to calm the frightened horse she attempted to climb on its back but It shied sideways almost pulling the reins from her grasp.

She persevered, and at the fourth attempt managed to stay on and with gentle urging she got the horse to move slowly forward.

An hour later head bent against the wind driven snow she became frightened and stopped the horse. It was impossible to see more than twenty metres surely she should have seen the small track to Kalow before this. Her heart sank. She must have passed it.

Turning round the going was easier now with the wind blowing from behind, but it was still twenty minutes before she found the right track. It was easily missed with the snow drifting to half a metre or more at the entrance. The horse refused to leave the road and enter the dark snow filled track. Izabel looked back into the blinding snowstorm realising she'd passed the point of no return, she had to go on.

Dismounting she took the lead and entered the track dragging the reluctant horse behind her but finding it hard going breaking in the virgin snow drifting above her knees. After a few hundred metres she was exhausted. Weakly she leaned against the horse feeling it shiver at her touch. They stood together as white statues in a white wilderness, the temperature was plummeting rapidly and when the daylight faded the wind increased, shrieking wildly through the tree tops driving the snow ever harder.

Whispering encouragement to the horse she climbed on its back only to find it start to shake with fatigue seemingly unable to go any further.

'Move, damn you move,' she shouted in desperation at the same time slamming her heels against its heaving flanks forcing it to lunge forward, breaking a path in the ever deepening snow.

Half an hour later it fell it's leg trapped in a hole and snapping like a twig. Izabel felt herself falling and she lay breathless in the snow listening to the horse screaming rolling in agony.

Staggering to her feet she ran crying to its side cradling its head until it lay quitely snorting heavily, its sides heaving as it fought the pain.

'Forgive me I'm sorry I brought you, Oh God it's not fair,' she sobbed bitterly looking around at the ever darkening forest.

The old horse was dying she knew it. It had given up lying still letting death take its course. Izabel watched tearfully as life finally left the pain filled eyes. She climbed unsteadily to her feet. How far to Kalow? half a kilometre, a kilometre? she had no way of knowing.

The daylight slowly faded to night and blinded by the wind driven snow she struggled to stay on the almost none existent track often falling and blundering into low overhanging branches. Her legs were numb and with feet weighing like lead she forced one foot after the other.

Her mind became blank, all fear had left and she just wanted to lay down in the soft snow and sleep. Twice she sank to her knees then will power alone dragged her back from the brink.

'Don't stop, don't stop or you'll die.' The words tumbled through gritted teeth. 'I will get there, I will'.

Once she thought she heard voices and called out asking for help but there was only the howling of the wind in reply. A light ahead or was her mind playing tricks again. She peered uncertainly into darkness yes there it was, she was sure.

It had stopped snowing she hadn't realised. There ahead was the clearing Kalow, its lights from the houses burning a warm welcome. Crying with relief she tried to run only to fall over on the uneven ground her legs not having the strength to support her. A door opened and a shaft of light illuminated her struggling figure attempting to rise. Dimly she heard a shout then she felt herself being gently lifted and carried inside, the sudden heat making her swoon. Placed on a soft warm bed her mind seemed to float away as she spiralled into an exhausted sleep.

Kalow

Marian and her mother gently shook the sleeping figur, she had been asleep for over fourteen hours and they were getting worried. Izabel blinked and sat up staring around her, her mind not registering.

'We had to wake you we were getting concerned. You've slept for such a long time.'

Izabel blinked back the tears. 'Oh Marian it was a terrible journey. My horse died, it broke its leg and I could do nothing for it.'.

Marian nodded in sympathy, 'We heard you talking in your sleep, Marek and my father are very angry with Curen for letting you come knowing what the weather can be like.'

Izabel became alert. 'Marek is here what about Rance and Don?

Marek came this morning with your brother and three others.' Marian hesitated. 'There was a fight with the Germans. Marek had to get the wounded to a doctor. Rance and Don with some of the others stayed behind to cover their retreat.'

Hurriedly Izabel got up and went looking for Marek finding him deep in conversation with Jozef.

Seeing her Marek looked relieved and Jozef beamed his pleasure.

Izabel's lip trembled. 'Marek, it's good to see your safe, and I'm happy that you brought my brother here. I must see him we have so much to talk about. She looked at him in anguish. 'What about Rance and Don will they be all right, when do you think they'll get here?.

They'll be fine I'm expecting them anytime now. I'm pleased you seem none the worse after your journey. I'm angry with Curen for sending you. He becomes harder everyday, this war is effecting everyone the longer it goes on.'

'It wasn't his fault. I knew the risks or thought I did. I have the details of an arms convoy leaving shortly for a garrison in Radom. Curen said it's the best yet and shouldn't be missed.'

Marek suddenly looked tired and far older than his years making Izabel suddenly realise what pressure these men must be under.

'When? that's important. We have to organise and plan,' he said the tiredness fading into the background.

'In four days' time'.

Marek looked at Jozef. 'We will need horses, wagons and more men. Do you think we can get more men?'

'Yes, Radice will send his sons into the villages. We'll get all the help we need, have no fear.'

Izabel stared into Marek's bloodshot tired eyes. 'You should get some rest yourself,' she said softly.

'When the Germans have left,' he answered curtly.

Izabel's reunion with her brother was full of joy, and for a brief moment Izabel was happy. Her brother was safe the news would also bring happiness to her mother. Thinking of her mother brought her back to reality. She couldn't stay any longer than tomorrow aware her mother needed food and was all alone.

She kept staring into the forest worrying about Rance fearing for his safety. Restlessly she walked from one house to the next anything to keep her mind busy. It was one of Radice's sons who saw them first. 'Here they come,' he shouted loudly, knocking vigorously on Jozef's door.

Izabel flew out onto the porch hand on her throat staring into the gloom of the sun dappled forest. She watched the four men slowly enter the clearing and unable to contain herself any longer ran to meet them stopping a few feet from Rance, suddenly shy. What if he didn't want her anymore?

For a few heart stopping moments he hesitated. Breathless Izabel looked up at his face and the laughter dried up inside her. Thick stubble covering his chin failed to hide the sunken cheeks or disguise the exhaustion in his eyes. She looked at Cross who was glancing hopefully around looking for Maria.

'I'm sorry Don, she's not here,' she said.

Cross tried to smile, 'Nice to see you Izabel,' he said shouldering his rifle and walking passed into Jozef's house.

Rance looked questioningly at her.

'I was going to stay at Maria's house then bring her with me the next day, but the Germans and the weather was against me,' she explained feeling guilty about it now.

Rance walked with her to the house. 'I'll explain to Don don't worry,' he said.

Marek looked up as they entered hand in hand. 'Glad to see you back where are the other two?'

'They didn't make it,' answered Krolik coming in behind them.

Marek got up and walked outside slamming the door.

Rance felt sorry for him. Every time one of his men died so did he a little.

'We lost a lot of men this time,' he said to her.

Izabel kissed him. 'Get some rest, I'll see you later,' and went in search of Marek.

She found him standing by the spring water pool which glistened with reflected sunlight off the thin sheet of ice laying on its surface.

He turned at her approach. 'A lot of good men died because of me,' he said in way of a greeting his voice sounding harsh and unforgiving.

Izabel's eyes flashed, her exasperation reflected in the tone of her voice. 'That's nonsense all the men would follow you anywhere. They didn't die because of you,' she snapped. 'Most of them are alive because of you.'

She smiled, touching his arm to give him support and understanding. 'Rance and Don think very highly of your leadership Marek. I know because they've told me so.'

Marek looked surprised. 'Rance doesn't like me because of my feelings for you.'

Izabel became angry. 'Sometimes you men are like children. You never grow up. Before you start feeling sorry for yourself, just remember this:

Those two Englishmen are not fighting for their country, at this moment in time they're fighting for Poland and us. You and I Marek. Remember they were given a choice. To stay in hiding or fight, and although hundreds of kilometres from their home country in a strange land with no knowledge of the language, it was they who chose to fight.' She stopped for breath. 'And fight they have side by side with you, as hard as any Pole. Their chances of surviving this war are far less than ours, but they don't whine Marek, they fight.'

Staring into his flushed face she knew that her words had struck home. Gone was the self-pity his eyes were now full of anger.

'Izabel, don't ever again accuse me of whining,' turning he stalked off, his back ramrod straight.

She bit her lower lip thinking her words were too harsh and that she'd overdone it.

He turned and came back his face grey. She stood her ground ready for him and as he bent towards her she flinched.

To her surprise he kissed her cheek. Flushing, she saw his eyes were smiling.

'Thank you for bringing home the realities of what I was doing Izabel. You're not only very beautiful but you're also wise far beyond your years.'

She flushed again, and feeling pleased with herself went to find Marian.

Rance and Cross had been given a room belonging to one of Radice's sons and after a long sleep they had just finished bathing and shaving when Izabel knocked on the door.

Hurriedly Cross excused himself, mumbling something about seeing Jozef before dashing off. Rance stood unsure of himself, her stunning beauty making him shy and uncomfortably. She leaned with her back to the now closed door her large dark eyes seeming to overwhelm him. He couldn't move. Silently he cursed himself for being a coward.

She hesitated then said simply, 'Forgive me Rance for that day in Piotrkow. I love you and I said those things out of fear that you were risking your life for me,' her eyes became misty with the hint of tears.

His choked reply was lost when she moved towards him. He became aware that he still held the wet towel and hurriedly threw it behind him. With a cry he crushed her to his body and kissing her neck could smell the cleanness of her hair.

Their lips moved hungrily together with pent up passion making them sway gasping for breath. He picked her up and carried her effortlessly to the bed.

CHAPTER 15

'What news of the girl'? Schneller stood with his back to Schmidt, looking out the window and down at the half tracks and trucks lining the main street.

'I tried to look after her,' answered Schmidt thankful that Schneller was not facing him. 'I even took her food which she almost killed me with'.

Schneller turned, looking at him with a bemused expression.

Schmidt stammered on, 'She threw it down out of the window. I was lucky it missed me.'

Schneller's eyes transfixed him, he felt like a petrified rabbit caught in the headlights of a car.

'Believe me Schmidt you will wish she had killed you.' He turned back to the scene outside. The officers and sergeants had all but finished loading the troops on board where they sat motionless, twelve to a truck facing each other. Two hundred of them. Schneller was pleased.

'So Schmidt, you say she has disappeared along with her mother. How can that be with no papers, where would she go?.'

Schmidt stayed silent wishing he was back in Germany.

'Have the police check the food queues pass the word to our informers and spies, they will be here in Piotrkow somewhere.'

He watched the column slowly move out with Lieutenant Lohr sitting in the leading halftrack.

The convoy trundled though Sulejow and out onto the Kiel road, such was the size the few people that were about stopped and stare at such a large body of troops.

With the road being partly blocked by snow drifts Lohr found it slow and boring, 'Can't we go any faster?' he snapped.

'Yes sir if you wish but the trucks behind wouldn't be able to keep up,' answered the driver. 'Do you wish me to go faster sir?.

Lohr studied the map on his lap and picked his target.

Lesznowola a large village, with plenty of people.

'Forget it we'll be turning left soon. Here is the turning now,- go left.'

The road was rutted and full of potholes Lohr hung on grimly to his seat staring out at the countryside which was all farmland dotted with the occasional farm buildings. Lohr shook his head. It was impossible to visit them all.

The convoy entered the village slowly and Lohr watched from the cab as the villagers hurried inside shutting their doors. At the far end of the village he stopped and climbing down walked back along the long line of vehicles carrying his pistol low down at his side.

The soldiers spread out amongst the houses beating and kicking at the doors until the villagers were gathered into a large group before him.

They stood and watched horrified when their livestock, pigs, cattle, and sheep were slaughtered and loaded into the waiting trucks.

There was a murmur of discontent when the soldiers started throwing their furniture into piles and setting light to it. Lohr watched cold eyed a trooper dragging an old lady from her house before dropping her in the snow. A young teenage girl broke away from the villagers and ran to the trooper hitting out hysterically, crying for him to leave her alone.

The man stepped back in astonishment and lifted his rifle.

'Leave her',

Lohr's voice cracked hard and the man hurriedly lowered his gun.

The Lieutenant strode across to the defiant girl grasping her arm and smiling calling for an interpreter.

Holding her arm and still smiling he faced the villagers who were now standing with their backs to the vehicles in the centre of the road.

'We have come here today because our friends that live amongst you have informed us that you've been aiding the bandits that live in this area'. He stopped waiting for it to be translated before pushing the now frightened girl in front of him.

'This is a grave offence punishable by death as is striking a German soldier.' He forced the crying girl to her knees.

'We'll come amongst you asking for information about these criminals,' he said pointing his pistol at the girls head.

'In future anyone caught helping the bandits will suffer the consequences like so,' he pulled the trigger.

Women and children screamed in horror and their men surged forward in anger only to be beaten back with rifle butts.

Lohr raised his voice over the screaming. 'Let it begin', he shouted.

The soldiers split the villagers into small groups and one at a time they were dragged to one side questioned, savagely beaten and left lying in the snow. Picking people at random the villagers were forced to watch the torture of their friends and loved ones.

After two hours it was over. Blood covered the snow throughout the village it was a testimony to the horror that had happened that day and would stay frozen as a monument until the thaw next spring.

The Germans withdrew, leaving behind the stunned, bewildered, and horror struck villagers who rushed to help the survivors.

Gently they pulled a man from his dead wife who silently shook them off, walked into his wrecked house and started to pack a small bag.

'Tdeusz what are you doing?' asked a neighbour.

'Now it's time to fight,' He answered, his voice showing no emotion. Shouldering his bag he brushed past without another word.

Silently, other men started to leave watched by their families, who were afraid but knew in their hearts that there was no other way.

Kalow

Rance and Cross stood watching Marek, Jozef and Krolik studying a map of an area northwest of Piotrkow. Marek threw down the pencil he was using and shook his head his voice showing exasperation.

'The convoy of arms will be heavily guarded. We have men, horses and carts to move the arms but not enough weapons to make the attack.'

The room fell silent. Jozef leaned back in his chair, 'Perhaps Losos and his men could help, they have weapons together we could do it.'

Marek shook his head. 'Losos has his own problems in the Konski area at the moment. Even if he could help there wouldn't be enough time to organise and get here.' He stared down at the map frowning. 'There has got to be a way to do this.'

'We have a plan, Don and me,' said Rance from the back of the room and for twenty minutes they outlined it with Izabel helping the translation if they faltered.

Marek leaned forward his eyes gleaming. 'It could work it needs polishing but it could work'.

Dawn was breaking before they'd finished. Scraps of paper covered in scribble and drawings littered the floor. Jozef's wife and daughter passed around hot drinks and breakfast. Jozef looked at the plans and nodded.

'I will pass the word. Seven o'clock in the morning day after tomorrow.'

'I don't want you to leave now,' said Rance holding Izabel tightly in his arms.

'Rance, I have to, my mother needs me there is no food in Piotrkow and she isn't at all well'. Tomorrow who knows what it may bring. No, I have to leave this morning while I still can. Beside you'll be leaving yourself soon.'

'Get your things together,' he said taking her by the arm. 'I'll go with you as far as the road.'

Borrowing a new horse and Panje from Jozef and accompanied by Rance, Don, and her brother to help her she set off, stopping once to look with sadness at the old horse lying dead and frozen on the track. Reaching the road the men gave her a final push and stood watching until she was out of sight. She didn't look back for fear they would see the tears streaming down her face at the thought that she might never see them again.

Gestapo HQ Piotrkow.

'Why do I have to take the convoy to Radom? I've never had to do this sort of thing before,' moaned Lieutenant Adam Grieb, annoyed at being given such a task.

'Because Adam, Schneller has ordered it so.' Herman Braun idly flicked an imaginary piece of dust off his sleeve.

'You know the man is completely mad don't you,?' Grieb persisted.

'What has that got to do with you going to Radom?.

'Oh I don't know but I do know he hasn't given me enough men as escorts for these arms. What if we're attacked?'

Braun roared with laughter, 'So that's it, is it, you're afraid the bandits will get you.'

'No I'm not.' Grieb choked. 'It's just that it's not my normal job that's all.'

Braun could feel himself losing patience, he poked his finger hard into Adam Grebe's chest.

'Oh that hurt.'

'You've been given a direct order, not by me, by Major Schneller. Now if I were you I would be more afraid of Schneller than the bandits.'

Grieb rubbed his chest. 'I'm not worried about either of them'.

Braun smirked, 'Of course you're not, but to put your mind at rest you only have six trucks to guard and over forty SS troops going with you. All heavily armed I might add'.

He sighed as Adam Grieb still looked uneasy. 'Don't forget you'll be leading in an armoured halftrack.'

Grieb regained some of his composure.

'If he hadn't taken all the spare men for the village raids this wouldn't have happened,' he sniffed.

German arms convoy

Adam Grieb looked at his watch. Five am. It was a cold morning and he noticed there'd been a frost during the night leaving the snow hard and crisp underfoot. It didn't put him in a good mood. The going would be treacherous on the icy roads and he was thankful that he was in the half track. Walking down the length of the convoy he took stock.

Sitting in the back of the halftrack were six armed soldiers and a machine gunner with his ammunition feeder. Behind that another truck carrying twelve more. Then came the ammunition trucks with two guards on each. Last a small armed truck with a machine gunner and six more soldiers. It looked impressive even to Grieb.

Confidently he leaped into the passenger seat. 'Let's go I don't want to take all day with this.'

Stony-faced the driver threw the gear lever forward.

'Yes sir,' he said. He felt uneasy that he'd got Second Lieutenant Grieb all the way to Radom. He glanced sideways at the prim officer.

The rumours must be true he looked to pretty to be a man. He gripped the steering wheel tightly and tested the door handle.

Adam Grieb stared out of the window at the passing white countryside. What a sour faced man he was sat next to, just his luck.

He didn't look very clean either. He sighed. What a boring journey this was going to be.

Returning to Kalow Rance found Marek surrounded by a large group of men.

'They've brought bad news,' Marek said in anger, their village was attacked by a large force of German troops and more will be targeted.

The message is that they are looking for us. They are going to starve torture and kill as they have just done to these men and their families if they don't turn us in.'

Rance's eyes wander over the tired looking group who were of mixed ages. Farm workers, men that had never know anything else but back breaking work from dawn to dusk. Tough self-reliant men.

The salt of the earth, with one thing in common: a hatred of the Germans.

It was Cross who voiced his thoughts. 'The Germans are giving us the men. Now all we need is the weapons.'

Marek issued orders to feed them and they were told to be ready to move in an hour.

Rance stood looking at a large wooden box that had been brought in from outside, smeared in dirt it had obviously been buried. Grinning, Marek threw open the lid and reaching inside withdrew a uniform before offering it to Rance who handled it gingerly. It was off a German policeman. He didn't need to ask how it was acquired when he poked his finger through a hole in the chest pocket. He grimaced, 'I think you should have had it cleaned before giving it to me to wear.'

Marek gave one to Cross, 'unfortunately this one has a few more holes as well.'

Rance counted eight uniforms in all. 'This is a bonus Marek why didn't you tell us about these before?'

'Under torture any man would break its best if everyone only knows a little.'

'Except you of course.'

'Except me, but then I would never be taken alive.'

Rance grunted, struggling to don the uniform, 'It's a bit small but it will do I must remember to hide the bullet hole.' Placing the cap on his head he stood awaiting their appraisal.

They stood in silence. It was Jozef who spoke. 'I could shoot you now. It's amazing how a uniform can change a man.'

Dawn came slowly over the Radom road, it had been a cold bitter night the coldest so far that winter. Marek had sent men ahead to Krolik and the rest of the waiting villagers to prepare them for the sight of the German uniforms that they were now wearing.

Rance looked at the work that had already been started men were lining both sides of the road, trees were being cut down and large fires lit. Snow was being carried and dumped in the middle of the road alongside a large hole. He walked down the centre amongst them searching for Krolik, finding him at the end of the working party.

'Where are the horses and carts?' Rance asked conscious of the uneasy stares of the men at his uniform.

Krolik nodded a sweat stained head towards the forest.

'They're well hidden don't worry.'

'Did we manage to get enough men?'

Krolik grinned. 'We think so at the last count it was seventy or eighty.'

'What about weapons'?

Krolik's grin faded.

CHAPTER 16

German arms convoy.

The heat in the cab of the halftrack was stifling, making Adam Grieb ease the collar of his uniform jacket. He glanced at the driver. Neither had spoken since their journey began two hours ago. Fresh air was what he needed. The man stank, his sweaty body odour pervaded the whole cab. Progress had been slow up to now and his mood had darkened. At the first opportunity he would change drivers there was no way he could stand this all the way to Radom.

'There are road works ahead,' the driver muttered sullenly.

Grieb stiffened in alarm.

'What! Slow down you idiot, we have to be sure whats happening here.'

'It's difficult to see sir there's a lot of smoke drifting across the road, but I think it's a labour gang, there are German police guarding the workers.'

Grieb, peering intently through the grimy windscreen relaxed.

A German policeman signalled them to stop. Grieb, holding his pistol by his side half opened the cab door while the man outside stood stiffly to attention.

'Just what's going on here, how dare you stop us?' snapped Grieb his face flushed in anger.

'Sorry sir, but there's subsidence on the road,' said the man.

'Whats that! What's the matter with your voice man?'

'I have a cold sir.'

'Just get the hell out of my way,' Grieb shouted and the man jumped backwards when the halftrack moved on.

'Please sir, just go slowly,' said the man saluting.

'Do as the man said drive slowly, I don't want to fall down a stinking great hole,' Adam Grieb muttered impatiently to the driver while staring aggressively at the gangs of labourers lining either side of the road.

Smoke from the fire became thicker obstructing the driver's view who cursed when the visibility dropped to a few metres.

Another policeman stepped in front of the halftrack and one by one the trucks following ground to a halt.

'Now what's the matter?' Adam Grieb flung open the cab door in temper and leaned out. 'Get out of the way man. What's the matter with you?'

The policeman didn't speak instead he walked round to Greib's side of the half-track. Something was wrong,

Grieb looked at the hard eyes and unshaven face, the scruffy uniform with the bullet holes and his eyes widened in terror at the sudden realization of what was happening.

Desperately he tried to shut the door and at the same time lift his pistol. He didn't see the pitchfork that came from behind the policeman with such force that it went through his chest pinning him to his seat. The scream he started died as a gurgle in his throat and paralyzed with shock he clutched weakly at the door handle his pistol falling to the floor.

Slowly he felt his strength ebbing away as his hand fell loosely to his side. His head bent forward and he stared in disbelief at the two prongs sticking though his chest.

An explosion shook the half-track when the man dressed as a policeman tossed a hand-grenade amongst the soldiers sitting in the back. Dimly he was aware of the driver being dragged from the cab and a machine-gun opening up somewhere in the rear.

He watched though the wing mirror workers lining the road pulling pitchforks out of the snow and hurled them like spears into the backs of the trucks. Two more men dressed as police ran forward hurling more hand-grenades into the trucks.

Adam Grieb started to scream now as the pain came. It began slowly at first as a small fire in his chest before growing in waves overwhelming him in its intensity, he screamed louder his eyes bulging until the blood welled up into his mouth choking him, the last thing he saw were men leading horses and carts out from the trees.

Rance fought back the urge to be sick watching the pitchforks fly in the air and could hear Cross retching behind him. Now together they ran towards the rear of the convoy. Bullets cut the air sending them sprawling to the ground seeking shelter, and when the smoked cleared it revealed a small armoured truck with a machine-gunner crouched in the back.

The driver had tried to reverse when the attack began but in his panic ran it into a ditch. He was now shouting in terror with the wheels spinning themselves deeper into the snow.

To their right Rance could see Krolik and some of his men pinned down. Every time one moved the machine gunner's bullets hunted them out. A wind shift sent the smoke rolling in again hiding them from the gunner's eyes. Pulling pins from their grenades Rance and Cross ran forward throwing them at the truck, the gunner now in a blind panic was traversing his gun in a semi-circle but he was too late.

The first explosion blew him out of the truck, the second blew it apart. A silence descended on the column and with the smoke from the burned out fire slowly clearing it reveaed the true cost of their victory. Rance and Cross stared at the carnage. The German bodies grotesquely twisted at the violent death from the thrusting pitchforks, the blood soaked trucks with sprawling corpses and the Polish farmers laying machine gunned down at the side of the road.

Already the carts had moved in and the arms were being hurriedly loaded with the dead collected and piled on top.

Cross broke the silence, 'Well we did it Rance, but at what cost Just look at it! It's like a slaughter house like something out of hell?'

Rance stared at the scene his face expressionless. He looked at the carts now piled high with their dead, at the wounded that cried, and the ones that didn't, and was sickened. He knew it was a scene he would have to live with for the rest of his life. That is if he had a life. Closing his mind he went in search of Marek finding him on the tailgate of a truck.

Marek's face was devoid of any emotion not looking at the carnage around him. Instead he furiously attacked a long wooden box breaking the lid off.

Reaching inside he held up a brand new machine gun and turned to the silent men below him.

'You see this, this is what will end our suffering. It's this that will protect our families and our homes. It's what our brothers and friends have just died for and they won't have died in vain.'

He shook the gun above his head, his voice hoarse. 'Now we have the tools to do the job. Now it's our turn to rid ourselves of the murdering scum.'

Searching down the column they found Jarek with Krolik loading dead Germans into the backs of the now empty trucks, he seemed in shock his eyes dull and listless. Silently Rance helped him with the depressing task. Krolik staggered past and threw a body into the nearest truck then turning away he climbed into the leading halftrack.

Cursing, he jumped out again and walked round to the passenger seat. Leaning inside he pulled a pitchfork from the body of a dead German officer which slumped forward and fell out. Grabbing it by the legs he dragged it to the rear of the halftrack where Cross helped him throw it on board.

Walking back to the front he climbed in and started the engine, with a final wave he moved off followed by the rest of the convoy, complete with a new set of dummy German soldiers, each smart in their borrowed uniforms.

Gradually the signs of battle began to disappear. The hole was filled in and covered by a layer of snow beaten down so it blended with the rest of the road. All traces of the fires were hidden and the heavily laden carts spilt up disappearing down a several different tracks. Marek took a last look round and was satisfied.

'It wouldn't pass a close inspection but I think it will be enough,' he said, 'especially as the convoy will be found a long way from here.'

Rance watched the departing trucks rumble round a bend and out of sight. 'Has Krolik got a good place to hide them?'.

Marek nodded, 'Its excellent about five kilometres from here there is a swamp. With the ground frozen he hopes to hide them a long way from the road, if he can cover the tracks it might even be the spring before they're discovered. On the way he'll be driving through a German speaking village. Those Volksdeutches will see the German uniforms and will tell the Gestapo that the convoy was all right when it passed through. That will delay them even more.

Gestapo HQ.

'How could this happen, Major Schneller how could a whole convoy disappear with forty of the best troops in the area?' Claus Ritschel was angry, so angry his voice was heard by the desk sergeant down stairs.

Schneller stood facing him his eyes blazing in panic.

'I have men looking searching the road between here and Radom.'

Captain Herman Braun couldn't contain himself any longer.

'What about my second in command, Adam Grieb? He said there weren't enough troops acting as escorts.'

Lieutenant Schmidt was enjoying this hovering in the background watching Schneller squirm like he always had too, he gloated as Claus Ritschel turned almost purple.

'What does he mean Schneller, there weren't enough troops?'

Schmidt had never seen him in such a rage.

Schneller was almost beside himself, the white spittle forming at the side of his mouth was flying everywhere.

He pointed a trembling finger at Braun.

'There were enough troops and they were the best. Except of course the one officer who was supposed to be in charge and we all know who that was, don't we?' He spat the words with venom. Adam Grieb, that's who.'

Herman Braun jumped to his feet red in the face sending the chair crashing to the floor. 'How dare you try to blame him. The man's not here to defend himself. No! it's you we have to blame for this.'

Schmidt tried to look serious but inside he was jumping in delight.

'Oh me, oh my, now what, pistols at dawn,?' he hummed, keeping his finger's crossed.

Claus Ritschel stepped between them still seething.

'Enough of this you both know what this means don't you. We have trouble if these weapons are now in the hands of the local population.'

He stared hard at Schneller. 'You will stop at nothing to get those arms back where they belong, and you,' he turned his attention to Braun. 'You will put your troops on full alert. You will reinforce your're outposts and you will help Major Schneller in any way you can, is that understood?'

He scowled at them both and stormed out of the office and down the stairs, past the desk sergeant who wisely kept his head down and out to his waiting car.

Silence and tension gripped the room. Schmidt didn't know where to look so he studied his fingernails until Schneller's voice grated on his nerves.

'I will see you in my office Schmidt. In the meantime find Lieutenant Lohr and get him there as well.' He turned to Herman Braun. 'And you. You can go to hell.'

Schmidt stood by the office door watching Schneller pace up and down still smarting from his meeting with Claus Ritschel, he coughed discreetly.

'You have something to say Schmidt?'

'Yes sir, I have a report from one of our spies that there are only two Englishmen fighting with the partisans in the area, but as yet he can't find out where they operate from.'

'How many times have I told you not to call them partisans. They're bandits, nothing more,' Schneller snapped.

Schmidt remained silent.

'I don't suppose our so called spies know what these Englishmen are up to or even when they arrived here?'

'No sir, they don't know that.'

'Now Schmidt, make a note telling them to find out and while they're doing that I want to see one or more of them get close enough to kill them. I don't really care which comes first.'

Lieutenant Lohr knocked and entered the room. He'd obviously been drinking he stank of it. Schneller eyed him in disgust but shrugged. He was off duty. 'Tomorrow I want you to start taking the villages apart and I don't want any missed, you will do whatever is necessary. Above all I want you to take hostages. As many as you can find. You will tell everybody you leave alive that if they don't report the whereabouts of these bandits then we will begin to shoot ten a day, and if that isn't enough then we will come back for more.'

He turned to Schmidt. 'You are in charge of the labour camps so I want you to find one where we can keep these hostages, so when we start to shoot them they can be put on show. Is that understood?'

Schmidt nodded and vanished from the room. Stopping by the sergeant's desk he breathed deeply trying to calm his nerves his mind in turmoil. 'Surely, Schneller must have heard about the Russian front starting to move this way. What's he trying to do, fiddle while Rome burns. Was he mad, were they all mad, they think it's all one big game. Perhaps it was, perhaps it's a nightmare and in a minute he'd wake up.'

The desk sergeant was looking at him with a perplexed expression. 'Sorry sir, did you say something?'

Schmidt stared at him with unseeing eyes before turning and leaving the room. The sergeant shook his head and returned to the papers on his desk.

Day after day Lieutenant Lohr and his troops scoured the farms and villages southwest of the River Pilica leaving a trail of death and destruction through the countryside. Hostages were taken and loaded into waiting trucks, notices were pinned to the villager's homes.

A week later Schneller's hand shook in rage, holding the report on the finding of the convoy. Without a word he passed it on to Schmidt who read it in disbelief, when he came to the part on how some of the troops died including Lieutenant Grieb he sat down, his legs shaking.

Kalow

Became an armed camp, weary men came in from the destroyed villages bringing with them tales of torture and death at the hands of the SS Nazi Einsatzgruppen.

Rance and Cross worked none stop trying to train the new recruits on how to use their new weapons. News came in that people were now beginning to abandon their homes crossing the River Pilica in an attempt to escape from the terror on that side of the river.

Marek called a council of war.

They gathered in Jozef's house the strain was beginning to tell even more on Marek who looked tired with heavy shadows showing under his eyes giving him a fierce expression, he stood by the fireplace rubbing at the stubble on his chin.

'We can't let this go on any longer that's why I've called this meeting. We now number more than fifty men; it's too many for safety so we split into two groups.' He nodded at Krolik.

First, 'He'll take half, the rest stays with me and we'll keep in contact by courier. Second, the Germans have taken hostages, we don't know how many or where they're being held. We need to find out because it is my intention to rescue them. We can't sit here and watch them be shot or hung.'

'What about the villagers still on the southwest side of the River? they need help too,' said Jozef.

Marek's voice shook, 'I'm sorry but we must free the hostages first. If we do that we can help the others afterwards. If we don't they all die.'

Rance felt sorry for Marek decisions that leadership forced upon him were his and his alone.

Cross voiced his own thoughts. 'Can't Krolik and his men look after the villagers and we concentrate on the hostages.'

Marek answered with sudden irritation. 'No, I've made my decision, divided we risk all. This way, - he just stared

CHAPTER 17

Kalow

Rance sat at Jozef's kitchen table savouring the warmth that radiated from the stove against the far wall. Outside came the faint murmur of the new men being issued with their weapons. Looking at Cross sitting opposite he thought of what they'd been through together these last few months, most of it bad. Now his friend whom he looked on as more of a brother seemed relaxed for the first time since they'd been swimming with the girls way back in July, or was it August? he couldn't remember.

Cross sipped at the home made Vodka and for the first time didn't pull a face.

Rance smiled, 'Don, I'm beginning to think you're turning native, becoming a Pole'.

Cross laughed and swallowed the rest of the Vodka in one go.

'You know Rance you might be right. This stuff grows on you the more you drink it.'

He lifted the bottle and poured a generous portion for them both.

'Do you know what would make my day,' he stopped, blinking as it hit his stomach.

'And what would that be?' asked Rance through watery eyes his smile broadening on realizing his friend was getting drunk.

'That Maria and Izabel would come walking through that door right now.'

Rance lifted his glass. 'I toast your broad imagination my friend.- If only.

'Cross couldn't contain himself any longer. 'If only indeed,' and started to laugh with the two girls smiling in the doorway behind Rance.

Startled! He turned and almost choking, jumped to his feet to gather Izabel in his arms.

'I don't believe it, I really don't believe it, Rance kept repeating himself. Why wasn't I told that you were coming?'.

'Because, nobody knew until we walked into Kalow, that's why. I can't get over how much the place has grown. All these men everywhere.'

'What news Izabel, how is your mother?' he asked still with his arms around her slim waist.

She laughed. 'All these questions. First of all, mother is well now that we have a little food'.

She stroked the stubble on his chin. 'You'll have to have a shave you know,' she whispered mischievously.

He grinned. 'I thought you liked me like this.'

She quickly changed the subject.

'Curen has found out where the hostages are being held. They're in a place called Janowo. That's about ten kilometres north of Piotrkow. I've already given Marek the details.'

Jozef entered the house with his wife and daughter followed by Marek who nodded stiffly to Rance,

'We have a meeting in half hour about the hostages,' he said walking out again leaving the door open.

Izabel went to go after him and then changed her mind.

'I wish you two would be friends instead of walking around each other like a pair of dogs.'

Rance flushed, Jozef grinned, and Cross choked back a laugh.

Half an hour later they walked into the barn which Marek had turned into a briefing room. It was crowded with men and Rance noticed Jarek standing with Krolik and went over to join them. The barn was lit by six oil lamps swinging from the rafters. Their light made shadows dance across the bare wooden walls. Cigarette smoke curled upwards to mingle with the smoke from the oil lamps. He looked around at the faces of the men at their expressions, most of whom had never fired a shot in anger but had seen and felt the hand of German violence. Now it was to be their turn to fight.

The low murmuring of their voices ceased as Marek got up to speak.

'We now know where the hostages are being kept. Soon, within the next few days the Gestapo are going to start shooting them, ten at a time'.

He stopped as a rumble of anger reverberated around the barn.

'The day after tomorrow at approximately 22.00 hours with Commander Viktor and his group in charge, we're going to take the prison and free them all.'

He pointed to the spot on a large map pinned to the wall.

'Commander Vicktor has planned it well. The hostages have been located in the grounds of a country estate. It is well guarded at the perimeters complete with searchlights and dogs. To be completely successful we have to take all of it. There must be no one left to follow but in case things do go wrong we will leave a small group as a diversion to lead them away from the escaping hostages.

Rance tried to follow what was being said but Marek was speaking so fast he gave up and looked at Cross who was standing with a blank expression on his face. He caught his eye and shrugged. He would have to get the information from Izabel later. He turned his attention back to Marek who was drawing arrows on the map with a piece of charcoal.

'We can't do anything about their radio, not until we take the main house. We can't stop once we're committed to the attack, its speed that counts with this one.

Half an hour later the meeting broke up and Jozef invited Rance, Cross and the two girls to spend the evening with his family. After they'd eaten they were joined by Radice and his two sons. The appearance of the inevitable Vodka bottle didn't surprise Rance or Cross as they sat and talked about what was happening, how the war was progressing but It was disappointing to Rance, because nobody knew much about it. To the villagers it was a local war that was being fought to the death they had no time for anything else. There were odd rumours that the Russians had started to advance against the German divisions and that they were in retreat but it was all hearsay there had been rumours like it before which had come to nothing.

Nobody had heard about how England was doing with the rest of the war which Rance found frustrating. Jozef talked about his fear of the communists and what would happen if the Russians did come.

'I'm sure it would be civil war there are lots of people who want to be communists and that combined with the Russian troops nothing could stop them. He nodded at Rance and Cross. 'I fear that you two will be in great danger if that happens.'

'Why would that be surely they are on our side?' remarked Cross.

Jozef's smile was crooked. 'They're on their own side. You would be on your own, strangers, with no passports, carrying false papers.'

Izabel looked horrified. 'Jozef what are you saying, surely it wouldn't be as bad as that?'

Jozef shrugged, ' I'm sorry to say it, but I think it will.'

They exchanged glances, they hadn't thought about the Russians. Rance saw the look on Izabel's face and tried to make a joke of it

'I think me and Don would make very good communists if things got rough. I mean, up to now we're only been practising I suppose.'

Izabel squeezed his arm tightly. 'Don't joke, I'm more worried now than ever,' she whispered.

'Things have a habit of not turning out how you think they will, don't worry,' said Rance trying to reassure her

Reluctantly Rance and Cross took their leave. Knowing it wasn't possible to stay together with the girls with so many people around.

They walked back to the camp fire in silence. He glanced at Cross who appeared deep in thought.

'Are you all right Don?'

'Well, like you I'm disappointed at not staying with the girls but mainly it's this Russian thing that Jozef was talking about. Are we forever doomed to run, fight, or die? Are we fast using up our allotted time? Already we've lasted longer than most. I don't want to go through all this to fall with a Russian bullet in me.'

He looked depressed. 'Rance do you think we'll ever see England again?'.

Rance's mind was in turmoil he tried putting on a brave face but wasn't making a very good job of it. What about Izabel? what about England? The war, the Russians, will there be Polish communists, will they have to fight them all. Then what? His mind was spiralling out of control. With a shudder he realized what a mess they were all in. 'Of course we'll see England again, if the Germans can't kill us, no bloody Russian will either.'

He put his arm on Cross's shoulder. 'Come on, I have a full bottle of your favourite Vodka in my blanket.'

Cross's face showed a glimmer of a smile.
'Now whose turning native,' he answered.

22nd December 1943.

During the day Viktor arrived and the two groups moved out with the onset of darkness. Vicktor led taking with him Marek, Rance and Cross, having left Jarek to follow with Krolik's group.

Rance looked up through the tree tops towards the night sky seeing the stars shining in their millions with their hard bright light seeming to wink through the branches at the men stumbling in the blackness of the forest floor.

It was bitterly cold the temperature plummeting twenty degrees or more below freezing and the only sound was the heavy breathing of the men combined with the crunching of the crisp hard snow under their feet. It was never pleasant or easy moving through the forest at night, but Rance felt the friendly protective power of the trees, it gave him a sense of security not like the constant danger of moving in the open fields.

They crossed the River Luciaza just above Blezun, now the pace became slower and skirting the village they crossed the main Piotrkow road leaving the forest behind. They were now in open countryside he could feel the tension pulsing through him like an electric shock the air almost crackled with it leaving men nervously fingering their weapons while glancing warily back towards the road. The snow lay deeper away from the trees sometimes coming up to their knees, and the exertion of breaking through it brought beads of sweat to Rance's brow before running down his face and freezing into his stubble, and the warmth of his body heat woke the lice making him itch, driving him to distraction.

It was after midnight before they reached the edge of another forest. Vicktor called a halt and while they rested sent scouts ahead to find the safest route. Rance noticed the half-moon which was now high in the sky but its pale light still failed to penetrate the blackness of the forest floor.

The scouts returned reporting they were to close to Piotrkow and the tension grew. Vicktor decide to move, ordering the scouts to circle away from the danger. Two hours later they turned west and came to the main Warsaw road while they waited for the passing of a German patrol before crossing and turning east. An hour later they reached a small clearing and lit a fire waiting for Krolik.

With the temperature still minus twenty and the long march over Rance crouched over the fire, he was tired. Now they'd stopped his feet were beginning to freeze. Picking up a log he threw it on to the already large flames which exploded sending sparks into the frost filled air.

Sitting on his blanket he pushed his feet towards the warmth.

'You'll get them burned if you get any closer,' said Cross sitting down beside him the air from his breath turning to ice even as he spoke.

'You sound like my mother what's the matter, can't you sleep?'

Cross pulled a face, 'I never was any good at sleeping the night before a fight'.

He scrutinised Rance's face lit by the dancing flames.

'Are you ever afraid,- before a fight I mean?'

Rance drew his feet away from the fire rubbing at them to get the circulation back. 'Always. My gut turns into a knot and believe me I'm frightened. Anybody that says they aren't, is either lying through their teeth or is a moron without any feelings.'

Cross nodded, 'It's the waiting for me sometimes I feel as if I'm going to be sick. It isn't just the dying although that's bad enough. It's the thought of breaking under fire and running away that I'm most frightened of.

'We all feel like that sometimes Don, you'll never run except when we all do. Don't worry we'll both live to fight the Russians,'

Cross didn't appreciate Rance's attempt at a joke. He didn't think it funny either.

It was a bitterly cold cloudy day. The fire had now been put out at dawn to avoid the smoke giving away their position. He glanced at the low clouds drifting slowly over head and wondered if it would snow but decided it was too cold. They were joined by Krolik's' group and the whole day was spent cleaning weapons and sorting the ammunition.

Marek had acquired two carts during the morning, the spare ammunition hand-grenades and weapons were piled in the back. Rance caste an eye over the two horses and satisfied they were fit, ran his hand down the neck of the largest feeling it shiver at his touch. He nodded his approval a good strong horse, now he frowned at a fleeting memory of an old sergeant giving him his first lesson on one. He thrust the memory aside.

Darkness descended on the waiting men and Vicktor finally gave the order to move. There was no moon that night for which Rance was thankful but the temperature had now dropped below twenty degrees so he was careful not touch the bare metal of his gun. Silently they crossed the main railway line to Warsaw and quickly entering a new forest on the other side keeping to the abandoned, narrow tracks left by forestry workers.

The heavily snow laden branches closed just above their heads forming thick over-grown tunnels cutting out all light and sound. Vicktor called a halt saying they'd arrived. Rance wonder how he knew he couldn't see a thing while listening to him giving orders to Krolik.

Jarek came over with another man to see him. He could sense the fear in Jarek it reflected in his moist palm when he shook hands.

Rance said gruffly, 'Keep your head down don't play the hero. Remember you have a mother and sister at home'.

Jarek grinned the tension easing. 'Yes, and you remember you have a girlfriend, eh, I mean a woman waiting for you too. By the way, meet a new friend of mine his name is Sowa, he's normally with another group but can't get in touch with them at the moment so decided to join us.'

Rance grasped the man's hand finding it hard and strong, the man grinned.

'Pleased to meet you Englishman, you and your friend are becoming quite famous in the area. I wondered when we would get together.'

Rance instantly liked the man who had an air of confidence about him. 'Pleased to meet you, have you known Jarek long?

The man's grin widened, 'Oh I should think most of the day, I find him easy to get on with,' he answered, making them all laugh.

Vicktor despatched half of his group into the night and led the remainder down a narrow track. At last Rance saw the prison. It was an old manor type building sitting in its own grounds surrounded by a low wall. In front of the wall was a wire fence with barbed wire on the top. The whole area was lit with searchlights flickering across a row of wooden huts next to the house.

Guards with dogs patrolled between the wall and the wire. He looked at the dark forbidding windows of the house wondering if there were machine guns there. It wasn't going to be easy.

He checked the safety catch on his sub machine gun and felt for the extra ammunition and hand-grenades in his bag. His gut felt on fire again and his palms began to sweat as he nervously scratched at his lice.

Marek kept glancing at his watch and Rance could see his face lit by the prison lights a nerve jumping in his jaw his knuckles were white around the pistol grip of his gun while his lips moved counting down the seconds to zero. Rance looked for Cross and found him to his right.

At 22 00 hundred hours a white flare lit the sky and along all three sides of the prison machine gun fire shattered the once silent night with winking lights of death searching out and destroying men and dogs.

Heavy calibre bullets whined and screamed into the hapless guards tearing into buildings and bunkers hunting out and killing anything in their path. Suddenly the lights went out leaving everything in pitch-black confusion. At Marek's shout they ran for the fence quickly cutting through and reached the wall.

A German machine gun opened up from one of the upper floors of the main house, covering troops from a bunker spreading out to meet the attack. Another shout from Marek and Rance was over the wall and running with the others towards the house. A white star shell curved up into the night sky its brilliant light slowly floated towards the ground picking out the running figures. Rance dived to the ground when the German gunners found their targets and bullets cut the ground in front of him and a partisan died on his right. He rolled desperately away but the bullets chased after him hunting him down. The star shell flickered and died plunging the area back into darkness.

Reaching the bunker behind Cross he tossed a hand-grenade through one of the slits which seconds later blew up with a dull thud in the confined space and together they ran to the front of the house before crouching under a window while another star shell turned night into day, and a fierce fire-fight on the far perimeter intensified as men found new targets. The machine-gunner on the floor above leaned out of the window trying to direct his fire downwards pinning Rance and Cross against the wall.

A burst of gunfire coming from Sowa on their right caught the man who jerked and toppled out his scream ending abruptly when he bounced off the edge of a balcony on the way down.

The three now ran for the main door which was in a porch-way with large pillars on either side. Rance tried the handle of the solid double doors and found them locked. He and Sowa stood to one side while Cross emptied his magazine at the area around the lock. Wood splintered and the lock shattered.

Cross lifted his foot and kicked the door wide open quickly slipping into a large hallway. Rance and Sowa followed just in time to see Cross running down a narrow passage.

'Don, wait, don't go,' Rance shouted running after him. The narrow passage ended in another smaller hallway, the German machine-gunner sitting at the top of a flight of stairs couldn't miss.

Cross screamed as the bullets shattering his legs slicing into his groin and lower stomach flinging him against the wall. He slid sideways falling heavily onto the floor. He screamed again doubling up in shock and agony.

Rance ran down the corridor shouting a red haze of madness making him blind to any danger firing from the hip the noise from his machine pistol almost shattering his ear drums in the confined space.

Bullets smashed the wood panelling around him while he fired up at the German who suddenly reeled backwards toppling over.

Sowa came up behind Rance and dragged Cross down the corridor and into the main vestibule. Rance, covering their retreat tossed a hand grenade towards the stairs. It blew a hole at the base and the staircase collapsed trapping the remaining Germans on the upper floor.

A fire had started at the rear of the house and was now burning out of control. It spread through the hall and into the corridor bringing down the main ceiling before hungrily entering the upstairs apartments.

Coughing from the effects of the smoke Rance shouted for Marek as he desperately tried to stem the flow of blood from Cross's inner thighs and stomach. Marek knelt down and examined him quickly.

'Get him into a cart and hurry, you must find a doctor and stop the blood. Sowa will help. Now get moving we'll finish up here.

Sowa and Rance carried him to a waiting cart placing him in the back. Rance sat beside him and Sowa climbed up next to the driver who lashed the horse into a fast trot over the rough and uneven ground. Cross screamed in pain.

'Slow down man, slow down,' Rance shouted.

'We have to get to the village of Polichno there is a doctor, but we must hurry.' the driver shouted back.

Rance grasped Cross's wounds tightly, trying to stop the flow but could feel the blood oozing between his fingers. Cross now lay quietly his breathing uneven and shallow. Now and again he moaned softly as the cart jumped in the rutted track.

Rance whispered encouragement holding him still. The sound of the fighting faded when they entered deeper into the forest, now only the rattle of the wheels and the laboured breathing of the horse could be heard.

He felt Cross begin to shiver with the frost starting to form on their clothing. Removing his own coat he wrapped it round him and moved closer to give warmth..

'Here's the village of Pilichno,' Sowa called. The cart stopped outside one of the darkened houses and Sowa ran to the front-door hammering hard until it opened, the frightened face of a woman holding an oil lamp appeared round the edge.

There was a moment's conversation and Sowa came back to the cart.

'The doctor's wife said her husband is away on a call and won't be back for hours or even the next day. She said to bring him in she will tend the wound.'

They carried Cross inside and laid him on the bed. Rance helped her lift up Cross's shirt and jumper and together they peeled away his trousers exposing the wound.

Blood continued to seep from the many holes across the tops of his legs and lower stomach. Deftly the woman formed a pad by tearing up strips of cloth and placing it over the wounds finally securing them by tightly binding his body and legs. Satisfied, she stepped back looking with undisguised curiosity at Rance.

'You're the Englishman that everybody is talking about'. She said as a statement not a question.

Rance could only nod as he stared down at Cross. She touched his arm. 'There's another doctor at Barkowice Mokre five kilometres from here but you will have to hurry your friend is losing a lot of blood. I have slowed it down but it's not enough.'

Rance turned to Sowa. 'You know the way?'

Sowa nodded, 'I know the way come we must hurry.'

They started to carry Cross through the door when the woman called to him, 'Englishman.'

Rance turned his head and looked back to see her standing in the middle of the room, tears were in her eyes.

'We've all heard of you, and what you are doing for us.'

The words caught in her throat. 'We all love you for it. God go with you.'

For Rance sitting in the back of the cart, the journey to Barkowice Mokre seemed endless. His legs felt numb, the bitter cold penetrating to his very bones.

'How much longer have we to go,' his concern for Cross growing.

'Half an hour," Sowa shouted from his position on the front seat.

The driver lashed at the horse with his whip and the pace increased into a fast trot through the pitch blackness of the frozen track. Rance hung on bracing himself against the swaying cart.

Cross groaned softly. He looked down at his friend and was surprised to find his eyes open and fixed intently upon him, the eyes seemed large and luminous in his pinched white face, he moved his thinly drawn lips struggling to speak.

Rance bent his head close to Cross's mouth. The words came in a ragged whisper through the pain. 'Rance, don't let the Germans get me.' His breathing became uneven as he fought for air.

'Nobody is going to get you Don. Certainly not the bloody Germans. We're nearly there soon you'll be in the hands of a doctor.'

'No Rance I won't. Promise me you won't let them find me.'

'I promise Don, I promise, just hold on. We'll get you there. Just think, you and me, drinking our first pint of beer together in an English pub. Don I won't let,'-- his voice trailed away realising Cross could no longer hear him.

He gently closed Cross's eyes who now looked at peace with the world. Gone the harsh worries of trying to survive, his fight was over.

Rance cried, the tears unashamedly running down his face he had lost a friend and brother. He called to Sowa.

'You can slow down now. It doesn't matter anymore.'

The driver stopped the cart and both he and Sowa climbed in the back. Sowa examined Cross and gently prising his body from Rance's tight grasp laid him down covering his head with a coat.

'I'm sorry Rance he was a good man, a brave man, and your friend. I can only guess how you must feel.' He became lost for words and climbed back on the seat nudging the driver.

'Let's go,' he said abruptly.

Rance sat next to Cross's body his mind numbed by grief staring down, willing him to get up.

'Barkowice Mokre is ahead of us. What do you want to do Rance?' said Sowa from the front seat

'I want to bury Don where the Germans can't find him but the grounds frozen solid we need men with pick-axes'.

'The men from the village will gladly help, remember this is the village that held you in a shed and were going to shoot you. They at least owe you this.'

They stopped on the outskirts and Sowa walked in disturbing the dogs that barked their warning. Rance became edgy the minutes ticked by and the village continued to be in darkness.

Sowa eventually returned with two men carrying pickaxes and shovels. Rance recognised them as the ones that had first captured him

'Hello Englishman we're very pleased to see you, but not in these terrible circumstances please except our condolences for your loss, which I think is our loss too.' said one of them.

Climbing on the cart they directed the driver off the main track and onto a smaller one which was rougher.

'Where are we going?' Rance asked.

'Towards Kolo about two kilometres, there is a place we know. Don't worry my friend no one will find him there'.

Twenty minutes later they stopped the cart and carefully lifting Cross's body out they carried him into the forest for two hundred metres, where in a small clearing they started to dig. At first the frozen ground was stubborn and unyielding then as they got deeper it became easier. Finally it was deep enough. Sowa and one of the villagers bent to pick up the body.

'I'll help do it,' said Rance quietly and bending he lifted Cross with Sowa's help and they gently placed him the grave.

Silently, he stood looking down oblivious to the men around him. Now with his face devoid of any expression he turned and walked back to the cart, unable to watch them filling in the hole.

Chapter 18

Gestapo HQ Piotrekow

Schneller finished a long telephone conversation with Claus Ritschel and replacing the receiver said to Schmidt,
 'Fetch them in'.
 While he waited, he studied the reports of his two agents.

DECEMBER 22nd 1943..
 There are only two Englishmen. Rumours in the villages suggest that they came here especially to organise resistance to fight the Germans. People who have met them say they are skilful fighters. They help train the local men who are flocking to their side. The leader of their group goes under a code name of Marek, a highly dangerous man.
 They are fed information from a central source, as yet unknown. Their link to that source is a woman called Izabel, as yet we don't know her surname but she lives with her mother in Piotrkow. END OF REPORT.

The words blurred before his eyes, a cold shiver ran down his back. Izabel, it must be, there could be no other. His rage knew no bounds screaming obscenities he cleared his desk with one sweep of his arm pacing the room with white spittle running unheeded down his chin staring with unseeing eyes at Schmidt who entered the room closely followed by two dirty looking men.
 'Sir, this is Mueller and Kantor, they are our agents who live amongst the villagers southwest of here,' said Schmidt.
 The two agents looked at each other as the Major appeared not to hear.
 'Sir, are you all right?' said Schmidt not really caring but thought he ought to make the effort for his own sake.

He watched as Schneller visibly pulled himself together and sat down fixing them with his dead eyes while his lip curled in distaste at the sight of the two dirty men standing before him.

One tall and well-built with hard eyes in a well punished face, while the other was shorter and thinner with eyes that never stayed still. Schneller noticed that the smaller man couldn't look at him.

He picked up the report and put it down again as if it were red hot. Schmidt wondered what was in it. Perhaps the war was over and they could all go home. No such luck he thought glumly.

'Which one of you found out about the girl?' Schneller whispered.

Schmidt became alert. So that was it, the man had got news had he. Really bad news at that by the look of him, he fought to refrain from smiling in glee at Schneller's discomfort.

The tall man spoke for them both, his accent had a strong Polish inflection. We compiled the report together from scraps of information.' He shrugged. 'A word here a word there, you know the sort of thing.'

'No, I don't know about that sort of thing enlighten me,' said Schneller his voice low and menacing.

The tall man swallowed. There was more to this than he could understand. Something contained in their report.

'Well we mingle and work with the villagers, sit and drink Vodka together and we listen to them talking to each other. If there's anything we feel might be useful we pass it on'.

Schneller's eyes fixed unblinkingly on the man. 'Is there anything else you think you might have missed telling us. Is there anything, even if it's only something that you feel isn't important?'

The one with the shifty eyes spoke German with a heavy Polish accent. 'There has been talk that the girl knows one of the Englishmen better than most, if you understand my meaning,' he sniggered only to find it drying in his throat when he was transfixed by the round dead eyes.

'How dare you speak without my permission you obnoxious little man,' said Schneller.

The man squirmed suddenly frightened by something he didn't understand. Only the madman with the staring eyes in front of him knew what was going on.

Schneller fought hard to control his emotions he could feel his blood pressure rising. A pencil snapped in his hand. His mind was in turmoil.

That bitch, that bitch will pay, oh how she will pay. The Englishman he will pay he would make certain of that. He became aware of the three men staring uncomfortably at him and pulled himself together. It wasn't worth getting distracted over one worthless Polish girl but she would pay all the same, nobody makes a fool out of me he thought blackly.

'I have a mission a very important mission for you both you understand.'

His voice was toneless scarcely above a whisper. The three men had to strain their ears to hear him. Schmidt had never seen him as bad as this before.

'I want you no I order you to penetrate this gang of bandits and deliver them to me. His voice rose and became malevolent.

'If they can't be led into a trap then you must kill the Englishmen and the man they call Marek.'

The tall man nodded. 'It may be possible. What about the girl, do we kill her too?'

Schneller's lips curled back to his teeth. 'There's no need I have other plans for her.'

He climbed to his feet and pointed at a map on the wall.

'Do you know the village of Blezun?'

Again the tall man nodded.

'We have another agent living there with the villagers.

Lieutenant Schmidt will tell you where he lives. All the information you get will be passed through him. If you succeed you will be rewarded handsomely.'

If you fail,'-- he left the rest of the sentence unfinished.

Relieved the two men left the office.

On their departure Schmidt turned to leave.

'I haven't finished with you yet Schmidt,' Schneller said..

Stopped in mid-stride he hurriedly returned, standing in front of the desk. Schneller looked at the overweight slovenly figure in front of him and didn't bother to conceal his contempt.

'You're being relieved of your duties with the labour camps. From now on you'll concentrate on finding these two Englishmen and the woman. You will pass the word to all our agents here in Piotrkow that we want all the information they can find even if it's just rumour and gossip. She has still got to be here with her mother somewhere. Put more men on checking the houses street by street if that's what it takes, but I want her found!'

Schmidt hesitated finally plucking up the courage to speak.

'Sir, what if she's got hold of new identity papers?'.

'Then issue a description you idiot there can't be many like her,' Schneller fumed.

Izabel found the journey back from Kalow uneventful. After dropping Maria off at her house she returned through the village centre. The only person she saw was the man they suspected of being a German agent. Afraid to look at him she kept her head down and leaving the village she could still feel his eyes upon her.

With her new horse she made good progress passing through the road blocks unhindered ignoring the usual crude remarks from the soldiers.

Arriving in Piotrkow her grandfather's friend was highly delighted to get such a fine horse to replace the one he lost. On the way back to Krolik's flat she kept to the back streets seeing an increasing presence of German patrols stopping people and checking their papers.

Passing the ever present food queues the population was resigned to the fact that when they reached the front invariably there would be nothing left. She clutched her small bundle of food closer to her bust afraid someone would try to take it.

In the street ahead she noticed that there were more policemen who were only interested in women and examining their papers they forced them to remove their head scarves or hats.

A feeling of insecurity ran through her, she didn't know why but she could feel a sense of danger surround her, whether it was because she knew she had false papers or something else but she didn't want to stay on that street any longer.

Turning left under a small archway she found herself in a dark and dismal courtyard. Everywhere there was a sense of decay rubbish lay frozen to the old cobbled stones dumped there because there were no collections anymore. The shadows in the courtyard lengthened and Izabel glanced at her watch agonising on what to do. It was four o'clock, curfew in one hour.

Dare she risk the police inspections, perhaps her premonition was wrong. Perhaps she was losing her nerve. She shook her head. No, they were definitely looking for a woman, if it was her she was in grave danger. How far to Krolik's flat? ten minutes! she decided to wait and take her chances with the curfew.

While waiting for the streets to clear she wandered into the old buildings. Jewish families had lived here she used to pass them on the way back from school. Quiet friendly people now all gone driven out of their homes by the Gestapo, put into trucks early one morning, and never seen again.

Paper had started to peel off the walls and water had dripped through the ceilings freezing into giant icicles. All the rooms were now empty the furniture having been stolen a long time ago.

Izabel felt a sense of sadness trying to picture the happy families that once lived there but now no vision came.

A door banged upstairs caught by a sudden draught. She shuddered, it was if the ghosts of the people were telling her to leave them in peace. Hurriedly she left the dark and dismal place and returned to the courtyard.

Now it was dark and the curfew had started but she waited another half an hour before cautiously peering out into the side street, finding it deserted. She flitted from one shadow to the next down the narrow street.

A drunk staggered from a doorway weaving his way towards the main road she wanted to warn him but it was too late, he died like a stray dog shot down by a passing patrol. She stood helpless in the shadows mouthing words of hatred at the soldiers gathered round his twitching body wishing now she had risked the inspection of her papers. It was certain death out here and she still had the gauntlet of the main street to cross.

She decided it would be safer going through the cemetery, at least there were no lights and the main road was narrower at that end. Carefully picking her way through the grave stones she avoided the gravel pathway because of the noise.

A deep frost had settled on the headstones the reflected light of a half-moon now rising above the surrounding rooftops making them shine. She worried again perhaps it had been a mistake to come this way. A feeling of being exposed to any passing patrol made her almost choke in fear as the moon's glow bathed the cemetery in a cold pale light.

She crossed from the old part and entered the new leaving the marble headstones behind to be replaced by cheap wooden ones. There was only a few metres to the main road and when a German patrol walked past she lay alongside one of the earth mounds hardly daring to breathe hugging the earth, biting hard into her hand knowing that if they looked across she would be in full view.

There was no challenge, no gunfire, no pain no death. They hadn't seen her and she gave thanks to the mound that had hidden her body from from the troops.

Casually she looked at the name on the stake and went rigid with shock which struck like lightening. It was her grandfather lying there. Choking, she tried to fight back the sobs welling up from deep inside her small frame. She couldn't hold back and the tears fell onto the frozen earth where she lay shaking whispering her grandfather's name.

It was the cold that finally forced her to move her frozen limbs. She had no idea how long she'd lain there but the tears had gone, she felt drained hatred engulfing her.

Now there was no fear only a burning desire to stay alive and seek revenge for what they'd done and were still doing.

The main street was deserted and she quickly crossed and entered the street where Krolik lived. Her mother opened the door to Izabel's knock and stood in silent shock when Izabel fell into her arms.

'What's happened?' you look as if you've seen a ghost,' she said,

Izabel burst into tears, 'Oh mother a have. I've just found grandfather, he's buried in the cemetery and nobody told us. They killed him, I know it.'

Anya sank down on a kitchen chair and buried her head in her arms as the tears racked her body. Izabel finally pulled herself together saying softly, 'In two days' time it will be Christmas, after it's over we'll have to move from here.'

She put a finger to her mother's lips to deaden the protest forming there.

'I can't explain why mother but you must trust me. We're in danger if we stay,' she saw the fear beginning to grow in her mother's eyes.

'Don't worry we're not alone, as you know I have friends that will help. They won't desert us you'll see, but for now we must stay inside and wait for the new-year.'

Her mother jumped at the sudden burst of gunfire in the street below. Calmly Izabel stood up and turned out the light. Gone was the fear and worry only revenge mattered now.

She woke after a restless night, listening to her mother having a nightmare. Picking up a mirror she grimaced at her puffy bloodshot eyes while she tried running a comb through her lank dirty hair. She felt ashamed of herself. 'What would Rance think if he saw me like this?' she whispered to herself..

Shivering, she washed under the tap, there was no oil left for the heater and the water was freezing, there was also no soap so she wrapped her head in a towel and rubbed at it vigorously. Suddenly she stiffened at a gentle tapping on the flat door.

'Who is it?' Her voice was surprisingly calm.

The voice was muffled, 'Curen sent me.'

Quickly she opened the door and a little man slipped in under her arm before she could say a word.

'Thank goodness you're safe.' he said the relief on his face plain to see.

'Why shouldn't I be?'

'Curen said to tell you that the Gestapo have found out about you. Or at least suspect you which is the same thing as far as they're concerned.'

He lowered his voice, looking round with a theatrical expression as if the walls had ears.

'All hell has been let loose they seem to be taking the town apart. I don't know what you've done but it must be something big.'

Izabel's face gave nothing away at the devastating news.

'I would appreciate it if you didn't mention any of this to my mother.'

He winked as if taking part in a great conspiracy. 'My lips are sealed,' he replied, showing disappointment at her silence he was hoping she would expand on the subject.

Izabel smiled wanly. Where ever does Curen find them? She thought.

'Has Curen any plans for my mother and me?' she asked.

The little man reduced his voice to a whisper, 'He said to stay under cover until after Christmas and then he'll make arrangements to get you both out of Piotrkow'.

He then stood proudly to attention in front of her, 'I, Mysz, have been ordered to get you food or anything else you may need but you mustn't attempt to leave the flat unless you ask me first.'

Izabel couldn't help it, 'Yes sir,' she said.

The little man looked at her suspiciously before finally satisfied she was being serious, he nodded and walked towards the door.

'I want you to get me a gun.'

He stopped in mid-stride and spun round to face her. She was standing in the middle of the room her face giving nothing away except her eyes, which were cold and hard.

'A gun, what do want a gun for?' he stuttered.

'For my protection and to protect my mother, that's why.'

'Curen won't like that idea very much.'

'Tell Curen that he's not in my position and I won't take no for an answer,' she said firmly, 'also tell him that I won't let the Gestapo take me or my mother alive so I will need it if they come for me.'

The little man nodded his face white, as if only now he realised the dangerous game they were playing.

CHAPTER 19

After burying Cross, Rance felt only the numbness of pain and grief he sat in the back of the cart in silence, not listening to the men talking. They returned to the village of Barkowice Mokre and the two villagers shook his hand.

'Any time you need us Englishman just send a message and we'll come. Remember that,' one of them said with a nod.

'Where do you want to go now Rance?' Sowa cast him an enquiring look.

'Back to the fight.'

Sowa wasn't surprised. 'It'll be all over by now.'

'Maybe, maybe not, but I would like to go just the same,' said Rance.

Sowa shrugged. 'You heard the man driver, let's go'.

An hour later they met the first of the men coming out of the night running hard. Rance recognised some of the partisans, and the rest he took to be the ex-hostages. In the distance he could hear gunfire and grabbing a running man by the arm he shouted, 'Where's Marek?

'Back there with the diversionary group the man gasped we managed to free the hostages but the Germans brought in reinforcements.'

He shook his arm free and Rance watched him go.

The grey light of dawn made it easier to see Vicktor, Marek and the other men running towards him. Marek showed surprise.

'What the hell are you doing back here, come on run, they're right behind us.'

'Which way, to the left is the River Pilica to the right is Piotrkow?'

'We'll take our chance with the river,' ordered Marek.

Within an hour they were at the river's edge. Rance looked for Jarek and saw him with Krolik further down the bank he then looked at the river with about five inches of snow on the top realising it was frozen ice underneath.

Gingerly he stepped onto it and immediately it cracked, sending a sound like the twanging of a saw across the surface. He jumped back in alarm.

'How deep is it Marek?'

'It's very deep in parts, but not so deep in others. In this spot I don't know. If the ice breaks you will either die from drowning under the ice or a bullet from the Germans behind us.'

He shouted to the men lining the banks. 'Spread out, no two men together and run, if anyone goes in don't stop to help or you'll die too.'

Rance's nerves screamed danger when he ran out onto the ice. All along the frozen river he could hear it cracking into the distance, he tried to tread lightly. One man lost his nerve and stopped trying to retrace his steps, crying out when the ice broke from under him and for a few seconds he floundered on the surface before disappearing from sight.

Rance slipped and rolled never staying in the same place as the ice cracked sending fountains of water spilling across the surface. He was up and running again the will to live giving wings to his feet. A man on his right screamed in terror when the ice broke from under him and he landed waist deep in the freezing water.

Rance reached the other side, and flung himself down amongst the undergrowth watching the struggling man only twenty metres from the bank.

On the man's face was a look of grim determination, he was fighting for his life clawing at the broken edges, but each time he almost made it the ice grumbled under his weight. Rance ran back towards him and the man saw him coming, a look of hope spread into his eyes. The look was still there when a bullet fired by a German on the opposite bank caught him between the shoulder blades sending him flying forward where he slowly slithered backwards into the water turning it red.

Immediately Rance was running for cover with a fusillade of shots smasheing into the ice around him. Seconds later he reached the safety of the trees as the firing intensified on both sides.

Marek crawled up to him seething with anger.

'What the hell are you trying to do? get yourself killed. When will you learn to take orders? why can't you be like Cross? he understands the meaning of the word.'

'Cross is dead he bled to death in the back of the cart.'

The news shook Marek, only now did he see the grief on Rance's face.

'I'm sorry I didn't know.'

Grim faced Rance brushed passed him. 'Yes, we're all sorry,' he said.

Marek opened his mouth to speak thought better of it and turned back to the fighting.

Captain Braun fumed, staring across the frozen river towards the opposite bank. There was no way he was going to cross that river especially with armed men on the other side waiting for them to break cover. He thought of Schneller and what he would say if they got away. He looked at his new second in command with a twinge of remorse remembering his friend Adam Grieb. He felt guilty about that he should never have let him go, his anger turned on Schneller, that maniac had deliberately tried to split them up.

A sudden burst of firing brought his thoughts to an abrupt end, crouching in alarm he shouted for his men to move up river and make a crossing away from the firing line. Twenty minutes later they came to a bend in the river which hid them from view. Braun pointed his gun at the opposite bank, 'Right get some of them over, I'll cover you'.

Second Lieutenant Hans Biehaus looked at the Captain, hiding the contempt he felt for the immaculately dressed effeminate officer. His face showed no emotion, but he shuddered at the prospect of crossing that ice.

'Impatiently Braun snapped at him. 'Take some men, I'll give you covering fire, I don't think anyone will be waiting on the other side, so come on, we haven't got all day'.

Then you go you gutless pig, thought Bilhaus, he saluted straight faced. 'Yes sir,' he said pointing at the nearest men.

'You, you and you, follow me,' white faced they followed him out onto the ice. They hadn't gone ten metres before the ice claimed its first victim.

The man screamed when the ice gave way sending the others into a panic. They stopped in confusion causing the ice to crack in all directions, its sing song noise like a saw over the surface.

Krolik on the other bank sent there by Vicktor as back up for just such a situation lined his sights on the officer. He squeezed the trigger and missed, hitting the man directly behind who threw up his arms and fell backwards crashing through the ice. It split in all direction causing pandemonium. In blind panic the exposed men ran back towards the safety of the bank.

Grinning, Krolik retreated back into the forest confident they wouldn't follow.

Braun resigned himself to the fact that they weren't going to cross the river, not there anyway. Not after that last episode. Angrily he turned on his second Lieutenant.

'Well that was really impressive for your first command with me. I'm sure Major Schneller will be pleased when he reads my report.'

Sullenly the second Lieutenant stared, furious but careful not to show his feelings.

'I don't think it was my fault sir.'

'You don't eh, well we'll let Major Schneller decide that shall we,' snapped Braun, storming off up river. 'Come on we'll find another crossing, there's a bridge four kilometres from here but by the time we cross those bandits will be long gone.'

Hans Bilhaus stared at his Captain's retreating back seething with resentment. He knew Braun had ordered that crossing knowing what would happen just so he could put the blame on someone else for letting them get away. 'Just my luck to be under that spineless,'-- he was lost for words.

Janowo

Schneller sat hunched in the back of his staff car looking sourly at what remained of the prison camp. With a roar of flames and smoke what was left of the roof finally collapsed making him wince.

Slowly as if in a trance he walked amongst the empty prison quarters. All the German dead and wounded had now been removed, leaving a pile of bodies stacked near the perimeter fence. He refused to look at Braun standing by his side. 'How many of the dead pigs are here?'

Braun swallowed hard his throat dry. 'We didn't count them, perhaps nine or ten, no bandits only some of the prisoners.'

'I don't suppose you would know if the Englishmen are here either?'

'We checked all their pockets none of them had any identity papers, we don't know what they look like anyway.'

Schneller sighed, 'I knew it would be a waste of time asking you.'

Braun opened his mouth to speak before thinking better of it. Schneller was in a dangerous mood Braun had seen it all before. In silence they walked back to the staff car. Schneller sat down on the rear seat waving to Braun,

'Come, ride back to Piotrkow with me we have something to discuss.'

His voice sounded almost friendly, Braun hesitated eyeing him with suspicion. Schneller drummed his fingers on the side of the car impatiently. 'Well, come on what's the matter with you?' he growled.

Cautiously Braun sat opposite as the large car swept back through the ruined gates, finding himself transfixed by the deadly eyes of the man facing him.

'I've read your report Braun it made an interesting story especially how the bandits eluded your men. In it you blamed your second in command, what's his name?' Schneller's voice was silky soft. 'Oh yes, Bilhaus wasn't it?'

Braun could only nod.

Schneller leaned forward and his spittle felt wet on Braun's cheek. 'I think you're a stinking liar Braun.'

Braun went rigid with shock his face white. He wanted to smash the face in front of him but knew he hadn't the guts to do anything, he wriggled in helpless fury.

Schneller sat back relishing Braun's discomfort and they rode along in silence for five minutes before Schneller spoke again. 'I've decided to accept your report and give you the chance to put things right.'

Braun felt the glow of relief but he still looked at him suspiciously. 'What about Second Lieutenant Bilhaus?'

'I will recommend that he be transferred to the Russian front for his cowardice.'

Braun looked puzzled. 'What do you want from me?.'

'I want your complete obedience to any order I give. I want somebody out in the field of operations that I can rely on. Not some fat subhuman of a Lieutenant that's only used to sitting behind a desk.'

Braun knew he was referring to Schmidt. Schneller leaned closer Braun aware of his spittle leaned back.

'I want you to release some of your men from guarding our villagers and to concentrate on finding these Englishmen. We have two agents who are getting close. You will work with them and be ready to move as soon as they have news.'

Braun looked troubled. 'That could leave our villagers open to attack.'

Schneller ignored the remark. 'Lieutenant Lohr will make sure our agents get the information they need. Believe me when he's finished with the Poles they'll tell us all they know.'

Braun had his doubts but wasn't prepared to argue about it. Anything was better than being sent to the Russian front.

After leaving the river Marek kept them moving all that day well away from the German controlled villages. A game of hide and seek developed with numerous German patrols searching for them.

Rance's distraught mind still couldn't come to terms with Cross's death and he agonised over his movements. Could he have done more to save him. Should he have been moved from the village of Polichno. He shook his head as if to wipe away the vision. Suddenly he felt tired. Tired of the running, tired of the fighting, sickened by all the killing and the horrors of what he'd seen and been part of in Poland. Now all he wanted to do was to take Izabel and go home to England.

He disliked moving through the forest at night but it was secure, if he hated it, then he took small comfort in the knowledge that the Germans doubly so. At least Marek knew every inch of the territory and they didn't. Finally, wearily at dawn with the faintest glimmer of light on the horizon they walked into the clearing at Kalow where despite the early hour Jozef and Radice were there to greet them offering a bed for the next few hours.

It was mid-afternoon before they met together again, Jozef sat in shocked silence at the news of Cross's death.

He shook his head in disbelief,

'Was he the only one ?'

Yes,' answered Marek, 'it went remarkably well.'

Rance stood up and went outside unable to speak. He knew what Marek was trying to say that the cost in life could have been much higher and that they had been lucky, but it didn't make Cross's death any easier to bear. Jozef came out and sat beside him.

'Marek didn't mean what you're thinking you know, he asked me to tell you that.'

Rance nodded, ' Yes I know what he meant. I understand.'

Jozef hesitated, his face serious 'What I have to say now is just for you. The Gestapo know that Izabel is a courier and even now they are searching for her.'

For a second Rance stared, without at first comprehending what Jozef had said, as it sank home he jumped to his feet his mind in disarray.

'What! How could this happen, someone must have told them, how else would they know? He turned to leave, 'I must go to her.'

Patiently Jozef restrained him. 'Wait my friend Curen has already decided to get her and her mother out of Piotrykow after Christmas, but at the moment it's too dangerous for her to move. You would only make it worse.'

We have a young partisan with us who has a house and family in Piotrkow you know him as Golab. Marek and I think you should go with him for Christmas,' he put a friendly arm on Rance shoulder.

'After Don, you need a rest my friend, when Christmas is over you and Golab together with Krolik can bring Izabel and her mother back out with you.'

Rance stared at him in bewilderment. 'It would be suicide for all of us on the road together'.

'You wouldn't use the road. Near the outskirts of Piotrkow is where the forest starts. The main danger is getting from the town to the forest with the curfew on but don't worry my friend, Golab and Krolik are experts at that'.

It took Golab and Rance all day to walk the eighteen kilometres into Piotrkow having detoured off the main road into the small tracks and villages surrounding the town. Rance followed Golab blindly he seemed to know every path and track. He felt the familiar tightening of his stomach muscles on nearing the town as the German patrols became more numerous.

Twice they were stopped while he stood back letting Golab do the talking. Finally allowed to proceed they entered the town through the back streets, crossing the main square and passing the chemists shop.

Rance glanced through the window and saw the little chemist busy behind the counter, he wondered if the man would wet himself again if he suddenly entered the shop.

Leaving the square they came out onto the main road, Golab crossed over with Rance following fifty paces behind suddenly feeling nervous at the sight of two policemen standing on the pavement opposite watching him. Walking towards them he tried to behave naturally but feeling his palms becoming moist he started to perspire although he felt cold.

Golab had stopped and was fumbling for his papers so he went to walk past but found his way blocked by a heavy hand.

'Lass mich deine papiere sehen'. The man spoke in German, so Rance answered in German.

'Yes sir, they're here, you'll find them all in order.'

The policeman was surprised, 'Oh, you must be a Volksdeutche,' he ignored them, you'd better get going, remember the curfew'.

Golab had gone on ahead and Rance followed. On his right he saw the Gestapo HQ, so near, he became nervous again. Golab turned into a road that ran at right angles to the main street and knocked on the door of a small wooden house.

He followed somewhat self-consciously standing by the door watching the joyous welcome Golab was receiving from his wife and young son. His wife was young probably no more than twenty five or six but looked thin, so did the boy. Rance realised there must be very little food in the house. Golab broke away laughing and introduced Rance who smiling shook her hand and said hello to the boy who stared up at him in wonder.

'I've never seen a real Englishman before,' the boy exclaimed.

'Hush now,' his mother whispered, 'this is a real secret that you must never tell anyone, especially the Germans or they will come and take us away.'

The boy nodded wide eyed with his big secret.

Rance dug deep into the inside of his large overcoat pulling out a small parcel which he handed to the woman who flushed with delight at the unexpected gift.

'It's not much, but perhaps it will help,' he said.

Opening it she gasped and quickly hid it from her son.'

'Tomorrow is Christmas day. Now my son can have a present after all', she whispered with tears in her eyes.

Curiosity got the better of Golab. 'Well, what have you got woman? Show me,' he demanded, smiling. He looked stunned when she held out the contents.

'He gasped, staring at Rance.

'Eggs, you dared bring eggs all the way from Kalow.'

Rance shrugged, 'If I can bring a gun why not eggs?'

Golab grinned, 'Well, as being caught with either carries the death penalty I don't suppose it matters too much.'

He felt guilty about eating the meagre dinner that his host put before him. He knew they were desperately short of food but to refuse would hurt their feelings. Somehow he would make it up to them he promised himself.

After the meal, Golab's wife excused herself and went to put the little boy to bed while Golab broke open a bottle of his home made Vodka. 'Be careful of this stuff Rance, it's my best, quite strong even for me.'

Rance gingerly sipped at it, struggling not to pull a face when the powerful brew hit his stomach.

'The rumours are that the Russians have started to move this way Rance,' said Golab after tilting back the bottle.

Rance's throat was on fire. 'I've heard, but will they get this far? The Germans have a strong force throughout Poland'.

Golab looked grave. 'The communists are getting stronger all the time.' Now correcting himself when he saw Rance's puzzled expression.

'I mean the communist party here in Poland. Rumour has it that they are in contact with the Russians who are helping them organise groups of fighters by parachuting in weapons and men ahead of their advance.

Rance took another swig from the bottle and felt the warm glow.

'That can't be a bad thing surely, anything that helps get rid of the Nazis has to be good'.

Golab agreed, but added a word of caution.

'There's a possibility of civil war if the Polish communists use the Russian forces as a stepping stone to power'.

Rance stared at the troubled face on the opposite side of the table shaking his head. 'I can't believe the partisans will fight each other if the Russians do come though here.'

Golab looked back mournfully. 'I believe they will and you my friend will be right in the middle of it.'

Rance sat back his mind racing ahead to the future trying to picture the things to come. The Russians fighting the Germans and the none communist partisans. The Germans fighting both of them

The two partisan groups fighting each other, his mind spun and all he saw was a great abyss that he would surely fall into. He forced his mind back to the present.

'It may not happen like that we have to be positive about such things.'

Golab didn't look convinced. 'For all our sakes I really hope so. As Poles, my family and I stand a chance even if we have to live under the rule of the Russians, but for you it will be a time of great danger so you must be on your guard.'

Rance smile was grim. 'If I should live so long,' he muttered.

Golab's wife made him a bed in the attic it was warm lying there staring into the darkness of the rafters. He thought of Cross and the pain of his death came back to haunt him. He deliberated on what he would do if the Russians came. Even now he found it hard to believe, that after all he'd been through, he would still have to fight if the Germans were defeated.

His papers would be worthless he would only have to open his mouth and they would know he wasn't one of them. With a tormented mind he drifted into a restless sleep.

It was early afternoon before Rance woke. For a few seconds he tried to get his bearings relaxing when he remembered. Climbing down the rickety ladder he found Golab and his wife peering through the curtains at the sound of German voices outside.

Golab turned anger showing in his face. 'Even on Christmas day they have to search. This time it's the man opposite they've taken away. Why? who knows what the Gestapo think. He walked away from the window and sat down next to Rance near the fire poking at the ashes basking in its warm glow. 'There's a lot of intrigue here in Piotrkow nobody knows who to trust anymore.

The Germans have brought in many spies, Volksdeutche collaborators who live and work in the towns and surrounding countryside. People are becoming too frightened to do or say anything. Look at the man opposite he led a normal quiet life until he said something to somebody and was reported to the Gestapo. Something they didn't like it needn't be much. Even so they would come for him.'

Rance frowned. 'What can be done about it?'

There are more rumours amongst the partisans that Curen is going to order action against them, including the Gestapo.'

'What sort of action would that be?'

'I think he means to put execution squads into Piotrkow to hunt them down, to act as a warning to others'.

Golab threw another log on the fire and watched the sparks fly up the chimney. 'That's not all he will want us to move against the Volksdeutche villagers.'

Rance was horrified at the news. 'To do what, kill them? I could never do that, it would make us as bad as they are.'

Golab held up his hand. 'Steady there, he doesn't mean that. He means we should go in, deprive them of their food in tit for tat raids. Burn them out cause them trouble like they do to our people. That way they'll think twice before attacking more of our villages.'

'Most of the Volksdeutche villages are protected by German outposts,' retorted Rance.

'Now we have the weapons we will us them,' Golab replied.

Rance sat back in his chair thinking about that. They were reaching a new more dangerous episode in this nightmare he was in.

Stubbornly he again voiced his feelings, 'I will not fire on civilians, the Gestapo, yes, but not civilians'.

Golab nodded, 'None of us will do that, so stop worrying.'

Rance leaned forward, looking glum. 'Where the hell will it all end?' he said.

Almost a four days had passed, Rance was beginning to relax. He'd washed his clothes, getting rid of the tormenting lice. He felt clean and rested. Now all he wanted was to find Izabel. Golab had assured him that she and her mother were safe, that they would go the next day if the weather was reasonable.

He passed a restless night thinking of her worrying about the danger she was in. Dawn came agonisingly slowly before it was light enough for him to study the weather which seemed settled enough, with no sign of snow.

He waited by the door checking the comforting handle of his pistol buried deep in his overcoat pocket as Golab said his goodbyes to his wife.

They left the comfort and safety of the house making their way into the town centre going unnoticed amongst the early morning crowds. Twenty minutes later they entered Krolik's flat.

For a full five seconds Izabel stood routed to the spot with shock before flying across the room and into Rance's arms. Holding her he smelt the freshness of her hair and could feel the curve of her warm body against his. Choking with emotion he kissed her warm and willing lips.

A discreet cough from Golab made them break away smiling self-consciously at each other.

'We must wait for Krolik before we can leave,' said Golab, looking at the small bundles of spare clothes on the bed,

' I see you are ready to go, travelling light.'

'Izabel smiled crookedly, 'It's all we have left,' failing to mention the revolver hidden in her bag on the kitchen table. A present from Curen.

'I was devastated when Curen sent news about Don's death,' Izabel whispered holding his hand tightly. 'I'm so sorry. but I am overwhelmed with relief knowing you're safe. If anything ever happens to you, I would want to die too.'

He took her in his arms staring bleakly at the wall the image of Cross's death coming back once more to haunt him.

Golab interrupted. 'Kroliks here, it's time to go.

Franz Lohr hated Christmas, he was always relieved when it was over. New year's eve, now that was different. He looked at his watch, one thirty. Two more villages and he would be finished for the day just in time to get back to Piotrkow for the New Year's party. He felt like getting drunk he'd worked hard and deserved it.

Stopping the halftrack on the outskirts of a village he studied the map on his lap The village of Huta, of medium size, population about one hundred. Slowly the convoy edged into the deserted centre and Lohr looked around smiling to himself. He knew where to find them.

Stepping down onto the hard packed snow he watched his men kick down the doors pulling the villagers out from under beds, out of barns, and from under the hay storage sheds. They found people hidden under floor boards, and in the attics, while troops scoured the nearby forest bringing in groups of women and children. Lohr's lips peeled back in a smile watching them being lined up in a snow covered field and ordered to strip.

He nodded at his Sergeant to begin, the giant bull whips cracked loudly in the still winter air. 'Remember this,' Lohr shouted over the noise of the bull whips, 'if we don't find these bandits you're helping we will return. The sooner you tell us where they are, the better it will be for you, only afterwards, we will give you food and help.'

He looked at his watch, three o'clock, a record for one village, practice makes for speed he wrote in his diary.

Lohr nodded at his Sergeant. 'OK now we go to the village of Przvtyk, bring five men hostages with us,' he ordered and they left without a backward glance.

He entered the village half an hour later, grinning at the familiar deserted looking houses. Within twenty minutes he had sixty villagers gathered together in a semi-circle round his halftrack and ordered a soldier to fetch a wood cutting bench which he placed in the centre. He stood facing them, his hard features twisted in contempt.

'You are here today to witness what happens to people that give help to the bandits in your area. This punishment is only a warning in future it will be more severe. Within two days I want to know where the bandits are. If not, this is what will happen to you and your children.'

He raised his arm and one of the hostages was dragged forward.

'Tie his arm to the top of the bench,' ordered Lohr.

'Fetch an axe'.

The man tied to the bench started to cry and the villagers screamed their protest. A German soldier raised the axe above his head. Lohr wasn't looking at the victim he liked to watch the expressions on the face of the onlookers, anyone that turned away he lashed with his bull whip. 'Watch damn you,' he said. The axe slashed down cutting into muscle and bone, the man screamed like a wounded animal before finally fainting.

'Bring the next man'.

Weak with fear the next man had to be dragged to the work bench, his breathing ragged, his throat dry, and his chest heaved. The axe fell twice before the man twisted and rolled clear screaming grabbing at his bleeding stump. Lohr watched with growing satisfaction as the women started to faint and the children cried in terror.

He looked at his watch grimacing with annoyance, nearly five o'clock, he would be late for the New Year's Eve party.

'We haven't time for anymore, kill the rest of the hostages,' he ordered

The villagers pushed forward, only to fall back under the threat of the machine guns.

Now the villagers fell silent when the remaining hostages were brought forward, and as the axe rose and fell they lowered their eyes and prayed. Lohr strode amongst them lashing with his whip, ordering them to watch.

'Deliver the bandits to me and you'll be spared anymore of this. Remember. We'll be back.'

None of the villagers moved until the German convoy was out of sight. Silently they tended to the two men who were already dying from loss of blood carrying the other corpses into the houses.

The village men reacted by reaching into their hiding place's fetching out their hunting rifles, sharpening their axes, and found their pitch forks. In ones and twos they headed northwest towards Kalow joining on the way with the men from Huta.

CHAPTER 20

Piotrkow

'Its New Year's Eve?' It was more of a question. Golab had already anticipated the answer struggled into his large overcoat.

Krolik looked at him with an amused expression. 'You want to go to a party?'

Golab grinned in return. 'We haven't all got an invitation, I thought that's where we were going.'

Krolik became serious, 'Tonight is the best time for us to go. The Germans like their new year most will be drunk, also I suspect most of the patrols will stay near the town centre. They won't want to miss the fun either.'

He turned to Izabel and her mother, 'I'll lead one hundred metres ahead of you, Rance will be just behind and Golab will be one hundred metres behind him.'

He paused at the door. 'Remember, if we're caught, we fight. We have no choice. I must remind you of the consequences if anyone is taken alive.'

Anya caught her breath it sounded loud in the silent room. Izabel wished her mother hadn't heard that last remark.

Krolik opened the door to a dark and moonless night and Rance hoped the snow would hold off for the next few hours.

Slowly they made their way through the dark streets, Krolik's lead dropped to less than fifty metres. Four times they crouched in the shadows watching drunken soldiers stagger passed. A patrol entered the street and Krolik signalled for them to hide. Izabel, lying with her mother slowly brought back the hammer of her pistol gently placing the muzzle near the back of her mother's head and waited.

Rance, hiding two doorways down worried because he couldn't see them, his gun butt felt wet to his touch as he slid off the safety catch.

A door opened letting out a blast of laughter and music. The patrol hesitated arguing before drifting across to the door, a German soldier fell out into the road calling one of them by name. Two more followed bringing glasses of beer.

Another argument followed before they all decided to go back inside.

Relieved, Izabel eased the hammer of her pistol and hid it from her mother's sight.

Krolik led them through a maze of small lanes and overgrown paths to finally emerge onto open fields scattered with small hedgerows and farm buildings. From somewhere behind came the muted noise of a party.

He explained their next move, 'We have to go maybe a kilometre before we reach the safety of the forest. Now you must follow me closely the tracks are narrow and there is no moon. Its good news for us but the going will be hard.'

Rance felt the first flakes of snow brush his cheeks when moved silently across the open farmland the tension growing being so exposed.

Skirting the silent farm-houses looking for every scrap of cover took time, so it was nearly an hour before they entered the security of the trees. Izabel shivered as total blackness engulfed them all and she instinctively held on to Rance and her mother, waiting for Krolik and Golab to find the right track. Fifteen minutes later Golab reappeared.

'Come, we have decided to make for the village of Drzewica where Krolik has friends. It will break the journey and make things easier for Anya.'

Rance nodded, 'How long will we be staying?'

' It depends on the weather as usual. If it stops snowing we'll go on tomorrow night.'

The track they were using was no more than a metre wide with low overhanging branches heavily laden with snow. Rance guessed it was mainly used by foresters. Soon their black coated figures turned white with the snow filtering down through the trees.

He knew from experience that a snow storm raged above them with the great trees acting as a protective canopy. He also knew that if the wind increased anymore the snow would drift and they could be in trouble already having to support Anya as she was becoming weaker.

They emerged from the forest into the open, meeting the full force of the blizzard hurling a solid wall of ice and snow into their frozen faces.

Golab came back to help with Anya. 'We're nearly here this farmland belongs to the village.'

Krolik came out of the blizzard a white hunched figure without shape.

'Wait here, I'll go and warn them I don't want you to get a pitch fork in your gut.'

He was back within fifteen minutes grinning broadly.

'What luck, you won't believe this they're having a party. There's so much Vodka you could drown.'

Rance groaned he could already picture his hangover, now the savage spear of grief hit him, bringing back the memory of Cross and himself making jokes about the taste.

'That's all I need,' he said gruffly, 'let's get Anya out of this snow.'

They entered a small wooden house and were hit by a blast of overpowering hot air the smoke filled room was packed to overflowing with people of all ages. Anya was quickly taken off Rance and put in a bedroom.

A bottle was thrust into his hand with loud cries of happy new year and there were gasps of disbelief when they realised he was English. Some of them came up to him saying they'd heard rumours about him, but they hadn't believed them until now.

The Vodka hit his stomach like the usual ton of bricks bringing tears to his eyes, he walked amongst them pretending to smile whilst looking for Izabel but only saw Krolik and Golab talking to one of the villagers. He wandered over to join them and was introduced to the village leader, Pawel, a large tubby man of about sixty with a round wrinkled face covered in stubble.

'Rance, we're talking about the Russians,' said Krolik. 'All along the front line the Germans are pulling back and some sections are in full retreat.'

Pawel was frowning. 'Already we've had communist agents come looking for recruits to help them, when, or if the Russians get here.'

'What do they want them to do?' Rance asked.

'They want them armed to be ready to take over, that's what they're after.' Pawel laid his hand on Rance shoulder.

'They were asking about you my friend. Did we know where you could be found ?' He shrugged. 'For what purpose I could only guess at'.

'How do they know about me?'

Pawel grinned, 'Most of the area has heard the rumours about you and your friend. You two are becoming heroes to these people, although a few still think you're a figment of the imagination, such is the secret that surrounds you. By the way, where is your friend?'

Rance took a swig of Vodka before answering. 'He couldn't make it this time'.

He was puzzled, why did the communists want to know where he could be found? Were they to be friends or enemies?

The thought of the Russian advance brought back the unease in him. Another man joined them. Middle aged with wispy grey hair, he looked half starved. Pawel introduced him,

'This is a friend of mine from across the River Pilica. He fled with his family away from the German soldiers. He's not the only one, many have come to get away from the shooting and torture that's happening over there. Nearly all have lost loved ones and are now afraid that it will be their turn next.'

He lifted his bottle, 'So tonight we try to be happy for the year to come, who knows?' he let the fiery liquid run down the back of his throat before staggering off.

Rance watched him go his frown deepening.

'Marek will have to do something about it soon, those killers can't be allowed to go on decimating the villages like that.'

Krolik answered before putting his mouth round the neck of a Vodka bottle.

'I think Marek has a little surprise for those inhuman pigs,' he paused taking a long swig.

Rance watched in amazement when he emptied the bottle and wiped his mouth using the back of his hand.

'Or so he tells me'.

'You must have iron guts to drink like that'.

Krolik laughed, 'No, I'm just a good Pole'.

Rance shook his head and moved away.

Feeling a light touch on his back he turned to find Izabel by his side. 'Mother's asleep, she's exhausted. I'm so pleased we're out of Piotrkow things were getting desperate.' She clung to him, 'and to be here with you on New Year's Eve is a wonderful bonus'.

Together they sat arm in arm watching the party until the last guest staggered away, all except the ones that had passed out or were too drunk to move.

Pawel's wife offered to share her bed with Izabel leaving her husband who was too drunk to stand sharing the floor with Rance. Who, lying close to the fire was listening to the loud snores coming from the various parts of the room while the whistling wind tugged at the wooden shutters.

He felt hate for the men committing the atrocities across the river, he'd hated before, but now it was keeping him awake he knew he would have to control it or it would consume him.

'Good morning.' Izabel woke him with a beaming smile and a large hot drink. He stretched his aching muscles and accepted it gracefully concealing a shudder at the bitter taste, not being able to decide what it was supposed to be. Having got up and washed he and Izabel spent all morning greeting a stream of visitors, all wanting to meet the Englishman who'd come to help fight the Germans. Izabel laughed at his serious expression. 'Come on, try to look as if you're enjoying all this attention,' she teased. 'So it's true, all Englishmen are shy.' She prodded him in the ribs.

'Next thing I know, you'll be blushing.'

Rance managed a weak smile. 'If I ever get to be alone with you, I'll make you eat those words.'

She giggled, blushing herself.

With no reports of any troop movements in the area, Krolik decided it was safe to move out at mid-afternoon. Thanking their hosts they walked through the open fields and entered the forest again. Krolik was two hundred metres in the lead when he turned, hurriedly retracing his steps.

'Somebody is coming.'

Quietly they waited hidden by the trees, but whoever was coming their way was speaking in Polish. Rance, Krolik and Golab stepped out onto the track confronting a group of people who seeing the three armed men stopped in alarm and confusion.

It was Krolik who broke the silence when the men in the party pushed their women to the rear and closed ranks.

'Don't be alarmed we're from the Polish Home Army, we're on your side,' he said quietly.

Some of the women started to cry and one of the men answered,

'Where were you when we needed you.' his voice was full of bitterness. 'Everywhere across the river the Germans are torturing and killing. They destroy our families and burn our homes and all the time it's you they're after.'

Krolik grew angry, 'We can't be everywhere but we're all in this together, none of us asked the Germans to come here.' His tone softened, 'I'm sorry for what they've done to you, but believe me, we will take our revenge. All the time we're getting stronger, and one day we'll stop them.'

The man shook his head, 'That won't bring back my mother and father, nor any of the others.'

Krolik's eyes flashed, 'Well we need men with guts, and it's obvious you're not one of them'. He waved him on. 'Go on run, we'll do your fighting for you.'

The man flushed in anger, 'I didn't say I wasn't going to fight, but I must make sure my wife and children are in a place of safety first, afterwards I will come.'

Krolik modified his tone, 'We'll be pleased to see you. Come to Kalow they'll know where to find us,' he stepped to one side allowing the villagers to pass.

Rance looked dubiously at the retreating man's back.

'Do you think that was wise telling him about Kalow?'

Krolik shrugged, 'Nearly every village has at least one or two people that know about Kalow. It's no big secret except from the Germans.'

They approached the River Pilica and met more refugees struggling to cross the treacherous ice. One group had strung a thick rope between two trees and were gingerly hanging on as one by one they reached the safety of the other bank.

'You're going the wrong way,' a man shouted to them. The Einsatzgruppen killer squads are in that area.'

Krolik put his hand on the rope. 'Can we use this to get across?'

The man stared as if they were mad. 'Yes, if that's what you want, but if you take my advice you should come with us it will be safer.'

Krolik smiled. 'No, we prefer to go on.'

'Help yourself I only hope you know what you're doing,' he stood back and watched as they made their way to the other side.

Anya asked nervously, 'Are you sure we're doing the right thing'

'Don't worry Anya, said Krolik smiling reassuringly, we'll stay in the forest until we can get you to Izabel's friend in Blezun. There you'll be well looked after by Maria.'

'Does Maria know about Don?' asked Izabel.

'Yes she does I told her,' answered Krolik, 'She didn't take it very well so I think it's a good idea for you to be staying there.'

The two men stood in the shadow of the trees watching the refugees crossing the river and looked with puzzled interest at the small group going the other way. Mueller the tall hard faced man nudged his companion.

'Now why would anybody want to go that way when everybody else is in such a hurry to cross over here?'

'Shall we follow them,' asked Kantor.

'No, we'd never get across in time,' said Mueller pointing at the fleeing refugees. 'I feel we'll learn the answer from them.'

Walking silently together they joined the rear end of the line as the people headed towards Drezewica. After a few curious glances the villagers accepted the men's explanation that they'd fled from the Nazi troops further up river and had nowhere else to go.

The village was full to overflowing when they arrived. Pawel was at his wits end with so many people to find room for. He stood with some of the other villagers trying to direct them to the houses and barns scattered about. Now there was the food problem, there wasn't any. How would he be able to feed so many?

'You have a problem here perhaps it was unwise for us to come, but we didn't know where else to go,' the man said apologetically.

Pawel focused his attention on the two men standing in front of him.

'Oh, you two have just come in with this last group haven't you? Well, to tell you the truth it's been like this for the last two days and I don't know where it'll end I'm sure. Where have you come from?' Although he didn't really care. He'd asked the same question a hundred times before.

The tall hard faced man waved his hand back the way they'd come. 'Just across the river about two days walk, but the way my feet feel it seems longer. Seriously though we want to fight we've had enough of the Germans. They burnt my home and killed my friend's wife,' he said nodding towards his companion who looked suitably stricken with grief.

Pawel shook his head in sympathy. 'Yes there are so many tales coming across the river about that sort of thing. Please accept my condolences,' he said gruffly.

He hesitated before making up his mind. 'You're in luck I can put you in touch with the partisans. That's if you're really serious in what you say'.

'We are,' said the two men earnestly.

Pawel stuck out his chest, 'It's a pity you weren't here earlier,' he said confidentially. 'We had some of them staying with us. Important ones, some of their leaders I suspect.'

He lowered his voice. 'One of them was the Englishman everybody is talking about.'

The two men became excited, 'That's who we want to fight with,' the big man's face broke into an engaging smile.

'What luck meeting you now how do we make contact with them?' he asked casually.

Pawel went into his house and fetched out an old used map, pointing with a grubby finger.

'Kalow is the place to go they'll put you in contact. Not an easy place to find mind you.'

The two men studied the map eagerly memorising every detail.

'Not so far from here then?' said the smaller man.

'Maybe a day's walk,' agreed Pawel.

The tall man made a decision, 'We'll go now while we have daylight left,' he shook Pawel's hand warmly.

'Thank you for all your help we shall mention that you sent us if you don't mind.'

Pawel watched them out of sight his smile giving way to fingers of doubt. Had he done the right thing. He shook his head, yes he was sure, then his thoughts were interrupted by more arrivals.

Kalow

It was dusk when Rance and the others walked wearily into Kalow after an uneventful journey.

Jozef and his family welcomed them and were joined by Radice, his two sons, and their neighbour who presented them all with bottles of Vodka, soon the room was filled with cigarette smoke and laughter. Bowls of watery soup were placed in front of them along with the inevitable strips of pork in a large stew pot from which they all helped themselves.

'I've never seen such a feast in all my life,' Anya exclaimed in wonderment.

Jozef grinned, 'Yes you have but it's been such a long time that you've forgotten. Now make the most of it because that's all there is. Until I can steal some more off the Volksdeutche that is,' he said and they all laughed.

'Where's Marek? I didn't see him when we arrived, ' said Rance

'He's taken some men and gone out to the villages there's all hell let lose out there. He should be back soon,' said Jozef.

Rance felt Izabel's hand slide into his and felt her hot breath in his ear. 'I don't want to leave you tomorrow Rance,' she whispered.

He winced at the thought, 'I don't want you to go either, but we don't have any choice in the matter.'

He kissed her cheek, 'Krolik wants to go early in the morning.'

She snuggled up to him, 'We still have tonight.'

He held her close, 'Yes, we still have tonight,' and he was content.

The next morning Marek returned, Rance was shocked at his appearance he looked ill with his bloodshot eyes staring out of a thin gaunt face. He sank wearily into a chair and told them the news.

'The villages are being raided everyday now by the Gestapo they're after information about us as well as making room for their own people'.

He paused to rub his red rimmed eyes. 'I've seen things that have sickened me,' his expression one of hate.

'Viktor, me with the other Commanders are going to fight them, village for village. They attack ours, we attack theirs. Above all we intend to hunt down and fight their Einsatzgruppen. Mobile killer squads.'

He rose to his feet swaying with tiredness. 'Any man that wants to stay at home can do so but we're going to fight,' he said savagely.

'When will this be?' queried Jozef

'Any man that wants to go must be here by five o'clock tomorrow morning send out your sons with the message Jozef.'

Krolik and Rance escorted Izabel and her mother back to Maria's house in Blezun. A house full of sadness, Rance left feeling grim and despondent pausing on the river bank where the four of them swam together. The bitter sweet memories came flooding back to haunt him. Was it only six months ago? To Rance it seemed a lifetime.

He woke with a start the next morning back in Kalow and looked at his watch, four thirty. He heard the gentle murmur of men's voices outside, carried on the bitterly cold morning air. Stepping out on to the porch of Jozef's house he looked at the men gathering quietly in the clearing. Turning, he stared towards the edge of the forest seeing more men threading their way through the trees.

Jozef nudged him. 'Have you ever felt proud Rance, because seeing this makes me proud to be Polish.'

Rance stared at the incoming men, noticing only a few had hunting rifles while the rest carried axes and pitch forks.

'It certainly stirs the blood seeing them come like this,' he said, sitting on the edge of the porch and proceeding to take his machine pistol to pieces. Laying each part carefully in a line. He gently oiled each one before slowly putting it back together. He nodded towards the barn,

'You'd better wake Marek, it will cheer him up to see this.'

Marek left the barn blinking in the grey light of dawn, the men fell silent, waiting. Slowly his eyes roamed the clearing. Rance estimated there must be nearly one hundred determined men facing Marek who was visibly moved at the sight. Slowly his face changed and became alive. His eyes fixed on Rance and Krolik. 'Break out the new guns you have two hours to teach them how shoot.

The men formed two lines and each was given either a machine pistol or a rifle with a share of ammunition. Hand-grenades were placed in boxes for them to help themselves.

Two hours! Rance knew it was an impossible task and so did everyone else. It was just enough time to show them how to load and fire.

Everywhere was a flurry of activity men appeared on horseback, spoke to Marek and disappeared back into the forest.

Jozef came up to Rance carrying a brand new machine gun and Rance winced chiding him for leaving the safety catch off.

'Who do you want to shoot, us or them?' he said and asked, 'Why the men on horseback?'

It was Viktor's idea,' said Jozef fumbling with the safety catch. 'We're moving to where the Einsatzgruppen have been operating recently and the men with horses will spread out over the countryside to pin-point their movements.'

Rance looked dubiously at their ramshackle army.

'Setting a trap is the only way we stand a chance against them, out in the open they would slaughter us.'

'Thank God for the forest Rance,' answered Jozef, smiling..

The long column of men moved in silence down the forest track. Rance found himself in an advanced scouting party just ahead of the main group travelling abreast and in sight of one another.

He had Krolik on his right and Golab on his left he was in good company. He wondered where Izabel's brother was, the last time he saw him he was near the rear grinning and waving as if he was going on a holiday day trip.

He shivered in the bitterly cold air that funnelled through the trees stinging his face. Fumbling with his scarf he pulled it tight round his chin and nose so only his eyes were exposed. The forest although he looked upon it as a friend and protector was clad in its dismal winter clothing, dark greys and dirty whites with the snow lying heavy on the branches, while lying dormant it seemed to be waiting for something to happen.

It would be another three months before it would start to awake, its branches frozen in time. Rance wondered how many of these young men would be dead and frozen by the end of the day, including himself.

By mid-day they'd crossed the River Pilica and gathered with other groups in the middle of a large 'U' shaped piece of land formed by the river. At the entrance to the 'U' shape a narrow dirt road had been built between two now frozen swamps which led to a small chapel. The two senior Commanders chose to keep Marek and his men here while they waited for news of the enemy.

They didn't have to wait long before the first rider came down the narrow road at full gallop stopping in a lather of rising steam with news of a German column sighted moving through the village of Clew, appearing to be heading towards Tuszyn.

'That's south of here not that far,' said Marek pointing at the map.

'This village next to Kozenin has been abandoned and is now empty. Here we could make our stand but we need a bait, something that will make sure they come to Kozenin'.

He stared at Rance and Krolik. 'A human bait would be best'.

Rance felt the now familiar tightening of his gut and looked at Krolik with a crooked smile.

'Just you and me to take on the whole German army Krolik, I guess that's fair odds.'

Krolik ignored him, staring at Marek

'That's not fair on the Englishman why do you expect him to have all the dirty jobs, besides which I think the job should go to a Pole?'

Marek bridled at being questioned, 'Every one of these men would volunteer if I asked them, but I want the best for such an important job,' he snapped.

Rance shrugged, 'Leave it Krolik, what else am I here for.'

Marek relaxed, 'We'll need at least six to eight men to make it worthwhile for the Germans to take the bait. You can ask for volunteers if it will make it easier,' he said to Krolik.

Viktor issued orders to move out. An hour later they reached Kozenin. Rance thought the Commanders had chosen well with the forest interspersed with small fields coming almost up to the village outskirts.

They set up the machine gun-nests amongst the trees covering the approaches with just one dirt road running through the centre of the village.

Men were placed in the deserted houses and more men hidden amongst the undergrowth under the command of Golab. Marek stayed on the tree line in view of them all with twenty men armed with the new German rifles.

Marek turned to Rance, 'When you and Krolik have sprung the trap you'll be under his command as reserves along with the twenty men I shall give him. Do you understand?'

Rance nodded and Krolik grinned at him. 'If only you would learn to speak more Polish you could have men to command as well,' Krolik joked.

Rance didn't care, all these years of running, hiding, the torture Cross's death. His eyes were slate grey and hard when they met and held Krolik's eyes.

Krolik's grin faded he had to look away he could see death staring at him, 'I'm glad you're on my side today,' he mumbled,

They set off with the six volunteers towards Tuszyn.

CHAPTER 21

Lieutenant Lohr's convoy entered the village of Brzezie early in the afternoon, he climbed stiffly from the halftrack it had been a long day.

He found himself carrying his bull whip and threw it back in the cab. There wouldn't be time for any games today. His mouth tightened into a straight line watching his troops herded the villagers down to his end of the village.

Slowly he walked amongst them, sometimes stopping to smile or pat a child. 'Don't be afraid he shouted, 'We not here to harm you, we only want to know where the bandits are?'

He stared at his highly polished boots waiting for an answer and when none was forthcoming he continued his walk.

Stopping in front of a nineteen year old girl he called to his interpreter.

'Tell her that I think she's a very beautiful young lady'.

She flashed him a shy smile and hugged her young nine year old brother. 'Don't be frightened,' she said reassuringly to the boy, 'It's going to be all right.'

Returning to the halftrack he slumped heavily in the passenger seat and lit a cigarette. His voice was casual when he blew the smoke from his lungs. 'Shoot them'.

He leaned back resting his head, and closing his eyes listened to the heavy machine guns clatter drowning out the screams.

The sudden silence made him glance at his watch. Two minutes, it must be a record he thought.

A sergeant came up and saluted. 'We've counted thirty two dead sir. Our information is that there should have been more. Do you want us to search the area?'

'No, we haven't time sergeant, get the men back, we move on to Tuszyn because the other villagers will have heard the shots and will almost certainly be running.'

Lohr hung on tightly to the dash-board as the vehicle bounced over the rough dirt track. 'Mind the pot-holes man,' he shouted angrily at the driver, 'where the hell did you learn to drive.'

The driver winced fixing his eyes steadfastly on the road ahead.

Fifteen minutes later they swept into the village of Tuszyn, the troops leapt from their still moving vehicles and moved amongst the houses. Lohr climbed down into the road and watched the search with an angry expression.

The sergeant returned to report 'There's no one here sir'.

He swore his temper flaring. 'Burn the place down,' he raged .

The driver of the halftrack never heard the shot that killed him. The bullet smashed through the windscreen and took the top off his head splattering Lohr with blood and brains.

A fusillade of gunfire followed sending him scrabbling to the ground screaming in anger and wincing with fear with the bullets whining all around him.

It was over as quickly as it began. Stunned he cautiously raised his head listening to the shouts of confusion as his troops hunted for the attackers. Another burst of gunfire sent him crouching down again. He was sweating he could feel the perspiration on his face and wiped at it, nearly collapsing as his fingers showed traces of blood, he cursed realizing it belonged to his driver.

'Find them, find the swine, hunt them down,' he screamed his voice hoarse. 'Get me another driver quickly., He looked around wildly. 'Where the hell are these bandits?'

There were about six or eight of them sir,' said the sergeant, pointing at a track, 'They ran off down there'.

Lohr pulled the dead man unceremoniously from the driving seat.

'You drive, come on lets go,' he shouted at the startled sergeant who jumped in crashed the gears and leapt down the track after the rest of the convoy.

Rance ran like he'd never run before, he was annoyed he'd missed the Lieutenant his new rifle must be aiming high and to the left. Behind him he could hear the high pitched roar of an army truck. He turned and holding his rifle against a tree took careful aim at a bend in the track and waited.

The heavy truck hampered by its width lumbered into view. Making allowances for the faulty sight he squeezed the trigger shattering the windscreen then turned and ran. The driver cut by flying glass panicked and ran into a tree bringing the rest of the convoy to a sudden halt.

Hurriedly the driver cleared his vision and reversed, swinging back onto the track and increasing his speed rapidly starting to overtake the running men again.

Rance could now see Kozenin in front of him the trees giving way to open fields. His vision blurred, a combination of sweat, exertion and fear with bullets whining around him throwing up sheets of ice and snow from the road.

He twisted on the run firing blindly over his shoulder at the fast overtaking trucks. At last Rance reached the buildings and threw himself down out of sight gasping air into his tortured lungs, his job done.

The enraged German troops smelt blood and behaved like hunting dogs oblivious to anything around them but the kill, they raced into the village. Lieutenant Lohr near the last truck was unable to enter and jumped down into the road. 'Kill them all, burn them out,' he was shouting in fury.

The troops piled out of the trucks and ran for the houses. The Partisan Commanders watching from the tree line raised their arms and waited as the machine-gunners lined their sights on the running soldiers while their feeders watched for the signal.

They waited until the troops were within twenty paces of the houses before bringing their arms down. Their shouted commands were lost in the hideous clatter of the machine guns and the screams of the men. A virtual wall of death swept down through the village centre. Trucks and men disintegrated under the onslaught while the ones still outside the village scattered towards the trees searching for cover.

Rance joined Krolik and the other reserves as they moved silently between the buildings looking for any survivors. There would be no mercy. Time had no meaning now as men on both sides died around him. Gradually the Germans gave way then broke running for the tree line under covering fire from some of their comrades who had escaped the original trap.

The village was theirs a great cheer erupted with Marek leading them in hot pursuit across the open space towards the trees.

'Dear God have we gone mad?' Rance shouted at Krolik as they ran side by side.

Lieutenant Lohr reached the tree line choking for breath and joined his troops who were desperately trying to set up a machine gun.

'It only needs two to do that,' he ranted.

'Spread out use your rifles and machine pistols hurry they're nearly here'.

Sporadic fire swept into the partisans caught in the open and Rance saw men fall all around him before he reached the cover of the trees

The return fire from a machine pistol flung the earth in his face and he rolled away desperately seeking shelter behind a giant pine. The rapid clatter of a heavy machine gun rent the air and bullets flicked viciously through the trees. He found Krolik and Galab with two others crouched behind a fallen log and joined them. Silently he motioned to them pointing back the way he'd come and hastily reloaded, finding he was on his last magazine.

The Germans came quietly dodging from tree to tree and Rance knew these were the best of the Waffen SS, tough experienced men who would be hard to stop. Rifle fire smashed into and around the fallen log and Rance frantically tried to dig himself into the ground. A stick hand-grenade landed at Golab's feet and he scrambled for it with the others looking on their eyes widening in fear. Grasping the handle he flipped it over his head where it exploded in mid-air sending shrapnel slicing down amongst them.

Bullets started coming in from the sides and his gun grew hot when he realised they were being outflanked. keeping his head down he fired his machine pistol wildly over the top. Golab's gun jammed, leaving only Krolik with any fire power. Silently he held up his fingers, eight bullets left. Rance grasped his pistol looking at the chamber, three bullets.

They all knew the rule. He looked up to see Golab staring at him, resigned to his fate.

'I haven't a pistol Rance, so you'll have to do it,' he said.

The firing around them seemed to be one continuous sound when Rance pointed the pistol at Golab's head who never flinched as his finger tightened on the trigger.

Lieutenant Lohr's initial panic had given way to a feeling of confidence now they'd broken free of the trap. Quietly he gave orders watching as they started to drive the partisans back towards the open fields, knowing once he had them there victory would be his.

Their advance stopped he frowned, angrily urging his men forward. 'Sergeant, what's the delay, get them moving.'

'Resistance sir, I'll take some men and work behind them, together we'll drive them out'.

Lohr moved some more of his men to the forest edge and waited for the bandits to break cover.

Rance pulled the trigger and Golab jumped in shock, his eyes widening in disbelief that he was still alive. The bullet which was meant for him killed a German trooper that had leapt on top of the fallen log. It was pure instinct on Rance's part that a split second before he pulled the trigger the soldier appeared and the bullet fired from the ground upwards drove through the trooper's chest and out through his neck.

A fierce fire fight had broken out on his left and Rance saw Marek with a group of his men inching forward under cover of their heavy machine guns which were now turning the forest into match wood. He risked a quick glance over the log and saw the Germans in retreat. Moving round to his right he removed the spare ammunition from under the dead German and joined Marek running with him by his side until they came out into open fields noticing they'd come in a semi-circle and were heading back towards the trucks.

Lieutenant Lohr, realising he was in the wrong place and was in danger of being cut off ordered his men to retreat and ran for his halftrack.

Rance and Marek coming under fire from the retreating troops stayed in the forest running parallel with them until they reached the trucks.

Marek was almost beside himself with anger and madness.

"He's getting away, he's getting away,' he ranted.

Rance, dropping on one knee took careful aim but his breathing was ragged and his hand shook, he couldn't keep the sight on the running figure. Taking a deep breath he tried again estimating the distance at least three hundred yards an almost impossible shot he thought. This time the sight wandered across the man's body and his finger closed on the trigger. He felt the rifle butt rebound into his shoulder.

With more than half his men either dead or wounded, Lohr's one thought was escape as he ran in a half circle out into the open back towards the trucks. He'd almost made it when a bullet smashed his elbow, travelling up his arm and out through the other side the force of it jerked him off his feet. He felt the seething pain then the numbness as he rolled in the snow. Shock and fear brought him back on his feet and he staggered, reaching for the door handle of the halftrack.

He never knew that it was the second bullet ricocheting off the vehicles door that sliced through the bridge of his nose taking out his right eye. He screamed and fell to his knees before he was helped by his sergeant who physically picked him up and threw him into the cab where he writhed in agony as the halftrack leapt forward, disappearing out of the village with the terror struck driver crouching low over the wheel.

Of the remaining troops, only fifteen made it clear of the village with the rest dying in a blood bath of revenge.

The sudden silence came as a shock to Rance when the last Germans died in the snow filled field and two trucks disappeared out of sight. His gun felt hot to his touch, he hadn't noticed before when he looked at the partisans running into the open their shouting and cheering echoing around him. His legs felt weak and he sat on the ground wiping the sweat from his forehead not cheering with the rest of the men, he felt no elation looking at the dead, dying and wounded troops.

He watched as the partisans moved amongst them striping the corpses and trying on their boots and clothing. Walking into the village he wished he hadn't. Everywhere the dead lay where they'd fallen, the blood already frozen into the ground. Moving amongst them were the dogs, abandoned by the villagers they were starving. Sickened, Rance turned away and returned to the open fields. Already the partisans had dragged the naked bodies into groups and were arranging them in the shape of a swastika. He couldn't blame them, understanding the hate that turned men into savages they had seen things done to their families that no man should have to witness and he watched dispassionately as they moved into the village searching for any Germans left alive.

Gestapo HQ Piotrekow

Lieutenant Lohr nearly died on the return to Piotrkow with the pain and loss of blood he was in shock. So the report that Schmidt handed to Major Schneller had been written by his sergeant driver.
He had to read it twice before it sank in his face going white, he could feel the rage boiling inside himself like some unchained monster trying to get out. His bulbous eyes seemed to devour the hapless Schmidt as he stood frozen to the spot in front of the desk listening to the voice ranting and raving about incompetence, sending them to the Russian front, shooting them for cowardice. He nodded vigorously, happy in the knowledge that it wasn't him getting the blame for a change.
For five minutes with Schmidt scribbling furiously on his pad, Schneller spat and drooled out his orders on how many hostages to take and hang, how many villages to destroy. How many more troops to request to do the job. Schmidt smirked to himself over that last one. There was no way he would be given more troops they were all needed now for the Russian front. He suddenly stopped scribbling. 'What was that last order sir? he quavered.
'You heard me Schmidt I'm putting you in the field. You'll work with Captain Braun and the other squads.' He prodded him with a stiff finger. 'I'll leave it up to you which hostages to take and which villages to burn.'

Schmidt swallowed. 'Yes sir,' he said meekly. He was depressed why was Schneller so vindictive towards him giving him such a job? He didn't deserve this. The way things were going it was like sentencing him to death or worse. If only he could get back into favour that would be half the battle. He straightened up and tried to look Schneller in the eye failing miserably.

'Is that a good idea sir? I was so close to finding out about the girl, and the information should be coming shortly from our two spies.'

Schneller's voice hissed with venom. 'Don't ever question whether any of my orders are a good idea Schmidt. You have three days and if nothing has happened by then I'll personally feed you to the bandits. One other thing Schmidt. Rewrite that report about the fire-fight Lohr was in, I'll recommend to Berlin that he gets the iron cross for bravery against overwhelming odds.'

CHAPTER 22

With the massive German manhunt still in progress after their defeat at Kozenin Marek decided to lay low and ordered that they split into smaller groups of no more than twenty, with some hiding amongst the local villagers, while his group would stay near to Kalow.

Izabel brought news that more hostages had been hanged and that a village had been burned before sitting at Jozef's table with Marian.

Strange voices from outside brought their conversation to a halt. Together they peered through the window to see Jozef talking to two men one tall with a hard face and the other thinner and shorter with eyes that were never still.

'I don't like the look of those two,' Izabel whispered.

'Me neither,' agreed Marian, 'but it takes all sorts to fight this war. I've seen worse my Father will sort them out.'

Jozef eyed the two men suspiciously, 'Where did you say you came from?'.

'The village of Drzewica, we saw the Englishman there but we didn't have chance to talk to him,' said the hard faced man seemingly unperturbed by Jozef's hostile stand. 'Pawel, that's the village leader, said if we want to fight then we should come and see you. If he's wrong then we're sorry to have bothered you but we don't know where else to go.'

Jozef softened his attitude, 'I have to be cautious you understand, there are so many informers and spies about. I think you're alright because you knew where the Englishman was, you could only have come from Drzewica to know that.'

He held out his hand. 'Welcome to the Polish Home Army and to hell,' he joked wincing at the iron grip of the hard faced man.

'My name is Czeslaw and this is my companion is Konstanty.'

Jozef shook the smaller man's hand who's grip felt like a wet rag. He didn't like either of them, but they were here to fight that's all that mattered.

He took them over to Radice and asked if they could bed down in his barn until he could get word to the partisans. Radice agreed and settled them down with a hot meal. They thanked him and watched him leave before sitting back grinning at each other.

Two days later Marian walked into Marek's camp bringing with her the two new recruits.

'Jozef says they have been checked and are all right,' she said to Marek, who walked over and shook their hands.

He called to Rance, 'Come and meet the new men'.

Rance stared into the hard brown eyes of the tall man who must have been well over six feet he thought, while he studied his face and looked as if he could handle himself in a fight.

The smaller man avoided Rance's direct gaze and looked to other man for support. Rance didn't like what he saw.

'Can you use a gun?' he asked.

'Only a hunting rifle,' lied the big man and the other just nodded.

Rance spent the next hour or so showing them how to use the various weapons at their disposal. They were quick to learn and he nodded his approval.

Marek finally received his orders the next day. To make reprisal raids against the new Volksdeutche villages. As he put it 'They burn our villages, we burn theirs.'

Rance took Marek to one side, 'I've told you before Marek, I won't kill civilians. Marek looked at him reproachfully. 'You should know me better than that.'

Rance wasn't to be put off, 'It's not you that bothers me, but some of the others have suffered terribly at the hands of the Germans can you control them in the heat of the moment?'

Marek started to get angry his eyes flashing stabbing at Rance with his finger. 'Have you ever seen me lose control of my men, well have you?'

He slapped away the pointing finger, 'There's always a first time Marek'.

'Don't you ever question my authority again Englishman,' he hissed though clenched teeth and turning his back stormed off leaving Rance to stare angrily after him.

'A difference of opinion eh,' murmured a voice behind him.

Rance's reaction was fast spinning round he almost caught the hard faced man off guard but he wasn't quiet fast enough and found himself held in a tight bear hug. He'd never heard the man come up behind him and was angry at himself.

The big man grinned down the back of Rance neck he stunk of Vodka. 'Steady now Englishman, I'm on your side remember'.

Rance heel came down hard on the man's foot and at the same time his elbow slammed into the man's ribs. The man grunted and let go backing off with arms outstretched

'No harm meant to you my friend,' he said.

Rance was still angry at Marek's words. 'Don't ever come up on me like that again, do you understand?' he snapped.

The man stared at him his eyes dark and unfriendly. Rance could see danger there and realized that here was a man that would have to be watched.

'I think you should go and sleep off the effects of the Vodka,'

The man seemed to change, as if realizing he'd gone too far.

'Sorry, the Vodka has always been my failing,' he mumbled stumbling away.

Rance watched him leave with an uneasy feeling eating at him.

A thick layer of fresh snow made the going tough that night in the seemingly impenetrable darkness of the forest. Rance trod carefully in the footprints of the man in front. The temperature had plummeted to well below freezing in the last hour turning the snow into the crisp solidness of ice. Occasionally the sharp crack of a tree splitting one of its branches under the extra weight forced by the ice could be heard.

When he'd first heard that sound it had unnerved him but now he could tell the difference between that and the enemy. He was uneasy although he wasn't sure why, he felt the presence of the hard faced man behind him and it made his skin crawl, but some sixth sense worried him. Where was the smaller man? he hadn't come with them for some reason. He must ask Marek at the first rest time.

They skirted Sulejow, crossed the Kiele then the Radom road and stopped on the outskirts of a large village which was quiet except for a solitary barking dog somewhere amongst the houses.

Rance crawled through the snow to the edge of the forest and studied it. They were at a cross roads of four dirt tracks running through the centre and in the middle he could see the outline of a German outpost surrounded by barbed wire. All the houses and barns looked in good condition and he could hear the occasional noise of cattle inside, which was in sharp contrast to the Polish villages.

They edged their way forward using the houses as cover, Rance found himself in the company of Golab and Jarek. He couldn't see Marek or the hard faced man and was annoyed that he hadn't had a chance to speak to Marek about the man's partner.

It was a dog that gave them away let out by its owner it immediately attacked the nearest partisan who shot it dead. A star shell fired from the German outpost illuminated the whole area, showing several of the partisans already inside the wire compound. There were twelve soldiers ten sleeping in the bunker leaving two on sentry duty. Golab shot the one who had the flare gun still in his hand and the other died coming out the bunker carrying two hot drinks.

The men inside the bunker awoke panic stricken, scrambling around in the dark, searching for their clothes and weapons. Golab kicked open the door and stood to one side as Jarek threw in two hand-grenades.

Rance counted the seconds while listening to the screams of the men inside fighting each other to escape. The bunker erupted in fire and smoke blowing off the earth roof while exploding ammunition flew out the firing slits and door. All around the village partisans were kicking in the doors, dragging the frightened occupants out into the snow covered road.

A villager appeared with a hunting rifle and immediately dropped it thrusting his hands in the air as Marek fired a burst over his head.

The partisans then systematically wrecked every house and barn, before forcing the villagers to throw all their food onto the fiercely burning outpost. Rance tried to shut his ears to the sound of the women and children screaming in pure terror.

He felt sick. It didn't matter that the voices were Volksdeutsches, they were civilians. He walked down the long line of shivering villagers and forgetting himself called out in English that they weren't going to hurt them. Hearing an English voice they were stunned into silence and stared at him in frightened astonishment.

It had begun to snow again, great snowflakes swirled about them made more dramatic by the red glow of the fire and shooting sparks reaching up into the night sky. The sound of breaking glass made him turn. All the windows were being smashed throughout the village and a house went up in flames making the villagers cower back. He looked at the shivering crying children and shouted at Marek. 'Leave the houses intact man these children will surely die without shelter'.

Marek hesitated and seeing this Rance ran forward his face a mask of fury. 'I warn you Marek don't be like these bastards,' his voice shook with anger.

Marek shrugged and called his men to leave the houses, he walked down the line of silent shivering people.

'I want you to take a message to the Gestapo chiefs,' he shouted in their frightened faces,

'Tell them that from now on we have declared war on all German villages, and if they attack any more Polish ones then we attack in kind.'

He had to raise his voice now as the weather had worsened, blowing with blizzard conditions.

'If we have to come back we'll kill you all. You make sure they understand that.'

Rance felt depressed at the turn of events when Marek led them back into the forest away from the devastated village. This war had now degenerated into a savagery that he couldn't comprehend he forced himself to put it out of his mind concentrating instead on staying alive.

A gentle breeze stirred on the Central Siberian Plateau in Russia, swirling over the frozen wastes with temperatures reaching minus forty degrees. Slowly it moved west and gathering strength swept over and through the Ural Mountains, stripping clean the loose snow that had just fallen on its sides, all the time its power growing as it pushed on westwards freezing the people of Moscow and lashing at the two fighting armies of Russia and Germany bringing with it giant snow filled clouds that rose high in the air holding on to their heavy burden.

The wind now a frightening power of nature having freed itself from the confines of the mountains swept across Central Poland screaming in a blind fury finally letting go its snow and ice burden.

The almighty blizzard hit shrieking all around him making his face a mask of frozen ice, Rance staggered on desperately trying to follow the man in front and like ghosts dressed in white they crossed back over the Radom and Kiele roads knowing that no German patrols would be out. The wind howled in unbeatable fury hurtling snow into great drifts that would swallow a man in seconds if he fell.

A man did fall laying unnoticed until someone almost fell over him. Two men tried to pick him up, Rance stopped to help but the man had frozen to death before their eyes. Silently they dropped him back into his snowy grave and staggered on still trying to follow the man in front. Rance slipped on something which almost brought him down. Swaying he stared at a discarded rifle, not daring to pick it up knowing that if he fell he wouldn't have the strength to regain his feet.

A voice cried from somewhere in the night, 'Help me, oh please God help me.' Rance looked round but was blinded by the wind driven snow which closed his eyes to mere slits. He clung to a tree rubbing to clear them as the voice faded. He stared into the impenetrable freezing blackness but all around was nothing but the howling of the wind through the trees, he felt himself being pushed from behind and a voice growled at him to keep moving.

Kantor the German agent lay on his raft of branches pretending to be sleep, he'd only just got back in time from his trip to their man in Blezun. Now he lay watching as the partisans returned to the campfires. Looking at the condition they were in he was glad he hadn't gone with them although it had been tough enough for him. He saw Mueller staring in his direction and gave a brief nod as a signal of his success. Even now the agent would be getting the message to Braun. They hadn't found the girl yet, but two out of three wasn't bad going.

Kalow

It hadn't snowed for a week now and the weather had turned a few degrees warmer. They'd lost two men on their return journey from that fateful village and because Rance had been with Viktor's group for the last few days he'd forgotten to ask about the hard faced man's companion, and in the end thought it possible he'd been there after all. German patrols had increased since the raid with the main aim of finding the partisans. Jozef met Izabel on his porch. Her face was red from the keen wind and the exertion of her walk from Przglow 'And what good news do you bring to-day?' was his opening remark.

Izabel smiled and followed him inside where she met Marian,

'I've brought orders for Marek. It's a small factory north of Piotrkow. Curen wants it raided because the Volksdeutche have taken it over. Where's your wife, Jozef?' she asked.

Jozef's face became tense, 'I've sent her over the river to stay with friends just as a precaution you understand, but now I think the danger of reprisals have passed.'

He nodded at Marian, 'She's like you stubborn, and refused to go. So, Marian will stay and keep you company until you leave and I'll take the message to Marek, I want to see him anyway.'

They spent a pleasant evening together with Radice and his boys talking and joking almost forgetting the war.

Jozef got up early the next morning and left to find Marek. Izabel watched him go then said goodbye to Marian, kissing her on the cheek.

'Are you sure you'll be all right here on your own?'

Marian smiled, 'I'm not on my own I have Radice and his two sons here and also there is our other neighbour he's like an uncle to me. My father wouldn't have left me otherwise so don't worry,' she answered. 'Now you get along while the weather's good'.

Reluctantly Izabel left. The once firm snow had turned to slush in the warmer weather and the track had become muddy and uncomfortable to walk on so she kept to the edge of the forest, preferring to walk between the trees.

An hour later she heard German voices and moved further away from the track and hid behind a tree praying they wouldn't notice her footprints in the snow. They walked past and risking a glance at the retreating figures she bit her lip when she recognised Lieutenant Schmidt with another officer in the lead, and counted at least fifty soldiers dressed in full white camouflage uniforms. She made a mental note to tell Curen because that was a new development then became frightened when she realised where they were heading.

There could be only one place on that track. Kalow, she panicked, she had to get ahead of them to warn Marian and the others.

She went deeper into the forest in an attempt to go in a semi-circle trying to beat them but came to a dead end, her way blocked by fallen trees and impenetrable undergrowth. Twice she slipped and fell in the melting snow before finally being reduced to a walk. Tears came to her eyes. She knew she wouldn't get there in time.

Kalow

Captain Braun halted before they reached the clearing and ordered his men to spread out. Silently they moved forward amongst the trees, almost invisible in their camouflage uniforms against the snow. Schmidt trembling with fatigue wiped his sweating face. He cursed Schneller and Braun for ordering him to do this he wasn't built for it and all the horrible mud and snow was ruining his new boots. Ahead he could see a clearing and in it there were people moving about. Two men chopping wood and a young girl stacking it into piles against a small wooden house. Nervously he looked for armed guards but couldn't see any. He began to feel more confident and checked once again to see his safety catch was off.

It was Radice's sixteen year old son who first saw the troops silently crossing the open clearing.

'Father,' his voice trailed to a whisper.

Startled! Radice straightened still holding the axe and looked for an escape route but found none. He dropped the axe, trying not to show fear. 'Welcome to our houses, can we help you in anyway?' he asked politely.

There were two officers, one Captain and one fat slovenly looking Lieutenant. The Captain immaculately dressed as if he'd just come on parade smiled. 'Who might you be? introduce yourselves,' he said.

Radice clenched his fists feeling his palms becoming moist. Slowly he gave the officer their names, waiting while the fat Lieutenant wrote them down in a small note book.

"Where is everyone else?'

'There is no one else'.

The officer's smile turned to a scowl. 'Search the houses,' he snapped.

Radice watched the soldiers in consternation as they searched inside the houses throwing everything outside into the snow. A sergeant came up and saluted, 'Nothing here sir, no weapons or people'.

Braun looked around and pointed to the giant oak standing stark and naked against the grey overcast winter sky.

'Take them over there,' he ordered.

Radice swallowed hard his throat suddenly dry finding it hard to breath.

'I won't beg for myself but leave the girl and my sons they're young and have done nothing wrong,' he exclaimed.

Skubisz, their neighbour stood rigidly to attention his face impassive before saying, 'If you want hostages then take me and leave the others alone.'

Braun smirked, 'How very touching'.

Izabel arrived at the edge of the clearing her breast heaving, fighting air into her tortured lungs as she watched the scene unfold.

Herman Braun nodded to Marian standing next to Radice.

'Stand in the centre next to the tree'.

'Radice put his arms around his son's shoulders.

'Face them bravely boys don't let them see your afraid,' he whispered.

The youngest whimpered and became still.

Marian blinked back the tears that had started to trickle down her cheeks her eyes never leaving the face of the immaculately dressed officer in front of her when he lifted his machine pistol level with his waist.

In her mind everything seemed to be in slow motion watching the man's eyes narrow to dark cold pools of death as he pulled the trigger. The clatter of the machine gun made her scream and closing her eyes tightly she could feel wetness on her face and neck as she slid down the tree trunk and on to the ground.

Izabel watching forced a fist into her mouth to stop the scream escaping, for to do so would bring about her own death. Feeling sick she looked on at the horror which had unfolded before her.

Gasping in shock she saw the officer grab Marian by the hair and drag her upright where she stood covered in blood swaying from side to side.

The Captain laughed, 'I haven't touched you bitch. That's the blood of your friends you're wearing. 'I've decided to let you live so you can say how generous we Germans are. How merciful.'

Schmidt sniggered. Now this was something to write home about, the first good deed of the war he thought.

Savagely Braun pushed the crying girl back on top of the dead bodies and without a backward glance ordered his men to move out..

Izabel waited until they were out of sight before running to Marian who jumped in fright at her touch. Izabel grasped the terrified girl whispering that they must flee in case the Germans returned. Together the two girls staggered back to the track and headed for Blezun.

CHAPTER 23

Jozef walked around the clearing at Kalow examining what was left of the houses and stopped at the four mounds of earth.

'One day I'll return and give them a decent burial,' he said bitterly.

'You must be thankful they spared your daughter, Jozef,' said Marek.

'They didn't do it to be merciful I'm sure. It's just another one of their sadistic ways, they like to play at being God deciding who will live and who will die'.

'One thing for sure, you won't be able to return here Jozef, not in the foreseeable future anyway, there are still a lot of patrols coming through this area.'

Jozef sighed, 'Your right about that now we can't use Kalow, I'll join you and the others we'll have to use another place for contact with Curen'.

"What about your daughter Marian?'

"I've arranged that she stays with Izabel and her friend Maria until I can get her to her mother across the river. In the meantime she will be safe there as anywhere else.'

Marek shouldered his machine pistol and they left. Jozef stopped at the edge of the clearing for one last look at the four graves under the giant oak before he turned and followed Marek into the forest.

The weather had turned cold again and Rance shivered as the temperature frequently dropped below freezing, he was suffering like the others in his group with frostbite, starvation and the never ending battle with the lice that drove him mad. He spent the time moving from Marek to Viktor's group and everywhere they went the Germans seemed to appear, bitter battles were fought which took its toll with men dying of their wounds through lack of medicine and food.

Izabel and Rance only met fleetingly when she delivered her messages at prearranged meeting places usually a foresters hut. She was shocked at Rance's appearance as time went by. Not just Rance, but all the men were tired or ill, looking dirty and unkempt always sleeping in their clothes never washing, only able to light small fires at night but as the reports came in she realised they still fought with a savagery that equally matched their enemy.

Mueller and Kantor were frustrated. Twice they'd attempted to follow the girl only to be waylaid by pressure from the group either moving out or other duties.

'We pass information one more time and if we can't trap them all we should take care of the Englishman and Marek,' Mueller declared.

Kantor agreed as he slowly horned his knife. 'Even Schneller could ask no more of us. How these bandits keep going I don't know, but I've had enough I can tell you.'

'They've received orders to sabotage and blow up a train south of Tomaszow in two days' time,' said Mueller 'I think we should try and get a message to the man in Blezun'.

Kantor wasn't happy about that and said so. 'There isn't much time and it will mean a daytime trip into the village. Very risky.'

'No more than going out on one of their patrols,' said Mueller.

'Then you do it,' countered Kantor, 'Why is it always me that has to go?'

'Because I'm fucking well telling you, that's why.'

'Why can't we just kill Marek and the Englishman and be done with it?' the small man grunted.

Mueller lost patience, 'Because you little rat Schneller is a madman, we both know it. Unfortunately he doesn't so we have to show that we've tried to trap them and find out where the girl is living.'

He spat on the ground in disgust. 'Do you want to face him and say we've failed?'

Kantor didn't like that idea and quietly slipped away.

Two hours later he approached the village of Przglow relieved there were very few people about. Somehow it looked different in daylight, perhaps it was because he felt more exposed. Cursing his luck he pulled his hat down lower and not daring to look round knocked gently on the agent's door.

He heard a child start to cry inside and a man swearing at it. The door remained shut. 'Who's that?' a voice queried.

'Open the door damn you and let me in,' Kantor snarled.

Cautiously the door opened slightly and Kantor pushed hard stepping quickly inside only to find a shotgun pressed against his nose. He stepped back in alarm.

'Put that fucking thing down,' he exclaimed his voice shaking.

'What the hell are you doing here in daylight you put us all at risk. These people don't play games,' countered the agent.

'Shut up and listen', Kantor fumed, ten minutes later with the information passed on Kantor stepped outside and turned to go and as the agent started to shut the door behind him Kantor went rigid with shock on seeing the girl they were after walking down the track past the house. For a second he panicked before throwing himself back inside passing the startled agent. Kantor stared his eyes still wide with shock

'That's her, that's the one outside what the hell is she doing here? he asked hoarsely.

The agent peered cautiously through the curtains. 'Oh her she lives at the other end of the village with her mother and a friend. She's been here since Christmas her papers are in order I had them checked without her knowing.

Kantor was beside himself with glee. 'Get a message to Major Schneller at Gestapo HQ immediately. Tell him that we've found the girl and make sure that you mention us you understand.

Kantor was sure the girl hadn't seen him and if she had would she recognise him? He shook his head. No he was certain.

'What luck, the Gods are with us this day,' he chortled.

Izabel walked on the other side of the track as she approached the suspected agent's house keeping her head lowered her eyes restlessly watching for any movement. It was always the same every time she passed that house he would always seem to appear never speaking, just staring. Unconsciously she quickened her pace groaning under her breath as the door opened. When the man the partisan's call Konstanty walked out she nearly died with shock and forced herself through sheer will power to act naturally. She carried on as if nothing was amiss but out of the corner of her eye she saw him turn and hurry back inside. Her legs felt weak but she refused to panic. At all costs she mustn't let him suspect she'd seen him.

Anya cried out in fright when Izabel bounded through the front door with Maria and Marian following close behind.

'Mother get your things together we have to move out,'

Anya's eyes widened with alarm 'What's happened, are the Germans coming?' she stammered.

'Not yet, but they soon will be,' said Izabel, stuffing the pistol Curen had given her into a coat pocket before pulling on a woollen hat.

'Now listen carefully mother, Maria and Marian are going to take you to a village called Aleksandrow.' She stopped her mother's protest by holding up her hand. 'Listen to me, Maria has relations there who help the partisans from time to time, you will be safe.'

Anya grabbed her daughter's arm tightly. 'What about you, where are you going?'.

'Jarek, Rance along with Marek and the others have been betrayed,' whispered Izabel tears in her eyes, 'I have to try and warn them. Even now it may be too late, but I must try.'

Krolik joined Marek and his men at the prearranged spot on the way to the railway line south of Tomaszow. With him were a dozen men. Rance shook hands with Jarek, slapping him on the back and recognised some of the others as having fought alongside them in previously battles. They welcomed him warmly. All except the hard faced man who called himself Czeslaw.

Krolik nudged Rance, 'What's the matter with him?'

'His friend's gone missing,' answered Golab, 'Marek is furious.'

Rance gave the hard face man a sideways glance. We should ask him, he should know. Czeslaw stepped forward with fists clenched, his face red with anger.

'What are you implying Englishman,' he hissed.

Marek jumped between them, 'That's enough. We have a job to do,' he gave Rance a warning look. 'Save your fighting for the Germans.'

Rance cursed himself for being a fool and antagonising the big man. Now he would have to watch his back more carefully than ever.

'Here comes Konstanty now,' shouted one of the sentries and when they all stared as he entered the camp he stared back with a puzzled expression on his face. 'Co jest takie smieszne?;

Jarek slapped him on the back grinning. 'Don't ask'.

The big man grunted and stumped into the forest Kantor went to follow. 'Kantor,' Marek's voice was clear but the tone was full of anger.

Kantor turned around and froze as he looked down the barrel of Marek's gun. The men fell silent watching the drama unfold. Rance looked at Marek aware of his finger tightening round the trigger of his rifle

'My orders were for you not to leave camp without consulting me first,' Marek said coldly.

Kantor backed away his face white. 'You didn't tell me that, or I didn't hear you. For God's sake don't shoot me.'

'You disobeyed an order,' and the retort of the rifle made every one flinch. A low murmur swept through the men as Kantor remained standing.

'You're not hurt, that was just a warning. Don't ever do that to me again,' snapped Marek.

Kantor swallowed hard and hurried after Mueller who stopped out of sight of the camp.

'Well, did you get the message out all right?' he enquired, completely oblivious to Kantor's shaking.

'I really thought he was going to shoot me,' stuttered Kantor.

'Never mind that,' said Mueller impatiently, 'What happened?'

Mueller's eyes gleamed at the news as Kantor related it to him.

'At last we can finish it. What a bit of luck, well done Kantor.'

Kantor seemed to forget his narrow escape with death, 'I want the Englishman,' he stated eagerly.

Mueller shook his head, 'No, I'm afraid not. He belongs in my gun sights. You can have Marek.'

'What will Schneller say?'

Mueller shrugged, 'We tell him we had no choice they were getting away.'

They returned to camp and silently walked behind Rance and Marek as they continued on their way towards the railway line.

Izabel studied the map in front of her finding the place where Marek was to sabotage the train. It was an ideal spot that Curen had picked, a small railway halt called Bratkow, situated just to the west of Tomasowek. It was surrounded on three sides by forest and a large swamp on the east side. She traced a small track on the map that led to some kind of building and thought perhaps it was a house or forester's hut. There they were going to rest while they waited for the train. She decided her best chance to find them would be there.

Time was running out and she forced herself to remain calm they had a head start but would be skirting the town of Sulejow. She could make up time by going directly through the town, although there was a large German garrison situated in the centre and a manned road block on the only bridge across the River Pilica.

The early morning air was cold and crisp. Dawn was just breaking into a cloudless sky when she set out. With only a day and night to get there she couldn't afford to lose any time so keeping off the main road she stayed with the local railway line that ran parallel with it and made good time with the track well-worn and free of any obstacles.

Arriving on the outskirts of Sulejow at ten o'clock and carefully avoiding the main road she wandered through the back streets of the small town. Very few people were about and she felt frightened and exposed, at the end of one of the streets she could see the bridge with its humped back in the centre and across the hump lay the road block with red and white barrels placed in the middle. It looked terrifying, not only were there guards on the bridge but also patrolling the streets on both sides of the river.

She thought of the pistol in her pocket, to be caught with that would mean certain death. Retracing her steps away from the bridge she found an overgrown garden, and pushing her way through the undergrowth until she was hidden from view she tore a strip of material from her underskirt and bound the pistol tightly to the top and back of her leg hoping it wouldn't show. Now walking slowly to keep the pistol in place she made her way back to the bridge.

It still wasn't busy enough with only a few people crossing so she wandered back into the side streets again and glanced at her watch. Eleven o'clock, she'd wasted an hour and feeling agitated made her way back again. It was slightly busier. Dare she risk it? She decided she had no choice it was either go over the bridge now or turn back. Feeling sick with nerves she ventured onto the bridge knowing she was in full view of the sentries and had past the point of no return. Walking in front of her was an old couple and a young girl so she stayed close to them. The barrier swung up and a German staff car crept around the barrels with a high ranking officer sitting in the back.

The four guards stood to attention and saluted. Izabel cringed at the raised arms, hating the sight. The young girl who looked to be about sixteen halted at the barrier and produced her papers. The guard said something and Izabel strained her ears trying to listen. It sounded as if the guard was being difficult twice going through her papers before making her stand over by the parapet where he forced her arms in the air and ran searching hands over her body, watched by his grinning colleges.

Izabel forced herself to remain calm although her heart was racing, she could almost taste the fear in her drying mouth. Desperately she looked for a way out. The old lady in front started to lean more heavily on her husband and quickly Izabel stepped forward,

'Here, let me help you, your wife looks tired,' she whispered.

Startled the old man replied, 'Yes she is, you see she is only just getting over an illness and I think this walk is too much for her'.

Izabel smiled at the old woman, 'Just lean on me and I'll help you across, by the way what's your name?'

The old woman gratefully transferred her weight to Izabel,

'Maria, and my husband's name is Jan,' she answered wearily 'What's your name?'

Izabel was watching the guards as she answered,

'Izabel, I'm going to visit friends on the other side of the river.'

'I'm going to see my sister,' said the old man, 'she hasn't been well either'.

The old woman started to get flustered, 'I hope everything is all right here. What are they doing to that poor girl?' she asked in a quavering voice.

'Don't you worry about that they're just searching her that's all', said Izabel.

'I hope they don't do that to me,' huffed the old woman.

One of the watching guards came over. 'What are you saying old woman?' his words were spoken in perfect Polish and Izabel flinched thinking her luck had just run out.

Startled, the old lady stared blankly at the soldier.

It was Izabel who spoke first. 'My friend Maria only said that she hoped the soldier wasn't going to do that to her,' and much to her surprise the man burst out laughing.

Turning the sentence round he shouted to the soldier mauling the young girl, 'Hey Carl, the old lady said she hopes you'll do that to her next'.

Carl turned, and seeing the old woman pretended to be sick. All four roared with laughter.

Izabel forced a false smile and the tension was broken, still chuckling they glanced at her papers and asked where they were going. Izabel answered, 'To see friends,' and they waved them through.

Izabel said goodbye to the elderly couple and chose the river road that led north from the town and into the forest. Once out of sight of the town she slipped the pistol back into her pocket and looked at her watch, one o'clock and with the weather still settled she was relieved it had gone so well.

She followed a forest road, occasionally having to detour round a village unsure whether they were Volksdeutche or Polish. Consulting her map she turned north east and within an hour she was lost. Frantically she looked for the right way but there were so many tracks more than on the map and all leading off in so many directions.

Gestapo HQ Piotrekow

Schmidt didn't attempt to conceal his delight while watching Major Schneller read the report. In it was all a man could hope for.

{ The discovery and subsequent destruction of the partisan's main recruitment centre and HQ at Kalow, the penetration of the main group of bandits by two agents. The discovery of the whereabouts of the girl and her mother. Finally, information about the forthcoming attack on a train at Bratkow.}

Schmidt all but rubbed his hands together his grin gradually fading as Schneller's face became uglier. What was the matter with the man was he never satisfied? Schmidt reverted back to his normally depressed self.
Schneller carefully placed the report down on his desk.
'Well Schmidt, what have you done about setting a trap for these bandits at Bratkow?' he enquired in a deceptively quiet voice.
'Why, as yet nothing sir, I thought I would await your orders on the subject,' Schmidt stuttered.
Seeing the thunder clouds start to build in Schneller's face he rushed on, 'I really didn't think I had the authority with something as important as this sir,' he said squirming uncomfortably under the gaze of the bulbous eyes.
Schneller relaxed but kept his eyes fixed on his sweating Lieutenant.
'You're quiet right Schmidt you haven't the intelligence for this sort of thing as you so elegantly put it.'
He climbed to his feet and walked over to a wall map beckoning Schmidt to join him, pointing at Bratkow.
'We'll let the train proceed on its journey but instead of carrying supplies we will fill it full of Waffen SS troops. You will inform Braun that he is to move his men at once to the forest around the area in question and so cut off any escape route they may try to take if there is any chance some of them surviving the main trap.'
Going back to his desk he shuffled the report back into its envelope.

'Are the agents still with the bandits?'

Schmidt shuffled his feet he hadn't asked about the agents,

'Of course sir,' he blustered.

'Do they still understand that I want the Englishmen alive if possible?'

'Of course sir, I made that most plain to them,' he mumbled, hoping Schneller believed him.

'You and I Schmidt are going to find that girl and her mother. It's time we brought everything to a logical conclusion don't you think?'

'When do we go sir?' Schmidt inquired.

'Why Schmidt, how keen of you to ask,' countered Schneller brightly. 'Tomorrow of course the day of the ambush. Rather appropriate don't you think?'

CHAPTER 24

Bratkow

Long shadows cast by the last of the weak winter sun turned the forest into gloom as Marek led his men into a building situated at the end of the track near Bratkow. It looked to Rance to have been used as a storage place for tree cutting machinery. Now because of the war it lay empty and deserted. The men lit a small fire outside as soon as it got dark and cooked their slices of dried pork.
While Marek posted sentries the rest of the men settled down inside and for the next two hours they stripped and cleaned their weapons.

Rance was annoyed at the hard faced man who called himself Czeslaw, he always seemed to be following him around. His annoyance had now turned to unease when twice in the last hour he'd caught the man staring at him. Mueller seeing he'd been noticed got up and ambled over to sit next to Kantor turning his back to Rance.

Kantor looked up with a quizzical expression, 'What's the matter with you?' he asked,.

'How can we get at Marek and the Englishman stuck in this barn with all the others?'

Kantor shrugged, 'I thought you were the clever one, you work it out.'

'Don't get clever with me', retorted Mueller angrily. 'If you haven't thought about it, then listen to me. Tomorrow the train comes and Schneller is bound to have troops on board. He'll also have troops come by road to cut off any chance of escape that way. Well, I don't know about you, but I don't want to be around when that happens.'

By the look on Kantor's face, Mueller realised the little man hadn't even given it any thought at all.

'We could be trapped right in the middle', Kantor groaned.

'Give the man a medal,' said Mueller despairingly.

'What shall we do?'

'I think we should wait until tomorrow there'll be no chance tonight. Sometime in the morning Marek and the Englishman will go to reconnoitre the area before the trains due. If we can kill them we'll leave immediately the train is sighted but If we can't manage to do it, we should leave anyway and certainly not wait for that train'.

Kantor nodded in agreement, 'What shall we do afterwards? Schneller won't be happy with that. Especially if they escape the trap'.

'There's no way they'll escape this time they haven't a chance, and not only that we make him a present of the girl. We know where she is so we just go and get her,' said Mueller.

Izabel saw the barn before she saw the two men repairing it, she hesitated, almost stopping, as if surprised to see them there.

With undisguised interest the two men ceased work to watch the approach of the young woman who even wearing a heavy overcoat walked with a feminine swing to her graceful figure.

'Now what would a young woman like that be doing here?' mused the older man of the two

Izabel tried to appear at ease in front of the men who were obviously farm workers by their appearance. The older man stepped forward into the centre of the track blocking her way.

'I haven't seen you around here before?' he said as a question raising one shaggy eyebrow. His Polish accent carried a hint of German. Volksdeutches! Her heart sank she put on a smile and tried to overcome his menacing attitude. 'Well no, I'm lost you see. I was trying to get to Smardzewice where I will be starting a new job'.

The other man joined them standing to one side.

'Now what would a peasant Polish girl like yourself be doing with a job in such a big town? Surely there must be hundreds of people who would love to have a job already living there, what makes you so special?'

He took a step closer, she took a step back, becoming alarmed at the way things were going.

The younger man interrupted, 'Where have you come from anyway?'

Izabel's eyes flashed in anger, 'Which question do I answer first,' she snapped instantly regretting losing her temper.

'Don't get clever with us my girl, snarled the older man, you're the one that's lost, not us.'

'If you can't be civil and help me, I'll be on my way,' she exclaimed.

'Where to you're lost remember?' retorted the younger one and stepped behind her.

Izabel quickly stepped to one side.

The older man glanced round with a theatrical expression.

'Well, well, now look whose lost and nobody knows you're here except us two fine men. We know where we are, don't we Mark?

Mark nodded no longer smiling, his face ugly.

Now alarmed Izabel twisted round and tried to leave.

The older one grabbed her left arm in a vice like grip making her cry out in pain, the other man lunged forward only to reel back in agony as her boot caught him in the groin.

Izabel saw the fist coming and rolled her head so the full force of the blow missed her face catching her on the side of the head.

In a daze she staggered almost falling to her knees. The older man laughed as he dragged her towards the barn with the younger one limping after them mouthing obscenities. Desperately she fumbled for the pistol in her pocket and slashed at the older man's face who screamed in pain instantly releasing his grip.

She lashed out again breaking his nose and blood spurted down his coat front. With her face twisted with rage she swung the pistol towards the younger man who on seeing it stopped dead in his tracks, his face suddenly grey.

Her rage knew no bounds she pulled back the hammer backing away from them both.

'Die you Volksdeutche pigs,' she screamed her vision clouding over in a red mist.

The younger man fell to his knees crying, leaving the older one to cower away holding his face and groaning,

'Please don't do it lady we were only joking.' His head sank to his chest which heaved in terror. Izabel stepped behind him forcing the barrel of the pistol against the back of his head. He screamed and wet himself, only stopping when she thrust the map under his bloody dripping nose.

'Now you snivelling little man, show me the way'.

With a shaking hand he pointed to where they were and traced a path to the Smardzewice road.

'It's not far only two kilometres,' he whispered kneeling and shaking in the mud.

Eighteen months ago she would have felt sorry for him she wouldn't even have been in this situation. War changes everything. She pulled the trigger, the loud report of the pistol shot was followed by his scream of agony as she'd shifted her aim and sliced his ear in half. He rolled on the wet earth convinced he was dying as blood flowed down his neck and over his collar. 'Help me, please don't shoot me again,' he cried looking up into the smoking barrel of the gun.

She turned to the younger man, who was watching with a feeling of dread, his eyes bulging. He shrank away paralysed and could only choke watching her finger tighten on the trigger again. Looking at his contorted face while he sat on the ground a stain covering the front of his trousers she slowly lost the red mist before her eyes.

The madness drained away leaving her feeling ashamed she could do such a thing. 'Help your friend into the barn,' she said woodenly.

Relieved, the young man half carried half dragged the wounded man inside where they both sat wide eyed in terror convinced she was still going to shoot them both.

Izabel levelled her pistol and they closed their eyes.

'For your information I'm not on my own soon I'll be meeting friends. If you attempt to leave this barn today they'll know and they'll kill you and any of your family, is that understood?'

They nodded vigorously.

She slammed the doors and because the lock was broken wedged them shut with a piece of timber. Walking all around the barn to satisfy herself that they couldn't escape quickly, she left.

On reaching a bend in the road she turned for one last glance at the silent barn still not believing what she'd just done. Gone was the young girl, now what had emerged was a confident and dangerous woman.

Rance spent the rest of the morning wandering around with Marek, Jozef and Krolik finalizing the details for their attack on the train. He pulled his coat belt tighter against the cold and wet. It had hardly stopped raining all night and the ground was sodden. Standing by the deserted station halt Rance stared across the track to the edge of the swamp watching thick wisps of fog swirl above the clumps of dead grasses and the stunted trees that clung to an uncertain life.

The water gleamed with an oily sheen while mud coloured bubbles slowly oozed to the surface and even from where he stood he could smell the decay. Rance thought he'd never seen such a cold and uninviting place and was glad to be on the other side of the track.

The fog closed in shutting it from his view. He turned away suddenly stopping to stare into the surrounding forest, he could have sworn there was a fleeting shadow amongst the undergrowth. The hairs stood up on the back of his neck he slipped the safety catch off his gun and listened to the sounds of the forest.

A flock of birds lifted off to his right, he knew someone was there and could sense he was being watched. Certainly not German troops he would be dead by now. Quietly he walked forward stopping every few metres to listen. Occasionally he heard the faintest of rustling sometimes on his right sometimes on his left. Two of them working ahead of him. Who? he pondered.

There was only two he could think of. The hard faced man, Czeslaw and his companion Konstanty but why play games?

He knew they didn't like him but they didn't seem to like anybody else either.

He listened, silence. Whoever it was had either gone or was waiting for him to approach them. He decided not to play their game, slowly backing away, his eyes restlessly covering every inch of ground.

Mueller cursed slowly lowering his rifle when his target disappeared from view, he should have fired earlier when he had the chance but he really wanted to do it quietly with his hands.

He looked across at Kantor who shrugged and put away his knife.

Rance went to meet Marek and Krolik.

'Somebody's been following me back there,' he said.
'We were just discussing the same thing,' echoed Marek.
'Did you see anybody?'
'No, perhaps just a shadow nothing more then a feeling of being watched ' said Rance.
'Well if there was anybody here they've gone now so let's get back to the men and plan the attack,' said Marek.

Marek looked at the men gathered around him in the barn, 'Where's Czeslaw and Konstanty,' he asked.

'They've been missing for the last hour we thought they were with you,' answered one of the partisans.

Annoyed, Marek ordered a search and after fifteen minutes of fruitless searching he came to one conclusion.

'They've deserted us like cowards we're better off without them,' he said bitterly. 'Forget them, we'd better get ready the train will soon be here.

'The sentry's coming in with a girl,' someone exclaimed.

Rance turned to watch the mud coated figure with the wild staring eyes running towards them and realised with a sudden shock that it was Izabel.

'Rance, Marek,' she screamed. They held her as she almost collapsed with exhaustion pointing behind her.

'Germans, German troops right behind me it's a trap,'

She started to be sick so Rance carried her to a nearbye tree and sat her down under it.

She became agitated. 'There's no time to waste there are two men with you who are enemy agents, I saw one of them in Przglow talking with that man we suspect.' She climbed to her feet.

'Those troops saw me running before them they won't wait for the train now,'

'The train. My God if it's a trap they'll have troops on board,' said Marek his face ashen.

The hollow sound of the train whistle in the distance galvanised them into action and they hurriedly started to gather their weapons. Gunfire shattered the silence and two men died caught out in the open while five others ran for the barn and the rest scattered.

Rance grabbed Izabel as the mottled shapes of camouflaged troops moved through the trees and they both ran. He stopped and looked back.

The barn was surrounded and from inside came the sound of firing from the men.

. 'Marek, some of the men are trapped,' he yelled in alarm. They both turned but were forced to the ground by fierce gunfire.

The barn had started to burn on three sides as the Germans set it alight and flames raced up and over the roof. Rance went cold in anguish, listening to the trapped partisans screaming inside.

Marek shouted, 'There's nothing we can do let's get out of here,' and they ran towards the railway line with bullets whipping the branches around them.

In full retreat the partisans fought and ran with individual fire fights breaking out as the Germans advanced. There was a sudden lull in the fighting when Rance heard the sound of the train whistle again, much nearer.

The troops had stopped their advance and it dawned on Rance why they weren't pushing their advantage.

'Marek, they're waiting for the train,' he shouted.

Marek's face showed the agony of indecision when they reached the railway line. Rance stepped on it and felt the vibration of the oncoming engine.

He glanced behind at the evil looking swamp, but Marek had already made the decision and together they wadded in. At first the soft sticky smelling mud only came to their calves but it sucked and held trying to drag them down. Rance held onto Izabel, his arm about her waist as they heaved themselves forward. In desperation they climbed on the clumps of marsh grasses trying to jump from one to the next. Bullets sent fountains of mud high in the air sounding like sharp smacks on flesh.

A curtain of fog closed around hiding them from view. Izabel sobbed, her strength all but gone as she fought to keep upright in the slime now above her knees and occasionally round their waists when they sank into holes beneath the cold brackish water.

From somewhere behind him Rance heard the train arrive its wheels shrieking on the wet rails and the sound of steam being released under pressure. It gave one long blast as if in anger at having failed to properly close the trap, the noise gradually dying away when they moved deeper into the swamp.

Izabel stopped to rest leaning heavily on Rance. 'Where's my brother? I didn't see him at the barn,'

'Don't worry I saw him with Krolik and Marek when we entered the swamp, I'm sure he'll be fine,' Rance tried to reassure her.

She wasn't convinced shivering with cold, 'Rance I must find him,' she whispered.

Gunfire sounded from behind and to their right and the renewed sound of German voices filled the air. Rance tried to stare into the swirling mist behind them.

'They've decided to follow I didn't think they would,' he said.

He continued to support Izabel with one arm while grasping his machine pistol in the other. A game of shadows developed in the swirling mist and stinking mud with gunfire sounding around them and the occasional shady camouflaged figure appearing then fading away.

Gradually the sound of firing and German voices ceased. He shouldered his gun having now to use both arms to help Izabel. His leaden feet at last found firm ground and he waded out onto dry land and laid her down.

Checking his machine pistol he walked carefully along the bank trying to stare into the swamp. He noticed on his right that the swamp had given way to firm sandy soil and the start of another forest.

Gradually men started to emerge one by one gathering uneasily together staring and listening. Jozef, Marek and Krolik appeared and they walked back to Izabel who was now sitting up. She stared at them wide eyed. 'Where's Jarek, where's my brother?'

'Krolik spoke first, 'He was behind me and when I looked round, seconds later when I looked round again he'd disappeared. I went back to find him and ran into German troops,' he stopped unable to say anymore.

Izabel clambered to her feet. 'I have to go back, I can't leave him he might be injured', Krolik and Marek grabbed her.

Marek's voice was harsh, 'You're not going back its suicide to return'.

He looked for Rance 'Stop, you're not to go,' he shouted seeing Rance disappearing back into the swamp his ears deaf to Marek's plea.

He searched through the dead trees and clumps of grasses, wading sometimes almost to his waist occasionally finding a body floating lifeless in the water, but not Jarek.

Through the mist he heard German voices. 'Have you found any of them alive?' one shouted.

'Nein, everyone we see is dead some even shot themselves, good riddance I say.'

Silently Rance backed away and retraced his steps back to firm ground and faced Izabel who buried her face into his coat and sobbed uncontrollable while the men looked on feeling helpless at her grief.

Marek looked at the darkening sky. 'We must move into the forest and get a fire going or we'll all freeze to death.' he counted the survivors. 'Fourteen, we lost fourteen men back there. His voice broke and he seemed to age again before Rance's eyes who guessed what he must be feeling. It was always the same after a battle he blamed himself for every death. He felt sorry for the man. Although they'd never got on because of Izabel he admired Marek for his courage and leadership.

'It's not you we blame Marek,' said Krolik, 'but the two who betrayed us, Czeslaw and Konstanty. We have a score to settle with those two.'

CHAPTER 25

Mueller and Kantor ceased their headlong flight and looked back towards the sound of gunfire.

'And so the trap closes,' Mueller said laughing.

'We don't need to run anymore they'll be far too busy trying to stay alive to worry about where we've gone.'

Kantor smirked, 'Are we still going after the girl?'

'We certainly are, there's no one left to stop us now.'

It was late afternoon when they reached the house in Blezun, Kantor stood to one side his gun drawn as Mueller carefully tried the door handle and found it locked. They walked around the yard and explored the barn and the rest of the outhouses before returning to the house. Mueller's face glowered in anger as he kicked at the door lock with his boot. They entered the dark kitchen and lit an oil lamp which illuminated the signs of a hurried departure with clothes scattered over the floor. Mueller swore smashing his hand down on the table top.

'She must have seen you at the agent's house you stupid little bastard,' he yelled at Kantor.

Kantor reddened in unbridled anger.

'You're only guessing about that there could be a thousand reasons for this mess.'

They stopped bickering and moved to the window at the sound of a car and trucks pulling up outside.

'I don't believe it,' Mueller said seeing Schneller and Schmidt sitting in the back of a staff car escorted by two halftracks full of troops.

The two men found themselves unceremoniously escorted outside, where they were thrust against the side of the car.

Schneller hadn't moved from the back seat and stared at them with his bleak emotionless eyes.

'Just what are you doing here?' he asked his voice ominously low.

Mueller shuffled his feet, 'We came to get the girl for you sir.'

'And?' said Schneller impatiently tapping his baton on the side of the car.

Mueller grew flustered, 'She's not here,' he stammered. 'She left in a hurry there are clothes all over the floor of the house.

Schneller's baton smashed into the side of Mueller's face drawing blood. He stood dazed too shocked to move while Kantor jumped backwards waiting for Schneller to turn on him.

'I didn't order you to take the girl I said find her and report back.' Schneller's voice was like a whiplash and white spittle flew in Mueller's face but he was too frightened to remove it.

'What about the Englishmen and their leader Marek? you must have killed them to be here.'

Mueller evaded the question. 'The trap was closed just as you planned sir. It was beautiful. They didn't stand a chance and they still thought our names were Czeslaw and Konstanty he declared, watching the look of elation cross Schneller's face.

'If you're deceiving me,-' Schneller's voice trailed away but the threat was there.

Mueller swallowed wincing as Schneller jabbed him hard in the chest with his baton,

'You will make enquires with their neighbours to see if they have relations or friends in the surrounding villages and you will report back to me or Lieutenant Schmidt at HQ.' Tapping his driver on the shoulder he motioned for him to drive on.

Mueller and Kantor stood rigidly to attention until Schneller was out of sight. 'Arrogant Pig', was all Mueller could think of to say.

Bratkow

Captain Braun walked down the line of corpses and noted that three were burnt beyond recognition. He didn't know if either the Englishmen or the leader was amongst them but he would report to Schneller that it was probable. There was no sign of the girl he'd seen running in front of them but she could well have been the one Schneller was looking for. That worried him it meant that some may have escaped. He walked over to the edge of the swamp and stared into the mist that still clung like a blanket on the surface. He hadn't lost any troops on the first assault but he'd lost three in the swamp before he'd called a halt.

He closed his eyes who knows what would have awaited them if they'd carried on going. Perhaps a trap, no he was right to stop. He issued orders to comb the countryside knowing it would be like looking for a needle in a haystack but he was satisfied they'd had a good day.

Marek called a council of war. It had been two weeks since they'd escaped from the trap and were now back using hit and run methods against the patrols roaming the villages.

Rance had taken off one of his boots and was busily examining a weeping sore just below his ankle. It had been nearly two weeks since his feet had seen the light of day and he was suffering. Even now he was taking a risk the Germans had an annoying habit of creeping up on them. To be caught without boots was something he wanted to avoid.

He was tired he still felt the loss of Cross missing him as a comrade but most of all as a friend and now Izabel was back in Krasne.

Even with the partisans around him he felt alone. There was no one to speak English with. He refused to make friends anymore it sickened him when they died, so now he took one day at a time not thinking of the future.

Marek's voice brought him back to reality.

'It's time we went on the offensive, Curen has ordered that he wants three man teams to go into the towns and start removing some of the worst Gestapo officers and their collaborators. We must show them that we can reach them anywhere. Everywhere they go they'll have to continually watch their backs because we'll be there waiting'.

Golab flicked a cigarette into the fire, 'How will we know where to find these people?' he asked seemingly unperturbed at the thought of such a dangerous game.

Rance wondered how he would fit into the scheme of things.

Marek paused. 'Curen has also got his spies and has compiled a list of the worst offenders. We'll know where they live, where they work what time they go and what time they return. In fact we'll know all about their habits so can plan on the best options to take.

The Nazi Gestapo officers on this list will be some of the worst killers and torturers that we'll have come across. They are in charge of the Einsatzgruppen squads. Their job is to make lebensraum, (living space for the Volksdeutsche) by enslaving, expelling or exterminating the local villagers, they show no mercy to anyone, and neither will we.'

It was late in the evening, Rance sat by the fire brooding about his last conversation with Cross when his thoughts were interrupted by the arrival of Marek and Jozef, who sat down opposite him.

Marek hesitated before speaking. 'Rance, this new order of Curen's is what we have come to talk to you about.

'I won't kill civilians you already know that,' he countered,

'I'm not asking you to,' said Marek..

'Well what do you want of me?'

'We want you to go after the Gestapo and leave the civilians to us,' said Jozef.

'Why me?' Rance was puzzled.

'Because you are a trained soldier and military man. Also you speak some of their language'.

It suddenly dawned on him what they were asking, he stared at them incredulously. 'You want me to dress up and impersonate a German soldier or officer, don't you?' he exclaimed.

'Well not all the time,' said Marek dryly.

Rance stared at him suspiciously, 'When would you like me to do this pantomime?'

Jozef looked at him with a puzzled expression. 'Pantomime what is this pantomime?'

Rance looked at him in amusement, his black mood gone.

'Never mind I'll tell you when the wars over,' he turned back to Marek with a raised eyebrow, 'Well, when?'

'Not yet, we want you to practice your German, maybe in a month, and at some time in the future you and I will go after the big one'.

'The big one?'

'Schneller,' said Marek.

For Rance the next few weeks were taken up with the never ending nerve racking patrols of ambush and counter ambush. In the villages he was becoming so well known that they would hide and feed him wherever he went.

The hiding places ranged from false bottoms in beds to barrels in barns. The worst one that Rance absolutely detested was the one hidden in the outside toilets where a hole had been dug under the lavatory seat alongside the main sewerage pit. The stench was indescribable especially when he used to lay there looking at the rear end of a German soldier caught short while searching the village he was in.

It was in such a village that he was approached by a young man. Rance knew him as Ston, one of their men who he'd fought alongside many times. The man was hesitant in speaking to him, clearly upset.

It was Rance that broke the ice. 'You look troubled isn't your wife looking after you?' he said jokingly thinking that Ston was going to cry.

'It's not my wife that's the problem, it's our priest,' the young man said despondently.

Rance nodded knowing they were a very religious people and that the church played a big part in their everyday life, he waited patiently for the man to calm down.

'He refuses to christen our baby and almost threw my wife and child out of the church saying that he won't have anything to do with bandits that cause trouble in the area.'

Rance grew angry, 'Why does he call you a bandit, does he know you fight with the partisans?

'All the priests know who the partisans are but they would never say anything to the Germans except this priest, who insists on calling us bandits. He doesn't understand.'

Rance fought to keep his temper under control, 'Where is your church Ston?'

'It's in the village of Dabrowa nad Czarna, about two kilometres from the Sulejow road.'

'Get your wife, baby and your relations into their carts and meet me here,' he said and waited impatiently for an hour before six carts turned up with at least six people in each. Ston sat on the front seat of the leading cart leaving room for Rance to sit beside him. His wife and mother sat in the back holding the baby. Rance swung his machine pistol over his shoulder and held out his arms. 'Give me the baby,' he said.

Ston's wife hesitated briefly before shyly handing him over. Rance held on tightly to the little bundle still fuming in anger, as the procession made its way to the church. The news was spreading fast. More people joined with some coming on horseback the column grew to nearly a hundred.

They reached the church only to discover another Christening was just finishing and it was busy. Holding the baby in one arm and his machine pistol in the other Rance ran up the steps closely followed by Ston, his wife and relatives while the rest of the onlookers waited expectantly outside.

He stormed through the large double doors and entered into the semi-darkness of the building that was dimly lit by hundreds of candles.

The priest, giving a sermon at the far end stopped in mid-sentence and he looked up angrily, his face full of annoyance at the rude interruption while the congregation turned to see what the commotion was about. Rance ignored them all striding purposely down the centre aisle, the priest's anger turned to one of alarm at the expression on the man's face coming towards him changing to pure terror at the sight of the sub-machine gun.

Rance thrust the baby into the terrified priest's arms and stuck the barrel of his gun against the man's head. Putting his lips close to the priest's ear he whispered.

'Now you scum, you'll Christen this baby or I'll take you outside and blow your fucking brains out, do you understand me?'

The priest was nodding his head so hard Rance thought it would fall off suddenly the church started to overflow with onlookers.

When the service began Rance stood to one side and let his anger evaporate and after it had finished he was startled at the great roar of delight from the watching congregation. The priest began to scurry towards a side room but stopped in alarm finding his way blocked by the grinning Englishman who prodded the man's belly with his gun, making him wince.

'I haven't finished with you yet,' he murmured.

By this time the priest was sure he was going to die and had starting to pray while looking appealingly at his executioner who was pushing him roughly into the vestibule.

' Where's your record book?' he heard the Englishman snarl.

With trembling hands he placed it on the table in front of him.

Grabbing a pen Rance signed it with a flourish in English. Before picking up his gun and thrusting it into the frightened priest's face.

'If I hear any more stories about you from my friends, I will come and kill you. Also you had better not let the Germans see this book or they will kill you. Do you understand me priest?'

The priest looked into the eyes of what he saw as the devil and seeing his own death written there whispered. 'Yes.'

Rance returned to Ston's village a hero and soon a party was in full swing with him as guest of honour. The home-made Vodka was poured out and people gathered outside Ston's little wooden house drinking and dancing until dusk and the curfew. Overnight Rance's fame spread far and wide and his exploits grew by the hour.

As Marek disdainfully put it, 'He's becoming a legend who could almost fight the Germans single handed, according to the villagers.'

The list that arrived by the new courier who had taken over from Izabel was long and detailed. How he got the information Rance could only guess. His spy network must be second to none he thought.

All the details of the traitors, collaborators, women who associated with the Germans and Gestapo officers were carefully outlined and graded according to their crimes.

Rance, at his own choosing picked only the Gestapo officers and men and so it was that he found himself sitting in a cafe overlooking the main square in Piotrkow. He was feeling uncomfortable in a German Major's uniform with trousers made for someone larger and the sleeves of the jacket a shade too long.

Three German soldiers were sitting at the next table but because he was an officer they didn't speak for which Rance was relieved. The cafe was next to the chemist shop that he'd raided the year before and he nearly choked on his drink when the little man and his bossy woman assistant bustled in ordered a drink and food before sitting down behind him.

Rance wondered idly if the man would wet himself again if he was to turn around and face him.

From where he was sitting he had a commanding view of the whole square. At the far end he could see Jozef and Golab standing with their backs to him watching through the reflection of a shop window. The man they were waiting for entered the café with a lady companion. Carefully groomed he was tall, with the rank of Lieutenant.

According to Rance's list he only used this cafe because it was in the town centre where he felt secure in the knowledge that there were so many troops about for anyone to risk an attack on his person. He was a cunning man who unaware of the fact had twice escaped an attempt on his life. This time Rance wanted to make sure. His target was the Gestapo's main interrogator with cells situated in the Gestapo HQ. Any prisoner he interviewed was never seen again and the reports about him and what he did made Rance sick with disgust.

The Lieutenant acknowledged Rance in his Major's uniform and sat down well away from the window paranoid about his own safety, he always sat amongst German soldiers.

It was a long wait as the lieutenant twice ordered more drinks before finally rising to leave. Idly Rance lifted his hat and wiped his brow which was the signal Jozef and Golab had been waiting for. Quickly they let off four shots in the general direction of the cafe before running off down a side street. Pandemonium and panic broke out with people diving for cover while the Gestapo officer flung himself into a corner. Rance jumped up and fired through the cafe window shattering the glass causing the small chemist to scream louder than his lady companion.

Rance shouted orders at the three German soldiers to chase the bandits and side-stepped out of their way as they rushed for the door and ran across the square.

Rance glanced across at the cowering chemist satisfied the man wasn't looking and walked over to the pale faced Lieutenant with his pretty girl friend. She stared at him wide eyed as he waved his pistol towards the door.

'Geh raus.' he said.

With a sob she fled and the Lieutenant got up to follow smiling weakly at Rance. 'That was close, I thought they'd got me,' he said.

'They have,' Rance said in English watching the shock spread over the man's face but he was surprised that the Lieutenant had already got his pistol out and was bringing it up pointing and firing, It was a pure reflex on Rance's part that he side-stepped, feeling the bullet brush his hair before firing back. Replacing the pistol in his holster he calmly walked out of the cafe into the nearest side street.

He felt no elation, but the man lying dead in the cafe was worse than an animal, a man that enjoyed torturing and killing others. There would be more, many more, and he wondered when it would be his turn to face a bullet, or worse the next Gestapo interrogator.

Piotrekow Square
.

Schmidt stepped back respectfully allowing Schneller and the police chief to enter the small cafe.

'Uncover the body Schmidt.' said Schneller.

With a flourish Schmidt pulled away the table cloth to reveal the Lieutenant who had been shot once through the head. The police chief pulled a face and turned his attention to the small chemist and his woman companion.

'What happened here, did you see?'

The chemist was still shaken by his ordeal and clung to the woman for support. 'Two men across the square fired shots towards us and everybody dived to the floor.'

'Not everybody,' interrupted the woman, 'The Major didn't, he got up and fired his pistol through the window then the three soldiers ran outside chasing the two men.

A look of annoyance crossed the policeman's face.

'One at a time please,' he motioned for the small man to continue.

'Well, that's all really, I heard two more shots and when I looked up the Lieutenant was lying on the floor and everyone had gone.

'It was the Major that shot the Lieutenant sir,' exclaimed the woman wanting to be heard.

'What was that!' echoed Schneller.

'The Major, he walked over to the couple and told the girl to go. The Lieutenant got up and said something to the Major who answered back, and then there was an exchange of shots sir.'

'You're sure about this, you saw it all?' said the Chief Of police.

'Yes sir, he didn't see me looking because I kept my head down, but there was something else sir.'

'Yes, go on,' snapped Schneller, impatiently.

'I thought it funny at the time, but the Major spoke in English sir,'

'What, he spoke what!'

'He spoke English sir, a second before they shot at each other.' she repeated.

Schneller's eyes bulged, his face went white.

Schmidt became frightened and looked nervously across the square. This war had entered a new dimension he thought. Now they were becoming the hunted and perhaps somebody had him in their sights.

He licked his lips that had suddenly become dry.

Schneller stared at the Police Chief with glazed eyes and the man watched him with a worried expression.

'I think we should go back to HQ and discuss this, don't you?' he said.

Schneller found his voice and turned to Schmidt.

'Get rid of the body and then find me Herman Braun, I want him in my office now.'

CHAPTER 26

Gestapo HQ Piotrekow

A sea of faces greeted Captain Herman Braun when he finally entered the operations room two hours later. Amongst them he saw Schneller standing in front of a large desk behind which was seated Claus Ritschel and on his right the Chief of Police. Scattered around the room were several high ranking officers and Schmidt, who stood quietly in the background.

Schneller signalled Braun to a chair near the front. Nervously Braun seated himself finding he was the centre of attention when addressed by Claus Ritschel.

'In your report about the action you fought with the bandits at Bratkow you stated, I quote:

It's my belief that the operation was a complete success and that the Englishman and the bandit leader called Marek were burned to death in the barn at Bratkow. Unquote:

How did you arrive at that conclusion?'

Braun became flustered his face reddening under the stare of his superior.

'The bodies answered the description of the wanted men sir, and from what my men said very few if any, escaped the trap.'

Claus Ritschel grunted and turned his attention to Schneller.

'Your report to me also states that they were dead, but from a different source'.

'Yes sir, my report came from two Volksdeutche agents that had infiltrated their organisation, their information has always been reliable in the past. Their names are Mueler and Kantor but undercover they were known to the bandits as Czeslaw and Konstanty

Braun echoed Schneller's last statement.

'Has been reliable in the past. Does that mean they're not dead and are still active?'.

'More than active I would say,' answered Claus Ritschel dryly. 'The Englishman has just killed one of our Gestapo officers in broad daylight right here in the centre of Piotrkow, not five hundred metres from this HQ.'

Schneller thought Braun was going to faint with shock and smiled maliciously at the man's discomfort, Claus Ritschel turned to the Chief of Police.

'What are your men doing about tightening security in the town?'

The Chief of Police gathered his notes and looked over the top of his glasses. 'We have received several reports of attacks on our policemen who have been actively engaged in counter espionage in the town limits.

Also,' he stopped to read his notes, 'There have been five of our collaborators shot and at least two have disappeared. I've mentioned this before but until now nothing has been done about it.'

'What do you suggest we do about it?' said Claus Ritschel leaning forward in his chair.

'My men have been asking for more protection from these killers, you have the troops, allocate some to me for bodyguard duties.'

Braun interrupted, 'Excuse me sir, but I have requested extra troops for my villagers who have been complaining about lack of protection from these bandits.'

Schneller snapped back, 'What's the matter with you all. You're running scared we're up against a few ill armed men who can't possible take on the might of the German Army. They're getting desperate that's all.'

'Well they're certainly tying down enough troops as it is,' remarked Claus Ritschel, 'I can't justify asking for more troops. The German high command needs every man they can get for the Russian front.'

Schneller turned to the Chief of Police, 'May I suggest you take hostages in the town, anyone will do.'

'How am I expected to do that without help from the Gestapo?' You're the ones with all the manpower it appears to me,' the Chief replied sardonically.

Schneller beamed with delight. Nobody in the room had ever seen this before and thought he'd finally gone mad.

'Well it just so happens I might be able to help you there,' he said relishing this moment. 'I've arrested the two men who fired the first shots at the cafe. They were picked up in the next street as they tried to get rid of their guns'.

'Have you got any information out of them yet?' asked the Police Chief eagerly.

'We haven't had time to question them. We'll keep them awake all night and start tomorrow. Don't worry they'll tell us all we want to know.'

'Well congratulations Major Schneller, that's at least a start,' said Claus Ritschel, 'In the meantime issue orders that all officers must never go out alone and that goes for the police too.'

'What about my villager's sir?' echoed Braun despairingly.

'We won't take on anymore Polish villages until we've solved the bandit problem, will that satisfy you?' said Claus Ritschel gruffly.

The meeting broke up leaving the Police Chief and Claus Ritschel alone.

'I don't like Schneller's methods,' complained the Chief of Police, he's a bit too crude for my liking.'

'Crude or not he gets results, I wouldn't complain too loudly if I were you, he has some powerful friends back in Berlin,' said Claus Ritschel.

'So have I,' exclaimed the Chief, far more than Schneller.

Claus Ritschel made a mental note to look after the Police Chief as he watched the portly figure depart down the stairs.

The Police Chief left the building shivering in the cold evening air and walked towards his car. The driver leaning on the bonnet hurriedly dropped his cigarette and ground it out with the heel of his shoe. That annoyed the Chief, he would have a word with the man later. The driver stood to attention and as he opened the rear door the Police Chief noticed another officer sitting in the back.

He frowned, casting an enquiring glance at the driver.

'The Major said he had a message from Herr Schneller to give you concerning the shooting earlier sir.' said the driver respectfully.

The Chief grunted and sat down heavily in the back seat next to the shadowy figure hunched in the corner, complaining that he would have to lose weight or get a bigger car. All the time he was staring at his silent companion, whose lower face was covered by his upturned collar and who's eyes were shrouded in shadow under his peaked cap which sported the deaths head badge of the SS.

'Well Major, what have you got for me that's so important that it can't wait until tomorrow?' the Chief said.

The shadowy figure ignored him instead giving orders to the driver to start the car and drive down the road. The voice was heavily accented, the sound sent alarm signals racing to the Police Chief's brain. 'Stop the car,' he shouted in sudden panic to the startled driver who caused the car to jump forward in fits and starts.

'Drive on, or I'll blow your head off.' The voice was barely a whisper in his ear but the driver knew who he was going to obey.

Eyes wide with fright the Police Chief stared with morbid horror at the pistol in the Major's hand.

'What do want from me?' he said trying control the quiver in his voice.

He was ignored the man sitting opposite was busy giving instructions to the driver who completely lost his bearings while they travel through the narrow streets. Eventually they turned into a deserted courtyard where the driver watched in his wing mirror the courtyard doors being closed by someone with a machine pistol slung over his shoulder.

The Police Chief found himself being pulled unceremoniously from the car and escorted to a small dimly lit room completely devoid of furniture.

He stared at the pistol, then into the hard, steel grey eyes of the Englishman. 'What do you want of me?' the chief asked in English.'

His captor looked surprised.

'I was educated in England and could tell by your accent that you're English,' he offered in way of an explanation.

'Your death perhaps,' answered the Englishman.

'Perhaps not, if you'd wanted that, you'd have done it by now,' said the Police Chief, regaining some of his composure.

'The man has brains,' murmured the Englishman to his companion, a scruffy looking man who had a baneful grin on his face.

'Perhaps we should shoot him in the legs instead,' suggested his companion.

The Police Chief grew fearful at the thought.

'Your men have arrested two friends of ours,' said the Englishman. 'We want them back. You, he pointed his pistol menacingly 'Will write a letter addressed to Claus Ritschel requesting an exchange. You for the two of them. They're to be driven west out of Piotrkow and released into the forest at night. We'll tell you where later. When that's done, we'll release you.'

The Englishman's lips tightened into a thin straight line and his tone of voice grew menacing. 'If they're harmed in anyway, then we'll execute you immediately. You must impress that upon him, especially Schneller.'

'How can they trust you not to kill me anyway after the release of your friends?'

'Tell them in the letter, that it's the Englishman holding you hostage and that they have my word.'

The Police Chief grimaced, 'Well, better that than a Pole's word I suppose. They'd never trust them.'

'What's he saying?' asked Krolik. 'Is he pleading for his life?'

'Yes,' grinned Rance, he's just about to write a letter'.

Claus Ritschel threw the letter on to Schneller's paper strewn desk. 'Read it,' he said grimly.

Schneller studied its contents, his face almost purple as his rage grew.

'When did this happen?. How could a thing like this happen?' he shouted the white spittle beginning to form at the edges of his mouth.

Claus Ritchel prudently stepped backwards out of the way.

'Last night after our meeting. The driver said a Major of the SS was sitting in the back of his car waiting for the Police Chief, he turns out to be the Englishman. It's perfectly true they released the driver to carry this letter.'

'They can go to hell as far as I'm concerned,' snapped Schneller, 'It's his stupid fault for not taking precautions in the first place.'

'Come now Schneller, who would have thought they would have the nerve for such a gamble,' said Claus Ritschel seriously.

'I've told you they're getting desperate they'll try anything.'

'We have to let the two bandits go,' countered Claus Ritschel, watching Schneller fighting to control his temper.

'At least let me interrogate them first. I'll personally do it,' Schneller fumed.

'No, we can't allow any harm to come to the Police Chief. Good God man can you imagine what it would do to the morale amongst the men, knowing that even the Police Chief isn't safe anymore.'

'In exchange for the Police Chief, can I bring in some extra troops that I have acquired from friends in Berlin?' asked Schneller.

'Now who might they be?' enquired Claus Ritschel his curiosity growing.

Schneller wiped the spittle off his lips. 'Cossacks, nearly two hundred of them. All primed and ready to go. They've been ordered to fight on the Russian front. I've a meeting to attend, just across the border in Germany and could arrange to have the use of them for almost two weeks as they pass through our area.'

Claus Ritschel looked dubious, 'They're absolute savages, wild and seemingly uncontrollable, can you handle them?'

Schneller's laugh was loud and unreal. 'Why sir, I've no wish to handle them. I've only got them for two weeks. I'll just tell them where to go and leave them to it'.

Claus Ritschel could imagine the terror they would strike into the hearts of the Polish villagers and partisans when they faced two hundred wild Cossacks.

'Where did you find them?' he asked.

Originally they were fighting with the Russians. We took them prisoner when we invaded Russia. Now they were given a choice, fight with us or die,' Schneller smirked. 'They hate the communists anyway so they chose to fight on our side. Better men you couldn't find anywhere it seems, they just like killing which is fine by me.'

'When do you propose to go?'

'I'll see the Police Chief back safely first although he doesn't deserve it'.

Krolik handed Rance a letter, 'The driver has returned with their reply it's written in German, what does it say?'

Rance glanced at it quickly, grinning broadly.

'They accept but want a straight exchange and at dawn', he frowned at the request. 'We should write back agreeing to their request but change the meeting to dusk. That way if they try and set a trap we'll have the cover of darkness on our side. Do you agree Krolik?'

'Yes, but I don't think we should go alone, we need Marek and the rest of the partisans in reserve somewhere in the background.'

Rance sat down and began to write.

Rance and Krolik stood with the shivering portly figure of the Police Chief at the end of a long straight piece of forest fire-break.

He looked behind him but couldn't see any of the partisans hidden in the rear. They watched the shadows lengthening as the sun started to set behind the tree tops.

They're late,' stated Krolik with growing unease. 'What's keeping them?'

'It's deliberate,' said Rance trying to remain calm, 'They're trying to scare us,' and succeeding he thought.

Krolik poked the unfortunate Police Chief in his rounded stomach with the barrel of his gun. 'You'd better pray that everything will go to plan. If they try anything,'-- his voice trailed away but the unfinished threat lingered on.

The Police Chief wet his dried lips sweat clung to his brow.

Dim figures appeared at the other end of the track and Rance could see the familiar shapes of Jozef and Golab standing amongst the grey uniforms of their German guards. A German officer in the black uniform of the SS stepped forward and walked with a curious rolling motion down the track towards them before stopping half way and beckoned for Rance to meet him. Rance walked to meet the officer ignoring Krolik's warning that it may be a trap.

They stood no more than ten feet apart, their eyes met. Rance fought to remain calm looking into the bulbous eyes which were totally devoid of any emotion.

Without asking he knew it was Schneller, the hate must have showed in his eyes because the German officer's hand unconscientiously moved towards his holster strapped to his waist. The thin lips twitched into what Rance took to be a smirk.

'You know after this Englishman that we will hunt you down like a dog,' Schneller hissed watching for a reaction from the hard eyed man facing him.

It never came. The Englishman seemed quite unmoved by the statement. Instead he said, 'You'll have to hurry or the Russians will beat you to it.' Annoyed at the coolness of the Englishman, Schneller snapped.

'Well, let's get on with it.'

Turning, he waved his arm. Immediately Jozef and Golab started down the track.

Rance waved and the Police Chief walked to join them.

Rance could feel his moist palms, his breath shortening as the tension mounted while he continued his eye contact with the Gestapo officer.

The prisoners met in the middle then each party slowly backed away.

'We'll meet again Englishman,' Schneller retorted.

Rance's nerves were stretched to the limit knowing a dozen rifles were centred on him, but he refused to let it show to the German officer slowly backing away.

'We certainly will pig,' he taunted.

Schneller was beside himself with fury. Nobody had ever spoken to him like that before, he felt humiliated by it.

It was almost dark before the exchange was completed and the partisans faded away into the forest leaving the Germans to vainly flounder after them. Within half an hour all signs of pursuit had disappeared.

Gestapo HQ Piotrekow

Schmidt wiped the sweat from his brow and stared in shocked surprise at the tall officer standing in front of him wearing a patch over one eye and sporting a massive scar across the bridge of his nose.

'I never expected to see you again, Lieutenant Lohr,' he declared trying not to stare at the man's face.

Lohr grunted, 'It was Schneller's idea and a direct order from Berlin.'

'Congratulations on getting the Iron Cross I always said you deserved it after fighting your way out of that ambush,' Schmidt rambled. 'There's been hell to pay since you left us, Schneller has become obsessed with catching the Englishman and the rest of the bandits round here. I suppose you have a score to settle too haven't you?'

Lohr scowled rubbing his finger across the bridge of his nose. Schmidt glanced at the thermometer hanging on the wall showing thirty two degrees. He felt uncomfortable in the humid atmosphere Lohr didn't seem affected by it.

'I don't know where the time goes,' Schmidt rattled on. 'One minute its winter, the next spring, and now summers here.'

Schmidt leaned forward beckoning for Lohr to come closer.

'I'm not supposed to tell you this but Schnellers gone to a meeting just across the border in Germany. Afterwards he'll be bringing back a company of Cossacks. He'll have them for two weeks before they move on to the Russian front.'

Lohr didn't look impressed by the news. 'You know the Russian front is only a hundred and fifty kilometres away and getting nearer all the time.'

Schmidt nodded he'd often woke up sweating in a panic, dreaming of Russian tanks crushing him to death.

'When will Schneller be back.?'

'In about a week I suppose he didn't really say. Things haven't been going his way lately.

Do you remember that girl he was after. Well, he found out she was in with the bandits, went absolutely mad and swore to teach her a lesson.' Schmidt sniggered. 'Now she's disappeared and despite having agents looking for her there's no sign.'

Lohr couldn't be bothered with such rubbish news, Schneller must be totally deranged. 'What are my orders, not chasing that girl I hope?'.

Schmidt picked up the telephone and spoke to Claus Ritschel.

'No, he want's you back in the villages, apparently the Russians have started to drop troops behind our lines with orders to arm the Polish communists. Your job is to find them.'

CHAPTER 27

A forest near Piotrekow

Rance could sense danger the atmosphere was wrong. These men looked tense and ill at ease.

'Who are they Marek?' Rance was curious that they should have met such a well-armed group of men.

Marek ignored him and spoke to their leader.

'I haven't seen you in these parts before, who are you?'

Their leader chose to by-pass the question.

'You are partisans yes,? well we're here to assist you in your fight with the Germans.'

The reply surprised Rance, even he could tell they weren't Polish.

He watched Marek stiffen then cautiously hold out his hand

'Welcome to Poland,' Marek said 'We've been expecting you.'

Now Rance understood, they were Russian paratroopers, flown in from the advancing front and no one looked very happy at the meeting.

The Russians eagerly accepted the partisan's offer of homemade Vodka and guzzled it down as if it was to be their last.

Their first question brought an end to any friendship there might have been. 'You are in the communist party?' asked their leader, smiling broadly.

'No we're not,' answered Marek, and lied, 'We're soldiers in the Polish Home army under orders from London'.

The smile faded from The Russian's face. 'Ah well, we're all still on the same side yes?' He lifted the bottle and toasted their health.

'Now we must move on, we have a lot to do.' He didn't offer the bottle back but pushed it inside his overcoat pocket.

'Goodbye my friends, we'll meet again soon I hope.'

Marek watched them leave with a worried expression.

'What was that all about?' asked Rance.

'It's what I've been afraid of. I think they're here to arm the communist party members who have been forming their own groups'.

'So what, they're on our side it's got to be good for us all surely?' countered Rance.

'I haven't told you this before but already there have been skirmishes between the groups who are not only fighting the Germans but are now starting to fight each other.'

Rance felt angry, 'Well thanks for finally telling me this. What else have you failed to tell me?'

Marek looked guilty, 'We don't know whom to trust anymore. We feel the communists want to take over when the Russians finally drive the Germans out, and the way they're advancing we know it won't be long.'

'How long do you think?'

Marek shrugged, 'Six months, who really knows. The Germans are fighting back fiercely which might slow them down.'

'The courier is here from Curen,' interrupted Jozef, and went with Marek to meet the young girl.

Rance felt the pain of longing, seeing her he was reminded of Izabel who he hadn't seen for weeks and was beginning to despair of ever seeing her again.

Half an hour later Marek returned and sat next to him as he lay in the shade of a tree, away from the hot July sun.

'We have another job,' he announced quietly.

Rance slowly regained a sitting position. 'And?'

Marek hesitated, 'This is entirely voluntary, you don't have to say yes to this one.'

Rance gave a mocking sigh, 'I've heard that one before. What is it, assassinate Hitler?'

'Almost as bad,' declared Marek.

Rance became wide awake. 'Tell me.'

'Apparently Schneller has gone across the border into Germany to some meeting. What it's about we don't know. Somehow he's managed to get the use of a company of Cossacks who were on their way to the Russian front, when this meeting finishes it's his intention to bring them here and let them loose amongst us and the local villages.'

He offered Rance a cigarette which he declined.

'Curen wants him eliminated, but not here. Not even in Poland. The retribution that the German high command would demand against the population would be too terrible to contemplate'.

Rance could again feel a knot tightening in his stomach.

'You want me to cross the border into Germany, assassinate a high ranking Gestapo officer and come back across that border again. What odds are you giving me?'

'You won't be on your own Rance, I'll be going with you,' declared Marek.

Rance's laugh sounded hollow, even to himself.

Marek jumped to his feet in anger. 'If you don't want to go, just say so. I can easily find a dozen volunteers.'

Rance waved him back down. 'Keep your shirt on how far are we from the border,' he asked.

Marek looked puzzled, 'I'm going to keep my shirt on, why did you say that?'

'Just an English figure of speech Marek, how far to the border?'

'Three days walk, then across the border, perhaps another day'.

'How would we get across?'

Curen knows someone who has contacts with black market smugglers near the Kemno border crossing. He will arrange for them to guide us over and back again.'

Rance still felt dubious and could feel the sweat on his brow.

'Well,' Marek was getting impatient.

Rance lay down again, his eyes staring up at the brilliant blue sky, he looked unhappy. 'Well Marek, why not. Anything to shorten this war,' again wishing he was back in England.

They set off early the next day each carrying a small bag of food packed in amongst four hand-grenades and spare ammunition for their sub-machine guns. Travelling only at night, keeping to the edge of the woods the two men headed west. On the third night it rained and they were forced to seek shelter just before dawn, choosing a small barn at the edge of a wood. Marek was guessing it was about two kilometres from the border. When dawn broke they found themselves near the main road which led from the border to Piotrkow and then further east towards the Russian front.

An unending stream of army trucks heading in both directions filled the road. Some going to the front carrying troop reinforcements and ammunition, others returning, carrying the wounded who were crammed into every available space.

Keeping the wood between them and the road they made their way to the rendezvous which looked to Rance like any other forester's hut he'd seen Together they stood watching the hut until they were satisfied it was safe to approach. It was empty almost falling down, its shutters barely hanging on to the one rotten window frame.

They glanced inside at the mounds of rubbish before deciding to wait back in the woods offering better cover. Now Rance could see the border crossing with its red and white striped barrier pointing straight in the air as if giving the Nazi salute to the never ending convoys. On his left stretched the border wire with cleared open ground on either side. He guessed there would be flood lights on parts of it at night.

Four hours later they watched the silent approach of three men who looked like Gypsies. Two were young the other considerably older. They had similar features which made Rance assume they were father and sons. None of the three had shaved for at least a week, which wasn't unusual.

What made the difference was their eyes, they carried a wildness about them, a lawlessness of never belonging.

Rance and Marek let them pass hidden in the undergrowth, then stepped out behind them.

'Looking for us?' said Marek cautiously.

Startled! The three men turned swiftly and seeing the guns their hands clawed high in the air.

'Your early, we weren't expecting you until tonight,' said the older man whose face reminded Rance of a very old pig.

'We made better time than we thought we would,' answered Marek.

'We haven't met any partisans before,' stated one of the younger men. who was smaller than his brother. The runt of the litter thought Rance.

' So how were you contacted?' asked Marek, frowning.

The older man answered, 'By a mutual friend who isn't a partisan, but he has a friend who is.'

'Why are you helping us in this way,' queried Rance.

The old man looked surprised. 'You're not Polish?' he said as a question.

'No I'm not,' said Rance, and didn't elaborate.

'We want to help you because we're Poles, we don't like the Germans in our country,' answered the taller of the two younger men.

'It wouldn't be because you received a considerably amount of money off us as well, would it?' questioned Marek.

'We have expenses to meet,' smiled the old man showing his rotten teeth. Other people to bribe, that sort of thing'.

They were nervous, continually searching the surrounding area with their restless wild eyes.

'Are you looking for someone? asked Rance.

'This is a dangerous area for us with hourly patrols, we must be very careful you understand,' said the old man frowning at Rance's tone.

He motioned for them to follow him to the hut.

'You will stay here until its dark afterwards we'll come to guide you across. You'll have seventy eight hours to do whatever you've come for. Afterwards we'll bring you back. If you're late we'll go without you.'

He turned to leave but what seemed as an after-thought he turned back. 'Whatever you do, don't leave this hut.'

Rance watched them go with a feeling of unease.

'I don't trust them Marek, they're doing it for the money,'

'Curen has been assured they're the best and have done this sort of thing before,' said Marek seemingly unperturbed.

Rance grunted still not convinced. 'Never trust a man who does this sort of thing just for the money. I think we should be very careful here.'

It was quiet in the woods. Rance sat in the open doorway to get some air, mid-afternoon in July the sun was at its hottest.

Listening to the humming of the insects and the whistling of the birds on that drowsy afternoon seemed out of place in this land of madness he thought. He looked across at the dozing figure of Marek, wishing it was Cross lying there. He found it hard to grasp that it was now 1944.

So much had happened things were becoming a blur and he wished he knew what was going on with the rest of the war. All they ever received were rumours and more rumours, until nobody believed in anything anymore.

He knew it was true about the Russians, already the Communist groups were on the move, helped by them.. To him the whole thing was becoming a mess and he imagined it becoming one big killing ground.

Now he worried for the safety of Izabel and her mother. The rumours were strong about the pillaging and rape of the Polish women as the Russians advanced towards them.

The sun slowly set behind the tree tops as he watched Marek yawn, and come awake smacking his lips.

'How long have I been asleep,' he groaned.

'Most of the afternoon you haven't missed anything,' said Rance, and left him on watch while he settled down to try and get some sleep before the return of the smugglers.

It seemed to be only a moment before he was being roughly shaken awake, feeling a hand over his mouth he opened his eyes into the darkness of the hut hearing Marek whisper in his ear.

'We have company and I don't think it's friendly.'

Rance reached for his sub-machine gun and lay alongside Marek on the dirt floor watching the doorway illuminated by the faint glow of the moon.

He stiffened hearing the faint whine of a dog. The dread of not knowing tied the familiar knot. He slipped the safety catch off his gun and pulled the bag of hand-grenades to his side. Taking one out he gripped the pin between his teeth and waited.

Krasne

Izabel, having established herself in Krasne was now receiving instructions from Curen on new operations to be carried out by the partisans under the temporary leadership of Krolik. She received orders to be passed on that they were to be on standby to go to the aid of Warsaw when and if an uprising began. It excited the men, but in the meantime they were to continue their operations against the Germans.

Daily, news came in about the Russian advances that the Germans were scouring the countryside for food leaving many of the Poles to starve and groups of desperate men were roaming the forests.

Izabel never travelled without her pistol anymore, because the communists Poles were now more active and several clashes had been reported.

Izabel had the latest task of conveying the news to Krolik about the return of Lieutenant Franz Lohr. The weekly rendezvous this time was near the village of Ostrow situated where two Rivers, The Pilica and the Czarna met.

She studied her map. By road the distance was approximately twelve kilometres, she decided that due to the increased patrols she would leave her bicycle and walk across country which was only eight kilometres.

Dawn was breaking when she picked up her small bag of food and pistol, which she carefully concealed under her dress with written instructions for Krolik, which were quite detailed concerning troop movements and food convoys going to the front through Piotrkow.

Already it was hot she glanced at her watch. Seven thirty AM, plenty of time she thought.

The long lush grasses of the pastureland came up to her knees and while walking she disturbed swarms of insects and butterflies which rose with dazzling displays of colour into the clean early morning air.

Looking across at the silent empty landscape, interspersed with forest, she noticed that there were no animals. No cows, pigs or sheep where before the war there were thousands.

Finding the path she was looking for she entered the first of the woodland, not as dense as the forest, but giving excellent cover for the wildlife that was being hunted to extinction by the starving population. Moving deeper into the woods she became aware of the silence, even the birds had ceased their dawn chorus. Here the bright sunlight faded into thin shafts of light that threw dappled shadows across her path. She shivered, suddenly feeling cooler, the sharp crack of a dried twig breaking made her jump.

Glancing apprehensively around and seeing nothing but trees and dense undergrowth she pulled herself together, deciding it was a wild animal, probable a deer.

A shadow moved to her right she realised that she wasn't alone any longer. A feeling of panic made her fight for air she wanted to run but forced herself to remain calm, she moved the bag of food to her front, so covering her movements when she undid the front of her dress and carefully felt for the butt of her pistol.

A feeling of being watched made her suddenly turn she confronted four men standing at the edge of the path. Hard looking men, some in uniform.

Alarmed, she realised they were Russian troops. Frightened by their silence she slowly backed away while they stood grinning at her.

'What are you doing here so far from the road ?' remarked a voice behind her.

Startled, she spun round, grasping the pistol butt tightly she was tempted to show it, but decided not to for the moment.

The man blocking her path was an officer in the Russian army, his Polish was perfect.

'I'm taking a short cut to work,' she stammered her mind racing as she looked for a way of escape.

'Let her go she's just a peasant girl,' said the man standing behind him.

Izabel had seen him before. He was a Pole recruiting for the communist party in the villages.

'She's seen us, that's not a good thing,' said the officer.

'Come now, news spreads quickly in the villages everybody knows that you're here,' protested the Pole.

Izabel realised now that the Pole was bargaining for her life, fear made her tremble and her body went cold,

'I already knew you were here,' she blustered.

The officer looked at her in surprise, 'And how did you know that?'

'I'm with the partisans, I'm a courier'.

The man laughed, 'You're not a communist though are you?'

She flushed in anger at his mocking laugh.

'No I'm not, but we're on the same side'.

The officer suddenly stopped laughing, 'Are we indeed, and what makes you think that?'

The Pole with him didn't look happy at the way things were going and shuffled his feet impatiently.

'Come on let her go,' he said quietly.

The officer rounded on him. 'When I'm good and ready,' he snapped his gaze travelled over her body.

'First we should find out which group she's with'.

He stepped towards her, his hand reaching out. 'Let's see if she is telling us the truth.'

CHAPTER 28

Polish-German border crossing Kepno

Rance lay quietly on the floor of the hut waiting. Would it just be the smugglers coming back? But what about the whining dog?

Dark figures filled the doorway and sheets of flame from their sub-machine guns lit the interior in a flickering glow aiming low as if a man were in a sitting position. They sprayed the room over their heads the bullets thudding and tearing into the back wall of the hut.

The flickering glowing shapes in the doorway made perfect targets when he and Marek pulled the triggers of their machine pistols hard on to automatic. The noise was deafening in the confined space and the figures screamed in agony before disappearing.

Rance and Marek pulled the pins from their grenades and threw them after the screaming men. Three seconds later the explosions almost burst their ear drums and the weak shutters of the hut blew inwards covering them in a cloud of dust.

Screams and shouts from the wounded and dying filled the night air, and a dog howled in mortal agony as it rolled next to its dead master. Rance and Marek ran outside their machine pistols blazing a way through the dazed survivors. Together they raced round the back of the hut running instinctively between the trees and vanished into the blackness of the night.

Changing direction once out of sight they turned left and worked their way towards the border. Seeing the flood lights ahead they again turned left and kept the wire parallel with them on their right careful to stay away from the illuminated area.

Twice they lay in the undergrowth and let the guards go past. By the shouting going on from the direction of the hut, Rance guessed the Germans were completely bewildered as to where they'd gone.

'We've missed our chance those Gypsies saw to that,' whispered Marek angrily. 'We'll have to return to Piotrkow if we can'.

'We'll have to move fast before they bring in the dogs,' said Rance.

All through the night they ran with only the occasional stop for rest and they both staggered with tiredness and fatigue.

The night dragged on in an endless nightmare of exhaustion trying to keep ahead of the torch lights and howling dogs following in the distance.

Looking back at the strung out lights behind them Rance knew that the dogs hadn't yet got their scent.

Dawn broke with fingers of sunlight heralding another hot day and they kept well south of the Piotrkow road wading into the shallow River Warta before turning downstream for a kilometre to try and throw off the dogs.

Striking out again across open country they were forced to stop through sheer exhaustion in a small wood but they could still hear the German troops moving in their direction. Rance's feet felt on fire in the heavy boots he was wearing but he knew that if he took them off they would never go back on.

The afternoon came as a challenge, with his feet swelling and his heels blistering so much that he felt the blood soaking into his boots. The shadows were lengthening with dusk approaching when they looked down on the River Widawka, another shallow river not as wide as the other but just as welcoming. Almost blindly they staggered down the bank falling face down in the cold slow moving water.

Rance slowly turned over closing his eyes letting the water gently lap over him. Now he could feel the pain and soreness in his feet when the water found its way into his boots. His face twisted with pain when he was forced to take them off and when he did he looked with dismay at his raw bleeding feet.

Gently he forced them into the water wincing as they began to cool and the swelling subside. He lay partly on the river bank with his waist and legs still in the water watching the sun finally sink below the horizon. He glanced over to Marek. 'How much further?'

'About twenty kilometres I suppose, maybe a little less'.

'Can we make it before dawn?'

'We have to they're gaining all the time. I have a new hiding place we can use. You may not like it but I think we'll be safe there.'

Rance gritted his teeth slowly pulling on his boots. It took all his will power to keep them on when the pain intensified.

He staggered after Marek until finally he went through the pain barrier and could no longer feel his feet.

They left behind the scattered woodland that had given them cover and moved out into open pasture-land that was dotted with isolated farmhouses and villages. Finding a rough track allowed them to make good progress until they arrived at the village of Kurnos at one o'clock in the morning.

Unable to get anyone to open their doors at that time of night they decided to keep on going not knowing how far the Germans were behind them. Twenty minutes later they stumbled on to the Belchatow to Piotrkow railway line.

'It doesn't seem to be used much,' said Rance stamping on the rusting track as if to test its strength.

'Very rarely nowadays,' answered Marek, 'But it will guide us straight into Piotrykow'.

Behind them they heard the faint but distinctive sound of a rifle shot. They listened, puzzled but heard no more.

'They must be searching the village,' remarked Marek.

'The dogs have lost our scent with so many others mixed in. It will delay them, and give us a little more time'.

'Why are they so persistent,'

'The smugglers told them who we are I suppose, and combined with the fact that we probably shot and blew half their friends up would give them an incentive,' answered Marek with a lop sided smile. 'We're lucky they weren't Gestapo or the SS and are only normal soldiers.'

Walking fast on the long straight track gave them renewed vigour, and they made good progress but they were aware that it would also help their pursuers. Dawn found them on the outskirts of Piotrkow, having left the railway line near the village of Gaski. In the distance coming the other way they saw the grey figures of more troops searching the track.

'It's a good job we left the line when we did,' remarked Marek, 'They must have radioed ahead and are trying to cut us off,'

'How much further to your hiding place?'

'Ten minutes that's all'.

They entered Piotrkow cautiously crossing behind the searching troops and walked into a cemetery. Marek motioned for Rance to wait before disappearing amongst the grave stones. He sat on a head stone too exhausted to move and groaned when Marek reappeared soon afterward bringing with him three other men each carrying crow bars.

Together they all moved off into the centre of the cemetery, Rance looked at the graves. They were the oldest headstones he'd ever seen, once clean-cut and sharp shaped by the mason's skill, now weathered and worn, crumbling with age. Some were obviously the graves of rich people their monuments towering above the great slabs of marble.

Stopping at one the three men dug their crowbars under a giant slab and with much straining managed to slide it over enough to leave a small gap. Rance could hear the sound of the dogs in the distance while the men looked at him nodding at the hole they'd uncovered. He tried to stare into the darkness but couldn't see anything he looked with consternation at Marek.

'We're not going down there surely?' Not believing that this would be their safe hiding place.

Marek nodded.

Rance looked towards the noise of the dogs. 'What about them?' he said nodding towards the sound.

'Don't worry these men will throw buckets of water everywhere to throw them off the scent, and it's surprising what a bit of meat will do dragged across the ground,' said Marek, 'but come, we must hurry if they're to do it in time.'

With one last look at the dawn sky, Rance swung his legs over the hole gingerly lowering himself inside. It was deep he couldn't feel the bottom even though he was now only supported by his elbows.

One of the men tried to push his arm off and he had visions of a body reaching out and dragging him in.

'Let go,' the grave digger whispered fiercely in his ear.

'Damn it man I can't feel the bottom,' he complained.

'It's not far just let go. Hurry,' said the man.

He let go and fell about a metre losing his balance landing heavily on a pile of rubbish. Marek followed him into the semi darkness. And Rance had only a few seconds to study their hiding place before the men swung the slab back. It was cramped about seven feet by five feet, but deep he could just about touch the slab grinding shut above his head. He looked at what he'd fallen on and froze in shock at what was left of a skeleton lying amongst the shell of a coffin. The skull reflecting in the early morning light grinned back in devilish delight at having company after so many years.

It was the last thing Rance saw before the giant slab of marble swung back into place leaving him in the blackness of the grave. He shuddered feeling the hairs on the back of neck tingle and so pulled his legs up to his chest as if afraid the bones would reach out and touch him.

'Marek,' he whispered making sure he wasn't alone.

'No noise until we're sure they've gone,' came Marek's hollow voice out of the blackness.

That made Rance feel better knowing Marek was suffering too.

It smelt old and musty in the hole, he put his hand on the wall and found it to be damp rough-hewn stone. Now feeling something come out of a crack and run lightly over his hand he involuntary swore and jerked his hand away.

'What's the matter, what is it'? Said Marek in a state of panic.

Rance couldn't help but smile to himself. 'The bones just got up and touched me,' he whispered back hoarsely.

'Don't joke about things like that,' exclaimed Marek, his voice tight with superstitious fear.

Rance felt cold sitting there as he tried to listen for any sound from above. Staring up towards the slab he was relieved to see a faint glimmer of light, not enough to see by but at least they wouldn't run out of air.

He gave up trying to see Marek in the total darkness all he could hear was his laboured breathing somewhere opposite him. At least, he hoped it was Marek. Now he knew what a blind man must feel like.

Time seemed to stand still and the rough-hewn stone dug into his back when he started to doze and stretch out his legs, hurriedly drawing them back when he found himself amongst the dry brittle bones.

A faint snore from Marek's direction irritated him, how could he get so comfortable to sleep. Putting his arms on his bent knees he rested his head, now thinking of Izabel made him settle, he wondered what she was doing now that she was reasonably safe. He would take her back to England if ever the war ended, but if she couldn't go he would stay here with her with or without the Communists. He tried to remember how long he'd been running and fighting but his tired mind and body gave up.

He was back in England with Izabel, it was spring time and the two of them were walking the cliffs in Cornwall, he showed her the wild Cowslips and Sea pinks waving their bright pink heads on their long slender stalks spreading themselves proudly amongst the grey granite outcrops of rocks coated with green lichens.

The sun was warm on his face and he stopped to shield his eyes against its glare, he saw someone approaching walking the same cliff path.

The stranger had a peculiar walk and held his head stiffly to one side. The figure came nearer and he realised with horror that it was Schneller who was grinning widely, his bulbous eyes glowing in madness with streams of white spittle pouring from the corners of his mouth.

In his hand was a giant pistol which he slowly lifted and pointed at Izabel. His lips moved but no sound came, with a cry Rance lunged forward and grabbed at his head which came away in his hand.

Quickly it changed to the smoothness of a skull his fingers disappearing into the eye sockets and in the darkness he found he was lying on the hard damp floor feeling the skull in his hand and with a cry threw it from him, causing Marek to yell out loud in fright when the skull landed in his lap.

'What the hell are you playing at you bloody stupid Englishman?' he snapped. 'You frightened me to death with your silly games, you think this is a joke?'

Rance found himself apologising that he'd had a dream about Schneller, but another grunt from the darkness told him that Marek didn't believe him.

He looked up towards the crack and panicked when he couldn't see it. 'Marek, I can't see daylight they've buried us alive,' he said hoarsely.

'I think you'll find its night time you've been asleep most of the day,' muttered Marek still upset about the skull.

'You haven't I suppose?' snapped Rance annoyed that he'd shown panic in Marek's company. He slowly stood up and stretched feeling his whole body stiffening. His mouth felt dry and hunger pains stabbed at his stomach.

Marek cursed and jumped about in the darkness, it was Rance's turn to be alarmed, 'What the hell's wrong with you,' he whispered.

'Just something in my shirt,' the voice groaned from across the dried bones.

Gingerly Rance sat down, now he could feel things running over his body, he grabbed something that was about two inches long with thousands of legs that reminded him of a hairy worm. He held on tightly to the squirming insect until it turned round and bit him. With a start he threw it away being careful not to throw it where he thought Marek was sitting.

'Have you a girlfriend back home Englishman?' The question coming suddenly out of the darkness startled him. It was something he wasn't expecting at this moment in time. He remained silent and still for a few seconds as the question brought back the painful memories of Anna in Boulogne.

'No, not in England, there was a girl once in France but-' his voice trailed away into silence.

Marek could sense the sorrow in Rance voice.

'You were in love with this girl?' he asked.

'Yes I think I was'.

'What happened to her if you don't mind me asking?'

'She was killed by the Gestapo for protecting me along with the rest of her family,' he answered bitterly.

'I'm so sorry Englishman, the Gestapo have a lot to answer for,' said Marek.

'The Germans have taken my family also, some say to a labour camp in Germany but for all I know none may be left alive. Yes they have a lot to answer for.'

He paused for a second. 'We could have been friends you and I Englishman, if it hadn't been for Izabel.'

Rance nodded forgetting Marek couldn't see him in the dark.

'Yes we could,' he admitted quietly, adding, 'we still can we've been through a lot together you and I. Is it really our fault that we had the luck to love the same woman. Neither of us would want to hurt her. After all in the end it's her choice not ours.'

Marek pondered on that before speaking again.

'Yes it's true either one of us would die for her and perhaps one of us will, but for now I would like to be your friend Rance, and if I could see your hand I would like to shake it.'

Rance thrust out his hand searching in the dark until they finally came together in the pitch-blackness.

The hours went by, seemingly endless hours of darkness, the crack appeared above their heads denoting the end of the night and the beginning of another hot day. For the two men their hiding place was quite cool almost cold in fact, Rance's whole body cried out for water and the pains of hunger still twisted in his stomach but his raging thirst was the worst to endure.

His mind shrieked for release from that place he could feel himself becoming claustrophobic as the hours slowly went by. His throat was now so parched he couldn't speak, the crack once again faded from view with still no sign of the grave diggers return. Although it was always dark in the hole the insects that lived there seemed to sense when the sun had set and night had returned.

Rance cringed whenever he felt them on him. Twice the long hairy ones ran along the back of his neck and down his collar before finding themselves trapped when that happened they would try and bit their way out which resulted in great contortions on his part to get rid of them.

'What's happened to the men who put us in here, where the hell are they?' croaked Marek.

Claustrophobia and fear was the factor now, had the grave diggers been arrested and shot? Were he and Marek entombed in this ghastly place to slowly die of hunger and thirst only to be eaten by these insects crawling all over them both?

He must have dozed because he felt himself coming awake. He sat up with a start and looking up at the slab was relieved to see the crack had returned denoting another day. He tried to remember how long they'd been there but gave up, feeling the insects still exploring his body he ignored them no longer caring.

His tongue was swollen and his lips felt cracked. Licking the damp rough-hewn stone trying to get moisture just filled his mouth with rot and decaying dirt, now he hadn't the energy to spit it out. He dozed again, for how long he couldn't tell when he opened his eyes.

This time the crack had again disappeared and by sheer will power he forced himself to his feet and found his way to Marek who jumped at his touch. Slowly he pulled Marek to his feet and like two drunken men they forced their legs to move until they sat down again exhausted.

The movement stirred Rance's blood helping his mind, because he was sure he was going insane and the urge to claw at the walls to get out was becoming unbearable.

For what seemed an eternity he lay on the cold floor of the grave his feet resting amongst the bones. Not caring anymore, all he wanted to do was escape from this hell he was in. Listening to Marek's laboured breathing he wondered if they were beginning to run out of air. Feeling something run over his face he forced himself into a sitting position and looking up he noticed the crack had reappeared. How many days and nights? he'd lost count.

Slowly the crack widened letting in a brilliant shaft of sunlight, its fierce rays almost blinding him when he rose to his feet and kicked his partner awake.

.'Come on Marek, we've just gone to heaven,' he choked.

Shading his burning eyes he stared at the silhouetted figure peering down at them.

"We're sorry you had to stay down there so long,' said the grave digger, 'but the Germans were around us and wouldn't go away until now. One of us got detained. Not because of you, something to do with the black-market, although I don't know why they want to be bothered with a poor grave digger.'

'Will you shut up and get us out of here,' croaked Marek impatiently.

A rope dropped down and they were hauled out into the pure fresh air where they lay panting on the ground.

Grunting with the weight of the slab the grave diggers started to slid the slab back into place. Rance sat up and glanced down into the hole, the last thing he saw was the skull staring up at him from the corner of the grave where Marek had thrown it. He shuddered as the slab finally hid it from his view forever.

They were taken to the grave diggers hut and given buckets full of fresh water which they tipped over their mouths letting it flow over their necks and down their fronts. He stared at Marek. He was a tramp, filthy and unshaven the lice in his hair plain to see, his eyes staring out of his strained face were red and bloodshot. He gingerly felt his own stubble, no not stubble, more of a beard and he could feel lice running over his own head and body.

'What time is it?' he asked scratching his head, making the lice run for cover down his shirt.

'Six thirty in the morning lots of people going to work we thought it best for you to mingle. The state you're in you'll easily pass as workmen going off shift.' The grave diggers were becoming agitated. 'We think you must go now, the Germans, well, you know-,'

Keeping to the forester's tracks they made good progress and reached the village of Leczno just before nightfall there they were welcomed by the villagers.

Fed on hot pork and forced to drink the inevitable bottle of Vodka, Rance and Marek fell asleep at the table.

CHAPTER 29

A forest near Piotrekow

The Russian officer caught Izabel's arm in a vice like grip and grinning broadly pulled her towards him, surprised when she came so willingly crushing herself close to his body.

His facial expression turned from lust to dread when he felt the barrel of a pistol pressed against his throat, he looked down into eyes that blazed with death, eyes of a woman that wouldn't hesitate to kill.

The rest of the men at first too startled to move watched in cold silence as the Pole tried to reason with her. 'Don't be foolish girl, nobody wants to hurt you. We're here to help.'

'I don't believe you,' she snapped. You're no better than the Germans'.

'Listen to comrade Piotr he's telling you the truth,' said the officer desperately trying to lean back from the barrel pressed hard against his neck.

Izabel's heart was thumping madly. She didn't want to die, but was determined not to back down. 'Comrade Piotr, as you call him is a traitor. He should be fighting the Germans with us, not forging an alliance with you.'

'When the Germans have gone it will be the Communist party running things here, so make it easy on yourself,' said the Pole in exasperation.

Seeing her hesitate, the officer tried to pull away before freezing in terror as she cocked the pistol. The sudden sound brought a deathly hush. Nobody moved except the officer who shut his eyes, waiting to die, the sweat running off his brow.

The fierce crackle of gunfire ended the stalemate, German troops broke cover and ran towards them. Izabel turned in confusion, before running headlong into the woods with bullets smashing into the trees around her. Risking a glance behind, she saw some of the Russians fighting while the rest were in full flight following her.

Of the Russian officer there was no sign, but she knew she'd made a deadly enemy there. Panic made her feet fly over the ground ignoring the branches that smacked her in the face drawing blood.

A bullet clipped a tree next to her and one hit the earth just ahead she guessed it to be one of the Russians who was firing, again glancing over her shoulder she noticed the Germans dropping back slightly.

She ran faster, running from the Russians, who in turn were running from the Germans, all heading in her direction.

Slowly she gained as the Russians stopped to fire back at their pursuers. All except the two who were intent on keeping contact, the officer and the Pole who had appeared as if from nowhere.

She was out of breath and exhausted but knew she was near the village of Ostrow. From behind her came the faint crackle of gunfire and the two shouting men who were gaining ground. The woodlands gave way to the River Czarna but she was too far upstream so she turned left and ran down the river bank. The two men saw this and raced to cut her off. She heard them coming and unable to run any further turned like a trapped animal ready to fight.

The two men also stopped, respectful of the pistol she carried. Slowly she raised the pistol trying to steady her shaking hand. Neither of the men made any move forward, instead they stared at something behind her. Puzzled she turned and found the tree-line full of heavily armed men their weapons pointing at the Russian troops.

Recognising Jozef and Krolik she ran to join them.

The Pole travelling with the Russians glanced nervously behind him before speaking 'We're being chased by the Germans, we're not after the girl. These Russians have been sent to help us. Now we need your help,' he shouted.

'Don't trust them,' Izabel said fiercely.

Krolik ignored her, instead issuing orders for his men to spread out, he waved the Russians forward as the firing intensified and the Russian rear guard came running out of the woods.

Throwing caution to the wind the German troops came on to the river bank. Izabel caught her breath standing on the edge of the woods partly screened she noticed a German officer with a patch over one eye but even that and the three hundred metres that separated them she recognised Lohr's figure before he turned and disappeared.

Krolik ordered some of his men to fan out to their rear to avoid being outflanked. The German troops out on the river bank looked to where the partisans lay concealed unsure on what to do next. Lieutenant Lohr hidden in the trees shouted for them to go on.

Krolik whispered to Jozef, 'He's not sure if the Russians are still here. Most of his men are with him in the woods. If we take the men on the river bank he'll circle us, but first he has to be sure.'

'You think he's offering his men as bait?' exclaimed Jozef incredulously.

'It's the sort of thing that he would do. Don't you think?'

'What shall we do now?' said Jozef.

Krolik smiled slyly, 'Two can play that game. We'll pull back, leaving some of the Russians as bait. When they close in we'll be behind them.'

An argument broke out between Krolik and the Russian officer who was at first reluctant to do it, but then it was agreed that some of the partisans would stay with them on the bank and some of the Russians would go with Krolik.

Izabel found herself next to the Russian officer and the communist Pole who stared at her with a frosty expression.

'We could do with people like you in the party comrade,' said the Pole, as a way of breaking the awkward silence.

'Why, so the Russians can rape me comrade,' said Izabel mockingly.

The Pole flushed and tried again. 'Honestly we didn't know you were with the partisans, we thought you were a German spy.'

Izabel grew angry, 'Not only did he want to rape me, but now you treat me like a fool'.

'Take no notice of her, she's just a bitch,' snapped the officer.

'A bitch that had you scared,' she snapped back.

Izabel thought he would explode with anger regretting opening her impulsive mouth once more. Now she'd only made the situation worse, it came as a relief when the firing started.

The Germans advancing along the river bank lost two men in the first volley of fire before going to ground amongst the reeds.

Lieutenant Lohr seeing the results, moved his remaining men in an outflanking movement to get behind them.

Krolik watched them come and signalled his men to close in but was dismayed at being only partly successful.

Lohr had now developed a healthy respect for the partisans and wasn't to be caught out so easily. He kept most of his men in reserve, only allowing eight to go forward. Three died, caught in the crossfire before Lohr attacked Krolik's left flank, forcing him to swing away towards the river.

Izabel watched him desperately trying to hold back the Germans while he directed Jozef to retreat across the river and set up his machine guns on the far bank.

Jozef beckoned her to follow and together with some of his men they crossed under covering fire and watched Krolik's men and the Russians make their break running from the cover of the trees and into the open.

They jumped down the shallow river bank and into the water which only came up to their knees. The uneven river bed with its loose slippery boulders took its toll men slipped and fell before staggering upright.

Jozef seeing what was happening directed his machine gunners to open fire even before they sighted the Germans. The thunderous clatter of the three machine guns almost split Izabel's ear drums. A withering hail of bullets whipped through the trees on the Germans side, tearing off clumps of bark, splitting branches and scything into the first of the pursuing troops who fell back in disarray.

Izabel watched in horror as the first mortars fell amongst the partisans and Russians caught out in the open. Two men died and Krolik fell with a piece of shrapnel slicing his cheek before he regained his feet and ran on. Another mortar landed in the river bed sending up a fountain of water, leaving a screaming Russian soldier floundering legless.

A single rifle shot rang out by Izabel's side and the man jerked with the force of the bullet in his head and slowly sank rolling along the river bed.

The Russian officer lowered his rifle and seeing her shocked face, mumbled that it was better than leaving him for the Germans.

Lohr, angry that they'd managed to cross the river had no intention of trying to follow, that would be suicide, so he was content to bombard their positions with mortar fire.

Krolik and the Russians withdrew by re-crossing the river and heading into the forest south of Sulejow where an hour later Krolik called a halt.

'Why have we stopped?' 'The Germans will be following us,' queried the Russian officer.

'Because we go our own way, we have things to do elsewhere,' answered Krolik.

The Russian officer and Piotr went into a whispered conversation, Izabel tried to listen as they appeared to be arguing while the Russian troops and the partisans split into two separate groups both nervously watching each other.

Piotr stepped towards Krolik. 'Comrade, you and your men are good fighters after all are we not on the same side.'

He looked at the partisans. 'Come you should join us as, together we can defeat our enemies and forge a great state for all our people to live as one.' He lifted his arms wide his eyes glowing with a fanatical light.

'Here we have our Russian friends who'll help us attain that when the Germans have gone.'

'A fine speech but we only take orders from the Polish Home Army HQ, based in London?' Lied Krolik, 'You may be assured that we'll pass on your message,' he add dryly.

Piotr's eyes narrowed. 'We don't like being made fools of comrade.'

Tension mounted amongst the men, Izabel felt the thumping of her heart when fingers curled around triggers and they moved further apart.

The seconds passed into eternity for Izabel watching the two sides nervously confronting each other. Krolik and the Russian officer were both aware that their men were waiting for them to decide on what to do next. If either one lifted or moved his weapon instant death would litter the forest floor with partisan and Russian alike, yet neither could back away.

Already the officer had lost face once that day and he wasn't going to do it a second time. Krolik had already decided he wasn't going to anyway. It was the Russian's guide, comrade Piotr that found the answer.

He spoke to Krolik, 'Comrade, why don't you let your men decide on what they want to do,'

Krolik didn't take his eyes off the Russian officer's face.

'They already have their orders,' he snapped.

'Ah yes, very commendable, but perhaps it may be the best way forward don't you think?' said the communist sagely.

Krolik realised he was being given a chance to avoid bloodshed.

Not taking his eyes off the officer he spoke to his men.

'If any of you are communists or would like to become one, step over to their side and no harm will befall you.'

The seconds ticked away, one man shuffled his feet but didn't move, the rest stared impassively at the Russian troops and stayed where they were.

'Are you happy now?' queried Krolik.

Seemingly relieved, the Russian officer relaxed and the tension disappeared.

'I think your men have made a mistake, but that's your affair now,' said Piotr. 'When the Germans have gone you will change your minds when you see what a wonderful country this will become.'

'Then I'll look forward to that day comrade,' countered Krolik, and ordered his men to move out.

The communist Pole watched him go with suspicion unsure if he was being taken seriously or not.

'So there was no sign of the Englishman or their leader Marek with that rabble,' frowned the officer, 'and are you sure that was the girl courier that has links with the Polish home Army HQ?'

'Yes I'm sure,' exclaimed Piotr annoyed that he'd been doubted. 'My agents are everywhere, we're getting to know everyone, friend and enemy alike. Already lists are being compiled on who is with us and who's against, I know which list they'll be on,' he said, nodding in the direction of the departing partisans.

Gestapo HQ Piotrekow

Claus Ritschel drummed his finger impatiently on the highly polished desk top and looked around at the assembled officers and the two agents, Mueller and Kantor, before his angry eyes came to rest on Schmidt.

'You told me Major Schneller had arrived back in Piotrkow over an hour ago. Well, where is he?'

Schmidt swallowed, 'I gave him your message that you wanted a meeting sir.'

He glanced back when the door opened, relieved at Schneller's sudden appearance walking in with that curious swinging motion and his head tilted to one side.

'I'm sorry to be late sir,' he breezed full of confidence, 'But I thought that seeing you I should make myself look presentable. I've had a very busy week and the train back was filthy.'

Still angry Claus Ritschel shuffled his papers and nodded curtly.

'Sit down Major Schneller and give us your report.'

'Sir, as you know the Russians are parachuting in troops, together with large amounts of guns and ammunition. Their aim, or so I'm informed is to equip and train the Polish members of the communist party to sabotage and delay our convoys going to the front line. My orders are to find and attack them wherever they may be found. I must also organise food collections from the local farmers, Poles and Volksdeutche alike for our troops fighting on the Russian front. To help us in this task I have on loan a company of Cossacks.'

He stopped with a lopsided smirk as a murmur of surprise swept the room. 'Nearly two hundred of them to be exact,' he continued 'They are under my command so I will tell them what areas to cover and let them get on with it. Which will leave us free to gather the food supplies and look for the Russian troops.'

'Where are they now?' enquired a Gestapo officer sitting behind him.

'Camped on the outskirts of Piotrkow,' said Schneller. 'I have my own officers and men with them, so don't be concerned about that.'

'What about their horses?' the officer persisted.

'And their horses, and their swords,' said Schneller plainly annoyed at the stupid questions.

Claus Ritschel pointed at Mueller and Kantor,

'These two have discovered two communist groups who are actively engaged recruiting men to their cause. One of the groups was seen southwest of Sulejow only yesterday.'

'So that's where we'll start with the Cossacks,' said Schneller.

'One more thing Major. It may interest you to know that two bandits were intercepted at the border post of Kepno. That was near your meeting place, wasn't it'.

Schneller nodded. "Yes why?'

'One of them was the Englishman.'

The news hit Schneller like a bullet, Schmidt watched him go white.

After a brief pause he managed to speak. 'It's good that he's been arrested. When can I interrogate the man?'

'You can't,' said Claus Ritschel, 'they eluded capture despite being chased all the way back to Piotrkow.'

'What fools let them get away like that?' exclaimed Schneller, plainly agitated. 'You realise it must have been me they were after?'

'I don't think there is any doubt about that,' said Claus Ritschel. 'I've arranged for you to have a bodyguard until we can deal with this problem. In the meantime we must protect the convoys and gather food supplies for the troops.'

After the meeting broke up the realisation that the bandits had even dared to try to cross into Germany shocked Schmidt. Making him wonder who would be next. Him perhaps? That bitch of a girl had been one of them all the time and already she might be planning her revenge. He felt his fingers shaking while gathering up the loose papers from the meeting. The Russians were slowly getting closer and soon he was sure he would be able to smell the dirty unwashed animals when they raped and killed their way across Poland. Things were getting out of hand now and he could see no escape.

CHAPTER 30

Major Schneller left his staff car at the edge of the Cossack encampment, and with Schmidt walking behind him he picked his way between the ragged tents towards the centre. Schmidt wrinkled his nose, almost choking at the smell of urine and raw sewage mixed in with the odour from the sweating horses that had obviously been ridden hard and now tethered up wind from the camp.

Gingerly he stepped over some of the Cossack troops languishing on the ground looking at them with distaste. They stared back with dark sullen eyes. So much for the Russian Cossacks of the Wehrmacht he thought nervously. He knew they hated Germans, and given the chance would slit his throat, but they hated the Russian communists more, much more.

Schneller stopped in front of a tent slightly larger than the others and called to the men inside. For a brief second there was silence then the flap was thrown back and out stepped a tall slim man with a long thin broken nose and a week's growth of stubble on his chin. His eyes were dark almost black, shining with a fierce light. He stared without blinking at Schneller reminding Schmidt of a wild animal.

'Du wills mich?' he said speaking German.

A small crowd gathered around them and Schmidt was conscious of their beady eyes boring into the back of his neck. All carried long slightly curved swords strapped to their waists with pistols pushed into their wide trouser belts. Some had rifles slung over their shoulders and others carried machine pistols across their fronts, while on their heads they wore the traditional black fur hats that looked out of place with their German uniforms. None of them had shaved and all had the same fierce look and wild eyes.

Schmidt felt a shiver run though him, thankful that at least they were on his side for the time being. He glanced at Schneller if he was nervous he didn't show it when he answered. 'I want you to scout the villages southwest of here. There are reports of Russian troops in the area also there are a number of bandit groups operating in the forests. I want them hunted down and destroyed. I give you complete freedom on how you go about it as long as you get results.'

He unfolded a map and laid it down on the ground pointing at Kalow. Every two days you will report here for fresh orders, if you can't make it yourself send one of your men. Is that understood?'

The Cossack leader drew his sword and without taking his eyes off Schneller pierced the map with its point and lifting it high in the air he passed it back to one of his men before answering.

'In case you want to know, my name is Gorecki I'm the leader of these men. At the beginning we were under your command for fourteen days. Now it is down to ten after that we go to the Russian front. Nothing has changed, or has it?'

Schneller shook his head. 'If you do your job right then ten days will be enough anyway but even if you haven't finished here you'll still go on to the front in ten days' time.'

Gorecki nodded and lifting his sword he shouted orders to his men.

The Cossacks broke camp, tents were struck and rolled into small bundles while strings of horses were run amongst them and loaded, leaving some of the Cossacks to race and jostled each other in mock skirmishes their swords clashing and flashing in the sunlight.

Schmidt dodged around like a frightened rabbit leaving Schneller to stand amongst all the turmoil.

The Cossack leader raced his half wild horse to the far end of the camp before turning and racing it back almost up to the waiting Germans.

The Major flinched, and seeing it the Cossack was satisfied, grinning widely his white teeth flashing. He screamed, wheeling away into the countryside followed by his two hundred strong men, until all that was left was the stink from the remains of their camp.

Schmidt wiped his sweating brow with relief at their departure. Bending down he picked up the trampled map. 'He forgot his map sir.'

'He can't read the fucking thing, that's why,' Schneller snapped disdainfully. 'I've arranged for a Volksdeutche and a cavalry officer to go with them. Damn him,' he muttered under his breath.

The village of Leczno

The noise of thunder woke Rance from a deep restful sleep he listened to the noise outside frowning trying to identify it.

Suddenly he knew, he'd heard it a thousand times before when the army had taught him to ride. It was the sound of charging horses, hundreds of horses. Leaping from his bed he peered through the window stunned in amazement at the sight of men on horseback sweeping in from the western end of the village swords slashing at anyone in their way.

A man died who he'd drunk Vodka with the night before. Another, caught outside the village was tied behind a horse and dragged bodily through the centre before being cut free and left to die. Two of the small wooden houses went up in flames, the occupants butchered as they ran.

Rance searched frantically for his machine pistol but couldn't find it, then he remembered the man lying dead outside had said he would clean it while he slept. He went back to the window and could only watch the carnage happening before him.

He picked out their leader a tall thin man sitting ramrod straight in his saddle directing his men from his position in the centre of the track. Satisfied they'd done enough he turned with a scream leading his men away as fast as they'd arrived leaving a shocked and horrified village to mourn their dead.

Rance went amongst the villagers helping where he could before finding Marek in a room full to overflowing with the wounded, dead and dying.

Marek looked up from a corpse. His hollow burnt out eyes glowing in anger. 'He's done it, Schnellers bought in the Cossacks,' slamming his fist against the door jam. 'We have to stop him what sort of animal is he?'

Rance could feel his own burning rage, a hatred that he had to fight to control while he surveyed the scene around him.

317

They did all they could for the villagers before reluctantly moving on across the River Pilica, entering the village of Krasne just after mid-night. Izabel told them about her brush with the Russians, keeping back the fact that they would have killed her if they'd had the chance. She told them about the uprising in Warsaw, apparently it had happened a few days ago but they'd only just heard the news.

Marek's eyes gleamed, 'That's tremendous news, have we received any orders about going to help them?'

Izabel shook her head. 'Curen said no. It would be suicide, the whole area between here and the Capital is full of German divisions. We must await the Russians, but in the meantime your orders are to harass the enemy supply lines wherever you can. Their outposts must be attacked and ammunition stores destroyed.'

'Has Curen said anything about the communist groups operating in the area?'

'There are stories emerging from behind the Russian lines that some of the partisans are joining the communist party and are turning on their own groups. But all are fighting the Germans. It's a mess,' said Izabel. 'A lot of the partisans are being arrested and are disappearing, some say to Siberia.'

'How far away is the Russian front now?' queried Rance.

'No more than a hundred kilometres,' replied Izabel, giving him a nervous glance.

'Where's Krolik?' asked Marek.

'He's left a message saying he'll be at the bridge near Czersko at mid-day tomorrow if you arrive back in time. He has orders to meet with your old friend Losos and his men. The two groups are going to attack an ammunition dump.'

Marek rose with a yawn, 'We must get some rest if we're to be there, it will mean an early start.'

Reluctantly Rance and Izabel parted once again having only a brief time together.

The meeting between Marek and his men was time for another celebration. Rance shook hands with Golab and Krolik and excepting a bottle of the usual Vodka, he took a deep swig before giving it back. He was sure it was getting worse as they didn't have time to distil it properly, he wondered if it ever made them ill, but as yet he'd seen no sign of it.

'Where do we meet Losos?' queried Marek in between swigs of the fiery liquid.

'Half a day's walk partly forest and open farmland, reasonable cover,' replied Krolik.

The heat of the mid-day sun was overpowering Rance shaded his eyes trying to stare into the shimmering distance of the open countryside. Crossing the open spaces was a time of extreme danger, he was nervous and the shimmering heat haze didn't help it distorted the skyline.

The sound of gunfire in the distance made them uneasy.

'It could be Losos and his men Marek,' said Krolik and they broke into a run with Rance pushing hard to keep up. Twenty minutes later they emerged on the other side of a small wood gazing out onto more open pasture-land.

On the horizon in the shimmering heat Rance could see figures grouped together on the ground while round them rode men on horseback. Lifting his field glasses he could make out the figure of Losos in the centre waving his giant machete. He watched spellbound as the Cossacks slowly cut off their retreat, driving them into the waiting guns of the German troops on their left.

Rance slowly traversed his glasses until he stopped on a German staff car parked on a rough farm track.

He nudged Marek and pointed, 'That's Schneller over there'

Rance turned back to the fighting to see that Losos had stopped running and formed a circle. The men became distorted again in the heat haze as the firing slackened to individual shots, figures began to fall in the circle one by one. Rance was puzzled he couldn't understand what was happening, but Marek knew crying out in anguish,

'Dear God, they're shooting themselves.'

Now Rance understood watching the scene unfold, he felt sick. They were obeying the one golden rule. Slowly he lowered the glasses unable to watch anymore.

Marek stayed hidden in the woods, setting up machine gun nests at fifty metre intervals as a precautionary measure while they waited for dusk. All afternoon the Cossacks stayed picking over what was left of Losos and his men, a temporary camp had been set up and the Cossacks rested while the Germans stayed together keeping their distance.

Rance studied the Cossacks through his glasses and lost count at a hundred and eighty and forty Germans. Of Schneller there was no sign.

Marek came and lay beside him offering a piece of dried pork.

'It's not our day,' he observed sourly, 'we need more men, twenty isn't enough and we need to be able to pick the place of our choosing to stand any chance against those animals'.

Rance took the pork and bit into the hard dried meat without saying a word. Was there to be no end to this, he thought.

In the late afternoon the Cossacks left, followed by the Germans in their halftracks. but Marek decided to wait until dark before approaching the killing ground. Rance was glad of that for he dreaded seeing what the Cossacks had done. The bodies lay close together and all had been stripped of their clothes and weapons. Someone lit a small lamp to examine a body and retched at what he saw.

Rance walked away unable to look. Silently they left the scene, there was nothing they could do. The nearest village would be informed and they would be buried where they'd fallen.

The next few days became a game of hide and attempted ambush. Endless kilometres of forced night marches followed by nervous days of trying to set traps for the Cossacks,

'It's an impossible task trying to catch them,' said Marek in frustration. 'No one knows where they will show up next. Four villages have been ransacked and twice we were almost caught off guard it's only because of our knowledge of the forest that's saved us.

Now it seems according to Curen that the Germans heartened by the Cossacks success have put more men in the field and are again raiding the farms and villages for food. Although this time they're making no attempt to move them out they seem to be collecting food from their own Volksdeutche farmers as well which shows how desperate they're getting to feed their the troops at the front

Two days later much to Marek's relief, Izabel brought news that the Cossacks had been moved to the Russian front and Curen had now ordered them to renew their attacks and harass the enemy supply lines again.

The long hot summer became a blur to Rance and the endless hunting and killing continued unabated, both sides fighting a savage and unforgiving war without mercy of any kind.

Desperately short of food Rance and the partisans raided the farms and villages of the Volksdeutches, walking twenty kilometres at night, blowing a railway line at dawn before walking another twenty kilometres the next night to attack a convoy.

He lost count of the men killed in his group but still they came, young men, some because their families had been killed or they were running away from the forced labour camps, but most just hated the Germans and what they were doing.

Jozef stood with Rance watching some of the new men arriving, wide eyed and unsure of themselves as Marek handed out weapons.

'More men for me to train and show how to die,' Rance spoke bitterly.

Jozef looked at him, 'Don't talk like that every one of these men have heard about you the Englishman with nine lives, now they want to fight with you and us so they can tell their grandchildren about how they fought with this Englishman'.

He knew different looking with bitter eyes at the eager young men knowing that most would last only a short time and he could only try and teach the ways to survive. But even that carried no guarantees for him. He was death, and could smell death, it pervaded the air around him. He dreamed of death and woke up screaming at the horrors he'd seen.

October 1944.

Rance stood in the middle of the main Piotrkow to Kielce road dressed as a German policeman. Being late afternoon with the shadows already lengthening it had started to get cold, he shivered despite the heavy overcoat he was wearing. He looked towards the sides of the road where Marek had set up two machine gun posts wondering how reliable the information they'd received about a food convoy due to pass their way, at the same time he glanced dubiously at the side road he was supposed to direct the convoy on to.

Marek had given orders to stop anything that came their way for it was bound to be German so they'd picked a sharp bend in the hope that the vehicles would be slow moving.

The first came faster than he'd expected, hurriedly he held up his police regulation red and white stick with a disc on the end forcing the saloon car to break fiercely. The occupants were a man and woman both well dressed and looking angry. He assumed they were Volkedeutches.

The man leaned out the window clearly agitated.

'That's a stupid place for a road block. I nearly ran over you, anyway you can clearly see who we are, so why stop us?'

Rance walked up and saluted. 'You should have carried on going Volkdeutche shouldn't you?' he said sticking his machine pistol in the man's face which immediately change colour to a deathly white.

The woman started to cry and the man froze at the wheel before two of the partisans pulled them out and a third drove the car off the road and under cover. Rance walked back into the road and waited.

Gestapo HQ Piotrekow

Lieutenant Schmidt smirked across the desk at the two agents who now were well dressed in the typical black raincoats of the Gestapo, he hardly recognised them.

Mueller and Kantor stared back impassively with nothing but contempt for the fat slovenly officer.

Schmidt slid a briefcase across his desk and sat back in his chair with arms folded. Neither of the two men attempted to pick it up, Schmidt sighed in annoyance.

'It's for you to deliver to the commander of the garrison at Sulejow. Its marked urgent'.

'Messengers now are we?' complained Mueller angry at being kept waiting so long.

'Why can't it go the normal way?' queried Kantor.

'You should know better than to ask questions like that especially from Major Schneller,' echoed Schmidt.

Mueller shrugged, 'Anything is better than running around with a bunch of Polish peasants, he lifted the case weighing it. 'There's not much in it'

'A few papers don't weigh a lot,' snapped Schmidt, 'you can take a car from the pool. Schneller's orders.'

Mueller glanced at his watch, 'You want us to go now? it will be dark in an hour.'

'Frightened of the dark are you?' countered Schmidt, now wishing he'd kept his mouth shut when they both glowered at him

They signed for the car and Kantor went to sit in the passenger seat.

'You drive,' snapped Mueller.

Kantor sighed, 'Why me all the time?'

'Because I'm telling you to that's why.

Kantor, still grumbling crashed the gears and turned onto the Sulejow road where the traffic had thinned out and they started to make good time.

'We'll be there before it gets dark,' mumbled Kantor, still annoyed that he'd got to drive, suddenly cursing when they came up at the rear end of a convoy of three trucks.

Every time he tried to pass another vehicle coming the other way forced him back. When the road became clear they found themselves approaching the brow of a hill. Mueller became impatient drumming his fingers on the briefcase sitting on his lap.

'Come on Kantor, stop messing about, move it,' he snapped.

Agitated by Mueller, Kantor put his foot down and swung out onto the other side of the road, surging passed the last truck then the second before being squeezed into the gap between the first and second as they approached a sharp right hand bend. The truck in front suddenly applied its brakes. Mueller cursed trying to see what was happening but the truck blocked his view. There was a slight delay before they were moving again with Mueller swearing profanely.

Before Kantor realised what was happening they found themselves being turned into a side road by the German police.

Mueller lowered his window to enquire what was happening and looked straight into the hard steel grey eyes of the Englishman.

'Bastard,' Mueller screamed, shouting at Kantor to go.

Startled! Kantor pushed hard down on the accelerator pedal and swung out onto the grass verge, narrowly missing an armed man pulling the first truck driver out of his cab.

The car wheels spun on the soft earth before finally taking hold and the car lurched forward onto the empty road ahead. Mueller ducked, screaming as a burst from a sub-machine gun shattered the rear window and front windscreen.

Rance ran with Golab and Krolik to the Volksdeutches car, and with wheels spinning went after them.

It was almost dark and the light was fading fast, Kantor tried desperately to stay on the road with bits of glass blowing back from the shattered windscreen cutting at his face, half blinding him.

Sheer terror forced his foot to the floor, he was dimly aware of Mueller hitting out screaming for him to slow down. Risking a glance into the rear view mirror he shouted out seeing the car behind gaining on them.

Rance hung onto the steering wheel forgetting his two passengers who were being bounced all over the inside of the car, it hit a ridge flying in the air before coming down with its wheels pounding the potholed road. Krolik and Golab shouted out in dismay swearing at him to slow down as he careered on.

He ignored them both he was gaining, now he could see Mueller's white strained face staring back at him through the shattered rear window.

Cantor's hands were wet with perspiration finding it hard to hold the steering wheel and his knuckles grew white. It was difficult to see now and he scrambled for the headlight switch.

'I can't find the lights,' he screamed at Mueller.

Cursing like a maniac Mueller bent forward to see the panel, as Kantor risked another glance in his rear view mirror and ran off the road.

The car hit the side of a bank and took off before somersaulting into a ditch. Mueller's head smashed into the panel and into the side window shattering it. Kantor pitched forward and screamed when the steering wheel splintered, impaling him through the chest.

The car lay on its roof with the engine pushed back pinning Mueller's legs into his seat the front door was bent open with the briefcase lying on the ground outside.

Frantically in a daze Mueller struggled to free himself ignoring Kantor's cries as he choked in his own blood. He could smell petrol leaking from the shattered engine and was dimly aware of figures racing towards him as he hung upside down. Now flames licked at his face scorching his hair. He started to scream when his flesh peeled and shrivelled sealing his eyelids.

Rance brought the car to a sliding halt and leapt out, racing towards the burning car only to be driven back by the intense heat. The three men stood and watched the funeral pyre before turning away and picking up the briefcase lying on the ground.

They returned to the road block and found that two of the trucks had been driven away, leaving the third for them to dispose of.

Rance gave the briefcase to Krolik for Marek's attention before climbing into the army truck and heading for Leczno having passed the burned out car without a second glance

He turned right at the cross-roads onto the village road. The engine missed a beat then slowed before picking up again he breathed a sigh of relief, but it was short lived. It coughed and slowed again before coming to a halt. He pulled the starter button time and time again making it whine in protest until eventually he gave up.

He realised he couldn't leave it there because it was too close to the village which the Germans would burn to the ground in retaliation. But still dressed as a German policeman he walked into the village.

On seeing him the young men ran into the forest, leaving the older ones to bolt their doors. It took him half an hour of going door to door to convince them of who he was and what he needed before they fetched the young men back.

Gathering together six horses to pull the truck they hauled it into the village. Rance stood on the tailboard, throwing cases of food and butter down to the villagers who had never seen such luxuries for years.

Within minutes the truck was empty so the villagers insisted he stay the night while the men towed the truck deep into the forest, well away from any village.

Tired as he was he couldn't help but join in the celebrations that drinking the usual bottles of Vodka led to. He lifted the home made brew and toasted everyone, before silently toasting his friend Cross.

Leczno

A hand grasped his shoulder shaking him awake, in a daze he struggled to sit up wincing at his thumping head before he realised it was morning. He stared at the old woman dancing around in front of him.

'Quickly,' she whispered you must hide the Germans are here and they're searching the village.

Rance, now fully awake followed her outside and into the back garden where she led him to the outside toilet just big enough for one person to sit in.

He groaned knowing what to expect every village seemed to have one. Lifting the lid he peered down into a big hole half full with sewage

He could see nothing until he bent his head inside and looked sideways. Now he could see his hiding place, a small space alongside the main hole. He lifted the top off and climbed inside choking and gagging as he could almost taste the smell.

The old lady gave him a smile of encouragement and replacing the lid proceed to drop her knickers and sit on the hole. Rance, already choking to death averted his eyes while listening to the Germans moving about outside.

The door to the toilet was pulled open and he heard the old lady scolding the hapless German soldier who opened it, much to the amusement of his companions. Rance silently thanked the old lady, realising what she had done to save his life

CHAPTER 31

The four Gestapo officers examined the burned out wreckage of the car.

'Was there a briefcase found amongst it?' Schneller asked the police guard.

'Not that I know of Sir.'

'Where are the bodies?' enquired Captain Braun.

'They were taken away for burial Sir.'

'On who's orders?'

'Why the lieutenant here Sir,' said the man pointing at Schmidt, who fidgeted under the gaze of the other three.

'I couldn't see the point of leaving them here Sir,' he said lamely.

Schneller turned away in disgust.

'Didn't you look for it when you first arrived?' countered Lohr, glaring at Schmidt with his one good eye.

Schmidt looked nervously at the burnt out car. 'Everything was such a mess the bodies had all but been cremated. I mean there wasn't much left of them. It was disgusting, they were burnt into the seats so much that you couldn't tell one from the other. When they left me Mueller sat with it on his lap, I'm sure that's where it would have stayed'.

'They were upside down, it could of fallen to the floor,' frowned Braun.

'Was the door open or shut when you arrived here first?' questioned Schneller.

'It was open Sir, but anyone of our troops could have done that before I arrived,'

'Where have you sent them for burial?'

'Well, they haven't actually been buried Sir'.

'Well at least that's something I suppose,' muttered Lohr.

'I had them cremated,' blurted the hapless Lieutenant. 'Well I thought being as they were almost there, we might as well finish it.' He cowered under the fury of their angry eyes.

The staff car sped away leaving him standing subdued next to the police guard who stared at the skyline trying to keep his face straight.

'If you so much as smile, 'I'll have you shot.' Schmidt snarled.

The three Gestapo officers sat in stony silence until they reached the main Piotrkow road.

'Do we still make the transfer?' queried Braun speaking to Schneller.

'I don't think we have much choice. Anyway, the odds are the briefcase burnt in the car but we'll compromise and wait another three weeks to be sure.'

'I don't think for one minute even if the bandits had the briefcase, they would be able to do anything about it. They haven't the manpower,' said Braun contemptuously.

Lohr rubbed at the scar on his nose. 'It would be a mistake to underestimate them,' he muttered sourly.

Rance returned to Krasne early in the afternoon and met Izabel gathering wood for the evening fire. With a cry of delight she ran into his arms, 'Rance, every time you go away I'm afraid you won't come back.'

He laughed as he swung her feet off the ground and kissed her soft full lips. Breathlessly she pulled away leaving him flushed with passion. Taking his arm they walked to the small house that was home to the three women. Anya greeted him with a kiss while and Marian hugged him.

'My, my,' murmured Izabel, tantalising him with her lips on his ear. 'Rance I'm getting jealous of all this attention you're receiving,' and they all laughed when he blushed profusely.

Izabel became serious, 'I have some bad news. The uprising in Warsaw has failed the city has been reduced to rubble by the Germans while the Russians sat on the outskirts and looked on, the few surviving partisans have surrendered'.

He felt dismayed he'd hoped that if they could have taken Warsaw then the end of the war would have been that much closer.

'There's some good news Rance', she continued, 'According to Curen the Germans have reduced their patrols and are having to send every available man to the front line. Apparently the Russians are again forcing them to retreat all along from Kielce to Radom.'

Marian placed a bowl of watery soup before him. He stirred the few vegetables round before cautiously sipping the brew. He'd had it before, Salivica or something, he wasn't sure but he remembered Cross hated it.

'Marek has informed us that we can return to Kalow at last, now that the Germans have all but stopped patrolling. It would seem that they're reluctant to take us on anymore,' said Marian.

Rance doubted that but was reluctant to say so.

'Where's Marek now?' he said instead.

'He's already returned to Kalow and wants you there as soon as possible,' Izabel answered giving his hand a squeeze.

'Tomorrow will be soon enough, don't you think?' she whispered.

Kalow

The next day Rance walked around the small wooden houses in disgust and looking at the mass of horse droppings in the clearing he guessed the Cossacks had used it as their base. The horses had used the outside while the Cossacks had used the inside. He couldn't bring himself to enter the houses so they stayed outside on the porch where Jozef offered him a bottle of Vodka which he declined.

Marek spread a map out on the floor and they all sat down.

'It's good news about that briefcase you found Rance. I sent the contents to Curen. It seems the Germans are moving their HQ to Sulejow or at least the Gestapo are. As you know it's on a major road junction both roads leading to the front he tapped the map to make his point.

'Anyway, Sulejow is becoming one of a group of main food and ammunition stores that will feed the troops on the front line and because of a shortage of troops the Gestapo are going to help man it.'

Marek grinned wolfishly. 'They'll all be there, Schneller, Braun, Lohr, the lot.' He stopped and swigged at the Vodka bottle.

Rance was puzzled, 'So what, do we wait for the Russians?' he said looking from one grinning face to the other.

Then with a shock it dawned on him. 'You must be mad.' he choked.

'No we're not,' said Marek, 'We're going to take the town, with Viktor and the others.'

Kalow

In the three weeks they'd been back at Kalow it was a changed place. Gone was the mess the Cossacks had made. In its place was a new order with men, ammunition, and guns pouring in, organised by Curen.

Other partisan groups continued to arrive brought in from fifty to a hundred kilometres away, some poorly armed, some with so much they could hardly carry it all.

There were so many men coming together that Marek had to split them into groups of a hundred, spreading them out through the forest for safety.

Food was a problem so raiding parties were despatched to the Volksdeutche farms and convoys were ambushed, with the food and ammunition found distributed amongst the various groups.

Farmers and their workers left their homes arriving in the camp in a never ending stream, while whole villages emptied of men young and old alike offering their services. Rance worked hard trying to teach the new recruits the basics of firing a machine gun, but in the end decided it was better if they stuck to a rifle.

The first snow had fallen and it was getting bitterly cold again as winter set in. Still only able to light fires at night they were forced into exercises to keep warm.

A plan of the town had been made showing the main eastern end with the garrison, Gestapo HQ, and the food stores attached with the ammunition dump on the outskirts complete with the bridge over the River Pilica which split the town from the western end.

Viktor and the other Commanders decided that one hundred men would attack the western end of the town to draw troops over the bridge, away from the main garrison and ammunition dump. When the troops crossed they would have to be delayed long enough over there for men already in the town to blow the bridge thus trapping the troops on the other side.

That would be the signal for the main frontal attack on the eastern end.

'What about the Gestapo HQ?' Krolik asked.

'Curen has given that to us,' answered Marek.

'When do we go in?'

'In three days' time regardless of the weather. The timing has to be right. From now until then we must infiltrate as many men as possible into the town. Some to get in place to blow the bridge, while others to cause as much chaos as they can in the town centre, they may even draw troops away from the ammunition dump but I doubt it.'

'How long do we stay in the town? They'll send for reinforcements,' said Golab.

Marek was cautious, 'Curen wants us there as long as possible but don't get trapped. We estimate twelve hours maximum.'

Rance again felt the now familiar bile rise up to the back of his throat. He knew it was nerves and fought to control it knowing the town wouldn't be an easy target. The garrison was still heavily armed with experienced fighting men. Men that had fought all over Europe and the Russian front.

Sulejow

Lieutenant Schmidt walked around his new desk. Looking out of the grimy window at the main street of Sulejow he saw the road was covered with a thin coating of snow. 'What a dreary place,' he said despondently to himself.

There seemed to be more people about than normal he thought, it must be market day although what they had to sell he couldn't imagine.

Certainly not food because the Gestapo had it all locked away in their warehouse.

Morosely he read the reports coming in about increased bandit attacks in the area but with all the troops needed at the front there was nothing they could do apart from scouring the streets and executing a few Poles in retaliation. He hadn't wanted to come to this town and his stomach had heaved in panic at being moved nearer the front, even if it was only twenty kilometres.

He'd seen the trucks bringing back the wounded, endless lines of them. There used to be endless lines going the other way but they had slowed to a trickle. He sighed trying to focus on his paper work.

'Who the hell wants this country anyway certainly not me,' he mumbled to himself.

He picked up a list of names and against each one was the sex, age, and health. It was his job to sort them out. The young and fit were to go to the labour camps in Germany, while the older ones if fit enough would work on the Volksdeutche farms, any others he would hold as hostages to be executed when needed.

He felt good doing this. He was in charge of who lived and who died. They couldn't boss him about this time he was the one to fear.

Sulejow

Rance stood hidden in a thicket some three hundred metres from the first building at the edge of the town. It was almost mid-day the time of the attack. His nerves were stretched to breaking point.

To his right he could see the ammunition dump which according to the plan he'd seen was surrounded by two lines of barbed wire. Concealed machine gun posts guarded the ten bunkers filled with ammunition bound for the front line. Inside at the far end he could see the three barracks of the Waffen SS with troops coming and going all the time.

Every one hundred metres stood a watch tower complete with the usual machine gun and guards. Marek had estimated there were probable about two hundred soldiers inside at any one time not counting the Garrison in the town which accounted for another thousand.

It looked a formidable target to take and he hoped the diversionary tactics would help. Glancing back along the thicket at the rows of silent motionless men he wondered how many would be left at the end of the day? How many women and children would they leave crying?

Behind the waiting men were positioned the rows of mortars, stolen long ago ready to be used in such a situation as this. He looked at the sky praying for a blizzard but the weather was on the Germans side, bright and clear.

He watched as carts pulled by horses loaded with oil soaked grass were wheeled upwind of the German positions. Lifting his binoculars he saw no sign of the men already in the town.

At five to twelve the men with the carts unhitched the horses and lit the oil soaked grass before walking casually back into the maze of side streets. Slowly the thick black oily smoke drifted across the open ground and the ammunition dump disappeared from sight shielding the partisans from the machine gunners sights.

At precisely mid-day the sound of mortars exploding on the west bank signalled the start, he waited impatiently for twenty minutes, listening to the sound of firing and explosions that filled the air from the furious battle on the other bank. Suddenly, the noise of the high explosives blowing the bridge shook the ground under him, He ran forward with Marek on his right and Golab on his left. He couldn't see Krolik but knew he was near.

They reached the first of the houses without incident hearing the machine guns of the Germans in the ammunition dump open up, firing blindly into the stinking smoke. The sheer fire power of the heavy calibre guns cut swaths of death through the partisans advancing on the front line, men fell screaming as their own mortars bombarded the enemy positions smashing the barbed wire and tearing into the machine gun nests.

From their position by the houses he watched as running men twenty metres from the wire fell writhing on the snow covered ground only to be replaced by others coming up behind until they reached the wire. Now throwing themselves on it they acted as a platform for others following close behind. The German defenders fought desperately to stop them, men died clinging to the wire before the partisans were in racing through the gaps and fighting hand to hand amongst the ammunition bunkers.

Satisfied that the dump had been breached Marek waved his men forward into the back streets where fierce house to house fighting began. Rance ran bent double with buildings blowing apart and gun fire sweeping the narrow streets leaving men crying and dying in the gutters.

He reached the main street as another high explosive charge blew like thunder and the debris fell amongst them, great pieces of stone clattering off roof tops and falling like rain into the street below.

Windows shattered about him and bullets peppered the walls burying deep into the masonry as the Waffen SS fought back. A hand- grenade exploded next to the corner where he stood the blast deflected, blowing out a shop window. He crouched down trying to locate where it came from. Another landed at his feet which he quickly threw back around the corner where it exploded harmlessly in the middle of the road. He again peered round the corner and saw movement in one of the upstairs windows.

Stepping out into the road he waited until the German looked down from his hideout then killed him with a short burst from his machine pistol. He ran on down the road and found Krolik where rifle fire pinned them down in a doorway coming from a house almost opposite. It forced them to abandon their position and break down the door behind where they were faced with a frightened family crouching terrified in one corner. With no time for anything but the fight they ignored them and ran out through the rear door and back down an alleyway into a street further up.

Schmidt in his new office jumped in alarm as the first explosions rattled the windows. Looking out he saw smoke billowing from a burning car on the opposite bank. More explosions followed, he realised it was mortars and with the guards on the bridge coming under sniper fire he watched as they ran for cover.

Hurriedly he buckled on his revolver with shaking fingers cursing out loud that it must be the Russians as men ran down the corridor shouting for the armoury to be opened. Someone shouted that the attack was on the other side of the river and not to worry. He ran back to the window in time to see reinforcements from the garrison coming over to the west bank to support the beleaguered outpost.

His confidence returned when he saw the attackers wore no Russian uniforms and were only partisans.

The next explosion that came was enormous. The partisans responsible had overestimated the strength of the charge and it blew before they had time to clear the area.

Schmidt threw himself down on the floor as his window frames and part of the front building collapsed into the street below leaving him lying in his shattered office in a cloud of dust. In a daze he scrambled to his feet and pulled the pistol from its holster, unsure what to do next his mind blank.

He ran down the stairs with the rest of the office personnel, noticing the bridge had disappeared and the fighting on the other side had intensified. .

Watching house to house fighting heading his way sent him panic stricken back inside only to find the Gestapo personnel burning piles of paper in the centre of the floor. With a sudden jolt he remembered his lists of hostages. He would have to destroy the evidence. Running back up the stairs and into his office he worked in feverish haste amongst the filing cabinets and drawers piling the papers in a heap.

The firing outside grew in volume and machine-gun bullets started to ricochet off the walls. He smelt burning as the building caught alight downstairs wisps of smoke drifted up the narrow stairway as he frantically searched for a match to light his papers. He stopped giggling uncontrollably.

What did he want a match for? Realizing the building was already alight.

Rance ended up at the end of a road in a large square next to the river. What was left of the bridge stuck out from the river bed like broken teeth in a wet running mouth. He took cover in a doorway when he came under attack from a machine-gun situated in the Gestapo HQ in front of him. Risking a glance he saw the machine-gunner in a smoke filled downstairs window near the main entrance. He watched as Krolik crawled along the pavement under the window and tossed in a hand-grenade which exploded with a dull thud and a scream came from the men inside.

Marek ran towards the front of the building and Rance joined him as a partisan with a Piat Mortar blew in the large double doors of the main entrance. Ignoring the entrance Rance and Marek preferred the bombed out window instead, clambering over what was left of a German gunner they crossed the room and entered a smoke filled passage which was filled with sheltering Gestapo personnel.

Bullets slammed into the door jamb above Rance's head as some of them opened fire. He and Marek pulled the triggers of their sub-machine guns onto full automatic.

The result in the confined space was devastating. Caught like rats in a trap the Gestapo screamed and died as the bullets smashed into them at point blank range starting at the front, while at the far end of the passage, they fought each other like animals to escape the murderous hail of death and destruction.

Schmidt cowering in his office above heard the firing while crouched in a corner behind a filing cabinet and his hand was shaking listening to the screaming coming from below. He snarled like a trapped animal dribbling in fear when he heard men running up the narrow stairs. Lifting his pistol he pointed it at the doorway.

Rance ran down the smoked filled corridor and entered the first room, finding it empty. Turning he ran to the next with Marek following close behind. He entered and quickly stepped to one side when he saw movement behind a filing cabinet.

The figure hiding behind the cabinet let out a scream and fired a single shot which caught Marek in the chest just as he entered the room behind Rance. The force of which from such close quarters, threw Marek against the open door breaking the glass. Rance opened fire and streams of lead tore into the fat slovenly figure of Schmidt who screamed in agony bouncing off the walls and cabinet before toppling out of the hole where the window had been and into the street below.

Fire now raged up the stairway filling the hall and rooms with thick acrid smoke. Marek lay groaning half in and half out of the room and as Rance bent down to help bullets fired from the other end of the smoked filled corridor smashed into the walls and door above his head

Instead of standing upright Rance carried on his downward movement and hit the floor before rolling and firing swiftly in the general direction of the attack. A choking cry echoed through the smoke followed by the sound of someone running away.

The heat had started blistering the paint work as Rance supported Marek in one arm and half dragged him away from the flames.

Marek took three steps and almost fell groaning through clenched teeth. They reached the end of the hallway and almost fell over the lifeless body of Braun who had been shot in the throat and was lying in a pool of blood. Behind him a second flight of stairs led to a small courtyard surrounded by warehouses.

On Rance's right a door blown off its hinges led out onto the square and as they reached the outside Marek collapsed. A harassed passing doctor bent over him and peeling off his coat cut through the blood soaked shirt.

Rance saw Krolik seemingly oblivious to the explosions around him setting up machine-guns along the river bank ready to repel any counter attack, now a fierce dual began across the river.

He looked at Marek's wound, at the bullet's point of entry the hole was small and round glistening with slowly oozing blood. The doctor turned him over to reveal a larger jagged hole where the bullet had passed through emerging out of his back. Rance knew it wasn't a clean wound. Somewhere inside the bullet must have hit a bone to make it spread like that.

Seeing there was nothing else he could do he went to find Krolik.

'Marek's been shot,' was all he could say. Now they were pinned down with fire from the other bank, Krolik turned his attention to the warehouse next to the burning Gestapo HQ. 'I think Schneller's in there,' he said.

Rance looked at the heavily shuttered windows. 'How do you know?'

'There are only three ways out of that HQ. Through the front door, which we know was impossible. Out the back but that was covered by Golab and the rest of our group or though the yard door which you brought Marek out of, but then I would have seen him.

So I'm pretty sure he's in there somewhere.'

'Is that the food warehouse?' Rance asked, Krolik shrugged,

'It must be, we haven't found any food in the last buildings we've searched.'

He looked around the ruined square, 'Where's the man with the Piat?'

'Down the street somewhere was the last place I saw him.'

Rance ran down the street, aware of the shrapnel and sniper fire all round him, he found the partisan dead with his arms curled tightly around his weapon.

He pulled it free and looked for the shells which he found in a case nearby. Returning to the square the fierce gun and mortar exchanges had doubled in their intensity with the partisans desperate to keep the Germans from crossing back over the river.

Rance, now joined by Jozef and Golab, set up the Piat and carefully lined it up on the large double doors.

CHAPTER 32

It was total darkness in the food warehouse, Schneller switched on his torch and looked at the boxes of German field rations piled almost to the wooden rafters above their heads. At the far end lay sacks of potatoes and other vegetables commandeered from local farmers which were going rotten having laid there for so long. He turned the torch on the frightened men around him, Franz Lohr stared back, his one eye looking baleful in the light from the powerful torch.

There were seven clerks who were nervously fidgeting with their pistols, five Gestapo officers and three guards who all carried machine pistols and spare ammunition.

With luck they may be able to hold out until reinforcements arrived, he reasoned.

'Check the rear of the warehouse,' he ordered an officer while supervising the stacking of food boxes to make their first line of defence.

He had the boxes placed two deep and four high with spaces to shoot though. Next they piled sacks of potatoes forming a circle behind the first defence to shelter from any hand-grenades.

Behind the circle they built the second line of boxes as their final defence. It was hot dusty work and the once immaculate officers were now covered in grime. The officer sent to inspect the rear of the warehouse returned.

'Sir, there's nothing really to report. Everything seems secure. There's only one window and that's covered by heavy shutters. I looked through a crack and the window leads directly out onto the river which is in full flood. There's no chance that they could come in that way.'

A mortar exploding against the outside wall made them flinch but the thick stone walls absorbed the shock, while another blew a hole in the roof near the door they had entered, letting in a little daylight and a fine dust filtering down through the musty atmosphere onto the waiting men below.

Schneller licked his thin dried lips his bulbous eyes seeming to reflect the dim light as he stared at the large warehouse door. For the waiting men hiding in the warehouse, the fighting outside seemed one continuous roar. The smell of burning flesh and traces of smoke from their HQ next door crept in through the hole in the roof. Schneller wrinkled his nose in distaste while a clerk stifled a whimper.

With a sudden roar the doors to the warehouse were blown off their hinges, large splinters of wood flew through the air in all directions. The defenders tensed, their fingers tightening on the triggers of their guns as they focused on the opening made by the Piat mortar.

Nothing happened. No one entered or tried to enter then without warning a shuttered window erupted in a welter of flying wood and glass followed by another and another.

Panicking, the Germans opened fire at the windows and door.

With seeming ease a hand-grenade landed amongst them. Schneller, Lohr, and three others made it into the inner circle of potato sacks before it exploded, sending white hot shards of metal into the remaining men.

Another came hurtling in and bounced off the sacks before exploding harmlessly behind the boxes.

'Where the hell are they coming from?' Lohr shouted.

One of the men pointed up to the hole in the roof and screamed, 'There, that's where they are'.

The trapped men directed their guns upwards and the roof slates shattered in the fusillade, flying in all directions.

Jozef rolled away from the hole where he'd been sitting and without anything to grab hold of he slid down the roof and into the gutter, before falling fifteen feet to the ground, breaking his leg.

Rance and Krolik threw more grenades through the windows, but when they tried to enter they were met with rapid return fire from the concealed men inside and were driven back.

'What about the Piat? we're running out of time here,' said Krolik.

'We've run out of ammunition for it,' exclaimed Rance. 'Let's burn them out'.

'What about the food?'

'We won't have time to remove it, so if we can't have it then neither shall they.'

Together they searched for something to burn, finding what they needed in a store room back of the burning HQ. Oil lamps put there for emergencies by the Germans.

Rance shook one and groaned, 'Only half full.'

'These others are empty, countered Krolik, but look what I have here, a drum, and it's full'.

Ten minutes later they were back at the warehouse with five full lanterns each.

Sowa met them, his face showing concern.

'We can't hold the river banks downstream much longer, more German troops have moved in from the north. We're having to withdraw.

Krolik cursed as they lit the wicks before running to the shattered windows and hurling them inside.

Schneller watched in dismay as the first of the lanterns came flying through a window and smashed in a roar of flames amongst the wooden boxes of food. More followed through the door spilling their burning fluid sending clouds of smoke drifting through the confined space making it impossible to see the entrance.

With tears streaming from his bulbous eyes, Schneller crawled towards the rear of the building the acrid smoke caught in the back of his throat sending him into a coughing fit.

Behind him he left total confusion and panic, the remaining men desperately searching with streaming eyes for a target to shoot at.

The last thing they saw was a hand clutching a hand-grenade, appear over the boxes and they screamed in terror as it rolled amongst them. Three men fought each other trying to pick it up but Rance had already counted to three after pulling the pin and the explosion in the confined space ripped through them.

Rance and Krolik climbed to their feet looking at the fire which had now taken hold and almost the whole of one side was starting to burn lighting the smoked filled interior with a dull red glow.

'Schnellers not here,' said Krolik sifting through the bodies.

'Neither is Lohr.' Cautiously they searched along the stacked boxes the heat forcing them to shield their faces.

Rance nodded towards the rear of the building,

'They must be back there, they certainly haven't come past us'.

Schneller found the shuttered window and tried to open it but it refused to move. Feeling someone behind him he whirled around lifting his pistol, only to find the glaring hostile eye of Lohr staring back at him.

'You're not leaving me behind,' Lohr growled, casting a backwards glance towards the heat and smoke of the fast approaching flames.

Together they heaved at the shutters sweating and cursing to no avail the shutters remained closed.

Rance and Krolik advanced further inside keeping low to avoid the choking smoke. It was becoming unbearably hot and darker as the smoke thickened above their heads. Rance glanced upwards and saw a dim orange glow flickering through the smoked filled air and realised the rafters were alight.

Schneller and Lohr lifting a heavy wooden food box and using it as a battering ram repeatedly slamming it against one of the shutters until it started to split before finally giving way and falling into the river.

The sudden back draft ignited the fire into a fury of flames. It went up with a roar lighting up the whole interior.

Rance and Krolik staggered back against the scorching heat and dimly heard Golab shouting from the doorway that the German reinforcements had broken through.

Schneller and Lohr fought each other to be the first to escape the flames that burned around them. Schneller screamed in agony as the flesh on his face blistered and his clothes started to smoulder. Lohr staggered about his clothes exploding in flames. Schneller savagely kicked out at him his boot sending the Lieutenant reeling back into the flames.

Schneller turned and with his clothes on fire leapt through the shattered window into the fast flowing river, he hit hard gasping in shock as the freezing water sucked him down. Panic stricken he struck out wildly for the surface feeling the tremendous power of the river trying to suck him back.

Lohr fell screaming to the floor before climbing back on his feet and running around in circles with his hair and clothes alight, feeling the flesh peeling from him in blistering agony. Blindly he staggered forward his face unrecognisable, apart from the burning patch over his eye socket.

Rance and Krolik stopped their retreat as a burning figure emerged from the flames vainly beating at the air before sinking to its knee in front of them.

With a groan of disgust Krolik kicked the figure over where it lay writhing on the ground. Krolik turned as his own clothes started to smoulder,

'Let's get out of here,' he shouted and together they ran for the unpredictable safety of the open air while behind them the rafters started to fall in a roaring curtain of fire.

They emerged coughing and choking into the fresh air, not even noticing that it was dark. They were guided by Golab down a side street packed with fleeing partisans forced to give ground to the German reinforcements.

His eyes beginning to clear, Rance looked around the street of running men, 'Where's Marek?' he shouted.

'Somewhere ahead in one of the carts, that was the last time I saw him,' said Golab.

Krolik grabbed Rance arm, 'You go and find him, I'll stay with Golab and organise a rear guard. When he's safe come to Kalow, we'll be there.'

He ran with the rest of the men while searching each cart until he found Merek lying unconscious with four others. Two of the men were groaning in pain as the cart bounced on the rough road while the others appeared to be dead. The horse pulling the cart was obviously terrified and had to be held by two men to stop it from bolting, Rance ran with it trying to calm the petrified animal.

They left the town and entered the forest as the ammunition dump blew, a tremendous roar of flames and rubble like an erupting Volcano sent shrapnel and earth raining down amongst the trees.

They emerged into open pasture-land and looking back all he could see was a dull red glow on the skyline. He thought of the burning figure of Lohr without pity, wondering what had happened to Schneller.

'Was he dead, burned to death in the blazing warehouse? Or maybe he wasn't there at all? Nobody had seen him, certainly he and Krolik hadn't. Rance shook his head. Now they would probably never know.

Urging the tired horse on, he decided to make for Krasne.

Schneller gasped for air before going down for the second time and with coldness of the water numbing his muscles he found it hard to move his legs. With a superhuman effort and the fear of drowning he resurfaced, choking out the dirty water from his lungs. He looked around with frantic staring eyes but all he saw was the black cold water in the darkness. He was alone in this freezing wet wilderness, and he screamed into the cold night air

With the Germans spreading out over the whole area, Rance stayed just long enough with Izabel at Krasne to make sure they would be able to hide the wounded before he joined Krolik and Golab at Kalow.

Once again they were forced to split into small groups of twenty, the night marches and dawn raids continued unabated.

The weather got progressively worse as Christmas came and went with Rance managing only a day with Izabel. Marek was unable to make any progress continually slipping in an out of a coma with Izabel tending to him day and night.

He tried to talk to Marek, and once got a flicker of recognition in reply before giving up. He returned to the forest and the fighting became more intense as German troops drifted back from the failing Russian front.

Unable to stay in one place they were forced to live rough out in the open, men suffered from frostbite afraid now to even light a fire as they slept using the branches of trees for cover against the freezing bitter elements.

Danger lay everywhere as men made their choice to fight with, or against the Russians and men died everyday through lack of medicine and food even the bandages of the dying were removed to give to the living that they may have a chance.

Gestapo HQ Piotrekow

Claus Ritschel read the signals arriving in his office almost hourly and as far as he was concerned it was the end. The Russians had at last broken though over running the front line all the way from Kielce to Radom, what was left of the German army was in full retreat and his orders were to move out.

Already his orderlies were burning papers and putting files into the waiting trucks. He'd sent orders for the recall of all patrols in the villages, and watched dispassionately from his office window as they returned and joined the exodus. He sighed, glad it was all over. He picked up his gloves and with one last look around walked slowly down the wide staircase ignoring the clerks feverishly running past carrying bundles of papers.

Nobody saluted him, he didn't care sitting in the back of his staff car he stared straight ahead when it swept out of the town joining the fleeing troops on the road back to Germany. Not once did he look back.

CHAPTER 33

'How is he today?' Izabel's mother asked watching her daughter carefully wiping the sweat from Marek's feverish body.

Izabel rinsed out the wet cloth, 'He's getting worse I think,' she answered. 'Do you think I should call out the doctor again?'

'The doctors said that he's done all he can, now it's up to him and you,'

Anya walked to the door, beckoning Izabel to follow.

Outside, she turned and faced her daughter.

'I didn't want to say anything in there because Marek might be able to hear. 'We've just received news that the Russians have made a breakthrough between Kielce and Radom.'

She paused biting her lip her eyes had a frightened haunted look about them. 'They're moving at tremendous speed it won't be long before they get here,' her hands were twisting nervously. 'I'm frightened for us all Izabel. Curen also said the retreating Germans are killing anyone they meet. There are also remnants of a large group of Cossacks who are raping and pillaging through the countryside, he thinks they're the same ones that passed through here before.'

Izabel forced herself to remain calm for her mother's sake. 'It doesn't mean they will automatically come this way, anything could happen'.

'Curen thinks they will because they know parts of this area. He wants us to move out.'

Izabel shook her head, 'I can't leave Marek here like this. I think that to move him would seriously endanger his life,'

She walked to the open door and looked at the still figure on the bed before returning to her mother. 'Marian must return to Kalow and get word to Rance, he will know what to do. Then she must get Krolik to hide everyone with Jozef in the forest before the Russians arrive. In the meantime I will stay here with Marek.'

It was Anya's turn to shake her head. 'No, I'm staying with you. You're all I have and that's final,' she said firmly. 'And one more thing, it's about Rance.'

'What about Rance? What's happened to him?' Izabel's voice was near to panic.

'Nothing yet but you know when the Russians finally come he'll be in great danger not only from the troops but more so from the men who will come afterwards. The communist state police and the Russian NKVD. Curen has detailed it all. Most partisans who have opposed them have simply disappeared.'

Izabel looked at her mother with horror struck eyes.

'What can he do? We mustn't let this happen,' she said desperately. 'He's a foreigner here with false papers, he can speak a little of our language but everyone can tell he's not Polish. Her eyes grew large with fright. 'Oh mother, they'll kill him out of hand.'

Anya nodded her eyes brimming with tears. 'He can't stay here after the Russians have arrived even if he wanted to. Somehow you must persuade him to go. To get out of Poland before it's too late.'

Izabel felt her world collapse the blood drained from her face as she realised she would lose him, but it had to be done.

I'll send a message with Marian for Rance to come quickly I'll tell him the Cossacks are coming, and when he gets here, I'll make him leave Poland somehow.

Kalow

Krolik came into Kalow just as Rance was tending to Jozef's broken leg. He was in a sombre mood staring at them both. 'I have some good news and some bad news which is it you want to hear first?'

'Get on with it,' snapped Jozef testily still sore from Rance prodding at his leg.

'The German patrols have gone, so have the Gestapo and the police. They're leaving Piotrkow like rats leaving a sinking ship. That's the good news.' The other news is that the Russians have broken through around Kielce and Radom and are on their way.

Already there's bitter fighting between some of the partisans and communists partisans even before they get here.

He shook his head. 'Where will it end?'

Jozef turned to Rance. 'You must get out of here before it's too late. We stand a chance but you're in danger.'

He doggedly shook his head. 'I'm staying, Izabel is here and that's where I'm staying as long as she needs me.'

Krolik shook his head and walked away. 'Stubborn bloody Englishman,' he muttered to himself.

The temperature was starting to plummet to well below freezing as the weak winter sun sank below the skyline. Marian came into Kalow, the horse lathered in its traces having pulled the small cart without stopping from Krasne.

Breathlessly she gave the message to Rance and the other two men sitting in Jozef's house.

He jumped to his feet, 'I must go to her now there's no time to lose,'

Krolik held out a restraining hand. 'Wait my friend we need to organise, we must get men together.'

He shook his arm free impatiently,

'You organise, I must go on ahead, meet me there.' and he turned to go.

'Wait,' Krolik again grabbed his arm. 'I and ten of the men will go with you, if you must go now. The rest we'll send out to the villages for reinforcements. We have men scattered everywhere.'

Hurriedly they loaded their weapons and spare ammunition into two carts and departed while the other men left behind were hurriedly preparing to go for help, saddling the remaining horses and leaving the carts behind to give them speed.

Rance felt it strange that they could use their horses more openly now. Even so Krolik sent scouts ahead to warn of any retreating German troops coming through. He felt a flurry of snow on his face and grew alarmed at the thought of a snow storm slowing them down. The moon became hidden behind the dark racing clouds that now filled the night sky. An hour later they were forced to shelter as the blizzard blew into a fury and the snow drifted, whipped by the biting wind. Lighting a fire they piled on the wood to keep out the bitter cold and sat hunched over it waiting for the storm to ease.

Krasne

Izabel stared out of the window looking for her mother who was fetching wood for the stove. It had been snowing most of the night and it lay thick upon the ground. She had lain awake for most of the night listening to what she had at first thought was thunder until she realised it was the sound of artillery guns in the distance. She had no idea how far away they were. Startled, she turned when Anya came running into the house carrying some logs and gasping for breath.

'There are men coming out of the forest behind the house but I don't think they're Germans,' she was stammering in alarm.

Izabel went to the dressing table and took out her pistol. Putting on her heavy coat she slipped the pistol into the deep pocket before stepping outside in the pretence of fetching more wood. Walking slowly to the wood pile she picked up four logs before taking out the pistol and thrusting it into the coat next to her bust. There she held it covered by the logs in her arms, pretending to have just noticed the approaching men she stopped and waited for them.

They were heavily wrapped with long coats and scarves and wore black fur hats. All carried sub-machine guns and pistols at their waists. She knew they were Russian all except one who was a Pole and her heart sank when she realised it was the same group as before. Her hand tightened its grip on the pistol butt inside her coat.

The Russian officer stepped forward but made sure he kept his distance, for he now had a healthy respect for the young woman standing defiantly before him.

'Well, we meet again I knew we would one day, it was inevitable, don't you think?' he said without a smile.

'What do you want from us?' she snapped Ignoring his remark.

'Take your hand out of your coat and do it slowly', he said his attitude hardening.

She stared at him unsure what do next, seeing her hesitate, he said loudly,

'If you don't, I'll shoot everyone in this village'.

' You'd be as bad as the Germans,' she retorted.

'You want to see, try pulling out that pistol in your coat,' he replied taunting her.

Releasing her grip she slowly pulled her hand free. Piotr stepped forward and removed the pistol.

The officer visibly relaxed. 'We have a list of names we would like you to see. They are of the local partisans in this area, so we only have their code names.'

'Why do you want them?'

'We need them to join us in our fight against the Germans'.

Izabel didn't believe him but kept her composure.

'None of them are here, and to tell you the truth I haven't seen any of them for weeks,' she lied.

'She's lying I have reports that they've been seen in this area,' said Piotr angrily.

'Have you been lying to me?' queried the officer beginning to lose patience.

Izabel appeared quite unmoved,

'I have no reason to lie, after all, didn't you say that you Russians were here to help us'.

He knew she was making fun of him, and in front of his men.

Angrily he shouted at his men to search the village.

'We'll see who's lying now,' he snarled, pointing his pistol in her face,

'And if it's you, I'll give you to my men.'

Krasne

Rance watched the Russians searching the village through his binoculars.

'What are they looking for?' he asked Krolik.

'Not what,' Krolik replied. 'Who, they're after us I think.'

Rance put away his binoculars, and took the safety catch off his sub machine gun. 'Then let's not disappoint them,' he said.

Using the houses for cover they entered the village and made for the rear of Izabel's house.

He looked through the window and saw Izabel talking to a Russian officer, gesturing towards the bed where Marek lay.

Suddenly the officer pushed her aside and pulled the bed clothes onto the floor. Rance ran to the rear door and quietly entered. The officer had his back to him, Izabel gave an involuntary gasp her eyes opening wide at his sudden appearance.

The officer turned quickly only to find a machine-gun at his head.

'I can just as easily kill a Russian as I can a German', Rance whispered in his ear.

The officer blanched, hastily letting Izabel go, and held up his hands. 'We've been looking for you to help us, we mean you no harm,' the officer exclaimed.

'Outside,' Rance snapped motioning towards the front door.

They stepped outside with him standing behind the officer.

'Call your men here,' he ordered.

The officer shouted and his men came to stand in front of the house. Rance counted fifteen and one civilian.

Krolik and his men joined them and the two groups once again faced each other.

'What do you really want?' said Krolik impatiently.

The Russian officer held out his arms appealingly.

'We come to you for help we need food and shelter that's why we're here, and look how you treat us your allies'.

'Don't trust them that's not what they're here for,' interrupted Izabel.

Krolik again chose to ignore her. 'We have no food but you can have shelter. You are our allies but only if you don't try anything stupid like trying to make us join you. We've told you before we only take orders from the Polish Home Army in London'.

The Russian officer saluted, 'You are indeed our allies, I will mention your actions in my report.'

Krolik motioned to a barn on the other side of the village.

'I'm sure you and your men will be comfortable over there, if we can find some food we'll send it over.'

'You are most generous,' said the officer backing away.

Turning, he walked into the barn with his men.

'When the time is right Piotr we will dispose of those trouble makers,' he said.

Krolik motion to his men, 'Organise a sentry watch, don't let them out of your sight whatever happens and don't let them approach this side of the village.'

He turned to Rance, 'I think one day soon we'll have to fight them'.

'You should have disarmed them,' said Izabel accusingly to Krolik.

'Oh yes and risk a blood bath,' he said frowning. 'No, that's not the answer we must play them at their own game. Soon there will be thousands more, and then where will we be?'

'You're giving in to them,' she cried.

'If you haven't forgotten we're still fighting the Germans we can't afford a second front right now,' he answered sarcastically. 'I must check the village and organise its defence if that's at all possible,' he muttered.

'What's the matter with him'? Izabel asked busily fussing over Marek who seemed to be in a shallow sleep.

'You mean Krolik?'

'Yes who do you think I meant?' she snapped.

Rance felt shock she'd never spoken to him like that before.

'Never mind,' he said softly 'Are you all right Izabel, is looking after Marek becoming too much for you?'

She turned to face him dreading this moment. 'Rance, I have something to say to you.'

Something in her voice told him it would be bad news.

'While I've been here looking after Marek and you've been away, it has given me time to gather my thoughts.' She paused swallowing hard before continuing. 'You know I was seeing Marek before you came along'.

He could only nod wishing the earth would open up beneath his feet, guessing what was coming next.

'Oh Rance, I'm so sorry to tell you it's Marek that I really love after all'.

She sobbed, turning away so as not to see the hurt on his face.

She felt like dying and wished she was, the pain of grief was unbearable twisting and turning inside her while waiting for his reply, but it didn't come instead she heard the door close quietly as he left without saying a word.

She sat at the bottom of Marek's bed and sobbed uncontrollably.

Rance walked outside in a daze and leaned against one of the carts that the men had brought into the village.

'You think they'll come?' said Krolik coming up behind him.

'What,' said Rance, his mind in turmoil.

'The Cossacks, do you think they'll come?'

'Oh, I don't suppose so, but I think we should put out sentries to be sure,' he said automatically not really listening, his mind full of grief.

Krolik stared at him. 'Are you all right Rance, you look ill ?'

Rance pushed away from the cart. 'Don't worry about me, I'm fine,' he said gruffly.

They both looked to the distant horizon as the rumbling thunder seemed to be getting nearer.

'I don't think we can defend this place Rance. Marek, Izabel, and her mother will stand a better chance in the forest away from everything. Especially if the Cossacks come,' said Krolik.

'Izabel thinks Marek is too ill to move and I think she's right.'

'None of them will stand a chance staying here, at least in the forest they can hide,' answered Krolik.

Rance looked dubious. 'Izabel won't go.'

'Have you ever seen what the Cossacks do to a woman they rape? Believe me it's not a pretty sight.'

Rance spoke to Izabel explaining the situation, and much to his relief she agreed to go and he helped her pad the bottom of the cart with bedding to make it as comfortable as possible.

Once when their hands met Izabel hurriedly drew back not looking at the misery on his face.

CHAPTER 34

Gorecki, the Cossack leader, reined in his tired horse and looked through the trees at a village that had perhaps thirty small wooden houses with smoke from the chimneys curling slowly up into the still afternoon air.

.He was pleased it had stopped snowing, his men were tired from running and so were the horses.

The loud thunder of the artillery guns weren't far behind now and the flat terrain was ideal for the Russian tanks as they overhauled the demoralised German army. There was so little time but his men needed food, perhaps the village had some and women which they could take with them.

He could see figures moving about between the houses. Lifting his binoculars he stared at the Russian troops standing near a large barn. For three days he and his men had been running from the advancing Russian front and now here were just a few. At the last count he still had over a hundred men under his command. More than enough.

He issued orders and they split into two groups, with one group moving to one side, half way around the village. He lifted his binoculars again and could now see other men and a woman loading a cart. All appeared armed. He lifted his sword and waited for a response from the waiting men already in position. When it came he brought it down in one slashing movement and together they charged silently down on the village.

The Russian officer stood with his men outside the barn watching the partisans loading the cart.

'It looks as if they're pulling out. are we going to stop them?' asked Piotr.

'The officer nodded, 'Listen to the sound of the front it can't be more than two kilometres away. Already I've seen German troops in the distance, running like mad dogs. It's only going to be a matter time before they start coming through here, and I don't want to be around when they do. Get some of the men to spread out through the village and keep a few in the barn while I call the partisans over for a talk.

Gorecki leaned low over his running horse his sword held at his side he felt the wind whip across his face as the snow deadened the sound of the charge. Now they were out of the tree line and almost at the houses before they were belatedly fired on by the sentries.

Men scattered as the thundering hooves could now be plainly heard and the Cossacks swerved between the houses, catching the Russians scattered throughout the village off guard.

Swords flashed down, slicing into the running men as the Cossacks wheeled about and came back coming under fire from within the barn bringing down five of the leading Cossacks while the rest instead of wheeling away leapt their fallen comrades and rode straight into the barn.

Gorecki screamed in savage delight when they jumped down from their horses and attacked the remaining men.

A Russian officer with a civilian ran outside. Gorecki remounted, and with two others chased them into the fields oblivious to the firing coming towards them from the other end of the village.

Now Gorecki was right behind the fleeing officer, who heard him coming and turned, lifting his pistol. Gorecki swept on his sword held above his head and bringing it down in one swift motion decapitated the man who ran three more step before falling headless into the snow.

Piotr seeing this, screamed for mercy and held up his hands.

Still grinning, Gorecki nodded to the remaining Cossack who reached down and ran him through with his sword.

Wheeling away they raced back towards the barn and with Gorecki screaming at his men they charged towards Rance crouched by the cart.

The partisans now warned and better placed opened up with a withering blast of gunfire decimating the front row bringing down horses and men alike before the remainder of the Cossacks were amongst them slashing and cutting until they swept passed before disappearing behind the houses to regroup.

Taking advantage of the respite, Rance and Krolik ran inside and carried Marek out placing him on the bedding in the cart.

'Quickly get your mother before they return,' Rance shouted at Izabel.

Anya sobbing with fright climbed in the back followed by Izabel.

Rance grabbed Krolik. 'Go with them they need your knowledge of the forest.'

Krolik pulled away. 'No, I stay.'

Rance rammed a gun hard into Krolik's stomach.

'Go damn you.

Startled at the savage response, he clambered into the driver's seat when someone screamed that they were coming back again. Rance lashed out at the two horses and they bolted towards the forest in a frenzied run. He was aware of Izabel screaming his name once, before they were gone.

Turning, he faced the charging horsemen who were keeping low, using their horses as cover when they swept back and ran amongst the few remaining partisans. They came at him on two sides, giving him no chance to reach the house. He rolled on the ground to avoid the slashing swords, coming up to a kneeling position firing from the hip with his sub-machine gun, making them swerve away once again.

The horsemen returned, their wild cries freezing his blood as they charged down on him. He waited not wanting to waste a single shot, now he could almost feel the horses breathe when he fired at point-blank range. Their leader, staring at him with wild eyes his sword poised, died instantly along with three others, Rance dived to the ground behind the cart trying to avoid the flashing swords which slashed and cut huge pieces from the woodwork.

His gun jammed and he turned it to use as a club twice fending off the sword thrusts.

Now men and horses fell screaming in front of him and in a daze he looked round to see dozens of men running out from the tree line firing as they ran. In the lead he saw the familiar figure of Golab and men he'd met in some of the villages, including the one whose baby he'd had baptised.

From the opposite side of the forest, men on horseback from other villages, from Barkowice, Mokre where they'd buried Cross, from Huta, Reczno and a dozen other villages, they came and their withering cross-fire tore into the Cossacks milling about in confusion before the remnants turned and raced away towards the tree line where they again started to regroup.

Rance could now see why they didn't continue their headlong flight the whole pasture-land round the village was full of running German troops complete with troop carriers and tanks that were in retreat from the Russian advance.

The Cossacks again started their run towards the village. Abandoning the use of their swords they turned to their machine pistols and firing over the heads of the horses they charged down on the villagers.

He searched for a gun amongst the dead in front of him picking up a rifle and running for cover when the first of the Russian artillery shells screamed down and exploded amongst the Cossacks smashing the charge sending men and horses crashing to the ground in bloody heaps.

Barrage after barrage blew apart houses and trees. Shells fell on the fleeing Germans and the villagers turning the pasture-land into a place full of craters, filled with dead and dying men.

He again prepared himself to fight when the first of the running German troops entered the village, but they totally ignored him their only thought to get away. He looked for the partisans and saw they had now scattered and were retreating back into the forest. Reaching the house which now had no roof he turned a heavy table made of solid oak on to its side propping it against a wall under the window. It left him just enough room to crawl under where he lay listening to the tanks rumbling past then the clatter of machine guns and the cries of men that lay wounded and forgotten in the blind rush to escape. The Russian army now began to pour out of the forest and into the village where fierce fire fights and hand to hand fighting broke out.

Part of the house collapsed as a Russian tank thundered through sending the wall down onto his hiding place. The table started to give way under the weight and he was forced to abandon it crawling out into the open where he stayed crouched under the window, partly concealed by the fallen wall.

A German soldier opened fire through the window above his head at a Russian coming in through the rear door. The man screamed and slumped to the ground as another replaced him and a gun battle commenced before the German vanished from sight. Rance and the remaining Russian stared at each other for a brief second as the man took in the crouched figure pointing a machine gun at him, then he was gone.

For the rest of the day and night he watched from his hideout the endless lines of tanks and artillery pieces passing through. Walking behind each with some sitting on the top were the infantry, many obviously too drunk to walk. He looked over at the pasture-land, watching the winking lights from the guns as they came line abreast, killing any wounded German they found.

The night sky was now lit from an almost continuous roar of guns that shook the earth until gradually they moved away west leaving him and what was left of the surviving villagers to pick their way out from amongst the half ruined buildings.

In the light of the dawn the full impact of the carnage hit him. The dead lay everywhere, mostly German who were scattered like confetti in the frozen snow. Amongst the houses he found what was left of his ten partisans. All had been executed by a shot in the back of the head.

Sickened by the sight he turned away shivering in the cold morning air, he lit a fire and huddled over it for warmth. He was now worried about Izabel and the others, praying that they'd been spared the savage onslaught. The warmth of the fire made his mind cry for sleep. He hadn't slept since when? He could not remember, perhaps it was just yesterday.

A forester's hut near Piotrekow

Izabel didn't sleep at all that night feeling sick with worry about Rance while she tended to Marek's wound. Examining it closely she saw it had become red and inflamed, he was again in fever. He shouted in his delirium sometimes becoming quiet before beginning to rave again, the sweat running from his body.

She sat by his side and re-lived leaving Rance, while he stood almost alone in the village waiting for the Cossacks to return. It was a memory that would be forever burnt into her brain.

She looked around the little forester's hut that Krolik had guided them to wishing Rance was with her now. Anya kept saying that it was the only thing she could have said to make him leave Poland.

Her mother was now asleep at last, her eyes twitching as if stirred by some bad dream.

She glanced down at Marek and stiffened. His eyes were open staring at her blankly, but she knew he could no longer feel the pain, that he was dead. Gently she leaned forward and kissed his cheek, before covering his tortured face. Now no longer able to contain her feelings she let the bitter tears fall unhindered over Marek's lifeless body.

Krolik stood outside amongst the trees watching the whole night sky light up, it was a dazzling rumbling display of fire power that seemed to shake the whole earth around him as the Russians pounded the remnants of the retreating German army.

Twice he heard voices in the darkness and the sound of machine gun fire making his finger tighten nervously on the trigger of his gun. He heard the door of the forester's hut open and close and watched the dim outline of Izabel approach.

'Marek's dead,' was all she could say.

Krolik only nodded, and avoided looking at her staring at the firefight display instead he too was feeling the pang of grief.

Tracers streaked unendingly across the night sky as if chasing each other in some sort of macabre game, the steady thunder of the guns rumbling away towards the west.

Izabel touched Krolik's arm. 'I'm frightened for Rance's safety, I have to go back.'

'No,' Krolik answered angrily. 'There's too much danger, everywhere there's killing and rape. Rance trusted me with your care and that's what I'm going to do.'

'I have to help him Krolik, he needs our help now, more than ever.'

'I'll take you and your mother into Piotrkow as soon as it's safe to travel, after that I'll try and get to Krasne. While I'm away you must find Curen and get him travel papers, and find out where the nearest British POW camp is.

If he can get back into a camp, the Russians will automatically repatriate him along with the rest.'

'You can't go alone, why can't I go with you.'

'I've already explained why,' he retorted sharply.

'If you see Rance, please don't tell him about Marek dying.' whispered Izabel

Krolik stared at her, 'Why not, what's happened?'

'I knew he wouldn't leave Poland without me. So I told him that I was in love with Marek. It was to make sure he went. He would die if he stayed.'

She stifled a sob, staring back at Krolik with tear stained eyes.

'That was harsh, but I understand what you're saying.' whispered Krolik, putting a hand on her arm. 'What a war. All our lives are nothing now.'

They buried Marek in a shallow grave behind the forester's hut, and waited three days before Krolik decided it was safe to move. Everywhere the Russians had set up road blocks on the road to Piotrkow and long queues had formed.

'So much for liberty,' growled Krolik sourly.

They entered the town, Izabel stared at the overcrowded streets, full of refugees with nowhere to go, but the town itself seemed to have suffered very little damage. The old Gestapo building now supported a huge red flag carrying the hammer and sickle of the USSR.

Russian soldiers stood on every street corner watching the NKVD state police begin their hunt for German deserters and any partisans that were on their list. They returned to their old apartment only to find it full of refugees whom Krolik persuaded to leave only after a violent argument and the brandishing of his pistol.

Krolik left to find Curen, returning two hours later with the promise of travel papers for Rance.

'I have some good news, Rance has been seen, still in Krasne. He told one of the men he would be making for Kalow where it would probably be safer. When asked what he would do then, he said he would probably follow the Russians all the way to Berlin.'

Izabel couldn't contain her delight at the news. Rance was still alive. Dancing round the room she hugged both her mother and Krolik. Krolik remained serious. 'There's something else. Curen also told me that Golab has been arrested by the NKVD police. At the moment no one knows where he is, so everyone must be very careful. Many have been taken like this, and it's worse in the countryside where they shoot first, then ask. 'Who was that.?'

'How long before you can get him papers?' Izabel asked..

'A week at the most, then I have to get them to him at Kalow. If he's still there. Another thing, the Germans blew the railway tracks as they retreated and no one knows how long it will take to repair them.'

Izabel stared at him, wide eyed in alarm.

'Krolik, I'm frightened, if you wait a week for the papers he will already have moved on and will certainly be caught. Will you go to him now. Please, for his sake and bring him to the edge of the forest near here. In the meantime I will get the papers which you can pick up so he can go straight to the station when the line is repaired. I'll ask Curen if he can find a guide that's willing to meet him and take him to wherever he will be safe.'

Krasne

It was bitterly cold the day Rance said goodbye to the surviving villagers before setting out for Kalow leaving behind a message, telling Izabel or Krolik if they came looking what his intentions were. It had been snowing again in the night, everywhere lay thick virgin snow.

Now it had stopped and the temperature had plummeted to minus fifteen degrees, freezing the top layer into a hard crisp surface which crunched under his feet.

He tightened the belt on his long heavy overcoat and pulling down his hat wrapped a scarf firmly over his mouth and nose. Discarding his sub-machine gun he kept only a pistol which he stuffed into his pocket. Everywhere were the signs of war. Burnt out tanks and halftracks littered the landscape filled with dead soldiers covered in a white shroud of snow making them appear grotesque and unreal.

Shell holes pitted the road in which the wounded had crawled seeking shelter, only to freeze to death in agony and despair. Houses lay in ruins and he could only guess at what had happened to their occupants.

Whole parts of the forest around him had been turned into match wood with frozen bodies lying scattered between the stumps their forms twisted and deformed by the manner of their deaths.

He reached the banks of the frozen River Pilica and watched a Russian patrol on the other side, who had lit a fire, gathering around it for warmth.

Backing away, he moved down stream until he was out of sight, before gingerly stepping out onto the singing treacherous ice. On reaching the other side he found a burnt out farmhouse and looking around he uncovered a dead horse lying on its back in the yard its legs stiff sticking straight up in the air.

There was no sign of the farmer and his family the place was deserted. In the partly destroyed barn he found an axe which he carried back to the horse, and swung it hard at one of the legs almost chopping off his own foot when it rebounded from the solid frozen flesh.

Again and again he swung the axe, his mouth watering at the thought of fresh meat, but to no avail, he gave up in disgust.

He hid once more from another Russian patrol, deciding to bypass what was left of the village of Karolinow. Striking out through the nearby forest he found what appeared to be a new road which he had never seen before.

Approaching closer he swept away the snow with his boot and saw to his horror that it was made of partly clothed German soldiers, their bodies placed with their feet towards the centre and their heads hanging outwards. Shuddering, he touched one finding it as hard as the horse he had tried to chop up. Brushing away more snow it became obvious they had been used as a road in which to run artillery pieces and trucks over to keep them out of the deep snow on either side.

He tried to walk on the road of bodies, but became ill feeling them underfoot. Retching in the snow his empty stomach gave up only a little liquid, which tasted foul and bitter. Now preferring to struggle in the deep snow at the side, he made slow progress and was beginning to tire rapidly.

He fell, lying in a drift trying to recover his strength, but with no food inside him he knew he wouldn't make it unless he got back on the road.

Slowly sitting up he managed to regain his feet and forced himself to walk on the tightly packed bodies.

Now he knew he was in hell his mind closed down shutting itself off from the sights and feel of the horror under his feet as he slipped and slithered for over two kilometres on the mangled frozen remains of what had once been men.

It eventually stopped and he thankfully left the road of bodies and joined a normal road, following it before turning onto a familiar track which he knew led to Kalow. Two hours later he walked into the clearing and was met by Jozef and Marian who Insisted he tell them everything that had happened, which he did, glossing over the story of the road for Marian's sake.

Two days later Krolik walked in carrying two bottles of Vodka which were worth a fortune on the black market. Rance was overwhelmed with relief that he'd got Izabel, her mother, and Marek to safety.

Krolik felt guilty about lying to the Englishman about Marek but knew it was for the man's own safety.

The next day they were visited by a Russian patrol with a group of communist partisans who were still scouring the countryside for German deserters and anyone on their lists.

Jozef entertained them with the last of the Vodka while Krolik and Rance hid amongst the rafters above their heads.

Two days later after Rance said his goodbyes to Jozef, and Marian, he and Krolik set off for Piotrkow. Staying clear of the main road they crossed the River Luciaza at night, arriving on the town's outskirts early the next morning. There Krolik left him promising to return in two hours. Rance spent the time watching the Russian troops using the main Piotrkow road.

In the distance he could see a road block with a long line of people waiting to go through while the Russian military police laboriously checked their papers.

Two hours passed, then three, he began to worry it seemed a lifetime and he was beginning to freeze in the sub-zero weather. Half an hour later Krolik appeared with the papers.

'I'm sorry I'm late but the papers have only just arrived. There was a slight problem concerning your photograph but we got over that by using your old one. Unfortunately due to time, you've changed a little but not enough to matter.'

'We hope.' muttered Rance looking at the papers which had been carefully soiled to look old and had him as a farm labourer.

'I thought Izabel might have come back with you,' said Rance unable to hide the disappointment from his voice.

'She has to organise a guide for you,' Krolik explained. 'The railway lines have been temporally repaired and a guide will meet you at the station entrance.'

He handed Rance a red scarf, 'Wear this so you'll be recognised. A man will ask you if the train goes all the way to Poznan'.

You will reply 'Yes and all the way back again.' After that do exactly as he says.'

Rance stared at Krolik and felt the pain of parting. 'We've seen and done much together, somethings we've seen, we can never forget, but all that is now over, I hope we never have to do or see such things again. Promise me, you and Marek will look after Izabel, make sure she comes to no harm.'

Krolik could only nod, unable to speak when he shook hands and watched Rance walked down to the road and through the road block.

CHAPTER 35

'Dokumenty Tozsamosci,' The Russian soldier's Polish was almost none existent which eased the tight feeling in Rance's gut when he handed them over.

The Russian was tired, he'd been on the road block four hours without a break. He glanced quickly at the photograph and then at the dirty looking Pole in front of him. The man looked ill, his unshaven face was thin and shallow, hardly surprising as nobody had seen any food for days. He handed them back and turned to the next dirty looking Pole.

'Documenty Tozsamosci,' he droned.

Rance walked into Piotrkow, mixing with the hundreds of refugees cramming the streets. He felt disheartened at not seeing Izabel and the urge to go to her apartment became almost unbearable, but he resisted the temptation knowing the danger he would be putting her and Marek in. Approaching the crowded railway station entrance he lingered near the railings that separated the platform from the road.

He felt ill at ease amongst the bustle going on around him. Russian troops mingled with the civilians, while the NKVD police were checking the papers and tickets at the station entrance.

A man came up to him looking at his watch. 'Excuse me does this train go all the way to Poznan?' he asked politely.

Rance stared at him. He was small, no more than five feet high with a large flat hat that seemed too big for him. His clothes were ill fitting and had seen better days. Even so he looked a prince compared with himself.

'Yes and all the way back again,' Rance dutifully replied.

The small man grinned and held out his hand. 'Good, my name is Jan, that's all you need to know. I have volunteered to be your guide to Poznan. Once there you will follow me fifty paces behind while I lead you to a British compound that the Russians have organised in that area. After that it will be up to you how you get in.'

'Can't I just walk in?'

'There are Russian troops guarding the entrance it seems there are a lot of people trying to leave Poland because of the communists, all the borders are closed, tight as a ducks arse to any refugees going west. Or anywhere else for that matter. Your only chance is to get into that compound and find a British uniform.'

All the time he was speaking he noticed Rance's eyes roaming ceaselessly over the crowds. 'Are you looking for someone?' inquired the guide frowning.

'I thought someone I knew might be here that's all,' answered Rance despondently.

The guide looked at his watch. 'Come, we must get on the platform'.

Disheartened, he moved behind the guide and they slowly edged forward in the line of disorganised humanity. The Russian NKVD scrutinised his papers and looked at his photograph then looked at him closely before looking again at his papers. One of them said something in Russian, pointing at his picture. Rance shrugged, holding his gut and rolled his eyes as if to say he'd been ill.

The NKVD man looked again, found a likeness and gave him back his papers, waving him through to the platform that was overflowing with people, some with piles of luggage, some with just bundles of rags.

He felt self-conscious with nothing to carry, feeling he should have had something to make him look more natural. The guide now stood to one side totally ignoring him while they waited for the train.

Rance looked for somewhere to sit but every seat on the platform was taken. A man sidled up to him and touched his arm.

'Follow me,' he whispered urgently. Not waiting for a reply he walked away from Rance and entered a waiting room.

Startled, Rance looked at the guide who shrugged, perplexed as he was. Slowly Rance followed, and entering the small crowded building, his heart missing a beat when he saw Izabel waiting for him at the other end of the room.

Overwhelmed with joy, he pushed his way through the motley collection of people, oblivious to their dirty looks and muttered curses.

He took her in his arms and they embraced each other, ignoring the stares of the people around them, her kiss felt hot on his lips before she gentle pulled away and held his hand.

At first she couldn't trust herself to speak. Then with a trembling voice she thanked God that he was alright. 'I've been so worried about you,' she whispered, squeezing his hand.

'I didn't think you were coming to see me leave,' he murmured softly, the grief of parting beginning to build up inside him.

She didn't answer, he could see she was close to crying.

'How is Marek?' he asked. 'With you to look after him, he can't help but get well.'

'Marek is fine, he's now sitting up and eating by himself. He sends his greetings, and wishes he could be here to see you off,' she lied blinking back the tears.

'That's good,' he said gruffly swallowing hard. 'Please wish him well for me won't you.' He hugged her hard against him. 'You have a good man there, but you already know that.'

The Poznan train crawled into the station, spewing its steam loudly over the passengers as they scrambled to get aboard.

Speech was now impossible, the guide arrived pulling at Rance's arm.

'We must go now or we may not have room there are so many people,' he shouted in his ear.

For a split second Rance and Izabel stared into each other's eyes, before he slowly backed away and was lost in the crowd.

Small as he was the guide pushed and shoved, making sure Rance got a place by the door. He struggled finally managing to lower the window. And looking out he saw Izabel standing almost alone on the near empty platform. He waved and she waved back furiously before slowly lowering her arm, she just stood there quietly watching him go fighting back the tears, afraid he'd see the truth.

The train started to move faster approaching the end of the platform, standing there were three men. Rance recognised Krolik, with two of the remaining partisans. They silently saluted him as the train picked up speed, sweeping him away.

Only then did Izabel let the tears flow, devastated and broken hearted, she stumbled away.

He closed the window, staring through misted eyes at the bulkhead opposite, not seeing anything, deep in his own misery and thoughts. He now felt tired and exhausted as the rocking train thundered on towards Poznan.

It was a long journey, with frequent stops for minor repairs to the damaged track, so it was mid-afternoon before the train pulled into the city of Poznan.

'Stay close behind me, but don't speak to me or anybody else That's important. They mustn't suspect that you're not a Pole,' said the guide seriously.

Rance stepped onto the platform which was lined with Russian troops. Long queues had formed when the passengers were forced to fill in forms which were written in Polish.

Some of the questions he couldn't understand. The guide walked clear and looked back in alarm when Rance was stopped and questioned.

Playing illiterate and slightly drunk he tried to fool them, but found himself being escorted into a building overlooking the main street. There he was ushered into an office which was crowded with displaced people.

He stood swaying in front of a desk with a Russian dressed in the uniform of a NKVD officer sitting behind it. Behind him stood a Polish Russian interpreter.

'Why have you come to Poznan?' the officer snapped staring with tired hard eyes.

'I'm looking for my family, I was told by someone that they'd been seen here,' he mumbled noticing the sudden startled glance the interpreter gave him.

He started to sweat, knowing the interpreter was now deeply suspicious.

'I need the toilet I'm desperate,' he stuttered, acting in a drunken stupor.

The officer grunted angrily, impatiently pointing down the hall.

'Don't be long, but better you piss there than in my office.'

He staggered out while the interpreter stared after him with a frown. Standing in the toilet he felt trapped. The windows were barred and covered in wire mesh. Coming out of the toilet he could see down the hall and out into the main street where his guide stood looking anxiously in. There were two Russian soldiers guarding the entrance stopping anybody entering or leaving without a pass. He slowly walked as far as the door to the office where he'd been questioned and saw the two men deep in conversation. Quickly dodging past he waited until the two guards faced the street then ran knocking them to one side before he was out, dodging through the crowds, losing himself in the small side streets aware of the shouting and screaming he'd left behind.

Where to go, he didn't know, he wandered about for an hour carefully avoiding any contact with the numerous patrols until he finally found his guide.

'You had me worried,' gasped the little man who was red and sweating who had obviously been running up and down the narrow streets in despair at not ever finding his Englishman.

Rance grunted back in relief. 'Believe me I had visions of going to Russia in chains or worse. Now where do we go from here?'

The little man beckoned, 'Follow me,' and led the way fifty paces ahead through the pushing throng of humanity and rubbish filled streets. Half an hour later the guide came to a large building and pointed to a narrow alley-way running alongside which was guarded by two bored looking Russian soldiers who stared morosely at the passers-by.

Rance walked nonchalantly passed the guards glancing casually down the ally, his heart pounded with excitement at the sight of the Union Jack flying proudly on a pole above a small door halfway down. It had been nearly five years since he'd last seen one and at times never expected to see one again.

There was a commotion at the far end of the main street they were in, someone was being arrested so he and the guide hurriedly departed into one of the numerous side streets. He could see the guide was getting nervous his job was now finished and he was anxious to go.

'Jan, I need one more favour from you,' he said trying to calm the man down, 'it won't involve you in any risk, but I need a diversion to draw the guards away from that ally for just a few seconds.'

Jan looked doubtful. 'What sort of diversion were you thinking of?'

'Have you friends here? Or anyone who could stage a fight with each other right in front of the guards, just long enough for me to get to that door. Once inside I'm safe and on my way home.'

Jan nodded thoughtfully. 'I can arrange that, we still have a few partisans left here.'

He had a sudden thought. 'What if that side door is locked?'

Rance shook his head. 'Then go home my friend because it will be too late for me.'

Three hours later. He approached the alleyway with trepidation feeling the sweat cold and clammy on his forehead while he wiped his moist palms on his overcoat. Coming in the opposite direction were two drunks arguing loudly before stopping in front of the Russian soldiers.

They continued to shout drawing a crowd. He drew nearer but the guards were too interested in the commotion to take any notice of him.

A fight broke out and the guards moved forward laughing and urging them on. He walked quickly behind them and down the narrow alleyway listening to the shouts of the soldiers when they finally pulled the two fighting men apart.

He was nearly there he could feel the tension and fear grow in him, fully expecting a shout from behind that would spell disaster.

Forcing himself not to run he risked a backward glance and the tension cut through him, making his pulse race when the guards returned to their post.

It only needed one to turn his head.

He approached the door, praying it wasn't locked. His legs felt weak and the sweat continued to run down his face. He turned the door handle but the door remained closed. Looking back at the Russians he saw them joined by two others, changing shifts.

Any second now one of them would look. With desperation borne of fear he lunged with his shoulder, the door was only slightly jammed and he fell inside.

He heard a shout from the street and turned quickly slamming the door shut. A British army officer and a sergeant looked up from a desk with startled expressions.

In front of them stood a scarecrow of a man dressed like a tramp, young maybe, they weren't sure. The scarecrow's eyes were steely grey and hard like steel. The scarecrow spoke in perfect English.

'Sir, Gunner Rance reporting for duty.'

They gaped at him open mouthed, his face broke into a smile, the hard eyes softening to a brilliant blue.

'Oh yes old boy,' said the officer, 'A likely story, you have you're ID papers with you of course'.

Rance stared at him in consternation. 'Why no sir, I lost them in 1940 when I was first captured.'

The officer smirked at the sergeant

'And of course you've just been walking around Poland ever since.'

'Not quite sir, I had a year in Boulogne and other POW camps, before arriving here a couple of years ago.

'So you've been sightseeing here for the last two and a half years'.

The officer's voice hardened. 'There are thousands of Poles like you all desperate to leave, coming up with all sorts of stories so why should we believe you?'

Rance rattled off his name rank and number.

'If you could possible check that sir, you'll find I'm telling you the truth.'

The officer looked dubious, Rance was becoming frustrated and angry. 'Check me out sir, what have you got to lose.'

'You realise you can't stay here if we do, it'll take at least three days to get a reply from the war office,' said the officer startled at his sharp tone.

'You want me to go back out there and face the Russians, I'll probably end up in Siberia or worse,' said Rance.

The officer shrugged, 'That's the way it is, but there's another door we keep locked which isn't guarded by the Russians, use that and report back in three days. If you check out then we'll let you in. If not-'. He left the sentence unfinished.

Rance stepped back onto the main street and the door closed behind him with the thud of sliding bolts, he glanced at the Russian guards standing in front of the alleyway fifty feet away. They ignored him so with relief he walked in the opposite direction. He was stunned it wasn't what he'd expected.

It had started to snow, he was hungry and had nowhere to go.

Everywhere there were Russian soldiers and he wondered if he could survive the next three days. Eventually having walked aimlessly around for an hour he reached a large open space that was obviously a bombsite crowded with refugees. In the centre were three small fires to keep warm. Rance reluctantly joined them, ever fearful of the Russian patrols.

For the next three days slowly starving and becoming weaker he waited impatiently until it was time to return.

It was mid-morning when he hammered on the British compound's door keeping a watchful eye on the Russians further down the street.

It opened cautiously and the Sergeant peered out grinning broadly at him.

'Welcome home lad,' the Sergeant said, 'Captain Grant wants to see you.'

He was ushered into an office where the officer rose from his desk with outstretched hand.

'Well old boy you checked out. welcome back, but I must say you were lucky to have been on the outside all this time. It's been absolutely awful stuck in a POW camp. We've almost died of boredom with nothing to do all day, but play cards and football.'

Rance stared at the officer, speechless. Now thinking of Izabel, answered, 'Yes Sir, For a short time I think I was.'

THE END

EPILOGUE

Rance was repatriated as a British prisoner of war by the Russians, arriving back in England in March 1945, five years after he was first captured in France.

I returned with Rance and my wife Lynn to Poland in the early nineties to do research for this novel, only to dicover that Izabel had died alone in Southern Poland eighteen months before our arrival. She had never married.

Marian lived alone as a recluse at a forest ranger station, she guided us to Donald Cross's grave. The villagers exhumed him in 1946 and reburied him in a Roman Catholic cemetery.

Marian explained that her father Josef was killed by the communists in 1971.

The baby that Rance had baptised by a priest at gunpoint was about fifty years old and lived in a different part of Poland we met his uncle who was present at the baptism.

We also met with some of the old partisans and villagers that remained. Bitter memories prevailed, but Rance they regarded as a legend.

Rance died in 2011 but before he died he was awarded two Polish war medals at a decoration ceremony at the Polish Embassy in London.